Rushmore G. Horton

The Life and Public Services of James Buchanan

President of the United States. Vol. 1

Rushmore G. Horton

The Life and Public Services of James Buchanan
President of the United States. Vol. 1

ISBN/EAN: 9783337402907

Printed in Europe, USA, Canada, Australia, Japan

Cover: Foto ©Raphael Reischuk / pixelio.de

More available books at **www.hansebooks.com**

THE

LIFE AND PUBLIC SERVICES

. OF

JAMES BUCHANAN,

PRESIDENT OF THE UNITED STATES;

INCLUDING HIS

INAUGURAL ADDRESS,

AND

THE MOST IMPORTANT OF HIS STATE PAPERS.

BY R. G. HORTON.

With an Accurate Portrait on Steel.

NEW YORK:

DERBY & JACKSON, 119 NASSAU ST.

1860.

PREFACE.

THE history of the statesmen of America is one of the most interesting and instructive studies that can well employ the mind of a citizen of this free and favored land. While nearly every other country presents, as far as political progress is concerned, little more than the dead calm of despotism, our own land, under the glorious principles of its free Constitution, has given every opportunity for that natural conflict between truth and error, which seems to be the established system of the moral universe, and the only means to insure the progress of wise and benificent reforms. Such a state of society has, we may say, almost created "a new heaven and a new earth," and though its convulsions are regarded with amazement by foreign nations, yet we may reasonably suppose, it is because they are comraratively strangers to the travail and pains necessary to the birth and establishment of new ideas. The prominent part which Democratic statesmen have acted in

5

all the leading questions of public policy, which have for seventy years divided political parties, and the fact that the doctrines they sustained, have without exception, now become the settled policy of our government, lend an additional interest to their history and opinions. Those who have preserved the purity of our republican institutions, and resisted every effort to model our laws after the example of foreign countries, deserve scarcely less honor than those who first established them. We think it will be shown in the following pages, that the distinguished individual whose life and public services have been, we are conscious, but feebly portrayed, has borne no humble or insignificant part in these patriotic and praiseworthy labors. Let no one, however, expect to find in them an elaborate work, or one even commensurate with the just importance of the subject.

The object of the volume is very simple and definite. When the Hon. James Buchanan was nominated on the 6th of June as a candidate for the Presidency, the public of course became interested to receive a more full and reliable account of his political opinions, than is usually afforded them in the various newspapers of the day. Immediately after his nomination, the writer was applied to, to furnish such an account of his LIFE AND PUBLIC SERVICES, as would promise to meet the demands of the time. The limited period allowed for the preparation of the volume, and the importance of its presentation to the public at as early a day as possible, precluded anything like a studied or careful effort, such, indeed, as its distinguished subject is eminently worthy of. The main point has therefore been to present merely the *facts* of Mr. Buchanan's career as a public man, and to show his position upon political questions as they have come before him for his consideration. As the limits of the volume did not admit of giving anything like a full report of his public speeches, it was thought advisable to present two or three of his prominent ones upon important public questions, and to limit the extracts from the others mainly to such matters as bear upon the issues now before the country.

As Mr. Buchanan has ever shunned publicity, and always been averse to courting public favor through the press, no account of his life and important public services to his country, through so many years of active and devoted labors, has been previously published. The writer has, therefore, been compelled to rely mostly upon the simple record of the Congressional proceedings, and a few leading facts which Mr. B. and some of his personal or political friends have been kind enough to furnish. It is proper to say, however, that while we are confident all the statements in this volume, in regard to Mr. Buchanan's private, professional or public life, may be fully relied on as correct, yet no one is responsible for a single line it contains except the writer.

New York, *July 4th*, 1856.

PREFACE TO SECOND EDITION.

THE election of Mr. Buchanan to the Presidency, and the continued demand for this volume, has rendered another edition necessary. The work has been carefully revised and brought down to the present time. Although prepared for a particular exigency, yet the author feels it has a standard value, and that it gives a correct and impartial review of the principal events of Mr. Buchanan's life. He has, also, the satisfaction to know that it has received this commendation from all parties in politics. He, therefore, desires that it may stand or fall upon its merits, whatever they are, without being prejudiced by the fact that it first appeared at a particular juncture. By avoiding excessive laudation, as being equally offensive to its distinguished subject as to the principles of good taste, and adhering strictly to the official record of Mr. Buchanan's political career, it is believed the public have, in the present volume, a faithful epitome of his most important services to his country, and an impartial history of the life of our new President. In this spirit it is commended to the favorable consideration of the sovereign American people.

NEW YORK, *March* 18*th*, 1857.

CONTENTS.

9

CHAPTER XVII.

CHAPTER XVIII.

CHAPTER XIX.

CHAPTER XX.

CHAPTER XXI.

CHAPTER XXII.

CHAPTER XXIII.

CHAPTER XXIV.

CHAPTER XXV.

ADDITIONAL.

THE

LIFE AND PUBLIC SERVICES

OF

JAMES BUCHANAN.

———◆◆◆———

CHAPTER I.

Mr. Buchanan's Birthplace—His Father and Mother—His Early Education—His College Life—Sporting in the Backwoods—Studies Law—Admission to the Bar—Unparralleled Success.

JAMES BUCHANAN was born at a place called Stony Batter, in Franklin County, Pennsylvania, at the foot of the eastern ridge of the Alleghanies, on the 23d day of April, 1791. Franklin County borders on the State of Maryland, and the greater part of it consists of a broad limestone valley, watered with copious and unfailing mountain springs, and having a soil of unsurpassed fertility. The immense range of mountains known as the Alleghanies, which commences in the northern part of Georgia and Alabama, and runs generally in uniform ridges to the northeastern part of New York, is in Franklin County divided into an irregular series of rocky, broken eminences. The South Mountain, a continuation of the Blue Ridge of Virginia, forms its boundary on the east, and Tuscarora or

Cove Mountain, on the northwest. The highest points of the Cove Mountain are estimated at fifteen hundred feet above the valley. The spot where Mr. Buchanan first saw the light of day is situated in a wild and romantic gorge of this mountain. The towering summits of the eternal hills surround it, and slope down like the sides of an amphitheatre. A beautiful stream of water, clear as the crystal fountain from which it flows, meanders through what was once a cleared field, not far from his humble birthplace. The remains of the old Buchanan cabin are still to be seen, although little is left but the chimney. They lie to the north of the Mercersburg and McConnellsburg turnpike, but within sight, and about three miles from the village of Mercersburg. It is a lovely spot, and the scenery has all those elements of grandeur and sublimity which serve to inspire in youthful minds noble aspirations and exalted patriotism. Such places have been those where a majority of our great men have been born and reared. The early struggles necessary to contend with the rugged inequalities of nature, have developed a hardy constitution, inspired them with honest ambition, and taught them in early life those invaluable lessons of self-denial which are the foundation of all true excellence of character.

Mr. Buchanan's father was James Buchanan, a native of the County of Donegal, in the north of Ireland, who emigrated to the United States in the year 1783. He was a poor man when he came to America, but with a vigorous arm, an industrious spirit, and untiring perseverance, he acquired before his death a handsome competency. Five years after his arrival he married Elizabeth Speer, the daughter of a respectable farmer of Adams County, Pennsylvania. At that time the broad and beautiful valleys of Franklin County were comparatively a wilderness, but Mr. Buchanan sought them, and with his young wife became a pioneer in American civilization. Having "staked his claim," and erected a rude log cabin, his own right arm felled the trees that allowed the sunlight of heaven to fall upon the little clearing that surrounded his humble home. In this log-cabin was the present James Buchanan born, and there he continued to reside until he was eight years of age. No one would have suspected, had they then seen the log-cabin boy wandering through the primeval forests, awe-struck at the strange, weird scenes which met his gaze, that he would one day hold listening Senates in attention, and stand among the leading statesmen of America. What a commentary do not such facts present upon our free and glorious institutions !

Mr. Buchanan's father was a prominent man in the county where he resided, and exercised a large share of influence. He had an excellent English education, and so fully understood the advantages to be derived from one of a more liberal character, that he early resolved that his son should receive it. The mother of Mr. Buchanan was a woman of uncommon intellect. Although she had not enjoyed the advantages of a superior education, she was distinguished for her masculine sense, and remarkable literary taste. It is a singular fact, that although she had never read a criticism on any of the standard poets, she had selected, and could repeat from memory all the striking passages in Pope, Cowper, Milton, and other prominent English poets. She was also a woman of the most exalted and enlightened piety, and to her influence in forming his character and implanting those fundamental principles of conduct which underlie all true greatness is her son, James Buchanan, indebted for his present distinction. It is a common remark, that all great men have superior mothers ; whether such be the fact, or whether the idea has arisen from a pardonable partiality of all men for one who was their earliest protector and most devoted friend, we cannot say. But surely in the case of James Buchanan, the remark is strictly true, and no unmeaning compliment.

In 1798, Mr. Buchanan's father removed with his family to the village of Mercersburg, where his son received his early education in English, Latin, and Greek. His progress in his studies was exceedingly rapid, and he early gave indications of a remarkably strong and comprehensive mind. At the age of fourteen, he entered Dickinson College at Carlisle, in Cumberland county, then under the presidency of Dr. Davidson. Here he immediately took rank among the most indefatigable students, and rapidly rose in the estimation of his teachers as well as his fellow pupils. The acquisition of learning was to him not at all difficult, and he mastered the most abstruse subjects with the utmost facility. The breadth and energy of his mind seemed to grasp everything as if by intuition, and to hold it with great tenacity. It was often remarked of him, that he never went to recitation unprepared. He did not merely learn his lesson, but he conquered it, and so fully and completely elaborated it, that it became his own. While, however, he was a great student, his exuberant flow of animal spirits made him enthusiastic in all kinds of relaxation and amusement. He sometimes surprised the faculty by his practical jokes, and upon one occasion was severely reprimanded for some youthful prank that was considered contrary to the strict rules of collegiate propriety. There was nothing, however, in his amusements, but what was strictly the result of a desire for mere fun ; the kindness of his disposition, and the evenness of his temper precluding any thought of anger or malignity.

While in college, he was a member of the Union P. Society, a literary body connected with the institution. All the members of this society were particularly attached to him, and he became its favorite, as, indeed, he was of the entire college. He enjoyed all the honors conferred by this society, and at Commencement was presented by its unanimous vote to the faculty for the highest collegiate honors. He graduated in 1809, at the age of eighteen.

At this period of his life, Mr. Buchanan was tall, slender, and graceful. He had been cradled in poverty, and at all times inured to hardships and toil. He exercised much in the open air, and the forests of Pennsylvania often resounded with the crack of the rifle of the young sportsman, who, at an early age, like nearly all Americans, learned how to use this sharp-shooting weapon. So dexterous was he with his rifle, that like a true back-woodsman, he considered it a disgrace to go home with squirrels or similar game, unless the ball had been sent with unerring precision directly through the head. His studies had expanded his mind, while his labors and recreations had given strength to his body, and already laid the firm foundation for a long life of uniform health. There can be no doubt that his vigorous, early training has been the means of giving him that wonderful endurance, which so remarkably distinguished him in after-life as a public man. The amount of labor he can perform is perfectly astonishing, and has always been remarked by all who have known him, both while engaged in his profession and in his duties in Congress.

In December, 1809, Mr. Buchanan commenced the study of the law in the office of James Hopkins, Esq., of Lancaster city, an eminent lawyer, and a prominent, valuable, and much-respected citizen. He was admitted to the bar November 17th, 1812, when he was a little over twenty-one years of age. He immediately rose rapidly in his profession. He came to the bar of his native State when Pennsylvania was distinguished far and wide for the superior ability of her lawyers. She could boast then of her Baldwins, her Gibsons, her Rosses, her Duncans, her Breckinridges, her Dallases, and her Semples, who shed not only honor upon their own State, but who added materially to the legal reputation of the whole country. With such men as these Mr. Buchanan was compelled to struggle for that eminence in his profession which he subsequently attained, and so firmly kept. Perhaps we do not go too far in saying, that there never has been in our country an instance of so rapid a rise in the legal profession as that afforded in his case. From the day he was admitted until he finally retired from the legal profession, his was a series of successive triumphs. He was poor, and necessity demanded that exertion which soon made him the rival and equal of the best lawyers in his State.   He was engaged in all important causes tried in Dauphin, York, and other neighboring counties, and his name appears in the Pennsylvania Reports more frequently than that of any other lawyer of his day.

In the session of 1816–17 of the Pennsylvania State Senate, when he was only twenty-six years of age, he defended, unassisted by senior counsel, a distinguished judge of his State, who was tried upon articles of impeachment, and was successful. At the age of thirty he had risen to the highest class of legal minds, and commanded a practice more enviable and more extensive than that of any other lawyer in the State.   At this time, however, he yielded to the urgent and repeated solicitations of his friends, and consented to become a candidate for Congress.   He was elected, and continued in the same position for ten years, when he peremptorily declined a re-election. He occasionally, during the vacations of Congress, tried some important cause, which, from past associations, or other reasons, he did not feel at liberty to decline.   He retired, however, from his profession altogether in 1831, having accumulated a competence by his steady devotion to business and the superiority in his profession, which his commanding talents had given him.   Avarice being no trait in Mr. Buchanan's character, he gladly sought repose from business, when Providence had blessed his labors with the realization of the sincere prayer of Agar, "give me neither poverty nor riches."   When he retired he left more business than any one man could attend to.   Thus had the log-cabin-boy, born in a wild and rocky gorge of the Alleghany Mountains, at the early age of forty years, been the architect of his own fortune, and become the admiration and pride of his native State.

Once only after he left his profession, could he be prevailed upon to again appear at the bar.   This was in the cause of an aged widow, where he was appealed to by the most earnest solicitations.   It was an action of ejectment which involved all her little property. The case was a difficult one, and technically decidedly against the unfortunate woman. To the surprise and astonishment of every one, he succeeded in establishing her title to the property in question. The poor woman was intoxicated with joy, and overwhelmed her benefactor with expressions of gratefulness, and offers of remuneration. Mr. Buchanan, however, would accept nothing for his services.

CHAPTER II.

MR. BUCHANAN early signalized his devotion to his country by acts as well as words. During the war of 1812 with Great Britain, the English army, after having sacked the city of Washington, threatened to attack Baltimore. The high-handed and outrageous act of destroying the public buildings at Washington lighted up a flame of indignant patriotism, which overspread the whole country. A public meeting was called in Lancaster in 1814, for the purpose of obtaining volunteers to march to the defence of Baltimore. On that occasion Mr. Buchanan addressed his fellow-citizens in a speech of great ability, in favor of a vigorous prosecution of the war, which he followed up by registering his name as a volunteer, the first with a number of other young and patriotic hearts. His country called for his services, and, throwing his law books aside, the stripling lawyer thus enrolled himself as a private soldier, willing to take any place if he could but defend the interests of his native land. The company was commanded by Judge Henry Shippen. They marched to Baltimore, and served under the command of Major Charles Sterret Ridgeley until they were honorably discharged This early stand of Mr. Buchanan in favor of the war of 1812, will show his feelings at that day, and at a time when the country needed the strong arms and stout hearts of its citizens. How senseless and calumnious, then, has been the story that Mr. Buchanan united with the federalists in opposing the war, and who, about the very time that he was shouldering his musket, and assisting to defend the honor and interests of his country, were meeting in a convention at Hartford to make peace with England without the consent of the United States! The whole cause of this calumny is noticed in a frank and manly letter written by Mr. Buchanan in 1847, after taking a seat in Mr. Polk's cabinet, as follows :

WASHINGTON, *April* 23, 1847.

"My DEAR SIR : I have this moment received you letter of the 15th inst., and hasten to return an answer.

" In one respect, I have been fortunate as a public man. My political enemies are obliged to go back for more than thirty years to find plausible charges against me.

" In 1814, when a very young man (being this day 56 years of age), I made my first public speech before a meeting of my fellow-citizens of Lancaster. The object of this speech was to urge upon them the duty of volunteering their services in defence of their invaded country. A volunteer company was raised upon the spot, in which I was the first, I believe, to enter my name as a private. We forthwith proceeded to Baltimore, and served until we were honorably discharged.

" In October, 1814, I was elected a member of the Pennsylvania legislature ; and in that body gave my support to every measure calculated, in my opinion, to aid the country against the common enemy.

" In 1815, after peace had been concluded, I did express opinions in relation to the causes and conduct of the war, which I very soon after regretted and recalled. Since that period I have been ten years a member of the House of Representatives, and an equal time of the Senate, acting a part on every great question. My political enemies, finding nothing assailable throughout this long public career, now resort back to my youthful years, for expressions to injure my political character. The brave and generous citizens of Tennessee, to whatever political party they may belong, will agree that this is a hard measure of justice ; and it is still harder that, for this reason, they should condemn the President for having voluntarily offered me a seat in his cabinet.

"I never deemed it proper, at any period of my life, whilst the country was actually engaged in a war with a foreign enemy to utter a sentiment which could interfere with its successful prosecution. Whilst the war with Great Britain was raging, I should have deemed it little better than moral treason to paralyze the arm of the government whilst dealing blows against the enemy. After peace was concluded, the case was then different. My enemies cannot point to an expression uttered by me, during the continuance of the war, which was not favorable to its vigorous prosecution.

"From your friend, very respectfully,

"JAMES BUCHANAN."

HON. GEORGE W. JONES.

Mr. Buchanan's active friendship in behalf of his country did not stop with his volunteer campaign. He was elected, in October, 1814, to the Legislature of Pennsylvania, and there assumed the same fearless and patriotic course which had distinguished him throughout the war. An attack was threatened against the city of Philadelphia. The general government was reduced nearly to a state of bankruptcy, and could scarcely raise sufficient money to maintain the regular troops on the remote frontiers of the country. Pennsylvania was obliged to rely upon her own resources for defence, and the people were ready to do their utmost in the cause. Two plans were proposed in the Legislature ; the one was what was called the "conscription bill," and similar to that which was rejected by Congress, by which it was proposed to divide the white male inhabitants of the State, above the age of eighteen, into classes of twenty-two men each, and to designate one man from the members of each class, who should serve one year, each class being compelled to raise a sum of money not exceeding $200, as a bounty to the conscript. During the discussion of these two plans, Mr. Buchanan took an active and highly patriotic stand. In the course of the debate, he said :

"Since, then, Congress has deserted us in our time of need, there is no alternative but either to protect ourselves by some efficient measures, or surrender up that independence which has been purchased by the blood of our forefathers. No American can hesitate which of these alternatives ought to be adopted. The invading enemy must be expelled from our shores ; he must be taught to respect the rights of freemen.

* * * * * *

"We need not be afraid to trust to the patriotism or courage of the people of this country when they are invaded. Let them have good militia officers, and they will soon be equal to any troops in the world. Have not our volunteers and militia under General Jackson covered themselves with glory? Have not our volunteers and militia on the Niagara frontier fought in such a manner as to merit the gratitude of the nation? Is it to be supposed that the same spirit of patriotism would animate the man who is dragged out by a conscription law to defend his country, that the volunteer or militia men would feel ?"

This noble stand, so early taken by Mr. Buchanan, displays a patriotic love of country and shows, even at this early time, his confidence in the people.

Mr. Buchanan assumed a position at this time, upon the question of the proscription of naturalized citizens, a position he has, through all the fluctuating changes of politics for forty years since, consistently adhered to. The governors of Massachusetts and Connecticut transmitted to the governor of Pennsylvania, and by him sent to the legislature of his own State, resolutions recommending certain amendments to the Constitution of the United States, among which was the following :

"That no person who shall be hereafter naturalized shall be eligible as a member of the Senate or the House of Representatives of the United States, nor capable of holding any civil office under the authority of the United States."

A committee was appointed to report upon this, among their other resolutions. They disapproved of every resolution sent ; but we only give as much of their report as relates to the one we have quoted. It is as follows :

"It may be fairly questioned whether the total exclusion proposed is generous to others, or wise to ourselves. The revolutions of Europe may hereafter drive, as they have already driven, many an honorable and distinguished exile to the shelter of our hospitality. The distance which separates him from his native country is some guarantee that he has not chosen his new residence from any motive of levity, but from deliberate choice, and when he has abjured his allegiance to that country, when his fortunes and family are fixed among us, when he has closed all the avenues to his return, when a long probation has evinced his attachment to our institutions, why should his mind continue still in exile and why should the natural and honorable ambition for political distinction be extinguished for ever in his breast? Why, too, should we deprive ourselves of the choice of such a man, whose European experience may be useful, if the deliberate voice of the community is in his favor? Other nations do not indulge in so jealous an exclusion There is scarcely a nation in Europe which does not habitually employ the talents of strangers, wherever they can be most useful.

"Even in England, the most fastidious of all the nations of Europe, with regard to strangers, naturalization is in many respects more easy than in the United States. Many of the restrictions on aliens may be at once removed by act of parliament, or by the mere wish of the crown; and we can readily call to our recollection, even within the present reign, several officers of high rank, both civil and military, employed in important and confidential stations, by the government of that country. In the United States, moreover, we enjoy a greater security than other nations, from the deliberation with which the choice of our country must be made; the probationary term of residence, and the certainty that no foreigner can rise to power, but by the voluntary suffrage of the community.

"The number of foreigners now in office does not threaten any inconvenience, and even that number will no doubt rapidly diminish. Out of 182 representatives in Congress, there are, it is believed, not more than four who were born out of the limits of the United States, and in the Senate, not one member. In one respect, too, the operation of the amendment would be injurious, by preventing the employment of American consuls, natives of the countries in which they reside—a practice almost universal among commercial nations. The natural and prudent precautions against foreign influence will, therefore, probably be satisfied, by requiring a long novitiate to wean a stranger from foreign modes of thinking, and insure his attachment to our institutions, and after that ordeal is past, leaving him a fair competition with native talents for political advancement; a competition in which the natural bias in favor of our own countrymen will insure them at least an equal chance of success. The committee therefore recommend a dissent from the proposed amendment."

The novitiate required at that time was five years, the same as at present, and yet this committee did not see fit to recommend any alteration, but even referred to five years as a long novitiate ; for it will be remembered that during a portion of Washington's administration the term had been but two years. Mr. Buchanan concurred fully in this report, indeed it was unanimously adopted in both houses.

In October, 1815, Mr. Buchanan was again elected to the legislature, and again he distinguished himself by a patriotic love of country, and by a devotion to its honor and interests which won for him the universal applause of his constituents. It is well known that no State has ever shown a more earnest love for the Union than Pennsylvania. Instead of endeavoring to embarrass the general government in its delicate and often difficult duties, it has when necessity demanded it, come to its assistance. At this session of the legislature a bill was brought in appropriating the sum of $300,000 as a loan to the United States to pay the militia and the volunteers of that State, in the United States service. The general government had been on the verge of bankruptcy, and this patriotic action on the part of Pennsylvania was as noble as its remembrance will ever be grateful, to every lover of his country. This appropriation received the warm support of Mr. Buchanan.

It was during this session that Mr. Buchanan became impressed with the danger, the inexpediency, and the unconstitutionality of a United States Bank, an opinion he has adhered to ever since, and in the defence of which he has rendered such lasting services to his country in the legislative halls of the nation.

After the conclusion of that session Mr. Buchanan applied himself to his profession with great assiduity, and accomplished in five years what it would have taken many men of considerable rank in the law three or four times that period to have achieved. We gave in the first chapter a very brief account of his rapid progress. The prosperity of his career can scarcely be exaggerated. In 1820 he yielded to the solicitations of his friends and became a candidate for Congress, to which position he was elected.

Before commencing the history of Mr. Buchanan's congressional career it may be well to notice some charges that have been brought forward tending to impeach the consistency of his political conduct. To pass them over in silence might give rise to the suspicion that his acts and opinions are not susceptible of defence, while we confidently assert that there is not one, which does not admit of the most thorough vindication, indeed which does not challenge the closest scrutiny and investigation. Prominent among the charges which have been flippantly made and perseveringly persisted in, is that of federalism. Now, we say most distinctly that had Mr. Buchanan been a federalist, it has nothing whatever to do with issues now before the public ; and if it could be shown that he gave good reasons for changing his opinions upon public questions it should not and would not militate against him in the opinion of any sensible man. If therefore, it were a truth that Mr. Buchanan had advocated any of the leading questions of public policy which that once very respectable party supported, we should so set down the fact, and consider him none the less worthy of support or confidence now, if he gave evidence of honesty of intention and stood upon principles essential to the safety and interests of his country. But as we have failed after a careful study of Mr. Buchanan's public life, to find any support for the charge brought against him by those who seem to be but indifferently acquainted with our political history, we have thought a notice of the matter in this place demanded by the integrity of history.

Originally, the name of federal was as honorable a designation as any other. It took its rise from those who approved of our federal Constitution, whilst those who felt that the government was too consolidated, called themselves anti-federalists or republicans ; but after the Constitution was adopted, and it was accepted as the fundamental, organic law of the land, as Jefferson truly remarked, " We are all federalists, we are all republicans." After the adoption of the Constitution, therefore, the term federal, so far as its primary signification was concerned, had no meaning. But in a few years it was soon discovered that the very men who had approved most earnestly of the Constitution, began to claim for it doubtful powers, and to give it a liberal construction. Mr. John Adams, the second President, was the first who boldly inaugurated this policy, and by the passage of the alien and sedition laws, overwhelmed himself and his party in disgrace. This was the first stain on the otherwise fair name of federal. Then came the war of 1812, when they completed their ruin as a party, not by opposing the war in a reasonable manner, but by an odious and unconstitional opposition, which finally terminated in a traitorous convention in New England, to make a separate peace with Great Britain. These two acts destroyed the federal party, and brought upon the name an odious reproach. It will not be pretended by any one that Mr. Buchanan approved either of the measures to which we have referred. The principles of the federal party were, however, as we have before observed, in favor of claiming from Congress the exercise of doubtful powers, in opposition to the doctrine of State rights as embraced in the Kentucky and Virginia resolutions of 1798. They also claimed the power in Congress to establish a United States bank. Yet, upon Mr. Buchanan's first appearance in public life, we find him announcing himself as opposed to a bank of this kind, and denying the power of Congress to establish such an institution. Now, there is no sense or propriety in calling any man a federalist, who has not advocated or supported federal doctrines. Yet there is not an enemy of Mr. Buchanan who can point to a single act of his life which is contrary to the doctrine of State rights, or to a strict construction of the Constitution. From first to last, from beginning to end, he has adhered steadily to this political faith. In the general disruption of parties after the war of 1812, he may have technically ranked with the federal party, but he certainly never supported a single one of its measures, as the reader who peruses the remaining pages of this volume will be fully convinced.

But even had Mr. Buchanan seen reasons for changing his opinions, and doubtless he has upon some public questions, who is there to reproach him for such a course? Where is the man, who in the period of forty years' experience in public life, has not changed? To suppose men not susceptible of an honest alteration of opinion, would be to expect that they come perfect from the hand of their Maker; or else that they were either so dull, that the instruction which experience furnishes, is incapable of making any impression upon them; or that they were so obstinate and self-willed, as to adhere to opinions after they had been convinced they were erroneous. Full-fledged Minervas do not, in these days, spring from Jupiter's head, any more than full-grown men, physically as well as mentally, enter the world to astonish those who have been exploring its mysteries, sometimes with only partial success, for years. All that the people can justly demand of any public man, is, that his course has not been erratic or irregular, and that, if upon any occasion he has changed his opinions, it has the appearance of honesty of purpose, and the excuse of public interest. But with all our study of Mr. Buchanan's career, and we say it without the least particle of anything like a partisan bias, we have failed to discover any change of any of the fundamental principles of his political action. In this respect he has not only been consistent, but exceedingly fortunate, for there are few persons

who do not imbibe some false principles, which more mature judgment convinces them are erroneous.   All who peruse Mr Buchanan's congressional career of twenty years, will be fully convinced that, for an exemplary devotion to great principles, and
a consistent and honorable bearing upon all questions, he is
not excelled by any living statesman.

CHAPTER III.

Military Appropriations—Bankrupt Bill—Internal Improvements—The Tariff Question.

THE year 1820 was one of great financial embarrassment. The Bank of the United States, which had been chartered in 1816, had in less than four years proved how delusive were the hopes and expectations of its friends. It had created one of those vast expansions of paper currency which are only the precursors of a calamity more wide-spread and destructive than any prosperity it could produce was satisfactory or desirable. The distress was universal, and pervaded public as well as private affairs. Mr. Benton in his "Thirty Years' View," speaking of this disastrous period of our national history, says: "No price for property or produce; no sales but those of the Sheriff and the Marshal; no purchasers at the executive sales but the creditor or some hoarder of money; no employment for industry, no demand for labor; no sale for the product of the farm; no sound of the hammer but that of the auctioneer knocking down property. Stop laws, property laws, replevin laws, stay laws, loan office laws, the intervention of the legislator between the creditor and the debtor—this was the business of legislation in three-fourths of the States of the Union of all south and west of New England. No medium of exchange but depreciated paper; no change even, but little bits of foul paper, marked so many cents, and signed by some trader, barber, or inn-keeper. Exchanges deranged to the extent of fifty or one hundred per cent. *Distress* the universal cry of the people , *relief* the universal demand thundered at the doors of all legislatures, State and Federal."

It was in such a social convulsion as this that the citizens of Lancaster county turned their thoughts upon James Buchanan, then only twenty-nine years of age, as their candidate for representative in Congress. Serious, thoughtful, and considerate, he was, wherever known, regarded as worthy of the utmost confidence. The warm and ardent friend of Mr. Monroe's administration, he contributed not a little in promoting that universal popularity which elevated that distinguished individual almost unanimously the second time to the presidential chair. Mr. Buchanan was elected in the fall of 1820, and took his seat in the seventeenth Congress, in December, 1821.

This was immediately succeeding the stormy session of 1820, when the difficulties in regard to the admission of Missouri had been adjusted, by the adoption of the first concession ever made to the anti-slavery or abolition sentiment of the country. The attempt was boldly made when Missouri applied for admission into the Union, to exclude her unless she would come in as a State with laws refusing to recognise the right of property interest in the labor and services of negroes. This unconstitutional demand upon her was successfully resisted, and finally only one clause in her Constitution was excepted to as constituting a ground of ultimate rejection. This was a section prohibiting the emigration of free negroes into the State. It was urged by the anti-slavery party of that day, that this was in contradiction to the clause of the Constitution of the United States, which guarantees to any citizen of any of the States of the Union equal privileges in all the States, of which privileges the right of emigration was one. It was held, that if negroes were admitted to citizenship in some States, they would be deprived of it by the terms of the Constitution of Missouri. It was successfully replied to this, that the Constitution did not regard persons of this race as citizens, and that the framers of the government expressly stated that it was formed " for

them and *their* posterity," of whom negroes could form no part
The objection, however, was a mere pretext, the real cause of
the opposition to the admission of Missouri being the existence
of negro servitude in the State. This is abundantly proved
from the fact that the anti-slavery party have long since abandoned the ground then assumed, and many of the western
States now have stringent laws in regard to the admission of
free negroes, without any objection being raised as to the right
of a State to pass such acts in regard to the *status* of the
negro, as it may in its sovereign capacity think proper for its
own welfare. Even the " Free State Constitution of Kansas,"
recently so earnestly advocated by the anti-slavery press of the
present day, contained an express prohibition to the immigration
of free negroes. The objectionable clause in the Constitution
of Missouri was finally so modified by the exertions of Mr.
Clay, that a resolution was reported in favor of the admission of
the State, upon condition that the legislature should first
declare that the clause in her Constitution relative to free
colored immigration should never be construed to authorize the
passage of any act by which any citizen of any of the States
of the Union should be excluded from the enjoyment of every
privilege to which he may be entitled under the Constitution
of the United States. When this was done, the President was
to declare Missouri admitted, by proclamation. This resolution
passed the House of Representatives by only four majority,
Mr. Randolph and other southern members opposing it with
all their might. The Missouri restriction bill of 36° 30', sometimes called " the Missouri Compromise," was also acquiesced in
by the same Congress, upon the supposition that this concession to the demands of the anti-slavery sentiment would be a
quietus to the agitation of the matter. Subsequent events,
however, proved how delusive was this hope, and how dangerous it is to yield even the slightest constitutional right to the
demands of a delusion which is propagated mainly for the purpose of acquiring political power. The overthrow of one right

2*

only paves the way for the destruction of another still more important ; and the party thus emboldened by success, will continue its lawlessness until it rides over every barrier of the Constitution, and prostrates every right which is not sanctioned by its own insane creed, or until it installs civil war in order to carry out its exclusive doctrines.

Mr. Buchanan's entrance to Congress was immediately subsequent to these events. The proclamation of Mr. Monroe had admitted Missouri as one of the States of the Confederacy during the summer of 1821. The country had been agitated with a long and fearful conflict, and all parties, after the settlement made by the preceding Congress, were but too glad to turn their attention from a subject which had threatened in so imminent a degree the safety of the Union, to others more practical in their character. The depression of the times suggested many of these, and the Congress of 1821—22 had therefore a great deal of business upon its hands which in the excited state of the public mind on the Missouri question, had been neglected.

The array of talent on the floor of Congress when Mr. Buchanan arrived in Washington was impressive and commanding. In the House were the ever memorable names of McDuffie, Joel R. Poinsett, John Randolph, Philip P. Barbour, Andrew Stevenson, Louis McLane, and others equally distinguished. In the Senate were Rufus King, Martin Van Buren, Mahlon Dickerson, Samuel L. Southard, Nathaniel Macon, and Richard M. Johnson. Mr. Buchanan immediately took rank among the most industrious and indefatigable members of the House. He was always in his seat, and generally participated in every debate upon any important public question. The first set speech which Mr. Buchanan delivered in Congress was upon a bill making appropriations to the military, for some deficiencies that had occurred in the Indian department. He so ably defended the course of Mr. Crawford, then Secretary of the Treasury, that the "National Intelligencer" at the request of severa. gentlemen departed from its usual course, and gave a verbatim report of his speech. As this was the first effort of Mr Buchanan on the floor of Congress, and as it gave an earnest of the future distinction that awaited him, we give it entire, with the exception of a small portion mostly taken up with statistics. It was delivered on the 11th of January, 1822. Mr. Buchanan rising said :—

"Mr. Chairman : On Friday last, when the House adjourned, I did believe that the subject now before the Committee was involved in doubt and in mystery. I thought that a dark cloud hung over the transaction, which ought to be cleared up before the House could give its sanction to this appropriation. After a careful examination the mystery has vanished—the cloud has been dispelled, and to my view the subject appears clear as the light of day. If it had not, my vote would be given against the appropriation, because in a Republican government doubt and mystery, in any measure proposed by the Executive department, should always be sufficient to prevent it from receiving the support of the House.

"In the remarks which I propose to submit, it will be my endeavor to communicate to the Committee the reasons upon which I have come to the determination to give this appropriation my unqualified support. If I should be wrong, there are many gentlemen in the House whose judgment and whose experience will enable them to correct my errors.

"Nice distinctions have been drawn between a just confidence in the Executive departments, and an unreasonable jealousy of their conduct, on the one side ; and on the other, between that confidence and a belief in their infallibility. Extremes in such case are very dangerous. Whilst unreasonable jealousy of men in power keeps the public mind in a state of constant agitation and alarm, a blind reliance upon their infallibility, may enable them to destroy the liberties of the people before they are aware of the existence of danger. At the same time, therefore, that I trust I am one of the last men in the

House who would consent to establish the office of dictator in the commonwealth, or to believe in the infallibility of mortals in politics more than in religion—yet I should think it wrong to withhold from a public officer that degree of confidence which assumes that he has acted correctly, until the contrary appears. It ought to be a maxim in politics, as well as in law, that an officer of your government, high in the confidence of the people, shall be presumed to have done his duty, until the reverse of the proposition is proved.

"These observations are made, not because I believe they have any bearing upon the present question, but simply in answer to those used by gentlemen who have argued upon the opposite side. The Secretary of War, upon the present occasion, requires not the aid of presumptions in his favor, because, to my mind at least, there is the most full, satisfactory, and self-evident proof.

"Before I come to the principal question, Mr. Chairman, permit me to answer one of the arguments which has been eloquently and ingeniously urged by the gentlemen opposed to this appropriation.

"It has been said, with truth, that the Constitution provides 'that no money shall be drawn from the treasury, but in consequence of appropriations made by law.' It is certain that this provision is the best security for the liberties of the people in the whole of the instrument. Once transfer this branch of power, vested in Congress by the Constitution, to the Executive, and your freedom is but an empty name. That department of the government, having then the command of the purse, might very soon assume the power of the sword.

"Has the Secretary of War violated this salutary provision? Has he drawn money out of the treasury without an appropriation made by law for that purpose? Unquestionably not. So far from asking you to sanction such an unconstitutional measure, he is now requesting you to make an appropriation to supply a deficiency in the means which you had provided to enable him to discharge positive duties, enjoined upon him by your own laws.

" Whether this deficiency shall be supplied out of the public purse, or the Secretary be made responsible in his private capacity to those with whom he has made contracts on the faith of the government, is the only question now before the committee.

" Here let me ask gentlemen why they are so much alarmed at the fact that the appropriation has proved deficient ? Deficiencies must and will occur so long as the men who wield the destinies of this government are fallible. Nothing short of the spirit of prophecy can prevent them from happening, unless Congress should think proper to make such overwhelming appropriations as would be sufficient to cover all contingencies, not only probable but possible. They existed even whilst the gentleman from Virginia .(Mr. Randolph) was chairman of the Committee of Ways and Means. 1 speak the honest sentiments of my heart, when I declare that, in my opinion, he possessed as much penetration as any gentleman who ever occupied that distinguished station. Calculate, with the nicest precision, the future probable expenses of any department of the government, and in the course of the year for which the estimate is made, suppose there should be no events of extraordinary occurrence, still it will be a miracle, if ever the appropriation shall be exactly equal to all the necessary expenditures.

" At the instant of time when the sum appropriated is expended in executing your laws, would you have the wheels of government to stop ? Would you declare that all your public agents who had served you faithfully should receive no compensation, merely because either you or your Secretary of War, in the beginning of the year, could not foresee the expenses which might be incurred before its end ?

" Take, for example, the army; admit, for the sake of argument, that which is impossible even in times of the most profound tranquillity—that you had estimated the future annual expense to a fraction, and had made an appropriation accordingly. Suppose, that during the recess of Congress, political storms should envelop your country, that treason at home, or war from abroad, were about to disturb your peace, and that the point of meditated attack was within the knowledge of your executive : under such circumstances, would the President of the United States be justified, either to his conscience or to his constituents, if he were not to march the army from all quarters of the Union to the district in danger ? What would you then think of his justification, if he informed you that he neglected to provide for the common defence, because the army appropriation was too small to enable him to embody the forces ? Such conduct would be treason against the Republic.

" Your security in all cases of this kind, arises from that admirable provision of the Constitution, which declares that no money shall be drawn from the treasury but under the authority of the law. When any officer of the government applies for the passage of a bill to supply a deficiency, you always inquire into the reasons why it has occurred ; and if his conduct upon examination is found to be correct, you will, as you have always hitherto done, supply the deficiency.

" This course of policy is not only necessary in itself, but it gives you a much greater control over the public purse, than if, in the beginning of the year, you were to make your appropriations sufficiently large to cover all contingencies. Such conduct would be a powerful temptation to the officer to become extravagant in the expenditure of public money.

" Let us then inquire, whether it was necessary that the sum of $170,000 should have been expended in the Indian department during the year 1821, to carry into effect the spirit and intention of the different acts of Congress ?

" It has been urged, that as Congress appropriated but $100,000 to defray the current expenses of that department during the last year, the Secretary was bound to confine himself within that amount. The necessary consequence would be, that the laws establishing that branch of our policy, were in this manner, at least in part, repealed.

" This is, I confess, the first occasion on which I have ever heard that a system of laws which had received a fixed construction by the practice of the nation for more than twenty years, could be repealed, not by withdrawing the whole, but a part of appropriation necessary to carry them into effect. If this were the case, it would give to estimates, uncertain in their very nature, the effect of expunging from our statute-book the most wholesome regulations. Nay, more, it would be delegating legislative powers to the head of a department, and would introduce the very evil against which gentlemen are so anxious to guard. By this construction, if there be laws in existence enjoining a variety of duties on any officer of the government, and if, to enable him to discharge all those duties, an annual expenditure of $170,000 is necessary, your appropriation of but $100,000 for that purpose would make him the legislator, instead of yourselves. You thus necessarily rest in him the power of deciding what parts of the system shall remain in vigor, and what part shall fall before his power. In order to ascertain what laws are repealed, you would be obliged to resort, not to your statute-book, but to the head of a department. Even then they would be forever varying, because, whilst he confined himself within his appropriation, he might at his pleasure range through the whole system as it originally stood, and select from it such parts as he thought proper to carry into effect. This is not the manner in which Congress ever will, or ever can, manifest their intention. If they desire to reduce the expenses of any department of the government, themselves will lop off every branch which they deem superfluous, and not leave it to the discretion of any executive officer, no matter how exalted his station. Whilst, however, certain duties are enjoined on any department of the government, by acts of Congress, or by treaties, we are bound to supply the officer with the means necessary to the performance of those duties. If, in such a case, our appropriation has been insufficient, we ought at once to supply the deficiency.

"This system, so eminently calculated to preserve tranquillity around our borders, and to prevent the intrigues of another nation from obtaining for them an undue ascendency over the minds of the savages has been long established, and was as much incorporated into your policy as that of sending ambassadors to foreign courts. Did Congress express any disapprobation of this system. Did they destroy any part of it by the bill which appropriated $100,000 for the current expenses of the year? Did they intend that the Secretary should destroy the objects of ascertained or of contingent expense? Both had been equally provided for, by your laws, and by your treaties. Did Congress mean either that the Indians should receive no rations at your military posts, or that no presents should be given to them, or that they should be deprived of the benefit of receiving agricultural instruments from your hands? If they did, they have expressed no such determination by any law. The consequence of the construction contended for is, that if they intended anything, by appropriating but $100,000, it was to enable the Secretary to legislate in your behalf, and to repeal so much of existing laws and existing treaties as would reduce the expense to $100,000. This he had no power to do, and to allow him to exercise it would establish a most dangerous precedent against the liberties of this people. It would be to allow an officer to stop the wheels of government and paralyze the energies of the law the moment the appropriation which had been made was expended.

"Could the Secretary have ever supposed that you intended to destroy any part of this establishment? Certainly not, because the expenditures are most just as well as most politic. You have driven that noble race of men from the hunting grounds which God and nature intended for their support. You have caused intestine wars to rage continually among them, by driving remote tribes near together, and thus making it necessary to their existence that they should invade the hunting grounds of each other. During the very last year, it appears from the letter of the Secretary that the disbursements have been increased by the emigration of the Indians from the States of Ohio, Indiana, and Illinois, beyond the Mississippi. After thus crowding them together, you make them waste their scanty supply of game by inducing them to destroy it without necessity, so that you may obtain their fur to gratify your appetite for luxury. In this situation, to which they have been reduced by our policy, the laws have provided that, when the cravings of hunger shall drive these children of the forest to your military posts, either on the frontier or in their own territory they shall receive food ; that in order to preserve their existence and enable them to live upon the circumscribed limits within which they have been driven, they should be taught agriculture, and receive the implements of husbandry ; that, when their chiefs think proper to visit your metropolis, you will enable them to do so by paying their expenses, and thus manifest to them the extent of both your power and your friendship. In short, all the other provisions, which our laws and our treaties have made for them, and which I shall not detail, are founded, not only in the strictest justice, but in the wisest policy.

"Did Congress intend, by the mere act of appropriating $100,000 for the current expenses of the last year, that the head of a department should alter the laws of the land, and that he might at his will declare what part of the Indian system should be in force, and what part should be considered as repealed? Was it, for example, their determination that no treaties should be held with the Indians, however necessary they might have been, because the Secretary had thought proper to apply the whole of your appropriations to other objects? This never could have been their intention. Congress alone have the power of changing this system of policy, whenever they think proper to do so, by unequivocal legislative acts ; then, and not till then, does it become the duty of executive officers to obey. They dare not sooner neglect to carry existing laws and treaties into effect.

"Suppose the Secretary had thought proper materially to alter our policy towards the Indians, and the first information you had heard of the change was, as it probably would have been, the howl of savage warfare around your borders, and the shrieks of helpless women and children under the scalping-knife, could you then have justified his conduct? Would you then have told him that he had the power of altering the whole system, because a sufficient appropriation had not been made to keep it in motion till the end of the year? And this, too, when the very sentence before the appropriation of $100,000 provided that $130,205 44 should be drawn from the treasury to cover past arrearages in the Indian department? The legitimate meaning of a reduction in the appropriation was not to destroy any part of our policy towards the Indians, but to warn the Secretary to use the strictest economy in carrying every part of it into effect. It has produced that happy result. He has informed you that the expenses of the present year will not exceed $150,000. This sum is upwards of $85,000 less than, upon an average, was appropriated to the same purpose, in each year, from 1815 to 1820, both inclusive. It is but a few thousand dollars more than was expended for the use of the same department for each of the two last years of Mr. Jefferson. In the meantime, our relations with the Indians have been greatly extended with our extending frontier, and we have become acquainted with tribes, of which before we had never even heard the names. This great curtailment of expense places the character of the present Secretary, in this particular, upon an exalted eminence; and the more so, as it is well known that not one cent more of money was expended by the administration of Mr. Jefferson than was necessary to accomplish its objects.

"But suppose, for the sake of argument, that the Secretary ought to have inferred from your appropriation bill that you intended he should change the Indian system, still we should vote the $70,000 to supply the deficit. If we do not, we require that he should have performed miracles.

"This system has been in constant and in vigorous operation since 1802. For six years before the passage of the last appropriation bill, its average annual expense had been more than $235,000. That bill did not pass until the 3d of March. Before that time, it has not been alleged that there had been a whisper of disapprobation against the former appropriations for the Indian Department. On the contrary, during that period, $200,000 at least had been appropriated every year; and, in addition, large deficiencies had been supplied, without a murmur. The Secretary, acting under a firm conviction that the same system would be pursued, had taken the measures necessary to continue its motion for another year, some time before the passage of the bill. The places at which the money was principally to be expended, were agencies upon the borders of your vast empire, far beyond the utmost limits of civilization. The distance to many of them is so remote, and the communication so precarious, that the Secretary has informed you they cannot be heard from more than twice, and often but once, in the whole course of the year.

"Could the motion of this vast machinery be at once suspended? In the beautiful language of the gentleman from South Carolina (Mr. Lowndes) it had received its impulse before the passage of the bill, and the momentum could not be withdrawn from it in a shorter period of time than one year. To require the Secretary, therefore to stop it immediately, would have been asking him to do that which was utterly impossible.

These, Mr. Chairman, are the remarks which I conceived it to be my duty to make on the subject now before the committee. I have, personally, no feeling of partiality for the Secretary of War, nor of prejudice against him. I view him merely as a public character, and in that capacity I conscientiously believe that upon the present occasion he has done his duty, and acted in the only manner in which he could constitutionally act. In my opinion, therefore, he deserves applause, instead of censure.

"One other view of the subject, Mr. Chairman, and I shall have done. In whatever light the conduct of the secretary may appear, still the deficit ought to be supplied. This case does not require such an argument ; but suppose, for a moment he had acted improperly, is this one of those extreme cases—for I admit that such may possibly exist—in which the House should withhold an appropriation to supply a deficiency ? Will any gentleman say, that individuals who have fairly and honestly entered into contracts with your Secretary of War on the faith of the government shall suffer ? Surely, you would not impose the task on every person who binds himself by agreement, to perform services for the government, to inquire whether the appropriation made by Congress justified his employment. If you did, he then becomes responsible for what in the nature of things cannot be within his knowledge. To enable him to ascertain whether he might safely contract with the head of one your executive departments, he should be informed, not only of the amount of appropriations, but in what manner their expenditure has proceeded, and is proceeding, in every part of the Union. It would be crying injustice to inform the men who have abandoned civilized life, and undergone all the dangers, the hardships and the privations of dwelling among savages in the wilderness, for the purpose of promoting the interest and the glory of their country, that they shall receive no compensation for their services, because the secretary who employed them has exceeded his appropriation. This would be making the innocent suffer instead of the guilty ; if, therefore, there has been any impropriety in the conduct of the Secretary, as some gentlemen have insinuated, but which I utterly deny, it is a question which should be settled between you and him, and one in the decision of which the rights of the persons employed under his authority ought not to be involved. Indeed, no gentlemen has yet said that these men ought not to be paid out of the public treasury. Why then, considering this question in every point of view, in which it can be presented, is there any objection against voting $70,000 to supply the deficiency in the appropriation of the last year? I hope it will pass without further difficulty."

Mr. Buchanan seems to have been uncommonly active during the whole period of the first session he was in Congress. Nothing that affected the interests of his constituents was allowed to pass unnoticed. Indeed Mr. B. seems to have entertained from the start the idea that he was strictly the servant of the people who had elected him, and that in his capacity of representative in Congress, he was bound to attend, first of all, to the concerns of his immediate district. While he was strict in the expenditure of money he was liberal where patriotism made the demand. When some members found fault with a bill authorizing the relief of soldiers disabled in the revolutionary war, Mr. Buchanan met the opposition with the remark that the amount the bill proposed to appropriate "was a scanty pittance for the war-worn soldier," and that he was altogether averse to opposing a matter of so trifling a character, where the demands of patriotism were so imperative. Among other things which engaged his attention, and upon which he made speeches, were the Apportionment Bill, Transactions in Florida, the Bankrupt Bill, Appropriation Bill, and other matters of minor importance. Various charges had been brought against Gen. Jackson's conduct in Florida, the most prominent of which were that he had usurped authority and actually violated the laws of his country. Mr. Buchanan, then a warm friend of Gen. Jackson, was among the most earnest to have them investigated. Speaking upon this subject, he remarked, "that the most serious consequences might be expected to result, if, after charges of this sort were made against an individual, the House should avoid meeting the question—should put them to sleep by permanently laying them on the table. He, for one, was willing to meet the proper responsibility of declaring his opinion, either of the guilt or innocence of this distinguished individual." It is scarcely necessary to remark that these charges trumped up against Gen. Jackson by his enemies were not sustained.

The most important speech that Mr. Buchanan made at this session of Congress was one on a Bankrupt Law, which was powerfully advocated by several of the most distinguished debaters on the floor of the House. There probably never has been a time in the history of our country so opportune as the one which the opponents of the democracy of that day took to bring about "a uniform system of bankruptcy." The universal prostration of commercial affairs, the general and wide spread disasters which seemed to be the inevitable fate of all classes, and the constant cry for relief which was thundering at the doors of every legislative body were enough to make the best grounded in democratic principles waver. The bill was drawn up in the most seductive form. Its operation was to continue only three years, when it expired, unless all branches of the government should concur in re-enacting it. It was shown by the friends of the bill that there was an unexampled number of insolvent debtors, and they contended that a large majority of these individuals were really innocent, and merely unfortunate men, reduced to their embarrassments by the unforeseen disasters of the times. It was shown, that by a rapid transition the country had passed from a state of unexampled prosperity to a condition of commercial and financial ruin, to which no precedent could be shown in the history of the nation. England and all the continental countries had Bankrupt laws, and why should not the United States? The law was held up as a benefit to all classes, and one imperatively demanded by the peculiar condition of the times. Mr. Buchanan did not participate in the debate, which was long and very animated, until late in the session and just before the bill came up for final reading. Then he delivered one of the most powerful and eloquent speeches of the session, taking decided ground against so unequal and unjust a law—one intended merely to encourage the wildest speculations, and tending to destroy public as well as private credit. The speech is quite a lengthy one, but it will amply repay perusal, as well for the just sentiments it contains as for its eloquent and triumphant vindication of public and private honesty, and the rights of the people. It was delivered on the 12th of March, 1822.

"Mr. Speaker: Before the amendment proposed by the gentleman from Kentucky had obtained the sanction of this House, the question whether the bill should be engrossed for a third reading was one of very great importance. That question has, however, dwindled into insignificance compared with the one at present under consideration. We are now called upon to decide the fate of a measure of awful importance. The most dreadful responsibility rests upon us. We are not now to determine merely whether a bankrupt law shall be extended to the trading classes of the community but whether it shall embrace every citizen of this Union and spread its demoralizing influence over the whole surface of society.

"The amendment which has been adopted to-day makes it my imperative duty, even at this protracted period of the debate, to trespass upon the patience of the House. I have the honor in part of representing an honest, a wealthy, and a respectable, agricultural community. I owe to them, to my conscience and to my God not to suffer this bill to pass, which I conceive to be now fraught with destruction to their best interests, both moral and political, without entering my solemn protest against its provisions. We have heard it repeated over and over again by the friends of a bankrupt bill that it should be confined by the mercantile classes. One of the principal arguments urged in its favor by its eloquent supporters, was that merchants from the nature of their pursuits were exposed to the vicissitudes of fortune more than other men, and that, therefore, their situation required a peculiar system of laws.

"That in this country their fortunes had not only been exposed to the dangers commonly incident to their profession, but that the commercial regulations of the government, the embargo, the non-intercourse laws, and, finally the war, had brought ruin upon thousands. It was, therefore, inferred that Congress were under a moral obligation to pass a bankrupt law for their relief. The policy of all the modern commercial nations in the world was presented before us for our imitation ; England, France, Scotland, Ireland, Holland, and Spain, we had been told, each extended a bankrupt law to the merchant, and absolved him from the payment of his debts upon certain conditions. Indeed, a great portion of the argument consisted in drawing a line of distinction between traders and the remaining classes of society. Judge then, Mr. Speaker, of my astonishment when, to-day, I found these gentlemen voting in favor of introducing an amendment extending the provisions of this bill to every individual in society who might ask to become its object. Will you pass a bankrupt law for the farmer ? Will you teach that vast body of your best citizens to disregard the faith of contracts ? Are you prepared to sanction a principle by which the whole mass of society will be in danger of being demoralized ? and it will be left to an election by every man's creditors, in which a majority of two-thirds in number and value against the consent of the remainder, shall have the power of discharging him from the obligation of all his contracts. Surely the House of Representatives are not prepared to answer these questions in the affirmative. No nation in the world, whether commercial or agricultural, whether civilized or savage, has ever for a moment entertained the idea of extending the operation of their bankrupt laws beyond the class of traders. Fortunately for our constituents, we have not the power of doing so. The Constitution correctly expounded has proclaimed, ' hitherto shalt thou go, but no further.'

"Nothing but a desperate effort to revive this expiring bill could have ever induced its friends to have adopted the amendment which has just now been carried. In the discussion of this question, I can assure the House, it is not my intention to travel over the ground which has been already occupied, or repeat the argument which has been already urged. The subject naturally divides itself into two questions—the one of Constitutional power, the other of policy. On the first, as the bill stood before the introduction of the last amendment, I had not a single doubt. Much as I would have deprecated the passage of the then bill, I should have been infinitely more alarmed if this House had determined that the enactment of such a law transcended the constitutional power of Congress. Upon this branch of the subject, the ingenious arguments of the gentleman from Virginia had not created a doubt in my mind.

" Where doubts before did exist, the argument of the gentleman from South Carolina (Mr. Lowndes), and of my honorable colleague (Mr. Sergeant) were, in my opinion, calculated entirely to remove them, and to carry conviction to every understanding. A new question of constitutional power has now arisen on the amendment. The Constitution declares that ' the Congress shall have power to establish uniform laws on the subject of bankruptcies throughout the United States.' To this provision I am willing to give a fair and a liberal construction. Congress have the power to discharge from their debts on the terms prescribed by the bill, all persons upon whom a law emanating from the clause of the Constitution may legitimately act.

But can Congress make a law extending the penalties and the privileges of a bankrupt system to every individual in society ? Can they embrace in its provision the farmer, the clergyman, the physician, or the lawyer? Such a proposition was never seriously contended for before this day.

" By considering the meaning of the term bankrupt, we shall be able at once to solve the difficulty. In adverting to its origin, we find the literal signification of the word to be a broken counter, which by a figure of speech has been applied in our language to a broken merchant. In the commercial laws

of all the nations of the continent of Europe, bankruptcy is
confined to merchants in the strictest sense of the word. The
operation of the bankrupt laws of England has been extended
by judicial construction somewhat further, and they now embrace
within their grasp, not only the merchant properly so called,
but all persons who are traders, and are concerned in buying
and selling any kind of merchandise, unless they have been
expressly excepted by some positive legislative provision. This
exposition of the law extends not only to those who sell any
commodity in the same state in which they purchase it, but
also to the manufacturer and the mechanic who bestow upon it
their labor and their skill, and thus render it more valuable.
The bill, as it formerly stood, confined itself strictly within this
range. Indeed, it was more circumscribed as to the persons
on whom it would have operated than the bankrupt laws of
England. I am willing, then, to expound the powers of Congress upon the subject liberally.

"In construing the Constitution, Congress ought not to be
fettered by nice technical rules. I admit that they have the
power, whenever they think proper to call it into exercise,
of establishing a system of bankruptcy which shall embrace all
persons who have ever been embraced even by the bankrupt laws
of England. Further than this they cannot proceed, without
extending the plain meaning of the word bankruptcy, as it has
been received by every commercial nation of Europe, and violating both the letter and the spirit of the Constitution. In
making this admission, I am sensible that many may suppose I
am giving a latitude of construction to the instrument which is
not warranted by its spirit.

"The authority to establish uniform laws on the subject of
bankruptcies throughout the United States, is contained in a
clause of the Constitution, which immediately follows, that to .
regulate commerce with Foreign Nations, and among the several States, and with the Indian tribes. The power over bankruptcy evidently originated from, and is closely connected with

that over commerce. This commerce which Congress has the power of regulating, is chiefly, if not exclusively, conducted by merchants, in the strictest sense of the term, and principally by that class of them denominated importers. They are the men most exposed to the vicissitudes of trade, and, on that account, are more properly the object of such a law than people of any other description. It might, therefore, with much plausibility, be contended, that the power of Congress over bankruptcy is confined to that description of merchants. Another argument, which would give additional strength to this construction, arises from the general spirit of the Federal Institutions. They do not propose to embrace the internal policy of the States. The jurisdiction of the federal courts is confined by the Constitution to controversies between citizens of the different States, and between foreigners and citizens of the United States. To such suits the men who carry on the intercourse with foreign nations, and between the different States, are most generally parties.

"The object which I have in view in using these arguments, is not to prove that the constitutional power of Congress is confined to such merchants, but to show that it is contrary to the nature and the spirit of our government to extend it to all classes of people in the community. The bill as it stood before the amendment, went quite far enough. It would even then have brought the operation of the law, and the jurisdiction of the federal courts into the bosom of every community. The bill, however, as it now stands, if it should pass, will entirely destroy the symmetry of our system, and make those courts the arbiters, in almost every case of contract to which any member of society, who thinks proper to become a bankrupt, may be a party. It will at once be, in a great degree, a judicial consolidation of the Union. This was never intended by the framers of the Constitution. Some of the terrible evils which would flow from such a system, I shall have reason to delineate, when I come to speak of the policy of its adoption.

* * * * * * * * *

"I shall now proceed to lay before the House my objections to the passage of this bill ; as it now stands, certain classes of society are exposed to its adverse operations upon the commission of any of the acts of bankruptcy described in its first section. Every individual in the community, including those embraced by the bill previous to the late amendment, may become voluntary bankrupts. It will be necessary here briefly to inquire who may be declared bankrupts against their will. The adverse operation of the law will not be confined to wholesale and retail merchants, strictly speaking, and to dealers in exchange, bankers, brokers, factors, underwriters, and marine insurers. By the construction which has been placed upon the words, "other persons actually using the trade of merchandise, by buying and selling in gross or by retail," not only every dealer in any article, but every manufacturer or mechanic who purchases any material, bestows his skill and labor upon it, and sells it in its improved state, falls within the compulsory branch of this bill, unless expressly excepted by the proviso in its first section. Thus, the distiller who purchases grain, converts it into whisky and sells the whisky, would clearly be within its operation. The miller, also, who buys wheat and sells it converted into flour, may be declared a bankrupt against his will. These cases are cited only as examples to illustrate the general rule. Each individual member can imagine many others.

"I will now proceed to that which strikes my mind as a radical objection to the existence of this or any other adversary bankrupt bill in the United States. It arises from the nature of our free institutions, and is one that exists in no other country on the globe. It springs out of the best principles of the Federal Constitution, and it cannot be removed without expunging them from the instrument. In what manner is a person to be declared a bankrupt by the bill now before the House ? On the petition of any creditor, accompanied by an affidavit of the truth of his debt, the circuit or district judge of the United States is authorized to issue a commission of bankruptcy. The alleged bankrupt may, however, appear before the commissioners, deny that he has committed any act of bankruptcy, and demand a trial by a jury of his country, before the judge who issues the commission. This is a right of which he cannot be deprived by the power of Congress. In the emphatic language of the Constitution, 'he shall not be deprived of his life, his liberty, or his property, without due process of law.' This trial before the circuit or district judge may and probably will, in a majority of cases, be delayed for years before its final termination.

" In free governments we cannot move with the celerity of despotism. During its pendency, what becomes of the property of the alleged bankrupt ? He cannot be dispossessed of it under the Constitution of the country, or by the provisions of this bill, until the jury shall have convicted him of its first section. But although it cannot be wrested from him until after the event, yet the moment the commission issues, he, in effect, loses all control over his estate. The reason of this is, that by the provisions of the bill all intermediate dispositions made by the debtor of his property are absolutely void, should he finally be declared a bankrupt. No person, therefore, would with safety in the meantime enter into any contracts with him, or purchase any part of his estate. From the very nature of an adverse bankrupt system, this must necessarily be the case. If it were not, every man charged with having committed an act of bankruptcy would demand a trial by jury before the district or circuit judge of the United States, so that during its pendency he might have an opportunity to dispose of his property as he thought proper. What, then, is the situation in which the bill places every man within its adverse provisions ?

" Any of his creditors or pretended creditors, by making an ex parte affidavit of the truth of his debt, without ever proving by his own oath or otherwise any act of bankruptcy against him, may bring upon him inevitable and overwhelming destruc-

tion. If envy or malice against him rankles in the soul of any
enemy who either is his creditor, or who will swear that he is,
that enemy may wreak his vengeance to the full extent of his
wishes, by having a commission of bankruptcy issued against
him. The commission itself would be the death-warrant of his
property, notwithstanding his property may have been sufficient
to discharge his debts, and he may have been guilty of no act
of bankruptcy. If he submits to the commission, his credit is
gone, and his power of exertion is at an end until he shall have
obtained his final discharge. If he does not, and demands a
trial, he is, during its pendency, in the situation of Tantalus in
the infernal regions. Although he may be surrounded by all
the comforts of life, and the means of extricating himself from
his difficulties, he has not the power of using them.

"If he should be a merchant, his counting-house must be
closed, and his capital remain idle, awaiting the result of a
tedious lawsuit. If he be a farmer who has carried on a distil-
lery, or who has been a miller, or retail merchant, he cannot
dispose of an acre of his land, or any of his personal property,
until the controversy is determined. Whether, therefore, he
submits to the commission, or does not, if he be an honest man,
he is exposed to inevitable ruin. If he be a fraudulent debtor,
the delay of the trial will afford him ample time and opportunity to secrete his property, and place it beyond the reach of
his creditors; and in this situation he will have the strongest
temptation to be guilty of fraud. The bankrupt law of England, the model from which the present bill has been drawn,
provides an effectual remedy for this evil. It is one, however,
which we have no constitutional power to adopt; and if we
had, it would be repugnant to every feeling of the hearts of
freemen. In that country the bare issuing of the commission is
itself equivalent to an execution.

"The debtor is at once deprived of the possession of all his
property, and it is vested in the commissioners. Although he
may declare he has never been guilty of an act of bankruptcy,

and petitions for a trial, he petitions in vain. The iron hand of the law is upon him, and no innocence can elude its grasp. In that country the law declares that ' caveats against commissions are not allowed, for they give too much time to a fraudulent debtor.' The proceedings under it resemble those of the judges in the infernal regions, who first condemn and afterwards hear. They first deprive a man of all his property by virtue of the commission, and after the evil has been done, allow him to apply to the chancellor to have it superseded. From the nature of those governments on the continent of Europe, under whose dominion bankrupt laws prevail, and from the peculiar character of these laws, and the commercial tribunals by whom they are administered, the same evils do not exist. I will not exhaust the patience of the House by detailing their different provisions.

" It may be said, as the bill provides, that the petitionary creditor, before the commission can issue, shall give bond to be taken by the circuit or district judge, in such penalty and with such security as he may direct, conditioned that the obliger shall prove the debtor to be a bankrupt, he will be enabled to recover damages to the extent of any injury which he may sustain in case the condition of the bond should be violated. The remedy, from its nature, could be no compensation for an injury sustained. To inform a man, after he had been arrested in the pursuit of his business by a commission of bankruptcy, after his prospects in life had been blasted, after his credit had been destroyed, and after he had been pursued for years in a course of litigation which had terminated in his favor, that he might then enter upon another law-suit, and bring his action upon the bond, would be laughing at his calamity.

" This would present no prospect of indemnity, even if the obligors should be solvent ; but from the ignorance of the judges, so far removed from the people, as those of the United States necessarily are, respecting the solvency of the sureties ; and from the lapse of time which must transpire before any suit

could be sustained upon his bond, it would in most instances be
of little or no value. These, then, would be the effects of the
bill on the persons within its adverse operations. Let us next
inquire what would be the moral and practical effects of this bill,
with the amendment just adopted, of the gentleman from Kentucky. Should it pass in its present shape, I should shudder
at the consequences. How will it affect the great agricultural
interests of the country?

"I have the honor, in part, to represent a district chiefly composed of farmers. They are honest, they are industrious, and
they esteem their contracts to be sacred and inviolable. The word
of each of them, could their existence be perpetuated, binds
them as forcibly as their bond. Have they, or have any other
agriculturists over the whole range of this extensive Union,
asked you to pass a bankrupt law in their favor? Have they
even petitioned you to discharge them from the obligation of their
contracts, which they feel themselves as much bound in conscience as in law to perform? It is certain that many honest
and respectable men of their valuable class of society have been
unfortunate, and I pity them from my inmost soul; but I
beseech you, spare them from a law for which they have never
asked, and which would tempt them to add guilt to misfortune.

"What then would be the necessary operation of such a law,
when brought home to those and every other member of society? Once declare that contracts shall be no longer sacred,
that any debtor, whether he has been a trader or not, by com-
plying with the provisions of the law, may have an election
held by his creditors, and if two-thirds of these in number
or value consent, may be relieved from all his debts against the
will of the remainder; and you make a direct attack on the
very first principles of moral honesty, by which the great mass
of the people have been hitherto directed. Let a bankrupt be
presented to the view of society, who has become wealthy since
his discharge, and who, after having ruined a number of his
creditors, shields himself from the payment of his honest debts

by his certificate, and what effects would such a spectacle be likely to produce? Examples of this nature must at length demoralize any people. The contagion introduced by the laws of the country, would for that very reason, spread like a pestilence, until honesty, honor, and faith will at length be swept from the intercourse of society. Leave the agricultural interest pure and uncorrupted, and they will forever form the basis on which the Constitution and liberties of your country may safely repose. Do not, I beseech you, teach them to think lightly of the solemn obligations of contracts. No government in earth, however corrupt, has ever enacted a bankrupt law for farmers; it would be a perfect monster in this country, where our institutions depend altogether on the virtue of the people. We have no constitutional power to pass the amendment proposed by the gentleman from Kentucky; and if we had we never should do so, because such a provision would spread a moral taint through society which would corrupt it to its very core.

" By the fifty-sixth section it is provided that any creditor of a bankrupt, appearing before the commissioners, may, at his election, have the validity of his claim determined in the circuit court of the district in which the bankrupt resides. The same privilege is extended to the assignee's objections to the validity of any claim upon the bankrupt, presented before the commissioners; in this manner every lawsuit which could arise in the settlement of a bankrupt's estate, respecting the demands of any of his creditors, would be drawn into the circuit court for decision. This would be the case whether he became a bankrupt voluntarily or by compulsion, and without any regard either to his occupation or place of residence, or that of his creditors. The whole structure of the national judiciary would be changed.

*　　*　　*　　*　　*　　*　　*

" Another serious objection to the passage of the bill is its manifest tendency to the perpetration of fraud. It is true it has been strenuously maintained by its friends, that it will, in a

3*

great degree, repress that evil. Has the experience of England justified them in making this prediction? Does not the testimony taken before the House of Commons prove clearly the contrary? Indeed so pressed down with weight was my honorable colleague (Mr. Sergeant) that he was obliged to attribute the innumerable frauds which had been committed under the bankrupt law of that country, not to the operation of the law itself, but to the general corruption that prevailed among the people. This bill, should it become a law, must be productive of innumerable frauds, unless it will have the power changing the nature of man, and rendering him the less criminal because he is the more tempted. He who created man, and therefore knew best his heart, directed him to pray that he might not be led into temptation. This bill informs the debtor, that if he will conform to its provisions, he shall obtain a certificate which will discharge him from all his debts. The State insolvent laws declare to him that when he has given up all his property for the use of his creditors, he has done no more than his duty, and that his future acquisitions shall be answerable until his debts are paid. If a debtor can pass the ordeal of this bankrupt law, and obtain his certificate, he may then in security enjoy that property which successful fraud has enabled him to conceal under the State insolvent laws ; however, he must know that the moment his concealed property is brought to light, it is liable to be seized by his creditors. Whilst, therefore, a bankrupt law holds out every temptation to make the debtor dishonest, an insolvent law presents him no such inducement. Indeed, his true policy is directly the reverse. Upon his good and fair conduct, and the consequent favorable discharge of his creditors, depends his hopes of a discharge.

* * * * * * *

" I shall now come to my concluding argument against the passage of this bill. It would tend again to arouse the spirit of wild and extravagant speculation, which has spread distress far and wide over the land. It will tend again to produce those

evils for which its friends say it is intended to provide a remedy. What has been the history of this country? Upon this
subject, let us not turn a deaf ear to the dictates of experience
It is the best teacher of political wisdom.

"Under our glorious Constitution, the human mind is unrestrained in the pursuit of happiness, the calm of despotism does
not rest upon us. Neither the institutions of the country, nor
the habits of society, have established any *castes* within the
limits of which man shall be confined. The human intellect
walks abroad in its majesty. This admirable system of government, which incorporates the rights of man into the Constitution of the country, develops all the latent resources of the
intellect, and brings them into active energy. The road to
wealth and to honor is not closed against the humblest citizen—
and Heaven forbid that it ever should be! It is however, the
destiny of man to learn that evil often treads closely upon the
footsteps of good. The very liberty we enjoy, unless restrained
by the dictates of morality and of prudence, has a tendency to
make us discontented with our condition. It often produces a
restless temper, and a disposition to be perpetually changing
our pursuits, for the purpose of becoming more wealthy and
more distinguished. The frame of mind produced by freedom,
if kept within proper bound, is a source of the greatest advantages to society and to individuals: if unrestrained, and suffered to run wild, it leads to every species of extravagance and
folly.

"A few merchants both in the cities and in the country have
amassed splendid and princely fortunes. These have glittered in
the fancy of the thoughtless and unsuspecting countryman, and
have moved his ambition or his avarice. He never calculated
that it requires a man of considerable parts with great experience to make an accomplished merchant; and that, with all
these advantages, but few comparatively are successful. His
son is taught book-keeping at a country school, and then he
abandons the pursuit of his fathers. He leaves the business of

agriculture, which is the most peaceful, the most happy, the most independent, and, I might add, the most respectable, in society, to become a merchant. He spurns the idea of treading in the path of his ancestors, and acquiring his living by the sweat of his brow. Wealth and distinction have become his idols, and turned his brain. Is not this the history of thousands in our country within the last twenty years? It was not difficult to predict what would be the melancholy catastrophe. Bankruptcy and ruin have fallen upon the thoughtless adventurers.

"Happy would it have been for the country had this spirit of speculation confined itself to the farmers who turned merchants. We have witnessed it spreading over every class of the community. We have, in innumerable instances, seen the plain, sober, industrious, and inexperienced farmer, converted into a speculator in bonds and stocks. We have lived in a time when the foundations of society appeared to be shaken, and when the love of gain seemed to swallow up every other passion of the heart. This disposition gave birth to hundreds and thousands of banks, which have spread themselves over the country. Their reaction upon the people doubled the force of the original cause which produced them. They deluged the country with bank paper. The price of land rose far above its real value; it commanded from $200 to $400 per acre in many parts of the district which I have the honor, in part, to represent; and I know one instance in which a man agreed to give $1,500 per acre for a tract of land, which he afterwards laid out in town lots. He sold the lots at so large a profit, that he would have accumulated an independent fortune by the speculation had not the times changed, and the lot-holders in consequence been unable to pay the purchase money.

"The universal delusion has vanished, the enchantment is at an end; the people have been restored to their sober senses. In the change, which was rapid, many honest and respectable citizens have been ruined. Among many, misery and want have usurped the abodes of happiness and plenty. I most sincerely deplore their situation ; but, as legislators, we should all have some compassion upon the community. Experience has taught us a lesson which, I trust, we shall never forget—that a wild and extravagant spirit of speculation is one of the greatest curses that can pervade our country. Do you wish again to raise it ? Do you wish again to witness the desolation which it has spread over the land, and which we now are slowly repairing ? Then pass this bankrupt bill ! Inform the farmer, who is now contented and happy, and whom experience has taught the danger of entering into trade, that he may become a merchant or a land jobber ; that he may proceed to any excess he thinks proper ; that he need confine the extravagance of his speculations within no other limit but the extent of his credit ; that if, at last, he should be successful, unbounded wealth will be his portion, if not, the law will discharge him from all his debts, and enable him to begin a new career. Hold out a lure to the industrious classes in society to abandon their useful and honorable pursuits, and enter into speculation of some kind or other, by proclaiming it as the law that, if they should prove unsuccessful, their debts shall be cancelled, and they shall be restored to their former situation. Such a law would present the strongest temptations to every man in society to become indolent and extravagant, because every man in society is embraced in its provisions. In these respects it is as novel as it is dangerous. Rest assured, Mr. Speaker, that our population require the curb more than the rein. If you hold out such encouragement to unbounded speculation as this bill presents, we shall, before many years, see all the occurrences again presented before us which have involved the country in unexampled distress. The time may come, in ages hence, when a bankrupt law may become necessary for the encouragement of commerce. History has instructed us, that nations, like men, rise, and flourish, and decay. At present our population possess all the vigor and enterprise of

youth. The stimulus of such a bill would drive us on to madness It would be putting into the hands of Phæton the reins
of the chariot of the sun The day will come, but I trust it
is now far distant, when old age shall fall upon us as a nation,
when wealth shall beget luxury and corruption, and when we
shall be enfeebled in all our exertions. Then it may be necessary to hold out extraordinary allurements to commercial enterprise. When that day shall arrive, when our country shall be
sinking into decline, when her energies shall be paralysed, and
when perhaps, a new Republic as vigorous as ours at present
may be her competitor in commerce, then and not till then,
will it be necessary that Congress should exercise the power
vested in them by the Constitution, and pass uniform laws on
the subject of bankruptcies."

The vote on the bankrupt bill was taken immediately after
the delivery of Mr. Buchanan's powerful argument against it,
and was defeated by a vote of 99 nays to 72 ayes. Of the
nays, fifty-four were from the southern States, while of the
ayes only fifteen were from that section of our country.

At this session, the question of internal improvements
by Congress was brought up in a formidable manner. The
presidential election was approaching, and the success of
De Witt Clinton in New York, who was receiving all the
honors of the day, created an intense desire in the minds of
public men to be imitators in some way of his acts, in hopes
that, at least, they might be able to catch a portion of the
popularity he had achieved. The question came before Congress in a definite form, in a bill for making appropriations to
repair the Cumberland road. Mr. Buchanan voted against the
appropriation, and introduced a resolution to cede the road to
the States in which it laid. The resolution was not, however,
then adopted, and the bill making appropriations for the repair
of the road passed both houses of Congress, and was presented
to Mr. Monroe for his signature. It drew from that distin-

guished man his celebrated Veto-Message upon internal improvements, in which he went into a thorough review of the entire constitutional question, showing how far the jurisdiction and authority of the Federal government extended in such matters. This able and convincing State-paper has never been answered, and it may be said to have settled the position of the democratic party on this important question of politics. Mr. Adams undertook to question Monroe's view of this subject in his inaugural address, but it only served to awaken public discussion upon the extent of constitutional power in the matter, and thus the sooner settle the true interpretation of the organic law.

The second session of the seventeenth Congress commenced on the 2d of December, 1822, and ended on the 3d of March, 1823. There were a number of very important subjects brought before it for consideration, and among the acts passed were several of national interest. Among others was one to regulate the collection of duties, imposts, and tonnage, which excited considerable discussion. During this session an act was passed regulating our commercial intercourse with the British colonial possessions in the West Indies, Nova Scotia, and New Brunswick. The most important discussion of this session was, however, on the tariff question. The general prostration of mechanical industry, consequent upon the previous period of inordinate speculation, had rendered the people clamorous for some relief. We were just recovering from the effects of a war, and there seemed to be not only a universal demand, but a general want of some measure which would restore a healthy and prosperous tone to business. That party which contend that it is the duty of government to pass protective duties in order to foster manufacturing industry, were unceasing in their demands for a new tariff bill. One was accordingly introduced, but as it did not seem to please either the friends or enemies of protection, it did not pass. Mr. Buchanan did not hesitate to express his opinion freely in regard to it. In some respects he approved of the measure, but not as a protective act. He expressly stated that we were only authorized to impose a tariff for revenue and as such he advocated the bill before Congress. He showed, in the first place, the alarming deficit in the annual revenue of $1,250,000. Besides this, there was a permanent debt of over forty millions of dollars which must be met by some measure which it was the duty of Congress to pass.

"There can be no doubt," said Mr. Buchanan, "but that every member of this committee will concur with me in opinion, that our debt ought, if possible, to be discharged as soon as it shall be redeemable. No one will contend that a public debt is a public blessing. The payment of the national debt is one of the best means of preparing for war. The resources of the nation ought not to continue mortgaged to the public creditor ; but they should be ready to be applied at all times towards the defence of the country. This, at least, is my system of policy. Under this view of the subject, we are brought irresistibly to the conclusion, that revenue must be raised, at least that it ought to be raised. The question then is, from what objects shall we derive the means necessary to extinguish the national debt ? It is admitted by all that a duty upon imports is the most economical and least oppressive mode of raising revenue. It is the mode most in consonance with the character of a free people. It does not require the agency of the tax-gatherer or the excise-man. The practice of the government for more than thirty years has sanctified this method in the minds of the people. They will not now readily submit to direct taxes or to excises when the country is at peace,—I say, emphatically, when the country is at peace—because I know that in times of actual war, or of approaching danger, the American people will cheerfully submit to any sacrifices which may be necessary to provide for the common defence, and promote the security and glory of the nation."

"The necessity of adopting a new tariff, for the purpose of

raising revenue, has not only been stated by the Secretary of
the Treasury, but he has distinctly recommended many of the
articles on the importation of which additional duties should be
imposed. These are all embraced in the provisions of the present bill, though the increase of duty is in several instances
greater than what he recommended. Yet, notwithstanding its
friends have declared their intention to amend it, and make it
conform more nearly with that recommendation, this is the
measure whose blasting influence, if adopted, gentlemen declare,
will paralyze agriculture, ruin commerce, and destroy the navy.
Phantoms the most deadly and destructive, have been presented
before the committee, as the natural offspring of this measure.
One would almost be led to believe, that the bill now under
consideration was the true box of Pandora, from which, if
enacted into a law, all the evils that can invade the human race
would proceed. The gentlemen from Georgia and Massachusetts (Mr. Tattnall and Mr. Gorham) have proclaimed it tyranny,
and tyranny which ought to be resisted. Yet all this mighty
conflagration has been raised to intimidate us from adopting a
system, which in substance has been recommended by the intelligent and independent officer at the head of the treasury, merely
because in its indirect operation it may benefit certain necessary domestic manufactures. I confess I never did expect to
hear inflammatory speeches of this kind within these walls,
which ought to be sacred to union ; I never did expect to hear
the East counselling the South to resistance, that we might
thus be deterred from prosecuting a measure of policy, urged
upon us by the necessities of the country. *If I know myself,
I am a politician neither of the East, nor of the West, of the
North, nor the South : I therefore shall forever avoid any expressions, the direct tendency of which, must be to create sectional jealousies, sectional divisions, and at length disunion, that worst and
last of all political calamities.*"

In the same speech, Mr. Buchanan took occasion to repeat

that he considered the bill as a revenue measure. "Money" said he, "must be collected—the public debt must be paid," and to do this he knew of no better or more equitable method, than to raise it by the imposition of duties upon foreign importations. In the course of this speech he paid the following eloquent tribute to the agricultural portion of society :

"Gentleman have contended that should this bill be adopted, the agricultural interest of the country will be greatly injured. If this were the case, it would be a conclusive objection to its passage. The farmers are the most useful, as they are the most numerous class of society. No measure ought ever to be adopted by the government that will bear hardly upon them They are the body of men, among whom you may expect to find in an eminent degree that virtue without which your American institutions could not continue to exist. Agriculture is the most noble employment of men. It communicates vigor to the body and independence to the mind. My constituents are principally farmers, and I should feel it both my duty and my inclination to resist any measure which would be pernicious to their interests. The agriculturists are the great body of consumers. It is from them that the revenue must be derived, no matter what may be the mode by which it is collected. They must equally pay it, whether in the shape of an excise, a land tax, or an impost on the importation of foreign articles. I will never consent to adopt a general restrictive system, because that class of the community would then be left at the mercy of the manufacturers. The interest of the many would be sacrificed to promote the wealth of the few. The farmer, then, in addition to the payment which he would be thus compelled to pay the manufacturer, would have also to sustain the expenses of the government. If this bill proposed a system which would lead to such abuses, it should not receive my support."

The sessions of the seventeenth Congress were of more than

ordinary importance. There had been a number of questions before that body which commanded a wide-spread and general attention. The bankrupt law, the question of internal improvements, and the doctrine of protection to manufactures, had all been ably and fully discussed. The friends of the bankrupt law had assailed the fortress of democracy and equal rights in vain. They had been put to flight in their determined and arduous attempts to model our institutions upon the basis of the worn-out, effete, aristocratic, and special-privileged governments of Europe, where the masses are the machines of the ruling classes. Among those who contributed in an eminent degree to achieve this result stands James Buchanan. At this day it is a gratification to look over the records of the proceedings in Congress, and mark the names of those devoted friends to democratic doctrines, who so nobly and heroically preserved them in the outset of our history as a nation, from the combined forces which federalism brought to bear against them. It is a lamentable fact that while our people have paid due homage to those who achieved by their swords our democratic institutions, they have not given the meed of honest, deserving praise to the men who immediately succeeded them, and who preserved this noble inheritance on the floor of our national legislature against all the arts which eloquence could master or sophistry invent. Among these names ought to stand forever remembered those of John Randolph, Nathaniel Macon, John Taylor, George McDuffie, Andrew Stevenson, James Buchanan, and others equally deserving of honorable remembrance.

CHAPTER IV.

The Tariff Act—Reception of Lafayette—The Niagara Sufferers—The Election of John Quincy Adams.

THE eighteenth Congress opened on the 1st of December, 1823. Mr. Buchanan had been re-elected, and found upon his arrival at the capital, a number of new individuals whom he had not previously encountered in public life. Among these were Mr. Webster, of Massachusetts, then in the vigor of his youth ; Henry Clay, of Kentucky, overflowing with the grand conceptions he had formed of the great "American System ;" and Edward Livingston, of Louisiana, the eloquent lawyer, the polished orator, and profound statesman. In the Senate, Hon. Thomas H. Benton, of Missouri, had made his appearance, hailing from the Kansas of 1820, then the *ultima thule* of our western advancement. General Jackson had been elected Senator from the State of Tennessee, and contributed not a little to the attraction of Washington society, by the prominent position in which he stood before the country, and the hopes which already many of his friends were forming of him for the future. Mr. Clay was chosen Speaker on the first day of the session, by a vote of 139 to 42, his opponent being the Hon. P. P. Barbour, of Virginia. Mr. Buchanan was placed on the Judiciary Committee, of which Mr. Webster was chairman ; a position for which he was eminently qualified by his careful and accurate reading in all the details of law and jurisprudence.

At this session the tariff bill came up again under the lead of Mr. Clay, who brought to its support all the power of his oratory, and all the influence which his personal character could produce. He had christened it "The American System ;" and such, in the depressed condition of the country, there was some plausibility in calling it. The bill was contested inch by inch, Mr. Webster, afterwards a high tariff man, opposing it with all his power. Besides Mr. Webster, there were other able and distinguished advocates of free trade—Mr. Baylies, from his own State ; Mr. C. C. Cambreleng, of New York ; Messrs. Randolph, Barbour, Stevenson, Rives, and Archer, of Virginia ; Messrs. Mangum and Saunders, of North Carolina ; Messrs. McDuffie, Hamilton, and Poinsett, of South Carolina ; Messrs. Forsyth and Cuthbert of Georgia ; Mr. Edward Livingston, of Louisiana, and others. Mr. Clay was the leading speaker on the other side of the question ; and after a protracted contest of ten weeks the bill was finally carried by only five majority. In the Senate the vote was still closer, where it stood twenty-five to twenty-three. The bill never could have passed, had it not been for the depressed condition of the country, and the pressing demands upon the treasury for more revenue, in order to pay the public debt, if possible, as fast as it became due. As a revenue measure, it was voted for by Gen. Jackson in the Senate, by Mr. Buchanan in the House, and by other democratic members, who expressly stated their opposition to a tariff whose object was simply protection. Congress adjourned on the 27th of May, 1824. It had passed two hundred and eleven acts, and been a session of great activity and considerable importance. Mr. Buchanan had participated generally in the discussions, and measured his powers with Mr. Webster in debate, and proved that even the youthful giant of Massachusetts found his peer, at least, in the stately and careful logic of the son of Pennsylvania. There was at this session a great deal of president-making, the members of Congress then having more to do with the matter than at present. Mr. Buchanan's preferences were well known to be in favor of Gen. Jackson, of whom he was an early

and devoted friend.   Gen. Jackson, Henry Clay, W. H. Crawford, and John Quincy Adams were the candidates, and all parties were preparing for a vigorous and determined campaign.
It is well known, neither candidate received a majority of the
electoral votes.   It accordingly devolved upon the House of
Representatives, at its next session, to elect a President.

The second session of the eighteenth Congress was therefore
looked forward to with great interest.   It assembled at Washington on the 6th of December, 1824.   The very first event for
which it was distinguished was the reception of Gen. Lafayette,
then on a visit to the land which he had so nobly assisted in
wresting from the grasp of a tyrannical oppressor.   As Lafayette was one of those unfortunate men who happened to be born
on foreign soil, and who in these later days, it is asserted, have
become so inimical and dangerous to American liberty, it may
be interesting to recur to the speech he delivered upon the
august occasion when he was received by both houses of Congress.   Mr. Clay was Speaker of the House, and in welcoming
the illustrious stranger, in his most eloquent and imaginative
strain, he said, " General, you are in the midst of posterity !"
Lafayette, after saying that it had been his happiness to be
adopted as a young soldier, a favored son of America, remarked :
" No, Mr. Speaker, posterity has not begun for me ; since in the
sons of my companions and friends I find the same public feelings, and permit me to add, the same feelings in my behalf
which I have had the happiness to experience in their fathers.
Sir, I have been allowed, forty years ago, before a committee
of Congress of thirteen States, to express the fond wishes of an
American heart.   On this day I have the honor to enjoy the
delight, to congratulate the representatives of the Union so
vastly enlarged, in the realization of those wishes, even beyond
every human expectation, and upon the almost infinite prospects
we can with certainty anticipate."

. If Lafayette were " in the midst of posterity," at the present
day, and surrounded with the cry of " America for Americans,"

he could hardly say, " that he found the same public feelings, which he had the happiness to experience in our fathers."

One of the first matters brought before Congress at this session, was a bill to indemnify the sufferers on our Niagara frontier, caused by the wanton devastation of the British troops during the war of 1812. Mr. Buchanan took the ground that if the property was destroyed in accordance with the rules of civilized warfare, then we were bound to indemnify the individuals who had been injured. If such, however, were not the case, every motive of public policy forbade it. Mr. B. went on to show that if the bill then before the House should pass, we would stand before the world as having justified Great Britain in her lawless and inhuman conduct—conduct that had met the reprobation of the civilized world. A short extract from Mr. Buchanan's speech on this subject, will show the perfidious conduct of the British troops, as well as his own exact position upon the bill :

Mr. B. said, " There was another view which this subject presents, which adds the guilt of perfidy to that of violation of the laws of war. Whilst the village of Buffalo still presented a hostile front to the enemy, a capitulation was entered into by Col. Chapin, of our army, with Gen. Rail, who commanded the British forces. By that instrument, it was solely agreed, 'that private property and private persons should not be molested or injured.' Upon the faith of this capitulation, the British forces entered the town. The testimony proves that before its date they were all acquainted with the fact that a large body of the United States troops had been quartered there, and that many of the houses were places of military deposit. With a full knowledge of these circumstances, they entered into the capitulation. What was then their subsequent conduct ? Instead of separating the military stores from the houses in which they were deposited, instead of destroying public property, they involved the whole village in one common conflagration. At the most inclement season of the year in a northern climate, regardless of their faith, they set fire to the town, and drove its inhabitants to seek shelter and bread from the compassion of strangers. And this, under pretence of what they well knew before the capitulation, that there were military stores deposited in many of the private houses. And yet this destruction is attempted to be justified by the laws of war established among civilized nations. Sir," said Mr. B., " I may be asked if I am willing to afford these sufferers any relief ? I answer without hesitation, I am not. They have claims upon our generosity, not upon our justice. I would mitigate their calamities, not indemnify them for their losses. They have suffered more than the common misfortunes of war—they are therefore entitled to the compassion of paternal government."

The most exciting, and indeed, important business, before this Congress, was the election of President. A long debate ensued upon the rules to be adopted in conducting the election by the House of Representatives. In the course of the discussion, it was proposed to sit in secret conclave, if the delegation of any one State demanded it. This Mr. Buchanan opposed with indignant eloquence, showing most conclusively how firm was his reliance on the popular intelligence, and how earnest his devotion to the rights of the people.

" The American people," said Mr. B., " have a right to be present and inspect all the proceedings of their representatives, unless their own interests forbid it. In relation to our concerns with foreign governments, it may become necessary to close our galleries. Our designs in such cases might be frustrated if secrecy were not for a time preserved. Whenever there shall be disorder in the gallery, we have also a right to clear it, and are not bound to suffer our proceedings to be interrupted. Except in these cases he at present could recollect none which would justify the House in excluding the people.

"In electing a President of the United States," said Mr. B., "we are, in my opinion, peculiarly the representatives of the the people. On that important occasion, we shall emphatically represent their majesty. We do not make a President for ourselves only, but also for the whole people of the United States. They have a right that it shall be done in public. He therefore protested against going into a secret conclave when the House should decide this all-important question. He said that the doctrine of the gentleman from Delaware (Mr. McLane) was altogether new to his mind. That gentleman has alleged that we are called upon to elect a President, not as the representatives of the people, but by virtue of the Constitution. Sir," said Mr. B., "who created the Constitution? Was it not the people of the United States? And did they not by this very instrument delegate us as representatives, the power of electing a President for them? It is by virtue of this instrument we hold our seats here. And, if there be any case in which we are bound to obey their will, this is peculiarly that one. To them we must be answerable for the proper exercise of this duty.

"What are the consequences which will result from closing the doors of the gallery? We shall impart to the election an air of mystery. We shall give exercise to the imaginations of the multitude in conjecturing what scenes are acting within the hall. Busy Rumor, with her hundred tongues, will circulate reports of wicked combination, and of corruptions which have no existence. Let the people see what we are doing ; let them know that it is neither more nor less than putting our ballots into our boxes, and they will soon become satisfied with the spectacle and retire. The gentleman from Delaware (Mr. McLane) has urged upon us the precedent which now exists on this subject. Mr. Buchanan said he revered the men of former days by whom this precedent was established. He had good reason, however, to believe that the intense excitement which existed at that time among the people at the seat of govern-

ment was occasioned in a considerable degree by their exclusion
from the gallery. They came in crowds into the house, but were
prohibited from entering the hall. Currents and counter-cur-
rents of feeling kept them continually agitated. New conjec-
tures of what was doing within were constantly spreading among
them. Mystery always gives birth to suspicion. If those people
had been permitted to enter, much of the excitement which
then prevailed would never have existed.

"It has been said that there might and probably would be
disorder if we admitted the people into the gallery. Mr. B.
could scarcely believe this possible. He had too high an opinion
of the American people to suffer himself to entertain such an
apprehension. Should we, however, be mistaken, where is the
power of the Speaker? Where that of the House? We can
turn them out, and we shall then have a sufficient apology for
doing so. But to declare in the first instance that they shall
be excluded upon the request of any one out of twenty-four
States would be a libel both on the people of the United States
and the members of the House. Mr. B. asked pardon for the
expression if it were considered too harsh.

"Mr. B. said he knew well his friend from Delaware was
willing that all his conduct in regard to the presidential question should be exhibited before the public, and that it was
principle and principle alone which had suggested his remarks.
That which gives this subject its chief importance, Mr. B. said,
is the precedent. He was anxious that it should be settled on
sure foundations. If the rule in its present form should be
adopted, it may and probably will be dangerous in future
times. At present our republic is in its infancy. At this
time he entertained no fear of corruption. In the approaching
election it can, therefore, make but little difference whether the
gallery shall be opened or closed. But the days of darkness
may, and, unless we shall escape the fate of all other Republics,
will, come upon us. Corruption may yet stalk abroad over our
happy land. When she aims a blow against the liberties of

the people it will be done in secret. Such deeds always show the light of day. They can be perpetrated with a much greater chance of success, in the secrecy of an electoral conclave, than when the proceedings of the House are fully exposed to public view. Let us then establish a precedent, which will have a strong tendency to prevent corrupt practices hereafter."

The result of the election is well known to every one at all acquainted with political history. In the electoral college John Quincy Adams received 84 votes, William H. Crawford 41, Andrew Jackson 99, and Henry Clay 37. Adams, Crawford, and Jackson being the three candidates who had received the highest number of votes, and neither a majority, it devolved upon the House of Representatives to make a choice of a President. There were at that time twenty-four States, and Mr. Adams received the votes of thirteen, Mr. Crawford of four, and Gen. Jackson of seven. Thus, though Gen. Jackson was without doubt the popular choice, he was defeated, as was generally charged at that time, by an arrangement between the friends of Mr. Clay and Mr. Adams, by which the former was to receive the position of Secretary of State under the new administration. This charge was indignantly repelled by Mr. Clay and his friends, and as Mr. Buchanan has been stoutly charged with having originated the report, the facts of the case should be known. The truth is, that the idea of the friends of Mr. Clay and Mr. Adams uniting, originated in Washington, at first from surmises, founded as much as any-thing upon the well-known hostility of Mr. Clay to "a military candidate." These Washington rumors were first communi-cated to the public by Hon. George Kremer, of Pennsylvania, in a letter to a western newspaper, and they were mentioned by Mr. Buchanan to Gen. Jackson, with whom he was on terms of much intimacy, and whose election he greatly desired. In the course of the conversation, Gen. Jackson indignantly re-marked, that before he would "be guilty of such an act, he would see the earth open and *swallow up* both Mr. Clay and his friends and himself with them." The fact, however, that Mr. Clay accepted office in Mr. Adams's administration, was the principal ground upon which the charge was grounded. They had been opposing candidates at the presidential election, and, however pure may have been the acts both of Mr. Adams and Mr. Clay, the fact of the latter going into Mr. Adams' cabinet, and the fact of his friends having been the means of placing Mr. Adams in his distinguished position, could not be separated in the minds of the people. It is doubtless true that no bargain existed. Mr. Benton in his "Thirty Years' View" does Mr. Clay the justice to say that he knew of his determination to vote for Mr. Adams, and not for Gen. Jackson, before the 12th of December, 1824. Mr. Clay's friends have always complained bitterly of the injustice done him by this rumor, and a few of the more malevolent have tried to connect Mr. Buchanan with it, but without the least foundation. He merely stated rumors to Gen. Jackson, which were current in private circles, and which had even been published in the public journals. The fact is, that it was not so much the rumor of "bargain and sale" that injured Mr. Clay, as it was the disregard of the will of the people in the election of Mr. Adams. Gen. Jackson had the highest number of votes of any of the candidates, and the preferences of some of the States which had voted for Mr. Clay himself, it was well known were for Gen. Jackson as their second choice. Yet the friends of Mr. Clay in Congress assumed to virtually decide that "military Presidents" were dangerous, or, in other words, that the people did not know enough to choose their own public officers. Whatever may be said about the "bargain and sale" story, this was the real issue in the election, and this disregard for the popular will, was doubtless *the* error of Mr. Clay's life, for he soon after joined the whigs (then called national republicans), and entirely lost the position in the democratic party he once occupied. The election of Mr. Adams was, of course, perfectly legal, but the will of the people had neverthe-less been defeated, and most proudly did they vindicate their sovereignty at the next election, when they sent " the hero of New Orleans" to the presidential chair with a majority which no trafficking could destroy, or no chicanery evade. Mr. Buchanan, in a speech in Congress in 1828, referring to Mr. Clay's accepting office in Mr. Adams's cabinet, exclaimed with true prophetic inspiration, " What brilliant prospects has that man not sacrificed !"

CHAPTER V.

THE nineteenth Congress met on the 5th of December, 1825. Mr. Clay, having taken a seat in Mr. Adams's cabinet, was not a member of the House. Hon. John W. Taylor of New York, was chosen Speaker. Mr. Buchanan had been reëlected, and was now commencing his third term. Messrs. Levi Woodbury, and Samuel Bell of New Hampshire, made their appearance in the Senate at this session. John Randolph, by the favor of the Virginia Legislature, had been transferred from the House ; Mr. Berrien of Georgia, was there for the first time, as was Gen. Harrison of Ohio, afterwards President. In the House, among the new members, were Hon. Gulian C. Verplanck, and Gen. Aaron Ward, of New York, W. C. Rives of Virginia, and W. P. Mangum of North Carolina.

An important discussion took place during this session upon the Judiciary System. It arose upon a bill reported by Mr. Webster from the Judiciary Committee, of which Mr. Buchanan was a member, for the appointment of three new judges, for the purpose of relieving the pressing demands of business in the western States. The bill was, for some reasons, vehemently opposed. During the debate, the whole question of our judiciary system passed under discussion, and on the 9th and 10th of January, Mr. Buchanan made a long and elaborate speech upon the bill, evincing profound acquaintance with the whole range of law and jurisprudence. No speech, probably, was ever delivered ou the same subject on the floor of Congress which showed greater familiarity with all the details of law. It was a convincing proof of the possession of that accuracy of mind and discrimination of intellect which are the foundation of all true greatness. No man can be truly famous who neglects details ; upon these, as upon the concrete mass of the granite, rests the superstructure which commands the respect and admiration of the beholder.

The mission to the Congress of Panama, proposed by Mr. Adams, was, however, the exciting topic of discussion during the session. The independence of the South American Republics had been recognized during the preceding session, Mr. Buchanan as a devoted friend of liberty and free institutions giving it his most cordial support. The mission to Panama was, however, quite another affair. Mr. Clay, with all the ardor of his impulsive nature, had become an enthusiast in regard to the Southern Republics which had just then thrown off that yoke of oppression which Spain had so long laid upon them. He seemed to have conceived a kind of "holy alliance" among the Republics of this continent somewhat similar to the one which existed in Europe, among the royal robbers and despots for the subjugation of the people The idea was at least romantic. Here was one Republic, already a great nation, which had thrown off the power of George III., and which had, after thirty years, again driven invaders from the same country from its soil. The colonial dependencies of Spain had followed the example, and emerging from the long night of Spanish despotism, had asserted the glorious and sublime truth of freedom and equality. Why should not these young nations, just beginning to tread the virgin soil of a new era in the world's history, unite in alliance to protect and defend liberal institutions on this continent? What reasonable objection could be urged against a course which seemed so palpably the dictate as well of duty as of patriotism? It is proper to say, that the first view of the question was a favorable one for the course recommended by Mr. Adams and Mr. Clay. It was popular. It appealed to the warmest and holiest sentiment, next to love to God, which animates all American bosoms—the love of liberty.

Considering that Mr. Buchanan was among the first to desire the recognition of the independence of these Republics, it may seem strange that he opposed Mr. Clay's brilliant scheme ; yet he did, and as it has turned out, he may well congratulate himself upon the stand he then assumed. And this country may well congratulate itself that it never consented to be mingled up with these hybrid Republics, where liberty has been but a name, and where those distinctions of race which the Almighty has so indelibly marked upon the human family have been disregarded, and, as a consequence, most of these countries this day present scarcely more than a mass of diseased and bestialized mongrelism, lamentable evidence of God's punishment and vengeance upon all nations which dare to disregard his laws. The following extracts from Mr. Buchanan's speech on this subject delivered on the 11th of April, 1826, shows with what profound sagacity he saw and comprehended the future.

"Mr. Chairman : I cannot say, with the gentleman from Virginia (Mr. Powell), who spoke first in this debate, that I am no party man. To a certain extent I am a party man. It is well known, that, at the last presidential election, I gave my warm and decided support to the distinguished individual whom the people of this country sent to the House of Representatives with a large plurality of electoral votes. It is my fixed purpose to give the same individual my feeble support in the next contest. I shall consider the next election as an appeal from the House of Representatives to the people, for the purpose of traversing a precedent which I consider dangerous to their liberties. To this extent I am willing to confess myself a party man, as I never wish even to be suspected of fighting under false colors.

"If, however, any gentleman upon this floor has intended to charge me with being engaged in a factious opposition to the measures of the present administration, I now indignantly cast back the charge upon him, and pronounce it to be unfounded. A factious opposition consists in opposing wise measures, because they have been recommended by particular men. I never have and never shall pursue this course. It would be as impolitic as it is unjust. The people of the United States will never sustain such an opposition. If any circumstance in which he had no concern could, in my native State, prostrate the illustrious individual whom she still delights to honor, it would be, that his friends in Congress were concerned in factiously opposing the measures recommended by the present administration. But do gentlemen expect to *carry everything* in this House which *may* be proposed by the executive, merely by attempting to brand the opposition with the name of faction? I trust that such is not their intention. I feel certain if it be, *they* will be disappointed.

"I protest against the measure now before the committee being considered a party measure. I am willing to follow the example of the individual to whom I have already alluded, and judge the tree by its fruits. I have not a single feeling of personal hostility against the present chief magistrate of this Union I shall always endeavor to do him justice. There is, however, in my opinion, just cause of complaint against his friends on this floor, for endeavoring to make the subject before the committee a party question. The cause of liberty in South America is the cause of the whole American people not of any party. An opposition to that sacred cause never will, never can, be cherished by the friends of that individual who refused to accept a mission to Mexico, merely because Mexico was then suffering under the despotic sway of a tyrant and a usurper. Nothing but a strong sense of duty will induce any gentleman upon this floor to resist his own inclinations, and to stem what seems to be the popular current, by giving his vote against this mission.

* * * * * *

4*

"It will here be necessary to take a short historical view of our relations with the Southern Republics. Within the last few years we have seen in this hemisphere seven new republics emerging from the chaos of Spanish colonial despotism. The whole American people beheld this cheering spectacle with heartfelt satisfaction. We watched their progress with the most intense anxiety, and, marching in the van of nations, we first declared them to be free, sovereign, and independent. This declaration now is, and will for ever continue to be, one of the most glorious events in our annals. It was made on the 4th of March, 1822, and all hailed it with pride and with pleasure. In the summer of 1823, the Holy Alliance, at the request of Spain, were called upon to assist in subjugating what she was pleased to call her revolted colonies. The most serious apprehensions were then entertained that an unholy crusade was to be proclaimed against the cause of liberty and republican government, wherever they existed, over the whole earth. In this alarming posture of affairs, did we give any pledge to foreign nations? Did we commit the faith of the country to all or any of the Southern Republics? Certainly not. We maintained the same independent position which we had always occupied in our relations with foreign nations. The celebrated message of Mr. Monroe, of December 2d, 1823, announced to the Holy Alliance and to the world that we could not view with indifference the hostile interposition of any European power against the independence of the Southern Republics, but would consider such an attempt as dangerous to our own peace and safety. This declaration was re-echoed by millions of freemen.

    *   *   *   *   *   *

"The President, in his message to the Senate, distinctly stated, that one object which he had in view in accepting the invitation, was to influence the Southern nations to change their political constitutions in regard to their established religion, and to introduce universal toleration. From the state of public opinion in those countries, an attempt of this nature would spread one universal flame over the whole Southern continent. With whatever justice the enemies of the Catholic religion may say it has been a scourge to liberty in other countries, it has certainly been a blessing to the Southern Republics. Its ministry, so far from having set themselves in array against the principles of liberty, took a leading and an efficient part in accomplishing the revolution. This assertion is true, in its utmost extent, in relation to Mexico. The President, having discovered the danger of such an interference at the present time, very prudently changed his attitude in his message to this House, and now only intends to ask, at Panama, what I feel confident all the nations will grant without the least difficulty—the liberty to our citizens, while they reside within any of the Republics, of worshipping their God according to the dictates of their own conscience.

" I come now to speak of a subject deeply interesting to my own constituents, and the State which I have the honor, in part, to represent, as well as the rest of the Union. We have often been told, as an argument against these amendments, that they imply a want of confidence in the executive. Judging from their conduct in relation to the Island of Cuba, I am justified in declaring that my confidence in them is shaking in everything which regards the Southern Republics. England and France have been warned by our government, in the most solemn and formal manner, that we could not consent to the occupation of that island by any other European power than Spain, under any contingency whatever. Ought not the same course to have been pursued towards the South American Republics? The reasons for adopting this policy, as I shall presently show, are at least as strong in the one case as in the other ; but, yet, the documents prove that the Cabinet had arrived at a different conclusion. From them, it is evident that our government did not intend to interfere for the purpose of preventing an invasion of that island by Mexico and Colombia. Mr. Clay, in his letter of December last, to the ministers of these two nations, requested only that their invasion of Cuba might be suspended until the result of our interference in their favor with the European powers should be ascertained. In his letter to Mr. Middleton, our minister at St. Petersburgh, dated in May last, which he read to the minsters of Mexico and Columbia, he entered into a long argument to justify an invasion of that island by these Republics, in case Spain should prove obstinate, and not recognise their independence. I will not trouble the committee by reading this despatch to them, as it is in the hands of every member.

"The vast importance of the Island of Cuba to the people of the United States, may not be generally known. The commerce of this island is of immense value, particularly to the agricultural and navigating interests of the country. Its importance has been rapidly increasing for a number of years. To the middle, or grain-growing States, this commerce is almost indispensable. The aggregate value of goods, wares, merchandise, the growth, produce and manufacture of the United States exported annually to that island, now exceeds three millions and a half of dollars. Of this amount, more than the one-third consists of two articles, of pork and flour. The chief of the other products of domestic origin, are fish, fish-oil, spermaceti-candles, timber, beef, butter and cheese, rice, tallow-candles and soap. Our principal imports from that island are coffee, sugar, and molasses, articles which may almost be considered necessaries of life. The whole amount of our exports to it, foreign and domestic, is nearly six millions, and our imports nearly eight millions of dollars. The articles which constitute the medium of this commerce, are both bulky and ponderous, and their transportation employs a large portion of our foreign tonnage. More than one-seventh of the whole tonnage engaged in foreign trade, which entered the ports of the United States during the year ending the last day of September, 1824, came from Cuba ; and but little less than that proportion of the tonnage employed in our export trade sailed for that island

Its commerce is at present more valuable to the United States than that of all the Southern Republics united. How, then, can the American people even agree that this island shall be invaded by Colombia and Mexico, and pass under their dominion! Ought we not to avert its impending fate, if possible?

"Important as the island may be to us in a commercial, it is still more important in a political, view. From its position it commands the entrance to the Gulf both of Mexico and Florida. The report of our Committee of Foreign Relations, truly says, 'that the Moro may be regarded as a fortress at the mouth of the Mississippi.' Any power in possession of this island, even with a small naval force, could hermetically seal the mouth of the Mississippi. Thus the vast agricultural productions of that valley, which is drained by the father of rivers, might be deprived of the channel which nature intended for their passage. A large portion of the people of the State, one of whose representatives I am, find their way to market by the Mississippi. For this reason I feel particularly interested in this part of the subject. The great law of self-preservation, which is equally binding on individuals and nations, commands us, if we cannot obtain possession of this island ourselves, not to suffer it to pass from Spain, under whose dominion it will be harmless, and yet our government have never even protested against its invasion by Mexico and Colombia.

"There is still another view of the subject in relation to this island, which demands particular attention. Let us for a moment look at the spectacle which it will probably present in case Mexico and Colombia should attempt to revolutionize it. Have they not always marched under the standard of universal emancipation? Have they not always conquered by proclaiming liberty to the slave? In the present condition of this island what shall be the probable consequence? A servile war, which in every age has been the most barbarous and destructive, and which spares neither age nor sex. Revenge, urged on by

cruelty and ignorance, would desolate the land.   The dreadful
scenes of St. Domingo would again be presented to our view,
and would again be acted almost within sight of our own
shores.   Cuba would be a vast magazine in the vicinity of the
southern States, whose explosion would be dangerous to their
tranquillity and peace.   Is there any man in this Union who
could for one moment indulge the horrid idea of abolishing
slavery by the massacre of the highminded and chivalrous race
of men in the south ?   I trust there is not one.   For my own
part, I would without hesitation, buckle on my knapsack and
march in company with my friend from Massachusetts (Mr.
Everett) in defence of their cause."

The consent of Congress for the appointment of the mission
to Panama, was at length obtained, though in a modified form
from what was first asked.   Few questions ever before Congress attracted for the time more attention than this proposed
mission.   It was the Monroe doctrine, and a step beyond, and
was opposed by the democracy of that day, simply because
they saw and knew it was only an effort of Mr. Adams to secure
popularity, and that he himself, as it afterwards appeared, had
no idea of entering into such "entangling alliances" as was
unavoidable if the mission were carried out as at first suggested.   It was, in fact, one of those false excitements raised by
the enemies of democracy to divert the public mind from real
issues.   It had its day, like many others which have been born
and nursed since, producing for the time excited and even intemperate discussion, but finally leaving the principles of genuine democracy only the clearer and brighter, on account of the
transitory storm that had darkened the political atmosphere.

The reader will not fail to notice by the above speech of Mr.
Buchanan, that the importance of allowing no nation to take
possession of Cuba in place of Spain, is no new doctrine of his.
When it was delivered in 1826, it was considered too conserva-

tive, now the same patriotic views are denounced as "filibus-
terism."

"The second session of the nineteenth Congress commenced
on the 1st of December, 1826, and ended on the 3d of March,
1827. Almost the first business that came before it was a bill
for the relief of the surviving officers of the Revolution. It was
opposed by many members, but sustained by Mr. Buchanan, in
a speech of great eloquence and power, in which he triumphantly vindicated the duty of government in providing for the
wants of its defenders. Upon an amendment to extend the
provisions to the State militia, and which was intended to kill
the bill, Mr. Buchanan said:

"Sir, has it ever been the practice of this government to provide for the militia? Are they before you asking for any such
provision? The wealth of Crœsus would have been as that of
a beggar—the riches of Plutus would have been exhausted, in
pensioning all the militia who served during the war of independence. I feel as much gratitude to them for their services
as any man. A recollection of their glorious achievements must
warm the breast of every patriot. They have given renown to
their country; but their occasional service of a few months does
not, cannot, place them upon an equality with the soldiers who
fought, and suffered, and bled, for years in the sacred cause of
liberty. The regular soldier was continually subject to martial
law; he was compelled to remain in the service summer and
winter; and, as the gentleman from Rhode Island had eloquently said, he had marked the frozen soil of his country with
the blood which flowed from his unshod feet.

"Who are before you asking for relief? They are the rem-
nants of the band who achieved your independence. They are
now suffering the evils both of age and poverty. They have
lived so long as to be forgotten; it would seem that they had
become pilgrims and sojourners in the land. The beautiful and
bountiful feast which they have purchased for the American

people, with their sufferings and with their blood, is open to all but to them. The few veterans who survive their generation again ask—what they have hitherto asked in vain—relief from their country. This has never been hitherto granted ; nay, more, we have refused to make any direct decision on their claims. Let us not shrink from meeting the case fairly ; let them know their fate."

The bill finally became a law, and the worthy veterans who sustained the doubtful and arduous struggle for independence were at least partially rewarded for their trials and their sacrifices. The business of this session was not very important, and although there were many minor subjects of discussion, in most of which Mr. Buchanan, as usual, took a prominent and leading part, yet, as a whole, the proceedings of the session are barren of historical interest.

CHAPTER VI.

Retrenchment—Mr. Adams' Administration—Dress of Foreign Ministers—Naturalizatio: Laws—Retirement of Mr. Macon.

THE Twentieth Congress convened on the 3d of December 1827. Hon. Andrew Stevenson, of Virginia, was chosen Speaker. In the Senate were such able debaters as Woodbury, Webster, Van Buren, Macon, Hayne, Berrien, and Benton. In the House were John Davis, Edward Everett, C. Mallory, Cambreleng, Michael Hoffman, Silas Wright, W. S. Archer, P. P. Barbour, John Randolph, George McDuffie, John Bell, James K. Polk, Edward Livingston, and Edward Bates. A new Tariff bill was introduced at this session, and was contested inch by inch, but finally passed the House by eleven and the Senate by four majority. Mr. Buchanan participated fully in the discussion ; but as we have, in a previous chapter, given his opinions on this question, it is unnecessary to repeat them. Retrenchment was another subject which engaged the attention of this Congress. It is very common for Congressmen to talk a great deal on this point, but they seldom advocate any practical method in order to reach the desired object without delay or difficulty. Not so, however, Mr. Buchanan ; he proposed a measure, which by simplicity of operation, laid the axe at the root of the tree. In the course of the debate, he remarked :—

" I have a word to say to the gentleman from Maryland (Mr. Barney) before I take my seat. I am prepared at this time, and at all times, to act upon the subject of reducing our own pay. In relation to this question, I formed a deliberate opinion six years ago, which my experience ever since has served to strengthen and confirm, that the per diem allowance of members of Congress ought to be reduced. As a compensation for our loss of time, it is at present wholly inadequate. There is no gentleman fit to be in Congress, who pursues any active business at home, who does not sustain a clear loss by his attendance here. If we consider our pay in reference to our individual expenses, it is too much. It is more than sufficient to cover our expenses. I believe that the best interests of the country require that it should be reduced to a sum no more than sufficient to enable us to live comfortably whilst we are here. For my own part, I do not, like the gentleman from Maryland, give away to my constituents my per diem allowance. I receive it and use it for my own benefit. It seems that gentleman uses the surplus of his pay, in displaying his liberality to his constituents ; by making donations to churches and charitable institutions at public expense. In this manner he may use it most effectually for his own advantage ; but still I am inclined to believe his constituents, as well as mine, would be quite as well satisfied, if the surplus were allowed to remain in the treasury for the benefit of the nation. If the government of this country should ever want almoners to distribute their bounty, the last men whom the people should desire to employ in this office, would be members of Congress. It might be dangerous to trust them with the performance of such duty."

During the course of the same debate on the subject of "Retrenchment," Mr. Buchanan took occasion to explain more fully his reasons for advocating a reduction of pay.

Said Mr. B., " when I expressed myself friendly to a reduction of our own per diem allowance, I trust neither the gentleman from Maryland (Mr. Barney), nor any other upon this floor, attributed my remarks to the grovelling and selfish desire of courting popularity. The people of this country are too clear-sighted and too intelligent to be deceived by such pretences. I here distinctly avow the saving of money to the public treasury was far from being the chief reason which influenced my mind in arriving at the conclusion that our per diem should be reduced. I firmly believe that my own constituents would not regard it a single straw, whether I voted for eight or four dollars per day. My motive was of a higher nature. My remarks, I trust, sprung from a noble source. If the gentleman from North Carolina (Mr. Culpepper) had reasoned upon the fact which he stated, and had drawn the fair deduction from it, he would, I think, feel the force of the remarks which I intend to make. He says that but one bill has passed into a law during the present Congress. I would ask this gentleman, why is this the case? Why has not more business been done? If he had asked himself these questions, he would probably have discovered the true origin of my remarks. I wish to speak with all due deference to the members of this house, when I say it is my desire, by reducing our wages, to make it our interest as well as our duty, to do the business of the country as it arises, and go home as soon as possible. I do not wish to be in a hurry—I do not wish to act without due deliberation; and yet, I firmly believe that the public business might be better transacted than it is at present, in little more than half the period of our long sessions. I do not profess to be "an aged gentleman," but yet, upon this subject, I can speak in the language of experience, and am glad that there are many gentlemen around me who can correct me if I should fall in error. I would ask, what has been the course of legislation which we have heretofore pursued? What have we done through the first half of every long session? I answer, comparatively nothing. The fact stated by the gentleman from North Carolina in regard to the business which has been transacted during the present session, is substantially true of those that are past. But I do not complain of the waste of time alone. The necessary consequence of this manner of proceeding is to force the whole business of the House near its close. Then we have so much to do, that we can do nothing well. There is neither time nor opportunity for investigation ; and measures are adopted the nature and character of which cannot be understood by the House."

On the 4th of February in a debate upon the very same bill which drew forth the remarks just quoted, Mr. Buchanan went into a thorough and searching review of Mr. Adams' administration. The presidential election of 1828 was approaching, and General Jackson, who had been defeated in 1825, was the candidate of the democracy. The people had already become tired of Mr. Adams' management of affairs. When a resolution was introduced in the House to inquire into abuses which were said to exist, some of the friends of the President opposed it. How different from the course of Mr. Buchanan in a former Congress where the conduct of his friend, General Jackson, had been assailed ! To those who thus proposed to stifle investigation, Mr. Buchanan indignantly replied :—" Against this position I take leave to enter my solemn protest. Is it the Republican doctrine? What, sir, are we told that we shall not inquire into the existence of abuses in this government, because such an inquiry might tend to make the government less popular ? This is new doctrine to me—doctrine that I have never heard before on this floor. Liberty, sir, is a precious gift, which can never long be enjoyed to any people, without the most watchful jealousy. It is Hesperian fruit, which the ever-wakeful jealousy of the people can alone preserve. The very possession of power has a strong—a natural tendency, to corrupt the heart. * * * If the government has been administered upon correct principles, an intelligent people will do justice to their rulers ; if not they will take care that every abuse shall be corrected."

In the same speech he made a reference to General Jackson,

which will show not only the early, but the devoted support he rendered to that distinguished democrat, to whom the people are indebted for the destruction of that gigantic monopoly, the United States Bank. Alluding to the taunt Mr. Clay cast upon General Jackson that he was simply "a military chieftain," Mr. Buchanan remarked :—" I thank Heaven, that in these days, a 'military chieftain' has arisen whose name is familiar to the lips of even the humblest citizen of this country, because his services live in their hearts, who will be able, by the suffrages of the people, to wrest the power of this government from the hands of its present possessors. No one else could, at this time, have successfully opposed the immense patronage and power of the administration. * * * I trust and believe, that the people of the United States will elevate 'the citizen soldier' to the supreme magistracy of the Union. In that event, and after he shall have been tried by them, I venture to predict, that their award will entwine the civic wreath with the laurel crown, and that Jackson will live in the history of his country as the man of the present age, 'first in war, first in peace, and first in the hearts of his countrymen.'" It is unnecessary to remark how abundantly this prediction has been verified.

Mr. Buchanan's love for genuine republican simplicity has always been something more than a mere name. Residing in a portion of the country which retains more of the simple, unostentatious habits of rural life than any other agricultural district of such wealth, it is not surprising that he should repudiate all those badges of distinction and inferiority, which are so contrary of that spirit of equality which democracy inculcates. He held up to just derision and contempt the attiring of our foreign ministers in a military coat covered with glittering gold lace, and decking them with a chapeau and small sword ! When it was called by some member of Congress "the livery of the American people," Mr. Buchanan remarked :—

"I protest against this dress being called the livery of the

American people : it is the livery of the last and the present administration. No gentleman who valued his standing with the people of this country, would ever appear before them in such a garb. The people of the United States do not even know that such a dress has been prescribed for their ministers abroad. In many instances it must make us appear ridiculous in the eyes of foreign nations. Imagine to yourself a grave and venerable statesman, who never attended a militia training in his life, but who has been elevated to the station of a foreign minister in consequence of his civil attainments, appearing at court arrayed in this military coat, with a chapeau under his arm, and a small sword dangling at his side ! Is not such a man compelled, by conformity to this regulation, to render himself ridiculous ? 'A military chieftain' who, in early life, had received his education at West Point, not the old citizen soldier who resides upon his farm, might sport a dress of this kind with some degree of grace ; but what a ridiculous spectacle would a grave lawyer, or judge, of sixty years of age, present, arrayed in such a costume ! If the salary of our foreign ministers be not sufficient to enable them to exercise that liberal but plain hospitality which belongs to the character of their country, I say, again, let it be increased ; but let them never forget, in their dress or in their manners, the simple grandeur which belongs to the character of republicans."

It is but proper to say that Mr. Buchanan has since practised what he advocated upon this occasion ; and during his recent residence as minister at the court of St. James, among all the gewgaws and trappings of royalty, he appeared in the simple, unpretending garb of an American citizen ; thus upholding the simplicity of republican institutions, and forcibly rebuking the spirit of monarchy which decks one man with badges of superiority, and fastens upon another the symbols of degradation.

During this session Mr. Buchanan reported an important and much needed amendment to our naturalization laws, from the

Judiciary Committee, of which he still continued a member. Under the law as it then stood, an alien could not be legally naturalized, unless he could produce a certificate that he had gone before a court and registered himself ; and this certificate was to be the evidence of the time of his arrival in the United States. The law also required that this certificate of registry should be recited in the certificate of naturalization. It will thus be seen that according to this law, no matter how long a man had been in this country, or how irrefragably he could prove it, he could not be legally naturalized, if he had neglected to make the registry of his arrival. This neglect was very common, on account of aliens upon their arrival here, not being acquainted with the law on the subject. The bill which Mr. Buchanan reported proposed to do away with this registry. There was also another section of the law which required every alien who arrived in this country after April 14th, 1802, to exhibit a certificate of the declaration of his intention to become a citizen, made two years before his application to be naturalized.

"It was believed," Mr. B. said, "by the committee, "that if an alien could establish, by clear and indifferent testimony, that he had arrived in this country previous to the late war (of 1812), and continued to reside in it ever since, this condition might, in such case, with propriety be dispensed with. He had reason to believe that there were many persons in the country, particularly Irishmen, who served as soldiers during the late war, who have hitherto neglected to make declaration of their intention to become citizens ; and we thought it right to provide for this class of cases, more especially as such persons must prove, by clear and indifferent testimony, that they have ever since resided in the United States."

These amendments to our naturalization laws, so just and proper, were, by the exertions of Mr. Buchanan, adopted. Congress adjourned on the 26th of May, 1828, and met again on the 1st of December following.   In the meantime the presidential election had taken place, and Gen. Jackson triumphantly elected, according to the predictions of Mr. Buchanan. The principal topics of discussion before Congress were the occupation of the Oregon river, the Cumberland road, and an amendment to the Constitution introduced by Mr. Smyth, of Virginia, to the effect that no person who should have been once elected President of the United States shall be again eligible to that office.   Mr. Buchanan opposed this upon true democratic grounds, which will at once commend themselves to the reason of every intelligent person.   He said " he would incline to leave to the people of the United States, without incorporating it in the Constitution, to decide whether a President should serve more than one term.   The day may come when dangers shall lower over us, and when we may have a President at the helm of state who possesses the confidence of the country, and is better able to weather the storm than any other pilot ; shall we then, under such circumstances, deprive the people of the United States of the power of obtaining his services for a second term ? Shall we pass a decree, as fixed as fate, to bind the American people, and prevent them from ever re-electing such a man ?   I am not afraid to trust them with this power."

Mr. Buchanan delivered an elaborate speech upon the Cumberland Road Bill, in which he discussed the subject of internal improvements by the general government, adhering strictly to the doctrine on this subject laid down in Mr. Monroe's celebrated message, to which reference has already been made.   The proceedings of this session are not voluminous or important. They embrace a large number of private bills, but none of important historical interest.   The country was anxiously awaiting the commencement of Gen. Jackson's administration, which was inaugurated on the 4th of March, 1829, the termination of the present Congress.

This session of Congress was distinguished for the retirement from public life of that remarkable man, Nathaniel Macon, of

North Carolina. Stern in his integrity, devoted to duty, ready to accept any office, even to justice of peace, within the gift of the people, but disdaining a seat in the Cabinet of Mr. Jefferson, where it could only come as an appointment, he presented one of the most noted examples of that illustrious patriotism, and rigid self-denial which was a leading trait in the character of all the more eminent founders of our democratic institutions. He had fixed in his own mind for many years previous to his retirement, that he would do so when he arrived at the age of three score and ten, and he was equal to his determination. When remonstrated with by his friends and assured that he was still in the vigor of his intellect, which was the fact, he remarked "that his mind was still good enough to tell him that he ought to quit office before his mind quit him, and that he did not mean to risk the fate of the Archbishop of Granada." Quietly and meekly he left the Senate, retired to his home in North Carolina, and on the 29th of June, 1837, died, full of years and full of honors. Jefferson, in speaking of him, used to say that he was "the last of the Romans."

CHAPTER VII.

Election of Gen. Jackson to the Presidency—The Impeachment of Judge Peck—Mr.
Buchanan's Celebrated Speech thereupon.

THE first session of Congress under the administration of Gen.
Jackson assembled on the 7th of December, 1829. In the
Senate were Samuel Bell and Levi Woodbury of New Hampshire, Daniel Webster of Massachusetts, Theodore Frelinghuysen and Mahlon Dickerson of New Jersey, John M. Clayton
of Delaware, John Tyler of Virginia, Robert Y. Hayne of South
Carolina, George M. Troup and John Forsyth of Georgia,
Edward Livingston of Louisiana, William R. King of Alabama,
and Thomas H. Benton of Missouri. In the House may be men-
tioned among the prominent names those of Edward Everett of
Massachusetts, Tristam Burgess of Rhode Island, C. C. Cambre-
leng, Henry B. Cowles, Michael Hoffman, Ambrose Spencer,
John W. Taylor, and Gulian C. Verplanck of New York, James
Buchanan, Joseph Hemphill of Pennsylvania, P. P. Barbour,
Charles F. Mercer and Andrew Stevenson of Virginia, George
McDuffie of South Carolina, R. M. Johnson, R. P. Letcher, and
C. A. Wickliffe of Kentucky, John Bell and James K. Polk of
Tennessee, and C. C. Clay and Dixon H. Lewis of Alabama.
Seldom in our history has the floor of either house of Congress
shown a greater array of talent or more sterling integrity than
upon this occasion. A large number of the members were fresh
from the people, and had been elected in that sweep of popular
enthusiasm which had placed "the hero of New Orleans" in
the presidential chair

And here it is proper to refer to Mr. Buchanan's part in that celebrated contest. From the prominent position he had taken as the friend of Gen. Jackson, he was the especial mark of the malignity of his enemies. He was assailed with all the bitterness which the most intense party spirit could invoke, but firm in his confidence in the ability of the distinguished man whom he supported for the highest office in the gift of a free people, he never wavered for a moment in his support. Through all the storms of detraction and abuse which were poured upon him as no man had ever before been assailed in this country, Mr Buchanan stood his firm, unwavering friend. The campaign of 1828 was a memorable one in the annals of the democratic party, as well as in the politics of the entire country. The power and influence of the administration were opposed to the success of Gen. Jackson, and his friends were compelled to contend with this and more than all with the systematic course of detraction that was pursued against their candidate. They triumphed, however, over every obstacle, and inaugurated the most glorious democratic administration since the days of Jefferson. M. de Tocqueville, about as wise as most European writers on our institutions, has said that Gen. Jackson was "raised to the Presidency and maintained there solely by the recollection of the victory of New Orleans!" This imputation upon the intelligence of the people in choosing their public servants, of course could only come from a disbeliever in popular government, and probably it never was repeated by a single person in our own country who was sincerely a believer in the capacity of the people for self-government. M. de Tocqueville has made another remark in regard to Gen. Jackson, which was, accidentally, true. He says, "the majority of the enlightened classes were always opposed to him;" and he might have added, that those he calls "enlightened" have always opposed democracy. Imbibing their notions of government from British writers, and contemning the doctrines of Jefferson, Madison and Jackson, it is no wonder they have no sympathy with the strong hearts, earnest impulses and unperverted sentiments of the masses who grasp as if by instinct their leader. In the early and strong attachment which Mr. Buchanan exhibited for Gen. Jackson, we see this impulse of democracy called forth, in all its power ; and the ratification it met from the suffrages of the people, gives it the stamp of unequivocal genuineness

Mr. Buchanan was selected at this session for the important position of Chairman of the Judiciary Committee, which had been held by Mr. Webster when he was a member of the House. Mr. B. had for several sessions been a member of this Committee, and no man in the House was probably better qualified for the place. There was too, at this time, one of the most important matters before this Committee which can possibly fall to the consideration of a legislative body. It was no less than the impeachment of a judicial officer, James H. Peck, Judge of the District Court of the United States for the District of Missouri. No matter may be considered of a more serious character, or one which requires a greater degree of prudence and discrimination, than the solemn duty of the impeachment of a judge. To keep inviolate the dignity and authority of the judicial bench, and at the same time preserve a jealous regard for the rights of the citizen, embrace points of constitutional law of a most delicate and important character. Fortunately, instances where the Senate of the United States has been called upon to resolve itself into a High Court of Impeachment, and to exercise the constitutional functions thereby conferred upon it, have been exceedingly rare ; only three previous to this case have occurred in our history as a nation. But the very fact that these cases have been rare, is the reason that makes them more difficult of adjudication. We have few or no precedents to guide us, except those we find in English reports, which, under a republican form of government are, or at least ought to be, mostly inapplicable. Hence, such cases require some qualification in a prosecutor beyond the mere fact of being a lawyer. They call for a profound acquaintance not only with the theory, but above all, with the spirit of our institutions. They need a mind gifted with sufficient power of originality to break away from the musty traditions of English precedents, and, in conformity with the new spirit implanted by republican principles, judge of facts by the unerring standard of rigid common sense, instead of following the decisions of the judicial sycophants of royalty. Are not men of the present day equally as able to judge of what is right or wrong as Scroggs and Jeffries, or even, with all due respect, "my Lord Chief Justice Mansfield?" At least so thought Mr. Buchanan in the argument he delivered in the Senate on that celebrated trial, and there is no man in whose bosom there beats an American heart who will not thank him for the noble sentiments he then uttered before the assembled talent of the nation.

The articles of impeachment against Judge Peck passed the House of Representatives at the first session of this, the twentieth Congress, but the trial did not take place before the Senate until the opening of the second session. The circumstances which gave rise to this celebrated prosecution were briefly as follows. In December, 1825, Judge Peck in the United States District Court of Missouri decided against the claims of the widow and children of one Antoine Soulard, to certain land within the State of Missouri and the then Territory of Arkansas. Luke E. Lawless, Esq., of St. Louis, had been one of the counsel for prosecuting the claims before Judge Peck, and when the decision of the judge in regard to the matter was published, Mr. Lawless wrote a brief article to one of the newspapers in St. Louis, in which he enumerated the errors into which the judge had fallen. These were stated in respectful language, and confined solely to a notice of the case in issue. Judge Peck chose to consider the communication of Mr. Lawless a contempt of court, and having summoned him before him, not only deprived him of his right to act in his profession, but even went so far as to commit him to prison, for exercising the right every citizen enjoys of criticising the decisions of our courts. Mr. Lawless made complaint to the House of Representatives. His memorial was referred to the Judiciary Committee of which Mr. Buchanan was chairman. After a full and deliberate consideration of the case, the Committee unanimously reported articles of impeachment against Judge Peck, which were adopted by the House, and thereupon presented to the Senate, which resolved into a Court of Impeachment for the trial of the accused judge.

There were five managers chosen by ballot on the part of the House of Representatives to conduct the prosecution. They were James Buchanan of Pennsylvania, Henry R. Storrs of New York, George McDuffie of South Carolina, Ambrose Spencer of New York, and Charles Wickliffe of Kentucky. Hon. William Wirt and Hon. Jonathan Meredith were the counsel of Judge Peck. The trial opened on the 13th of December, 1830, at noon. The Senators were arranged on two sets of benches, covered with green cloth, to the right and left of the Vice President, the Hon. John C. Calhoun of South Carolina. Judge Peck and his counsel, Mr. Wirt and Mr. Meredith, entered and were conducted to a table prepared for their convenience. Soon after, the managers appointed on the part of the House of Representatives to conduct the impeachment came in and took seats prepared for them. Mr. Buchanan, who had been selected as chairman of the committee of managers, rose and stated that they were ready to proceed to trial. After the transaction of some preliminary business, the Court adjourned for one week. On the following Monday, the case was opened on the part of the prosecution, by Mr. McDuffie, in a speech of great learning, eloquence, and power. After the evidence of the prosecution had been submitted, Mr. Meredith opened for the defence in a learned and able argument, and upon the submission of the entire testimony, Mr. Storrs first, and Mr. Wickliffe afterwards, addressed the Court. Mr. Meredith opened his great speech for the defence on the 19th of January and continued four days. Once in the course of his argument he sank from physical exhaustion. On the 24th, Mr. Wirt followed him in one of the happiest and most eloquent efforts of his life. He occupied three days. The closing portion is still described by those who heard it as surpassingly beautiful. Wit, sarcasm, and impressive eloquence, as only a Wirt could use them, poured forth in streams, riveting the attention and eliciting the admiration of a crowded Senate chamber and galleries during the whole time he was speaking.

Mr. Buchanan closed the case. He did not bring to his task, perhaps, the graceful oratory of Wirt, or even the impulsive, indignant eloquence of McDuffie, but he presented an argument which, for a review of the principles of constitutional and judicial law, it may be said without offence, was certainly superior to Mr. Wirt's speech, and fully equal to that of Mr. McDuffie. Mr. Buchanan was at this time about forty years of age, and his mind had been thoroughly trained in debate on the floor of the House, with such men as Mr. Clay, Mr. Calhoun, Mr. Lowndes, Mr. Randolph, Mr. Webster, and others equally eminent in forensic ability. After opening his speech with a few preliminary remarks explanatory of the general nature of the case, Mr. Buchanan said :

" In the progress of this trial, we have made a long excursion to England. We have had the principles of the English government extensively discussed, and the court has been entertained with a minute account of the judicial history of that country, and what does it all prove towards the elucidation of this cause? I should not have cared if the gentlemen had succeeded in establishing that the offence of scandalizing a court, whether a cause was pending or not, is punishable in a summary manner in England. If it were so, what then? Are we to look to the laws of England, or to the Constitution and laws of the United States, for the power of our judges? At the revolution we separated ourselves from the mother country and we have established a republican form of government, securing to the citizens of this country other and greater personal rights, than those enjoyed under the British monarchy. The gentlemen have been discussing the extent of personal rights in England ; but that is not the standard of the rights of the people of this country. When we arrive at the proper stage of the cause, I think I shall then show that the language of the Constitution of the United States upon this subject is so plain, that he who runs may read. Judge Peck had no occasion to go to England and consult the common law to discover prerogatives for the courts of this country ; all he had to do, to ascertain the limits of their legitimate power over contempts, was to read the seventh section of the Judiciary Act of 1789, and the Constitution of the United States.

" In the further prosecution of this subject, I shall contend that under the Constitution and laws of the United States, the federal courts possess no power to punish in a summary manner, as contempts, publications reflecting on the court, whether in relation to a cause pending or one finally decided, and that in either case, such a power is equally at war both with the spirit and the letter of the Constitution.

" And here I will take leave to observe, that any one who has attended to the course of this trial, might alone imagine it was the impeachment of an English judge before the House of Lords, and not that of an American judge before the Senate of the United States. We have scarcely heard of our own Constitution or our own laws. This may have been accident, or it may have been design. If it has been by design, it shall not succeed. The gentleman shall not keep us pursuing the judicial history of England for the last five hundred years, and thus place out of view our own constitutional guarantees for the personal rights and personal liberty of our own citizens.

" If the courts of the United States do possess this power, it must be derived either from the common law or from the inherent powers which necessarily belong to all courts of justice, or from the Judiciary Act of 1789. If the power exists at all, it must come from one of these three sources.

"As regards the common law, I think it is now conclusively settled by the adjudged cases, that the courts of the United States possess no criminal common law jurisdiction. If any question can be considered at rest, it is this. It is utterly astonishing to me, that such a claim of jurisdiction should ever have been asserted for the judiciary. The Constitution of the United States called into existence a new government. Under its provisions, Congress established new courts of justice. To the legislature it belonged to declare what ought or what ought not to be the law by which these courts should be governed. The attempt to transfer from England to the United States the whole criminal code of common law, without the sanction of Congress, was the most extraordinary that will be conceived. I have ever been a friend to courts, and in an especial manner a friend to the Supreme Court of the United States, and I trust I have shown it by my public conduct ; but if ever they should attempt to usurp the legislative power of declaring any act to be a crime in this country, merely because it is a crime by the common law of England, I do not know but I should be willing to bring the judges of that court themselves before this tribunal. The Congress of the United States have ever legislated upon the principles, that an act must be declared a crime by law before the courts can notice it as such. In 1825, the chairman of the Committee on the Judiciary in the House of Representatives, who is now a distinguished member of this Court (Mr. Webster), reported a bill on the avowed principle that many actions manifestly of a criminal character had not been declared crimes by act of Congress, and it was necessary that this omission should be supplied, in order to give the courts of the United States the power of trying and punishing them. The bill thus reported was enacted into a law. This doctrine, which is clearly correct in reason and in principle, has been settled by the two adjudged cases, which have already been cited.

5*

Indeed, so clearly and firmly is it established, that the late Mr. Justice Washington, in delivering a charge to the grand jury at Philadelphia in 1822, laid it down as settled, that the courts of the United States have not cognizance of offences at common law, unless it be conferred on them by the laws of the United States.

* * * * * *

"I shall now proceed to prove that the power claimed and exercised by the respondent is in direct violation of the letter and spirit of the Constitution. In order to demonstrate this proposition, it is only necessary to contrast the provisions of the Constitution with the proceedings of the judge against Mr. Lawless. The Constitution declares that "in all criminal prosecutions the accused shall enjoy the right to a speedy and public trial, by an impartial jury." What does this mean? Does it not extend to all criminal prosecutions? and is it not established that the prosecution of a libel as a contempt is a criminal prosecution? In criminal prosecutions the rights of a citizen are never to be taken away, without a trial by an impartial jury. Impartiality is the attribute peculiarly required. But what does the law of contempts, as administered by Judge Peck, declare? That the dearest rights of a citizen may be taken away, without any trial by jury, and by the sole authority of any angry, offended, and therefore partial judge. Need I add another word?

"Again, the Constitution provides that 'no person shall be held to answer for a capital or otherwise infamous crime, unless on a presentment or indictment of a grand jury, except in cases arising in the land or naval forces,' &c. In England, where the power of punishing libels against judges in contempts came to the King's Bench from the Star Chamber, a man may be prosecuted criminally upon a mere information filed by the crown. But the Constitution of the United States explodes this doctrine, except in cases arising in the land and naval service. In all other cases a grand jury must pass upon

the accused, before he can be brought to trial. So careful
has the Constitution been of the liberty of the citizen, that it
has blotted out forever the proceeding by information ; although
before any punishment can be inflicted, even by this mode, a
petit jury must first have found the accused guilty. But what
is the process in the case of contempts? Without either an
information or an indictment, but merely on a simple rule to
show cause, drawn up in any form the judge may think proper,
a man is put upon his trial for an infamous offence, involving
in its punishment the loss both of liberty and property. He is
deprived both of petit jury and grand jury, and is tried by an
angry adversary prepared to sacrifice him and his rights on the
altar of his own vengeance.

" The Constitution declares, 'that no person shall be compelled, in any criminal case, to be witness against himself.'
Now I ask, can the English language furnish plainer words
than these? Did not the respondent know, when he called
upon Mr. Lawless to answer interrogatories upon oath, and on
his refusal inflicted an additional punishment, that the Constitution protected him against any such inquisition? If the Constitution does not apply to a case of this kind, in the name of
Heaven when or where will it apply? By the common law of
England, the refusal to answer interrogatories is itself 'a high
and repeated contempt, to be punished at the discretion of the
court :' and so thought Judge Peck ; but the Constitution inter-
poses its protection, and secures the citizen being called upon
to answer. Even the courtly Blackstone, the apologist of every
abuse under the British government, declares 'that this method
of making the defendant answer upon oath to a criminal charge
is not agreeable to the genius of the common law in any other
instance.' (4 Com. 287.) Now I verily believe that when the
framers of that sacred instrument inserted in it the provision
'that no person shall be compelled, in any criminal case, to be
witness against himself,' they had this very case of contempt
full in their view. The power which they have forbidden did,

in this case, exist in England ; but even there it 'is not agreeable to the genius of the common law in any other instance.' What case so proper could they have had in view when they inserted this clause ? They could never have intended that, notwithstanding the provision, unless the accused would himself humbly crouch at the foot of judicial power, and swear that he had no intention to give the slightest offence to the judge, he should be liable to be severely punished. Such a doctrine would be repugnant to every feeling of a freeman.

"Even the miserable pretext which existed for exercising this power in Pennsylvania and Tennessee, that the Constitutions of these respective States had sanctioned a pre-existing 'law of the land,' which prostrated the barriers erected by these very Constitutions for the protection of civil liberty, has no existence here. No law of the land for the United States existed previous to the adoption of the Federal Constitution. It declares that no man shall be compelled to bear witness against himself in a criminal charge ; and I put the question home to each member of this high and honorable court, whether the language must not be construed to extend to cases of this nature. Is there anything else to which the provision can apply ? This odious inquisition must certainly have been intended, as there is no other criminal accusation on which a man can, even by the common law, be required to bear witness against himself.

"Let me here bring into the view of the Senate a fact on which I shall comment hereafter. The counsel has told us that at first Judge Peck only intended to suspend Mr. Lawless ; but in consequence of his refusal to have interrogatories filed, and answer questions upon oath, which might require him to bear witness against himself, and of his reading a paper to the court in the character of a protest or bill of exceptions, his punishment was aggravated by the disgrace of imprisonment.

"Yes, sir, with this constitutional charter in his hand, the judge has branded Mr. Lawless with infamy (so far as his sentence of imprisonment could do so), for refusing to give evidence against himself. But I shall treat more fully of this point here-after.

"The Constitution further provides that no person, for the same offence, shall be twice put in jeopardy of life or limb. But the law of contempt, after a judge has first wreaked his own vengeance on the accused for the offence, considered as a contempt of court, the unhappy victim may afterwards be indicted for a libel, and thus again punished for the same offence.

"The Constitution of the United States does not contain the provision, which is to be found in almost every State Constitution in the Union, that, upon prosecution for a libel, the truth may be given in evidence. The reason of this omission doubtless was, that as this instrument did not confer upon Congress any power to punish libels, there was no necessity for the introduction of such a clause. If the power exercised by the respondent does not exist in the courts of the United States, I presume no man will be hardy enough to contend that the truth of an accusation against a judge cannot be given in evidence in a summary prosecution for a contempt. What a spectacle would then be presented on such a trial! For example, I believe that a judge has in a certain cause decided absurdly (and such a thing we know may happen). I review his decision in one of the public journals, and prove that he has shown himself to be a weak man, and charge him with having been wicked and partial. If such be the fact, I have a right to establish it anywhere, and the truth everywhere ought to protect me from punishment.

"I am called before this very judge, charged with a contempt of court, and the only issue to be tried by him is, whether he himself is not weak or is not wicked, whether he has not made an absurd or a partial decision. What an examination would this be in a land of liberty! Could it ever have been intended to confer a power so absurd and so dangerous upon an American court of justice?

"I now advance a little further in this argument (although

it is astonishing to me that any argument on such a subject can be necessary). That sacred ægis—the liberty of the press —a right which Congress, if they would, could not, and if they 'could,' dare not infringe—shields every citizen of this land from the blow of such judicial tyranny. No free government can long exist without a free press. Power is constantly stealing on. One implication involves another, until liberty may be lost before the people know it is in danger. To preserve this invaluable boon, it ought to be watched with greater jealousy than ever was excited by the fabled guardian of the Hesperian fruit. Its safest protector is a free press ; and the Constitution of the United States has therefore declared, that 'Congress shall make no law abridging the freedom of speech, or of the press.' What was the intention of this provision ? The framers of the Constitution well knew, that under the law of each of the States comprising this Union, libels were punishable. They, therefore, left the character of the officers created under the Constitution and laws of the United States, to be protected by the laws of the several States. They were afraid to give this government any authority over the subject of libels, lest its colossal power might be wielded against the liberty of the press. They have guarded it with a wholesome and commendable jealousy.

"In open violation of this provision, the sedition law was passed in 1798. This law, after having destroyed its authors, expired in March, 1801, by its own limitation. The gentleman who first addressed the Court in behalf of the respondent, has mistaken the argument of the managers in relation to this law. None of us contend that it was cruel and unjust in its provisions. It was more equitable than the common law, because in all cases it made an indictment necessary, and it permitted the truth to be given in evidence. The popular odium which attended this law was not excited by its particular provisions, but by the fact that any law upon the subject was a violation of the Constitution. Congress had no power to pass any law of the kind, good or bad. It is now, I believe, freely admitted by every person (I, at least, have not for several years conversed with any man who held a contrary opinion), that Congress, in passing this act, had transcended their powers. I have no doubt that the motives of many of those who passed it were perfectly pure ; but yet, if any principle has been established beyond a doubt, by the almost unanimous opinion of the people of the United States, it is, that the sedition law was unconstitutional. Such is the strong and universal feeling upon this subject, that if any attempt were now made to revive it, the authors would probably meet a similar fate with those deluded and desperate men in another country, who have themselves fallen victims upon the same altar on which they had determined to sacrifice the liberty of the press.

"Well, sir, and what then? It is contended by the respondent that although Congress could not bestow upon the courts of the United States the power of trying and punishing libels, yet that by implication he may exercise this authority and dominion over all men who may dare to discuss his pretensions in the public newspapers. That power which the legislature who created him could not confer upon him by express grant, he exercises by implication.

"Shall then a petty judge, a petty provincial judge (if it be lawful to use such language, after the rebuke my colleague received)—although Congress itself dare not pass a law for the punishment of libellers against its own members, or the President of the United States—be permitted to sit as the sole judge in his own cause, and in palpable violation of the Constitution, fine and imprison, at his own pleasure, the author of a libel against himself? When the express power cannot be delegated, shall he take it by implication? Shall courts of justice exercise a power as a bare incident, vastly beyond what their creators could confer upon them?

"If all courts do possess this authority, it may be wielded with vast power as an engine for the destruction of our liberties

We have always had in this country, and I suppose we shall always continue to have, angry political discussions. It would seem that such storms are necessary to purify the political atmosphere of the Republic (though they are sometimes much more violent than agreeable). Let me illustrate my views by putting a case in reference to the so much agitated question of our relations with the Southern Indians. This question has awakened intense feeling throughout the Union, and I doubt not has given birth to much honest difference of opinion. Some believe the President to be right in his views upon the subject, and others that he is entirely wrong. It would not become me here to express any opinion. But suppose the President of the United States were to institute suits against some one of the editors who have attacked his character and assailed his motives in relation to his conduct on the Indian question, what might be the consequence? The question then to be settled by such a suit would be, are these attacks true or false? Now you could not take up a paper in the District of Columbia which would not contain one or more articles discussing the general question, and having a direct bearing upon the public mind in relation to the cause pending. These publications upon the principles on which Judge Peck acted would all be contempts of court. You might as well attempt to stop the flowing tide, lest it might overwhelm the temporary hut of the fisherman upon the shore, as to arrest the march of public opinion in this country, because in its course it might incidentally affect the merits of a cause depending between individuals.

"Sir, is this a fancy picture? When a man so distinguished as to be a prominent candidate before the people of the United States for the highest office in the country, undertakes to redress his wrongs by an action for a libel, he attaches to himself the whole politics of the country, and thus all the publications in the papers of the United States on the subject out of which the suit arose are converted into contempts against the court in which it is pending.

"I know something about a governor's election in New York and Pennsylvania. The liberty of the press is on such occasions carried to its utmost limits. Charges are very freely made and very freely urged against the opposing candidates ; and all the people of the State are deeply interested in knowing their truth or falsehood. The candidate who fears the public discussion of any charge made against him, has nothing to do but bring a suit, and then, according to the doctrine of contempts now asserted, all future publications upon that subject become contempts of court, and may be punished with severity by the judges before whom the action is depending. The current of public opinion must be stopped ; the merits or demerits of the candidate must not be discussed ; there must be an awful pause to await the event of a little libel cause in an inferior court. Such a doctrine cannot exist in this country. Carry it out to its practicable consequences, and it becomes appalling. By a politic application of it, every judge in the land may become the tool of executive power, or the instrument of preventing all attacks against his political favorites who may be candidates for office. These are not mere fanciful cases. They may occur in practice ; and if the power should be sanctioned and established by the decision of this court, the day may arrive when it will be resorted to for the most dangerous purposes. The time may come when it shall be considered very necessary and proper to shield some future President from public discussion by the exercise of this power.

"Why, sir, at this very time, from one end of the Union to the other, we find the public papers of a particular complexion ringing with attacks on the character and conduct of the Chief Justice of the United States, in relation to the Indian question now pending before the Supreme Court. I think these attacks are unjust ; but to check them, would you silence the public press? Would you say that the Supreme Court ought to drag before it every editor in the country, and thus put an end to the discussion? I know that even if the court possessed this power, it would never be invoked by the present Chief Justice—a man upon whom any eulogy of mine would be lost. But if he resembled a Scroggs or a Jefferies (and such men may yet hold that office), he would never rest content until he had inflicted vengeance, through the agency of this power, upon those who dared to attack his judicial character.

" I have been considering the consequences of this power in regard to cases pending ; but it would be infinitely worse in its application to cases which have been decided. The Supreme Court of the United States is vested with power in the last resort, to construe the Constitution ; constitutional questions are brought before it almost every term, involving great and extensive interests, and in some cases the rights of sovereign States. Its jurisdiction is co-extensive with the Union, and from the very nature of things, its decisions must agitate and inflame large masses of the people of this country. Judgment is pronounced, and the reasons for it go forth to the world in the form of an opinion. Is not this opinion as fair a subject of criticism as any other public paper ? And will not, and ought not such opinions to be freely criticised as long as liberty shall endure in this country ? And yet upon the principles which governed the respondent's conduct, the Supreme Court possess the power to bring all the editors throughout the Union before them, who have dared to impute errors to their opinions, and punish them by fine and imprisonment at their pleasure. The bare attempt to exercise such a power would convulse the people of this country.

" I recollect a case in my own State, which may serve to illustrate the absurdity of this claim of power. The Chief Justice of Pennsylvania delivered an opinion that the Supreme Court of that State had no right to declare a State law unconstitutional. A United States judge took up this opinion, and in one of the periodicals of the day handled it very severely ; more so, beyond all comparison, than Mr. Lawless criticised the opinion of Judge Peck. If such a power had existed, here was a case for its exercise. The Supreme Court might have brought the District Judge of the United States before them on an attachment, and sentenced him to fine and imprisonment for scandalizing the Chief Justice, and endeavoring to bring him into odium and disgrace before the people.

"If a judge be corrupt or partial in his judicial conduct, or should chance to be a fool, (a case which sometimes happens) it is not only the right, but the bounden duty of his fellow-citizens to expose his errors. If a man should be notoriously incompetent for the judicial station which he occupies, though this may be no ground for an impeachment, yet it is a state of things on which the force of public opinion may rightfully be exerted, for the purpose of driving him from the bench. I admit that the case ought to be an extreme one to justify such a resort. But then, if this power to punish libels does exist, a judge may decide as he pleases without regard either to honesty or law ; and then silence the public press in relation to his conduct, by denouncing fine and imprisonment against all those who shall dare to expose the errors of his opinion. In such a case, upon the hearing before the judge, the greater the truth, the greater would be the libel. A weak judge, when his capacity is called in question, would always be the most cruel and oppressive.

"As I have already referred to the Supreme Court of the United States, let me do it again. That illustrious tribunal, in the honest and fearless discharge of its duties, has come into collision with many of the States of this Union—with Pennsylvania, with Virginia, with Georgia, with Massachusetts, with New York, and with Kentucky. It has been abused and vilified from one end of the continent to the other. This has been its history since the foundation of the federal government. Has any man ever heard that the judges of this court claimed the power of punishing these revilers in a summary manner by fine and imprisonment? Have we, at any period of its history, heard the slightest intimation to that effect from any of these men? Not one. That court has often been in the storm. It has been assailed by the minds and waves of popular opinion ; but it has gone on in an honest and fearless course, and trusted for a safe deliverance to the good sense and patriotism of the American people.   That tribunal needs no such power as has been claimed by this judge in Missouri, and has never thought of resorting to the arbitrary and vindictive conduct, which has brought him to your bar.

"I trust I have now succeeded in proving, that the courts of the United States can neither derive this power from the common law, nor from the Judiciary Act of 1789, nor from necessity ; and that its exercise is in direct violation of the Constitution of the United States.   Another question now presents itself, on which it may be proper to make some additional remarks.

Had Judge Peck power in this case to suspend Mr. Lawless from practising his profession ?   It is of importance to us who belong to the bar to know whether or not—and to have the decision of this court upon the question.   If he had, the members of a profession which has ever stood foremost in this country, in the defence of civil liberty, are themselves the veriest slaves in existence.   I believe that I have as good a right to the exercise of my profession, as the mechanic has to follow his trade, or the merchant to engage in the pursuits of commerce.   I want then to know whether henceforward I must humble myself and become the sycophant of a judge, whom I may despise, under the penalty of being deprived of the right to practise my profession before him.   If a judge be weak, or if he be wicked, his judicial conduct is as fair a subject of discussion among lawyers, as among any other class of citizens ; and for exercising this right they incur no punishment, which cannot be inflicted on any other person.   If this proposition be not true, they become the mere creatures of the court. Instead of being the firm and fearless asserters of their clients' rights, often in opposition to the preconceived opinions of the bench, they must cringe and assent to any and every intimation of the judge at the risk of their ruin. The public have almost as deep an interest in the independence of the bar as of the bench. The rights of the citizens, under the complete systems of modern times, can only be asserted and maintained through the agency of the profession.

"Members of the profession may forfeit their right to practise, but this can only be done by the commission of some professional offence, or some crime of so black a character as shows them to be wholly unworthy to be trusted. For other offences they are subjected to the same punishments as their fellow citizens. Their official and their private acts are entirely distinct from each other. To show that Judge Peck has no right to suspend Mr. Lawless, I need not go further than 2d Petersdorff's Abridgment, 615, the book cited by the judge himself. It proves conclusively that the high prerogative of striking an attorney from the rolls has never been exercised, even in England, except for grossly dishonest professional misbehavior, or on a conviction of felony or other infamous crimes. This power has never been resorted to, except in extreme cases. I admit, that if in this country, where the two professions of attorney and counsellor are generally united in the same person, an attorney, in open court, will manifest by his conduct a total want of respect for the judges, and will pursue a course tending to obstruct the public business before the court, they must from necessity, possess the power of suspending him from practice. But it is not pretended, that Mr. Lawless has brought himself within this rule. Was it ever heard of in England, that an attorney was stricken from the rolls of the court for writing and publishing strictures, no matter how severe, upon the opinion of a judge? The research of the learned gentleman has not furnished us with a single case from the English book, nor a single dictum to that effect. If I write and publish an article which a judge may choose to consider as a libel upon himself, is it not enough that he may appeal like other citizes to the laws of his country for redress, and have me fined and imprisoned for the offence ?   Shall he be permitted to take the law into his own hands, and add to this punishment a forfeiture of my means of subsistence, by taking away from me my profession ?   Even the punishment of a libel as a contempt, by fine and imprisonment, would be mercy when compared with this power.

"The judge, in the same rule against Mr. Lawless, has embraced two things of an entirely different character.   No two subjects can be more distinct, in their nature, than a rule to show cause why an attachment should not issue for a contempt, and a rule against an attorney to show cause why he should not be stricken from the rolls.   In the first case, the court must proceed without delay.   Its progress, or its lawful command must be obeyed immediately, otherwise the progress of public business is arrested.   If the order of the court be obeyed, either there is no punishment at all inflicted, or it is generally very slight.   The suspension of an attorney from practice is of another character.   The question, then, to be decided is, has his conduct been of such a character, as to require his expulsion from the bar ?   This is a question which need not be determined in a day or in a month.   The spirit which dictated that provision of the common law, that the tools of an artificer shall not be distrained, ought to prevail upon such an occasion. When a man's all is at stake, or rather the means by which his all is acquired, there ought to be no haste in the proceeding, when no haste is necessary.   But here this infuriated judge had decided, from the very first moment, that Mr. Lawless should be suspended ; and it has been alleged that it was not till after his refusal to answer interrogatories that he determined to add the ignominious punishment of imprisonment.

*   *   *   *   *   *

"I come now to the vital and essential part of this cause, and I do contend, that if there were no evidence before the Senate but the opinion of the court, the article signed 'A Citizen,' and the fact of its author's imprisonment and suspension, these would be sufficient grounds to pronounce the res pondent guilty. If he had the heart to proceed coolly and deliberately, without passion, and to cloak his malice under a fair and kind exterior, I should not believe him to be the better man, for being able so well to play the hypocrite. But the facts of this case leave nothing for conjecture. They speak in a language which cannot be misunderstood. It will now be my endeavor to present them before this Court in a distinct and perspicuous manner, according to the order in which they occurred.

On Monday, the 17th of April, 1826, Judge Peck issued a rule against Stephen W. Foreman, the editor and publisher of the 'Missouri Advocate, and, St. Louis Inquirer,' commanding him to appear on the next morning, and show cause why an attachment should not issue against him for a contempt of court. The language of this rule is unmistakable, and discloses the source of the whole proceeding. In it the judge declares himself to be satisfied that the article signed 'A Citizen,' contained 'a false statement' of a judicial decision delivered by him in the case of Sowlard against the United States. He was not only satisfied in the first instance of the falsity of the statement, but that it tended 'to bring odium on the court, and to impair the confidence of the public in the purity of its decisions.'

"In the circumstances in which the judge was placed after he had determined to proceed, what ought to have been his course? He ought to have expressed no opinion, but merely called the editor before him on a general rule to show cause why he should not be attached for the publication. But before Mr. Foreman came before the court, or one word had been uttered in his defence, nay, before the issuing of the rule against him, the respondent had prejudged the cause. He had determined the publication to be 'a false statement, tending to bring odium upon the court, and to impair the confidence of the public in the purity of its decisions,' and this prejudication he grafted into the rule. *   *   *   *   *   *

"A rule is made upon Mr. Lawless to appear forthwith. That which was bad enough in the first rule now becomes much worse. 'The false statement' in it is now magnified into 'false and malicious statements.' The tendency of the article is not now merely stated as in the first rule, but the author himself is charged with an 'intent by its publication,' to impair the public confidence in the upright intentions of the said court, and to bring odium upon the court, and especially with intent to impress the public mind, and particularly many litigants in this court, that they are not to expect justice in the causes now pending therein, and with intent further to awaken hostile and angry feelings on the part of the said litigants against the said court, in contempt of the said court.' The conclusion of this rule is a still greater outrage. It calls upon Mr. Lawless 'forthwith' to 'show cause why he should not be suspended from practising in this court, as an attorney and counsellor therein, for the said contempt and evil intent.' Without one moment's delay he is called upon to answer, why he shall not be deprived of the exercise of that profession on which he and his family depended for existence. It is not merely why he should not be fined and imprisoned for a contempt, but this mild, placid, dovelike judge, as he has been represented, dictates also a rule against Mr. Lawless, to show cause forthwith why in effect his wife and children should not be made beggars.

"What! Is there any precedent of a proceeding like this? Had the judge but taken time to refer to 2 Petersdorff's Abridgement, the book which he has cited here, he would have found that a rule upon an attorney to show cause why he shall not be stricken from the roll, is a very different matter from an attachment. But his vengeance could not tarry. He was eager to inflict the double punishment of consigning Mr. Lawless to disgrace, by sending him to the common prison, and depriving him of the power of practising his profession so long as this land court should endure ; and yet we have been talk-about the quo animo of this transaction, and whether the whole might not have proceeded from a pure and disinterested, if not from a benevolent, motive. A picture has been presented to us of a man filled with the very milk of human kindness, with a heart pure, tender, and guileless as a child of three years old, and whose whole conduct has been so correct as to win for him the warm friendship of the counsel who last addressed you on behalf of the respondent. Of Mr. Lawless I will here take occasion to say what I believe to be strictly just ; I profess no friendship for him, for my friendships are not quite so sudden ; but from what I have seen of him (which has not been very much), he has exhibited the model of an Irish gentleman. That he has failings, I have no doubt ; I believe he has, but they proceed from the ardor and intensity of his feelings—feelings which belong to the brave and gallant nation from which he springs. He may be hasty and impetuous, but a braver or a warmer heart beats not in human bosom. I admire and respect him, and am so much his friend, that I wish to see him have justice, and so far as God shall give me ability, every effort of my mind shall be directed to the attainment of that object.

"On the 26th May, 1824, the act passed, enabling the District Court of the United States for the State of Missouri, to try the validity of those Spanish land claims. It required all claims to be presented to the court within two years. Any claim thus presented and not decided within three years after the passage of the act 'on account of the neglect or delay of the claimant,' was forever barred. The claims were to be filed before the 26th May, 1826, and to be decided before 26th May, 1827. To suspend Mr. Lawless for eighteen months, from 21st April, 1826, was to banish him forever from that court, if the law had not been afterwards extended.

"Some evidence has been given, but for what purpose I cannot conceive, unless to mortify the feelings of Mr. Lawless, that he had but little business in the court, excepting that arising

6

from the land claims. Be it so. He had devoted the whole energy of his mind to the investigation of the Spanish laws and customs, and of the treaties relating to these land titles. He naturally became concerned for most of the claimants, and interested in their claims. They were that on which he rested his hopes of fortune. Under this circumstance this judge called upon him to show cause forthwith why he should not be deprived of the opportunity of prosecuting any of these claims, and thus in fact lose nearly all his practice. Most truly may he be said to have been foredoomed. But we are told that the judge did grant him a delay until the afternoon. This is most true. He actually extended the rule for half a day, to enable him to attend to some urgent business in another court.

"After all these indications of the judge's feelings, what could we expect from the trial itself? Could it have been anything but what it was, an outrage on the Constitution and laws of the country? It was then high time for Mr. Lawless to take his stand. He then resolved upon his course, and to that resolution he stood firm and steadfast. As an American citizen, I rejoice at the determination which he exhibited. After his argument in behalf of the printer had been overruled with contumely, after he had been publicly insulted, and his character traduced, he acted as a man ought to have acted. Hitherto I have yielded, but henceforward I move not a step. I put it to each member of this court, whether it was not such a determination as he himself would have made? Mr. Lawless felt as he ought to have felt. He then gave instructions to his counsel to make no apology. The time for apology was over. When arguing the question for the printer before the judge, who then well knew that the article was written by Mr. Lawless, he repeatedly declared that the author had no intention to offend the court. These declarations were all made in vain; and the judge had exhibited such a spirit, that when he was called upon to answer in his own person, he felt it to be his duty to stand upon his rights as a man and as a citizen.

"The trial commenced on Thursday afternoon, and how? Mr. Magenis took up the article and attempted to prove that it contained no misrepresentation of the opinion. The judge immediately cried out, 'Stop, sir, that question has been already fully argued, and decided on the rule against the printer. I shall hear nothing further upon that point.' But had it been fully argued? No. Mr. Lawless had indeed attempted to argue it, but he had been interrupted and insulted at every step, until he became embarrassed, and sat down in despair before his argument was completed. And how had the question been decided? It is true the argument had been immediately overruled, but no opinion was given. Besides, this was on the rule against Mr. Foreman. Was not the rule against Foreman distinct from the rule against Lawless? Was it the same cause? Foreman had purged himself of the contempt and been discharged. Mr. Lawless was now the accused. Here was a new rule against a new man, the old one having been dismissed. Upon this new charge, Mr. Lawless had a constitutional right to be heard by counsel. Yet this judge determined that his opinion should remain a mystery—that it should not be analyzed and exposed to vulgar gaze. He stopped Mr. Magenis, and would not allow him to utter one word for his friend upon that point, which was all important for his defence against the prosecution. Has any case ever occurred in the United States, where, upon the trial of a criminal offence, such a high-handed course was attempted?

"But why should the judge have considered one question as open and the other not so? The counsel were not prohibited from arguing the question of jurisdiction. They were allowed to show that the proceedings of the court were unlawful and violated the Constitution, though these topics had been discussed on the former rule both by Mr. Lawless and Mr. Geyer. These were still held to be open points; but when the opinion, the sacred opinion was approached, the judge cries out, 'Forbear! You must not touch this monumentum ære perennius.

You may argue as long as you think proper to show that I am trampling upon the Constitution, and violating the dearest rights of an American citizen—that point is still open—but the opinion—do not venture to discuss it ; that door is forever closed.'

"Mr. Magenis and Mr. Geyer now argued the same questions, which the latter had argued on the rule against the printer. Mr. Geyer came better prepared to press his points than he had been before, and Judge Wash tells us his argument was methodically logical and well digested. Colonel Strather then rose and began to violate his instructions by making an apology for the article. He was stopped and privately requested to take his seat. One of the counsel (Mr. Meredith) asked Mr. Geyer 'what ground of argument was Colonel Strather taking when you interrupted him?' The answer was, 'He was taking none, as I thought. I considered him as making rather an apology than an argument. It was on that account that he was interrupted.' I shall never forget the air and the manner with which Mr. Geyer declared in the conclusion of his testimony that he thought it not a case for apology.

"Whether there was now a short recess of the court is uncertain. On this point the evidence is contradictory.

"A spectacle was afterwards presented, such as I trust will never again be witnessed in any part of these United States. The judge took off his goggles and bound up his eyes. God knows I do not attribute this weakness of his eyesight to him as a fault. I am sorry for his misfortune. But such was the fact. He sat upon the bench blindfold. Mr. Bates, the District Attorney, was then called upon to read the article of Mr. Lawless, paragraph by paragraph, and on each as it was read the judge commented. And such comments ! And that too from a court of justice ! Such was the impression made on the bystanders, that one of the witnesses tells us, that among the multitude which thronged the court, he did not hear a single man say the judge was doing right. Mr. Lawless, meanwhile, sat silent and submissive. He uttered not a word. He only showed by the flush upon his countenance the indignant feelings which were struggling in his heart. He remained until he could endure it no longer. But before he left the court-house, he consulted with his counsel, whether his withdrawal could be construed into a contempt. What was the answer? Either that he was not obliged to remain there and hear himself abused, or listen to such a torrent of abuse. It is stated in both ways by witnesses.

"As the judge proceeded he became more violent. Judge Wash, his leading witness, admits that he 'spoke in strong terms of the publication.' He used the words 'false' and 'malicious.' He frequently used expressions of this kind, 'that is wholly unfounded,' 'this is clearly false and without foundation, except in the malice of the author;' and he says that remarks like these occurred throughout the whole course of the analysis of the publication. They were not merely occasional bursts of passion, but it was a steady current of malicious and abusive language. The epithets used were very various. The words 'false,' 'scandalous,' 'libellous,' 'unfounded,' 'slanderous,' 'calumniator,' were all used over and over again in the course of this harangue, which lasted for about two hours. We may form some faint idea of what must have been its tenor and spirit, from the expression used by the judge in his answer to the article of impeachment. The terms embodied in that document have left a lasting monument to posterity of the temper and feeling under which this American judge must have acted.

' The Rev. Mr. Horrall, a gentleman who was merely passing by accident and had never been in the court before, and whose high character places him above all suspicion, says, that the judge appeared to be under vehement excitement. He used the words 'slanderer,' 'falsehood,' and 'misrepresentation,' and the witness thought he intended to apply these epithets to the

author of the publication. But why need I enumerate all the
witnesses who have given testimony of a similar character? As
if to cap the climax of abuse, the judge declared that such a
calumniator as the author of the article, had he lived in China,
would have had his house blackened, as an emblem of the blackness of his heart. Even Judge Peck himself could go no further. A large majority of the witnesses state the expression in
this or a similar manner. Two or three of them, however, say
that the terms used were not directly and personally applied to
Mr. Lawless, but they were used by the judge as an illustration of his argument. In every material part of their testimony,
however, there is no disagreement. Whether the one or the
other version be the truth, there can be no doubt but that it
was the judge's intention the audience should point to Mr.
Lawless as the black-hearted calumniator whom he had
described. Now I ask one and all of the members of this
court, whether, in the course of their experience, they have ever
known a man convicted, even of murder, and brought before the
court for his final sentence, to receive anything like such a cruel
and inhuman taunt, as that the very house in which he lived
ought to be painted black, as an emblem of the blackness of his
heart.

"I may be wrong in another particular. I have inquired of
many learned men whether they had ever heard or read of such
a custom in China as that to which the judge has adverted,
and the answer of them all has been in the negative. I may be
displaying my own ignorance, but I have certainly never met
with anything of the kind. The gentlemen on the other side
have referred us to no book asserting the existence of such a
custom. Still I might not be warranted in applying to Judge
Peck the language which he use to Mr. Lawless, and pronounc-
ing this Chinese custom to be without any foundation, except in
his own malice.

"When the dearest rights of an American citizen are at
stake, I will not stoop to answer such observations as have

been made by one of the gentlemen on this part of the case. What, sir, when this court is solemnly engaged in investigating an outrage committed against the liberties of this country, shall we suffer our attention to be led away to a farcical scene in a play of Kotzebue? Do gentlemen believe they can laugh out of court a fact, which every man who has a heart must feel to have been the extremest aggravation of insult and cruelty? Sir, under such circumstances, wit is out of place; and if, feeling strongly and as I think justly, I did often repeat the same question to the different witnesses, I did not expect to be treated with a sneer."

Mr. WIRT.—"The remark to which the gentleman seems to allude, was, I can assure him, perfectly sportive in its character, and that nothing like a sneer on the gentleman was thought of or intended."

"If so, I retract the remarks to which it gave rise.

"It is scarcely necessary to waste a word upon the question whether Judge Peck was in a passion whilst he was delivering this opinion against Mr. Lawless. All the circumstances of the case prove that he must have been. The mass of the testimony establishes the fact that he was vehement and excited to a degree beyond what the witnesses had ever seen him. Both Mr. Geyer and Judge Wash declare that they had never observed the judge's manner to be so impassioned as on this occasion. Whether he was in a passion or not is wholly immaterial; but were it otherwise, the fact has been clearly established. His passion is some little extenuation of his guilt. Had done what he did coolly and deliberately, the evidence of his malignity would have presented a still darker hue.

"I have now come to the last scene, an attachment issued against Mr. Lawless. He was brought into court in custody of the marshal. The judge then, with a good deal of formality (to use the language of Judge Wash), asked him if he wished to have interrogatories exhibited, and whether he would answer them if they were exhibited? To which he replied that he did

not require any interrogatories to be propounded, and if they
were he would not answer them.

"Now, sir, after the judge had occupied about two hours in
proving that the article of Mr. Lawless was false, scandalous
and malicious—that it had no foundation except in his own
malice—and that its character was so infamous that even in
China the man who could write it would have his nouse
painted black to denote the blackness of his heart, and to warn
the public against him ; after he had thus held Mr. Lawless up
before the assembled multitude, he asks him whether he will
not answer interrogatories, and purge himself upon oath of the
contempt. Sir, had he consented to answer them under such
circumstances the certificate of his naturalization which he had
exhibited with a decent pride before this court ought to be
destroyed, and the man who could have so disgraced it ought
to be driven back to the country from which he came there to
crouch and fawn before a lordly aristocracy. But no, sir, the
spirit of his 'father-land' beat high in his bosom :—a spirit
which the impression of centuries had not been able to subdue.
I trust and believe that rather than submit to such wantonness
of tyranny, he would have yielded up his life as a sacrifice. Yet
a gentleman whose name I believe is Carr, has told us that he
thought at the time Mr. Lawless refused to answer the interrogatories, there was something contemptuous in his manner, and
the witness has illustrated by exhibiting to the Senate the posture in which Mr. Lawless stood. He was asked whether Mr.
Lawless had used any disrespectful language, and the reply was
that his language was perfectly respectful, but there was a
something in his manner which did not accord with that respect,
which from the pre-conceived notions of the witness he thought
due to judicial dignity.

"I put it to the heart of every member of this most dignified court to say, whether under such aggravations he would
have answered interrogatories ? Did not the Constitution protect Mr. Lawless ? Was it not his right to refuse to be sworn

in a prosecution against himself? Yet we have been told that for his refusal to answer he was imprisoned twenty-four hours, and that until he had refused, it was the judge's intention to inflict no other punishment but that of a suspension from practice. Here then we have presented to our view an attempt made by an American judge to compel an American citizen to be a witness against himself, and for no other crime but because he stood upon his constitutional rights, and determined that he would not be sworn, we see him doomed to imprisonment long enough to brand him with disgrace so far as this could be inflicted by such a sentence.

"When Mr. Lawless was called upon to answer interrogatories, we are informed he was a good deal agitated. After his refusal, he read a paper to the court which he desired might be entered upon the record   That paper is in the following language :—

In the District Court for the District of Missouri, sitting at St. Louis, on the 21st day of April, 1826, for the decision of land titles.

THE UNITED STATES }
    vs.   }
L. E. LAWLESS.   }

'Be it remembered, that on the day and year aforesaid, " the said court called upon the said defendant to know whether if there were interrogatories filed in this cause he would answer them, which the said defendant declined for the following reasons, which he assigned to said court in the words following : First—I refuse to answer the above interrogatories, because this court has no jurisdiction of the offence charged upon me, in manner and form as the court has proceeded against me. Second—the positions ascribed in the article signed, ' A Citizen' are true and fairly inferred, and extracted from the opinion of this court in the case of Soulard's Widow and Heirs *vs.* The United States, as published."

6*

"To this request (I use the language of Judge Wash), the judge answered that it could not be put on the record, and that if it were it would answer no purpose, or something of that kind. On which Mr. Lawless remarked, it was of no great consequence, and then threw the paper down and seated himself. Mr Magenis then took up the paper, and asked the judge whether, if it should be signed by the bystanders, he would permit it to go on the record? The judge appeared to me to hesitate, and seemed for some time at a loss, and then replied, it would answer no purpose, and could not go on the record in that shape either. Whether this paper was called a bill of exceptions, or what name was given to it, the witness could not say.

"I have been thus particular in stating this transaction from the lips of the principal witness of the respondent, because it has been much relied upon both by him and by his counsel. But with what justice, let Judge Wash himself determine. The following question was propounded to him by the court:—'When Col. Lawless read the paper which had been called a bill of exceptions, was it pronounced by the judge, or supposed by you, to be intended as a new contempt?' To which he answered, 'i never regarded it in that light, nor was anything said by the court, that I remember, which induced me to believe that the court so regarded it.'

"Let me make a few observations in explanation of this part of the case. We have seen that under the law of Missouri a writ of error is allowed in cases of contempt, and the judges of the Court of Error may suspend the execution of the sentence by a supersedeas. Mr. Lawless, therefore, in the hurry and confusion of the moment, must have thought that he might derive some benefit before a superior court, from having this paper placed upon the record. It never occurred to any of the witnesses at the time that the reading of it was a contempt, and we have the oath of Mr. Lawless that he had no such intention.

"Another regular practice prevails under the laws of Missouri, which they have borrowed from Kentucky. When a judge refuses to sign a bill of exceptions, the party may appeal to the bystanders for their signatures. Mr. Magenis must have had this in view, when he asked the court if they would permit the paper to go upon the record, if it were signed by the bystanders. Upon this proposition the judge doubted. He at first hesitated, and seemed to be at a loss how to decide. But at all events, both the testimony of Judge Wash and Mr. Magenis prove conclusively that no insult to the judge was either given or intended by this proceeding

"The judge, without further delay, pronounced the fatal sentence against Mr. Lawless of imprisonment of twenty-four hours, and a forfeiture of his means of a livelihood for eighteen months

"Was not this 'a cruel and unusual punishment?' Does it not violate an express provision of the Constitution? Why should he not have been satisfied with the infliction of a fine? Why not punish Mr. Lawless through his pocket? It is not pretended that he had before ever shown any want of respect for that court. This was the first instance. Even if the judge had possessed the power, a fine of $50 or $100 would have answered every purpose of punishment, and would have been sufficient to warn others against offending in like manner. This, in every point of view, would have been infinitely better. But no! Mr. Lawless must be disgraced. He must be sent to gaol. He must never again appear in that court as the advocate of any of the land claims, to acquire a thorough knowledge of which he had devoted several of the best years of his life. I ask one and all of you to consider seriously the nature and extent of this punishment, and the provocation. Can it have proceeded from a pure motive and virtuous intention? Was it merely to vindicate the character of the court? the honor of the judiciary?

"But the vindictive feeling which urged the judge to inflict this punishment had not cooled even twenty-two months after. Mr. Lawless then went from his home at St. Louis to attend the session of the District Court at Jefferson City, a distance of 140 miles. He was there comparatively a stranger. When he modestly presented himself for admission, the judge immediately asked, in open court, whether the period of his suspension had expired. Is there a man within the sound of my voice who can for one moment suppose that the judge asked the question for the sake of information? Can that be possible? The punishment of Mr. Lawless was an era in his life; it was engraved upon his memory, and will remain there forever. Yet several months after this suspension had expired, when Mr. Lawless in a strange place, and before a multitude of people to whom he was unknown, asked for admission, he is treated with indignity. Judge Peck deemed it necessary, and becoming his judicial character, to inform the multitude that he had affixed a stigma upon this man.

"There is another circumstance to which I must advert before I conclude. A witness by the name of Walker has been examined. His testimony would never have been admitted by the court, save on the principle that it might tend to show the feelings of Mr. Lawless, and thus prove that he was a prejudiced witness. Having been received upon this ground, it was afterwards used by the counsel for a totally different purpose. After Mr. Lawless had been goaded by oppression into madness, and was actuated by those feelings which naturally belong to an injured and suffering man, the intemperate language which oppression provoked and extorted from him has been gravely urged as an argument to justify his oppression. The effect has been relied upon to justify the cause.

"Mr. Walker met Mr. Lawless in his garden in the spring after his suspension and imprisonment. Every object around was calculated to remind him of the punishment he had endured and was still enduring. Whilst showing Mr. Walker his improvements, he spoke of the hardship of his suspension. He observed, that it had done him much injury, and interfered essentially with his business. But for it, he said, his improvements would have been in a more advanced state. In the very bitterness of his soul, however, he was unwilling to take any unmanly advantage of Judge Peck. He exclaimed, that if the judge, after his eyesight should be restored, would meet him in the field of honor (of false honor, I admit), 'he would let him off from going to Washington.' This language wrung from him in his own garden, is brought here by Mr. Walker, who was subpœnaed to prove it, and this is the manner in which the respondent has been defended. Sir, no act of the life of Mr. Lawless subsequent to the punishment inflicted upon him can be proper evidence in this case, but I am astonished, considering the well known ardor of his temperament, that they have not been able to prove more declarations of a similar character. I have not a doubt, but that he has a thousand times expressed the most indignant feeling of his persecution

"I have now nearly done with this case ; and in conclusion, I shall strongly express what I strongly feel. I do most solemnly believe, if this judge shall escape punishment, the description which has often been contemptuously applied to the power of impeachment, that it is but the scare-crow of the Constitution, will be hereafter strictly just. But the acquittal of this man may have a still worse effect. If the power of impeachment presents no prospect to the people of removing an arbitrary and tyrannical judge, what will be the consequences? They will soon begin to inquire whether the judicial office ought not to be limited to a term of years ; at the commencement of this trial I should have shrunk with horror from such a proposition. But if there be no other alternative—if the people must either be cursed during a long life with an arbitrary and oppressive judge who has trampled upon their rights, or the Constitution must be so amended as to limit the term of office of the inferior judges, I should choose the last alternative, as the least of two very great evils. I say the inferior judges. God forbid that ever such a provision should extend to the judges of the Supreme Court of the United States.

"Impressed with a solemn belief of the respondent's guilt, I now respectfully ask his conviction. I have no regrets to express, no apologies to offer for the part which I have taken upon this trial. I have been acting in an office wholly unsought by myself and ungrateful to my feelings, but yet I enjoy the proud consciousness of reflecting, that I have done my duty ; I have urged the respondent's conviction with no feeling of personal animosity, but in the strong belief, that mercy to him will be cruelty to the American people. I ask for his conviction in the name of the Judiciary, whose pure character he has sullied, and whose independence he has endangered. I ask for it in the name of the people of the United States, whose Constitution and laws he has violated by tyranny and oppression. Should he be acquitted, I shall bow with the most profound respect to the judgment of this Court, but I shall never cease to believe, that it will establish a precedent dangerous in the extreme to the rights and liberties of the American people."

The counsel of Judge Peck contended, in opposition to the arguments of the prosecution, that the article published by Mr. Lawless was a gross and palpable misrepresentation of his opinion, and calculated to bring his court into disrespect. That he had given Mr. Lawless every opportunity to defend himself and to purge himself of all intentional disrespect, but that he refused to do so, and even reasserted the truth of his publication. They contended, that a contempt had been committed, and that the judge was right in asserting the authority and dignity of his court as he had done. The Senate refused to impeach Judge Peck, by a vote of twenty-one for bringing him in guilty, to twenty-two for not guilty. Whatever may have been the peculiar circumstances of the case which thus induced the Senate to decide, it is very evident, if Mr. Lawless was not justifiable in publishing the very temperate and considerate article he did, there are scores of individuals now who might be committed for contempts of judicial decisions, with tenfold more reason than the unlucky advocate of the St. Louis bar. The Senate, however, although refusing to impeach Judge Peck, shortly after, almost unanimously passed an act obviating whatever technical objections then stood in the way of his conviction, and placed the law on such a basis, that no judge has since ventured to punish a person upon so frivolous a pretext.

At the close of this session, March 3d, 1831, Mr. Buchanan voluntarily retired from Congress, of which he had now been a constant member since the 4th of March, 1821.

CHAPTER VIII.

Mr. Buchanan's Ten Years in Congress—New Issues—Opposition to Sectionalism—
Defence of the Freedom of the Press—Mission to Russia—Election to the United
States Senate.

TEN successive years of active service in the popular branch
of the national legislature, necessarily gives a man a thorough
acquaintance with the details of legislation, and if he be an
individual of even ordinary sagacity, he must be qualified for
more responsible positions. But if he unite to a vigorous mind
an originality of conception and an independence of thought,
which make him a man whose influence is felt, whose presence
is observed, and whose absence is lamented, we may conclude
that such a man is destined to occupy something beyond a circumscribed reputation in his country. It is not too much to say
that Mr. Buchanan has won his present position in the affections of the American people by the laborious industry of a
long life devoted to their interests, and by the possession of
those qualities both of head and heart, which have qualified
him for retaining in so remarkable a degree their confidence,
and in discharging with so much acceptance the responsible
duties with which he has been entrusted. A brief review of
his early Congressional career, a mere outline of which we have
only been able to give in the preceding chapters, will illustrate
more forcibly than words the truth of what we say. He
entered Congress at a period when party lines were not drawn
with that rigid exactness which has marked political life since
that time. Mr. Monroe had just been elevated a second time

to the presidential chair by the almost unanimous consent of the electors of all the States. The federal party had been dissolved immediately after the war of 1812, and political issues had not yet again assumed a definite form. New issues were arising, which it became every one to meet. What men had been previously was of no consequence, if they now should prove true to democratic principles in the new era which the progress of our national government was inaugurating. Unlike a despotism, where everything is governed by the voice of one man, we cannot expect that quietness and calmness where the conflicting forces of truth and error have fair play and every opportunity to combat each other.

Jefferson had fought one great battle for democratic institutions, and his enemies had sought refuge in annihilation, or what was the next thing to it, had denied their name. They were now coalescing under new leaders, and marshalling their forces to come forth and give battle to the friends of democracy, under other names and upon other questions. The first measure, as we have seen, which they brought up, was a bankrupt bill, or, in other words, an act declaring that a man need not pay his honest debts. A measure more unjust, more unfair, or more inimical to the whole spirit and tenor of our institutions can scarcely be conceived. Let those who accuse Mr. Buchanan of federalism read the noble speech of his upon this iniquitous measure. Upon his very first entrance into Congress we find him battling for the cause of equal rights—for special privileges to none, and for justice to all ; and opposing this bill with all the power of his logic, and with all the ability which his distinguished talents could bring to the consideration of the subject.

Even upon the question of internal improvements, then not yet definitely settled, as regards the constitutional principle involved in them, we find him instinctively adhering to the democratic doctrine of strict interpretation, and when Mr. Monroe's great message on this subject appeared, he had only to acknow ledge it as an endorsement of his own preconceived opinions. On the question of the tariff we find him with Gen. Jackson and the democracy generally, denying the right of Congress to levy duties except for revenue, but willing to grant, in levying such duties, that incidental protection which would be beneficial to the industry of the country, and not calculated to advance special interests to the injury of the general welfare. As early as 1823 we find him a foe to sectional strife, and an enemy to that spirit which seeks the destruction of our Constitution, that it may rule over its ruins. Ambition never so far enticed him from the path of rectitude as to enable him to contemplate the overthrow of this government, which had required so much blood and treasure to establish, without the most painful emotions. He was born too near the era when the noble spirit of republican freedom took its rise, and had caught somewhat of its holy inspiration from the lingering patriots of the revolution. More than thirty years ago he solemnly promised " that he should forever avoid any expression, the direct tendency of which must be to create sectional jealousies, sectional divisions, and at length, disunion, that worst and last of all political calamities." And who shall say that James Buchanan has not been faithful to this promise, made when he was a young man, on the floor of the House of Representatives? Let the captious fault-finder search his life, and he will—he must come to the conclusion, that for steady devotion to this sentiment, he stands before the country a model of consistency. Whatever may be the opinion of even his enemies in other respects, they must award him this praise. It is no trifling boast, therefore, to make, that in all that has been said by different parties to produce irritation between different sections of our country, no one can charge that one word has ever been uttered by James Buchanan. It is only proper to say, however, that no man in the midst of the excited discussions which have occurred for a quarter of a century, could have achieved this result merely from a settled design. It must have originated, as all who know Mr. Buchanan will testify, from his personal character, from that rigid sense of justice to all, and of devoted love for the institutions of his country, which is emphatically a part of his very nature.

Following his career in Congress a little further, we find him in 1826 expounding in an able speech of two days in length, the whole range of our judicial system, going into all minor details of legal formulæ, and evincing an acquaintance with jurisprudence which would have done credit to lawyers of twice his age. On the mission to Panama he delivers a speech full of the most patriotic Americanism, and taking a survey of the importance of the tropical regions of the Gulf of Mexico to this country, which seems at this day like the vision of the prophet penetrating futurity. Time has only served to confirm the truth of his statements, and yet we have some persons even yet, venerable fossils, who do not see the commercial and military value of " the gem of the Antilles."

Finally, as an appropriate close to his representative career, we see him selected as chairman of the Board of Managers, among whom such names as McDuffie, Wickliffe, and Spencer stand prominent, to conduct the impeachment of a high judicial functionary at the bar of the Senate of the United States. There he ranks second to none in the ability and vigor with which he supports the freedom of the press and the rights of the people. Indeed, through his whole ten years in the House of Representatives, we find him upon all occasions the defender of popular rights, the upholder of democratic doctrine, and the enemy of those who would turn the government into a machine for plundering instead of protecting the people.

Shortly after Mr. Buchanan's voluntary retirement from Congress, he was honored by President Jackson with the appointment of minister to Russia. How he filled this distinguished position the records of the State Department will show. His diplomatic life was marked by the same scrupulous regard for duty, and the same careful concern for the interests of his country. Among other valuable services which he performed for his country while on that mission, was the negotiation with Count Nesselrode on the part of the Czar, of the first commercial treaty between Russia and the United States, by which valuable advantages were secured for our commerce in the Baltic and Black Seas. In this connection it may not be improper to refer to the testimony of the venerable Judge Wilkins, his successor at St. Petersburg, formerly Secretary of War, senator in Congress, &c., as to the effect that Mr. Buchanan produced in Russia in favor of his country. On a recent occasion the judge remarked : " He had been associated with him, and had always had the highest respect for him as a citizen—as a professional man—and as a statesman. It had been his honor to follow in his footsteps. He had traced him through Europe. He had been at a foreign court, after Mr. Buchanan had represented the government of the United States there, with such unsullied and pre-eminent honor. Walking in his footsteps, many thousand miles from here, he could see, and plainly trace, the high respect which followed every official act of his, and the whole deportment of his private conduct. St. Petersburg was full of admiration for the American statesman ; and so effectually did he perform his duties there, and so effectually did he endear this government to Russia, and so effectually did he arrange the commercial and diplomatic concerns of the two countries, that he left nothing in the world for him (Mr. Wilkins) to do but to state that he was his humble successor. He had preoccupied the ground and filled the demands of his government."

After the return of Mr. Buchanan from Russia in 1833, he was elected to fill the vacancy in the United States Senate, caused by the resignation of the very Judge Wilkins who bears such a noble and voluntary testimony to his fidelity to duty He had left Congress just as the storm, which the rigid principles Gen. Jackson inaugurated, had been raised. He was destined to return to the theatre of his duties in time to come, to the rescue of his early friend, and bear a part in the memorable struggles that the democracy encountered during his administration. Mr. Buchanan left Congress just at the breaking out of the rupture between Mr. Calhoun and Gen. Jackson, which finally produced a dissolution of the Cabinet and much ill-feeling which it is now painful to contemplate. The great battle on the renewal of the charter of the United States Bank had been fought and won during the session of 1831–32. Mr. Buchanan had not participated in the struggle, but he returned in time to bear an honorable part in maintaining possession of the field, and in fortifying it against further assaults.

CHAPTER IX.

French Reprisals—Executive Patronage—Mr. Clay and Mr. Buchanan—Conclusion of Twenty-third Congress.

ON the 15th of December, 1834, Mr. Buchanan took his seat in the Senate of the United States. We may well say that "in those days there were giants in the land." Among the distinguished individuals, now numbered with the dead, whom Mr. Buchanan there met, were Daniel Webster, Silas Wright, John C. Calhoun, and Henry Clay. He had encountered all of these before, however, in the popular branch of the national legislature, and it was therefore but the reunion of old companions among whom, although they had often measured their strength in manly debate, nothing but the most kindly personal feelings existed. The era of malignant speeches, of crimination and recrimination, had not yet commenced. Massachusetts in those days delivered eulogiums upon South Carolina, and South Carolina, with the natural grace of her chivalric sons, did not hesitate to return the compliment. The intercourse which should distinguish gentlemen was not only strictly observed, but each one seemed to instinctively feel that a difference in education, habits and domestic institutions demanded a mutual respect for one another's feelings which no excitement should allow them to disregard. Unfortunately, a wretched delusion and the heat of party strife has now nearly destroyed the era of good fellowship, and has placed those in antagonistic positions who have no good reason to be anything but brothers. It is to be hoped, however, that the storm which for thirty years has been gathering, will pass away without injury to our institutions, leaving the political atmosphere all the more clear and transparent on account of the temporary clouds that have enveloped us.

Almost the first thing of national importance which came before Congress, was a resolution reported by Mr. Clay from the committee on Foreign Relations, to the effect that it was inexpedient to pass a law authorizing the President to make reprisals upon French property, to force that government to pay the indemnity stipulated by the treaty of 1831. We had waited for three years the tardy action of the French government until the claims began to be with us a question of honor. The President had repeatedly urged our demands upon the attention of France, but had only received promises which had never been fulfilled. At the risk, therefore, of the charge of desiring to involve the two countries in a war, he believed we ought to assert our rights and maintain them, as the very safest method even to avoid a conflict. Mr. Buchanan ably supported this decidedly American view of the subject. In the course of some remarks upon the resolution, he paid a handsome compliment to France, declaring " that she was a brave and chivalrous nation, whose whole history proves that she is not to be intimidated even by Europe in arms." But said he, " France is wise as well warlike ; and to inform her that our rights must be asserted, is to place her in the serious and solemn position of deciding whether she will, for the sake of a few millions of francs, resist the payment of a just debt by force." The matter, however, was postponed until the next Session of Congress, on account of the meeting of the French Chamber of Deputies.

Among the subjects of debate before the Senate at this session, was " Executive Patronage." Charges of the most indiscriminate and wholesale removals from office had been brought against General Jackson, and Mr. Clay opened upon his ancient enemy with all the force and power which the batteries of his eloquence could furnish. Mr. Buchanan delivered his speech

upon the subject on the 17th of February, showing the power
of removal from office was an indispensable requisite of the
executive department of the government, without which it could
not perform the duties imposed upon it by the Constitution.
After stating the plain import and meaning of the Constitution,
Mr. Buchanan observed :

" But, sir, if doubts could arise on the language of the Constitution itself, then it would become proper, for the purpose of
ascertaining the true meaning of the instrument, to retort to
arguments *ab inconvenienti*. The framers of the Constitution
never intended it to mean what would be absurd, or what would
defeat the very purposes which it was intended to accomplish. I
think I can prove that to deprive the President of the power
of removal would be fatal to the best interests of the country.

" And, first, the Senate cannot always be in session. I thank
Heaven for that. We must separate and attend to our ordinary
business. It is necessary for a healthy political Constitution that
we should breathe the fresh and pure air of the country. The
political excitement would rise too high if it were not cooled
off in this manner. The American people never will consent
and never ought to consent, that our sessions shall become perpetual. The framers of the Constitution never intended that
this should be the case. But once establish the principle that
the Senate must consent to removals, as well as to appoint-
ments, and this consequence is inevitable. A foreign minister in
a remote part of the world is pursuing a course dangerous to
the best interests, and ruinous to the character, of the country.
He is disgracing us abroad and endangering the public peace.
He has been intrusted with an important negotiation, and is betraying his trust. He has become corrupt, or is entirely incompetent. The information arrives at Washington, three or four
days after the adjournment of Congress on the 3d of March.
What is to be done ? is the President entirely powerless until
the succeeding December, when the Senate may meet again ?

Shall he be obliged to await until the mischief is entirely consummated—until the country is ruined—before he can recall
the corrupt or wicked minister? Or will any gentleman contend
that, upon every occasion, when a removal from office becomes
necessary, he shall call the senators from their homes throughout
this widely extended Republic? And yet this is the inevitable
consequence of the position contended for by gentlemen. Could
the framers of the Constitution ever have intended such an absurdity? This argument was also adverted to by Mr. Madison.

"But again, there are great numbers of disbursing officers
scattered over this Union. Information is received, during the
recess of the Senate, that one of them in Arkansas or at the
Rocky Mountains has been guilty of peculation, and is wast-
ing the public money. Must the President fold his arms, and
suffer him to proceed in his fraudulent course, until the next
meeting of the Senate? The truth is, that the President cannot
execute the laws of the Union without the power of removal.

"But cases still stronger may be presented. The heads of
departments are the confidential advisers of the President. It
is chiefly through their agency that he must conduct the great
operations of governments. Without a direct control over
them, it would be impossible for him to take care that the laws
should be faithfully executed. Suppose that one of them during the recess of the Senate, violates his instructions, refuses to
hold any intercourse with the President, and pursues a career
which he believes to be in opposition to the Constitution of the
country. Shall the executive arms be paralyzed, and in such
a case must he presently submit to all these evils until the
Senate can be convened? In time of war the country might
be ruined by a corrupt Secretary of War, before the Senate
could be assembled.

"It is not my intention on this occasion to discuss the question of the removal of the deposits from the Bank of the
United States. I merely wish to present it as a forcible illustration of my argument. Suppose the late Secretary of the

7*

Treasury had determined to remove the deposits, and the President had believed this measure would be as ruinous to the country, as the friends of the bank apprehended. If the secretary, notwithstanding the remonstrances of the President, had proceeded to issue the order for their removal, what should we have heard from those who were loudest in their denunciations against the executive, if he had said, *my arms are tied, I have no power to arrest the act*; the deposits must be removed, because I cannot remove my secretary? Here the evil would have been done before the Senate could possibly have been assembled. I am indebted to the speech of the senator from South Carolina (Mr. Calhoun) at the last session for this illustration. The truth is this, view the subject in any light you may, the power of removal is in its nature inseparable from the executive power."

The proposal of Mr. Clay doubtless originated more in a dislike to Gen. Jackson than to a really candid belief that such a measure as he proposed could or would be beneficial to the interests of the country. To deprive the President of the power of removal from office would, in effect, be depriving him of his executive functions. The bill was finally modified so as to limit the term of office of certain officers, and in this form passed the Senate. The decided stand which Mr. Buchanan took against this bill and the ardor with which Mr. Clay pressed it, brought them very often on the floor of the Senate into opposition to each other. They both, however, possessed too much dignity of character to allow themselves to resort to anything but the most courteous deportment in their public intercourse, which was as honorable and manly as their private relations were cordial and agreeable. And here it may be remarked that Mr. Clay and Mr. Buchanan were always personal friends, notwithstanding the efforts of many malicious persons to produce a rupture. During the debate upon this bill there occurred one of those agreeable episodes between them, which was so illustrative of their intercourse. Mr. Clay, in the closing portion of a speech denying the constitutional power to confer upon the President the power of removal from office without the consent of the Senate, remarked, " that when the subject should be resumed, he should expect to see (giving one of his searching glances towards the friends of Gen. Jackson) some of the leaders of the administration party come out, with book in hand, and show the text for this tremendous power."

Mr. Buchanan, who presumed he was meant, replied, " I am exceedingly sorry, Mr. President, that the senator from Kentucky appears to be disposed so often to pay his compliments to myself."

Mr. Clay gracefully disavowed " any allusion to the senator from Pennsylvania."

Mr. Buchanan remarked that " when the gentleman spoke of the leaders of the administration party, he looked at me, and I understood him as referring to me."

" I assure the gentleman," resumed Mr. Clay, " I had no allusion to him whatever. I might look at him as he looks at me sometimes ; but I think at the time I spoke of the leaders of a particular party, I was looking rather to the senator from New York (Mr. Wright) than to him."

Mr. Buchanan replied, " that without going further into the question of who the gentleman referred to in his remarks, I will state that, whenever he thinks proper to take up the subject and attempt to prove that the practice under which this government has flourished and which was sustained by Madison, is not founded in reason and justice, is not necessary for the proper administration of the government, and is not consistent with the Constitution, then I will be ready to meet him."

" We shall meet, then," said Mr. Clay, with admirable adroitness, " at Philippi."

The Senate, dignified and deliberate as it was in the trans

action of important business, was not always without its seasons of relaxation and even amusement. A pleasant scene occurred during the present session, upon the reception of some presents which the Emperor of Morocco had sent to the President. These testimonials of royal favor consisted of two Arabian horses and a lion ; but as our Constitution does not allow the Chief Magistrate to receive presents from a foreign potentate, some disposition had to be made of the munificence of the barbarian prince. A resolution had been reported by a committee that the lion and horses be sold by public auction. Mr. Frelinghuysen, the present venerable President of Princeton College, moved " that the lion be presented to the proprietor of Peale's Museum, in New York, and that the horses be given to some agricultural society."

Mr. Porter, of Louisiana, " objected to this, as New York State was already the richest in the Union. He would give the lion to the State of New Jersey if the gentleman desired it, but thought Louisiana ought to have the horses."

Mr. Poindexter, of Mississippi, considering our delicate relations with France, moved " that the lion be presented to Louis Philippe."

Mr. Buchanan said " he opposed this on the ground that it would be a declaration of war."

Mr. Shipley, of Maine, " desired to know where the gentlemen obtained their authority in the Constitution to give away the property of the United States."

Mr. Frelinghuysen replied, " that this question could be best settled on the principles of common law. In order to legally dispose of property, we must first be able to hold it ; and he did not see how we could hold the lion."

A resolution was finally adopted, authorizing the sale of the horses by public auction, and the presentation of his kingly majesty, the lion, to such person or persons as the President might designate.

The twenty-third Congress expired on the 3d of March,

1835.   On the very last day of the session a very excited
debate occurred upon the famous "expunging resolution"
introduced by Mr. Benton, by which it was desired to expunge
from the journal of the Senate a resolution adopted in March,
1834, censuring Gen. Jackson for removing the deposits from
the United States Bank.   Mr. Buchanan participated actively
in the discussion, and voted among the heroic band who were
determined to vindicate Gen. Jackson on the floor of the Senate
from the odium of a censure which had been the offspring of
momentary party exasperation.

CHAPTER X.

New Aspect of the Slavery Question—Incendiary Publications—Abolition of Slavery in the District of Columbia—Affairs of Texas—Sufferers by Great Fire in New York.

THE twenty-fourth Congress assembled on the 7th of December, 1835.   Among the new members who made their appearance in the Senate at this session were John Davis, of Massachusetts ; J. J. Crittenden of Kentucky ; and Robert J. Walker, of Mississippi.   Almost the first thing that came before the Senate was the subject of negro slavery.   It came up by a reference in the message of Gen. Jackson in regard to the circulation by the United States mail, of incendiary publications designed to excite insurrection in the Southern States, and upon memorials for the abolition of slavery in the District of Columbia. The question was then in most of its aspects a new one.   It had been before Congress previously, but simply as a measure for excluding it from further extension.   Now, however, the question was assuming a different form.   It had come from England, like most of our errors, covered with the conquests for " freedom " it had there made under the lead of such tories· as Wilberforce and Clarkson, and was about to be inaugurated as an element in our society.   " A slave could not breathe in England " had been sung by her poets, and repeated by her orators, until their strains for freedom had actually drowned the voices of the patriotic " sons of liberty " who in 1776 had ridiculed in poor doggerel, but full of magnificent patriotism, the tyranny of George the Third, and his unlucky generals, Burgoyne and Cornwallis.   The turning of a few negroes loose in Jamaica, to go back to the *fetichisms* of their ancestors, was heralded as an act' of devotion to the cause of human liberty which had made angels glad, and produced rapture even in heaven   The reception of this abolition exotic in our country was at first, however, cold and disdainful.   Its advocates were mobbed as readily at the North as they would now be at the South.   All regarded the doctrine of equality with negroes with something like indefinable horror ; and although the general sentiment of the community, both North and South, at that day was opposition to negro slavery in the abstract, yet anything that looked like placing white men and negroes upon terms of social and legal equality was instinctively rejected as outrageous and degrading.   There were but few men who then had the courage to call them-selves abolitionists ; and it is to be charitably supposed that those who did brave the odium of the charge were honest in their opinions, and actuated, if by a mistaken, certainly by a sin-cere desire to benefit the negro.   No one at this time probably denied the injustice of negro servitude in the abstract.   The demonstration of the incapacity of the negro race to retain the advantages of civilization, when left to itself, had not been afforded by the results of British emancipation in the West Indies ; and the unwilling conclusion had not been forced upon the minds of even the best and most benevolent men, that some legal *status* for the negro, different from that applied to white men, is absolutely essential for the welfare of every society where any considerable number of both races live in juxtaposition. Whatever, though, may be the opinion of any person upon this point, the constitutional guarantees between the States are plain and explicit ; and while Mr. Buchanan held to the view of the time in regard to slavery in the abstract, yet he went to the utmost limit of constitutional power in protecting the South-ern States from what was then thought to be the danger of incendiary publications.

The story of the St. Domingo massacres which had been duly told by British historians, and ascribed entirely to the negroes (which, if we may now believe reliable witnesses, were like the atrocities of the French Revolution, instigated

by British agents), had created a profound sensation through
out the Southern States.   President Jackson had recommended that some measures be taken to afford the South such
protection as seemed proper.   Mr. Buchanan, in the debate on
the subject, said he would be willing to go to the full constitutional power on the subject, and placed his advocacy of whatever
measure could be constitutionally adopted upon the ground that,
if the inflammatory publications and pictorial illustrations referred to were calculated to excite insurrection, the United States
ought not to allow its agents to knowingly be guilty of circulating them ; otherwise the Constitution formed for the purpose
of insuring domestic tranquillity becomes an agent for foment-
ing discord—in fact, was in effect, by its operation, destroying
itself, and instead of being a protection for the common defence,
was actually the worst enemy the States where slavery existed
could have.   If the danger of negro insurrections had been what
it was supposed to be at that time, these would have been very
just and proper views ; but a more extended acquaintance with
negro "slavery" has shown that no society which treats its
negroes with any proper degree of humanity need ever fear an
insurrection.   The attachment formed by these faithful and
devoted children of the sun to their masters, gives rise to no more
apprehensions of revolt than may be anticipated by a father of a
family among his children.

The abolition of slavery in the District of Columbia arose
from memorials for that object which had been presented by
societies of Friends in different portions of the country.   These
memorials had been received for many years from this peculiar
but worthy body of Christians, and had given rise to but little
or no debate.   Their manifestoes had been quietly consigned to
the tomb of the Capulets, and the public business duly proceeded with ; but in the excited state of public feeling which
now existed, they caused a long and animated discussion.   Mr.
Buchanan met the question in the outset in the following frank
and decided manner :

"What is now asked by these memorialists? That in this District of ten miles square—a District carved out of two slave-holding States, and surrounded by them on all sides, slavery shall be abolished! What would be the effects of granting their request? You would thus erect a citadel in the very hearts of these States, upon a territory which they have ceded to you for a far different purpose, from which abolitionists and incendiaries could securely attack the peace and safety of their citizens. You establish a spot within the slaveholding States which would be a city of refuge for runaway slaves. You create by law a central point from which trains of gunpowder may be securely laid, extending into the surrounding States, which may at any moment produce a fearful and destructive explosion. By passing such a law, you introduce the enemy into the very bosom of these two States, and afford him every opportunity to produce a servile insurrection. Is there any reasonable man who can for one moment suppose that Virginia and Maryland would have ceded the District of Columbia to the United States, if they had entertained the slightest idea that Congress would ever use it for any such purpose? They ceded it for your use, for your convenience, and not for their own destruction. When slavery ceases to exist under the laws of Virginia and Maryland, then, and not till then, ought it to be abolished in the District of Columbia."

In a further debate upon this subject, Mr. Buchanan more fully stated his position upon the question as follows :—

" I shall now proceed to defend my own motion from the attacks which have been made upon it. It has been equally opposed by both extremes. I have not found upon the present occasion, the maxim to be true, that ' *in medio tutissimus ibis.*' The senator from Louisiana (Mr. Porter), and the senator from Massachusetts (Mr. Webster), seem both to believe that little if any, difference exists between the refusal to receive a

7*

petition, and the rejection of its prayer after it has been received. Indeed, the gentleman from Louisiana, whom I am happy to call my friend, says he can see no difference at all between those motions. At the moment I heard this remark I was inclined to believe that it proceeded from that confusion of ideas which sometimes exists in the clearest heads of that country from which he derives his origin, and from which I am myself proud to be descended. What, sir! no difference between refusing to receive a request at all, and actually receiving it and considering it respectfully, and afterwards deciding, without delay, that it is not in your power to grant it! There is no man in the country acquainted with the meaning of the plainest words in the English language, who will not recognize the distinction in a moment.

" If a constituent of that gentleman should present to him a written request, and he should tell him to go about his business, and take his paper with him, that he would not have anything to do with him or it; this would be to refuse to receive the petition.

" On the other hand, if the gentleman should receive this written request of his constituent, read it over carefully and respectfully, and file it away among his papers, but, finding it was of an unreasonable or dangerous character, he should inform him, without taking further time to reflect upon it, that the case was a plain one, and that he could not, consistently with what he believed to be his duty, grant the request, this would be to reject the prayer of the petition.

" There is as much difference between the two cases as there would be between kicking a man down stairs who attempted to enter your house, and receiving him politely, examining his request, and then refusing to comply with it.

" It has been suggested, that the most proper course would be to refer his petition to a committee. What possible good can result from referring it? Is there a senator on this floor who has not long since determined whether he will vote to abolish slavery in the District or not? Does any gentleman require the report of a committee, in order to enable him to decide this question? Not one.

"By granting the prayer of this memorial, as I observed on a former occasion, you would establish a magazine of gunpowder here, from which trains might be laid into the surrounding States which would produce fearful explosions. In the very heart of the slaveholding States themselves you would erect an impregnable citadel, from whence the abolitionists might securely spread throughout these States by circulating their incendiary pamphlets and pictures, the seeds of disunion, insurrection, and servile war. You would thus take advantage of the generous confidence of Virginia and Maryland in ceding to you this District, without expressly forbidding Congress to abolish slavery here whilst it exists within their limits. No man can, for one moment, suppose that they would have made this upon any other terms, had they imagined that a necessity could ever exist for such a restriction. Whatever may be my opinion of the power of Congress under the Constitution, to interfere with this question about which at present I say nothing, I shall as steadily and as sternly oppose its exercise as if I believed no such power to exist.

"In making the motion now before the Senate, I intended to adopt as strong a measure as I could, consistently with the right of petition and a proper respect for the petitioners. I am the last man in the world who would intentionally treat these respectable constituents of my own with disrespect. I know them well, and prize them highly. On a former occasion, I did ample justice to their character. I deny that they are abolitionists. I cannot, however, conceive how any person could have supposed that it was disrespectful to them to refuse to grant their prayer in the first instance, and not disrespectful to refuse to grant it after their memorial had been referred to a committee. In the first case, their memorial will be received by the Senate, and will be filed among the records of the country. That it has already been the subject of sufficient deliberation and debate, that it has already occupied a due portion of the time of the Senate cannot be doubted or denied. Every one acquainted with the proceedings of our courts of justice must know that often, very often, when petitions are presented to them, the request is refused without any delay. This is always done in a plain case by a competent judge. And yet, who ever heard that this was treating the petition with disrespect? In order to be respectful to these memorialists, must we go through the unmeaning form in this case of referring the memorial to a committee, and pretending to deliberate, when we are now all fully prepared to decide?

"I repeat, too, that I intended to make as strong a motion in this case as the circumstances would justify. • It is necessary that we should use every constitutional effort to suppress the agitation which now disturbs the land. This is necessary, as much for the happiness and future prospects of the slave as for the security of the master. Before this storm began to rage, the laws in regard to slaves had been really ameliorated by the slave-holding States; they enjoyed many privileges which were unknown in former times. In some of the slave States prospective and gradual emancipation was publicly and seriously discussed. But now, thanks to the efforts of the abolitionists, the slaves have been deprived of these privileges, and, whilst the integrity of the Union is endangered, their prospect of final emancipation is delayed to an indefinite period. To leave this question where the Constitution has left it, to the slaveholding States themselves, is equally dictated by a humane regard for the slaves as well as for their masters."

During this session there was much discussion in regard to the affairs of Texas. This gallant State was then passing through its battle for independence, and Santa Anna with all the pomposity of his nature was endeavoring to compel his revolted province to return to its ancient allegiance. Mr. Buchanan was one of its earliest, most devoted friends and defenders. It was an odium then to sympathize with the heroic men who were rescuing the fair plains of Texas from the curse of Spanish-American despotism, and consecrating them to the genius of American liberty, and a man ran the risk of being called "a friend of adventurers," "a fillibuster," and other opprobrious epithets which have fortunately ceased to frighten those lovers of free institutions, who patriotically wish to see all nations enjoy the same blessing of civil and religious liberty which have made our country the pride of its citizens, and the terror of tyrants everywhere. Mr. Buchanan in the debate upon the affairs of Texas had early and nobly stated his sympathy with the heroic band struggling for liberty :

"In regard to Mexico, Mr. B. said, he looked upon Santa Anna as a usurper. The federal Constitution, established for the republic of Mexico, and which Texas as a part of that republic, had sworn to support, had been trampled on by him ; Texas, in his eyes, and in the eyes of all mankind, was justified in rebelling against him. Whether the Texans acted consistently with a true policy at the time, in declaring their independence, he should not discuss, nor should he decide ; but as a man and an American, he should be rejoiced to see them successful in maintaining their liberties, and he trusted in God they would be so. He would, however, leave them to rely on their own bravery, with every hope and prayer that the God of battles would shield them with His protection.

"If Santa Anna excited the Indians within our territory to deeds of massacre and blood ; if he should excite a spirit among them which he cannot restrain ; and if, in consequence the blood of our women and children on the frontiers shall flow, he undoubtedly ought to be held responsible. Mr. Buchanan saw a strong necessity for sending a force to the frontiers, not only to restrain the natural disposition of the Indians to deeds of violence, but because they could place no confidence in a man who had so little command of his temper, who had shown so cruel and sanguinary a disposition as Santa Anna had. He was for having a force speedily sent to that frontier, and a force of mounted men or dragoons, as suggested by the Senator from Missouri (Mr. Linn); but he was against interfering in the war now raging in Texas, unless an attack should be made on us."

In a more elaborate speech upon the same subject on the 9th of May, 1836, Mr. Buchanan said :

"In some remarks which he had submitted to the Senate a few days since, and which, like all other proceedings in this body, had been much misrepresented abroad, he had indulged the feelings of a man and an American. What he then had uttered were the sentiments of his heart in relation to the exist. ing struggle in Texas. But as to the independence of that country, he thought it prudent to refer back to the conduct of our ancestors, when placed in similar circumstances, and to derive lessons of wisdom from their example. If there was any one principle of our public policy which had been well settled—one which had been acted upon by every administration, and which had met the approbation not only of this country, but of every civilized government with which we have intercourse—it was, that we should never interfere in the domestic concerns of other nations. Recognizing in the people of every nation the absolute right to adopt such form of government as they thought proper, we have always preserved the strictest neutrality between the parties in every country, whilst engaged in civil war. We have left all nations perfectly free, so far as we are concerned, to establish, to maintain or to change their forms of government, according to their own sovereign will and pleasure.

"It would indeed be surprising, and more than this it would be unnatural, if the sympathies of the American people should not be deeply, earnestly enlisted in favor of those who drew the sword for liberty throughout the world, no matter where it was to strike. Beyond this we had never proceeded. The peaceful influence of our example upon other nations is much greater. The cause of free government is thus more efficiently promoted than if we should waste the blood and treasure of the people of the United States in foreign wars, waged even to maintain the sacred cause of liberty. The world must be persuaded—it cannot be conquered. Besides we can never, with any proper regard for the welfare of our constituents, devote their energies and their resources to the cause of planting and sustaining free institutions among the people of other nations.

"Acting upon these principles, we have always recognized existing governments, or governments *de facto*, whether they were constitutional or despotic. We have the same amicable relations with despotisms as with free governments, because we have no right to quarrel with the people of any nation on account of the form of their government which they may think proper to adopt or to sanction. It is their affair—not ours. We should not tolerate such interference from abroad, and we ought to demean ourselves towards foreign nations as we should require them to act towards ourselves.

"A very striking illustration of this principle has been presented during the present administration, in the case of Portugal. We recognized Don Miguel's government, because he was *de facto* in possession of the throne, apparently with the consent of the Portuguese people. In this respect Mr. B. believed we stood alone, or nearly alone, among the nations of the earth. When he was expelled from that country, and the present queen seemed firmly seated upon the throne, we had no difficulty in pursuing our established policy in recognizing her government.

"A still more striking case, and one to the very point in question, had occurred during Mr. Monroe's administration. The Spanish provinces throughout the whole continent of America had raised the standard of rebellion against the king of Spain ; they were struggling for liberty against oppression. The feelings of the American people were devotedly enlisted in their favor. Our ardent wishes and our prayers for their success continued throughout the whole long and bloody conflict ; but we took no other part in their cause, and we rendered them no assistance except the strong moral influence excited over the world by our well known feelings and opinions in their favor. When did we recognize their independence ? Not till they had achieved it by their arms ; not until the contest was over, and victory had perched upon their banners ; not until the good fight had been fought and won. We then led the van in acknowledging their independence.

"But let us not, by departing from our settled policy, give rise to the suspicion that we have got up this war for the purpose of wresting Texas from those to whom, under the faith of treaties it justly belongs. Since the treaty with Spain of 1819, there can no longer be any doubt but that this province is a part of Mexico. He was sorry for it ; but such was the undeniable fact. Let us then follow the course which we had pursued under similar circumstances in all other cases."

Among the bills discussed at this session, was one for the relief of the sufferers by the great fire in New York city, on the 16th of December, 1835. The generous manner in which Mr. Buchanan met this proposition for the relief of a city, the rival of the commercial emporium of his own State, deserves to be recorded. He brought no narrow-minded jealousy to the consideration of the subject. It was enough for him to know that prosperous merchants had been suddenly reduced to ruin ; that homeless families were suffering the inclemencies of a severe winter. The remarks he made upon the occasion referred to will ever entitle him to the gratitude of the mercantile classes of New York city.

He said, "it had not been his intention to say a single word upon this question. He would not do so now, but he distinctly perceived, that if the friends of the bill yielded to any one of the amendments which had been proposed, the bill was lost. We must take the bill as it now is, or none. For his own part, he took a much more liberal view of the question than some of those gentlemen who had addressed the Senate. What was the state of the case? On the 16th of December last a capital of between seventeen and eighteen millions of dollars had been in one day annihilated by fire, in our greatest commercial emporium. Notwithstanding this calamity, not a single failure had since taken place among the merchants of that city. He would say that he did not believe the history of the commercial world presented an example of such punctuality and such ability to comply with all engagements in the midst of such distress. It was highly honorable not only to New York, but to the American character. At the time of this destructive fire, the merchants of that city were indebted to the United States about $3,600,000. And what does this bill, first and second sections and all, propose to give? To give them this amount or any part of it? No, sir; all that is asked is, that you shall not in the midst of their distress extort this sum from them; which, at this moment, may save them from insolvency and ruin, for the purpose of placing it in an overflowing treasury, where it is not wanted. You are only asked to grant these suffering merchants time to pay their money, provided they give you ample security that the money shall be paid. Is there a single senator who would not most cheerfully comply with this request if he did not believe the Constitution to be in his way? Not one. He certainly should not go into the argument of the constitutional question after what had been already said. He felt confident that a large majority of the Senate were already convinced that the Constitution had nothing to do with the question. After the merchant had entered his goods at the custom house, and given bonds for the payment of the duties, he became a debtor to the government, with whom he might make any fair and reasonable terms, as we may do, and have done with our debtors. This, he was very clearly of opinion, would not be giving any preference by any regulation of commerce or revenue to the parts of one State over those of another.

"What is the present position of the mercantile community of New York? He had observed in the late public journals, that money was now worth one, one and a half, and two per cent. per month. The pressure was very great. The present state of tension could not long endure. Without some relief, some speedy relief, it was probable the merchants must yield. Let a single failure take place to the amount of a million, half a million, or a quarter of a million, and, in its consequences it would produce such ruin in New York as would be felt to the very extremities of the Union. We might then see that the forbearance which the bill proposes to extend to the merchants, is the very best bargain for ourselves which we can make."

CHAPTER XI.

Twenty-fourth Congress continued—Relations with France—Specie Payments—Admission of Michigan and Arkansas.

Our relations with France, on account of her neglect to comply with the terms of the treaty of 1831, and pay the indemnity so long due our citizens, caused a long and excited discussion during the first session of the twenty-fourth Congress. The object of the French government in delaying to do what was simply an act of justice, had fairly given rise to suspicions in regard to her ultimate designs. The king, in his opening speech to the Chamber of Deputies, had barely alluded to the subject, and his failure to ask for the sum necessary to liquidate our claims, whilst at the same time he had called for appropriations for other and apparently less important objects, had served to still more embarrass the question. The President, in view of all the circumstances, and particularly of the necessity of an increase of the navy to meet the constantly expanding demands of the country, had recommended an augmentation of that arm of our defence, and also some improvement of the forts, &c., of our maritime frontier. The proposition was opposed by Mr. Clay and all the anti-administration party on the floor of the Senate. Mr. Buchanan, on the 1st of February, 1836, in a speech of great length and extraordinary ability, reviewed the whole question of national defence, and the entire range of our difficulties with France. He gave a complete history of the negotiations between our own and the French government, and showed in a most conclusive manner that our citizens had been shamefully used, had

been denied for years their just rights without a shadow of ex
cuse, and that longer acquiescence in such manifest injustice
would brand us with pusillanimity and even cowardice. We
shall give only a portion of this speech, much of which is historical, but sufficient to show with what ardent patriotism Mr.
Buchanan has always contended for the interests and honor of
his country. The following extract embraces the opening
portion :

"Mr. President : I am much better pleased with the first
resolution offered by the senator from Missouri (Mr. Benton)
since he has modified it upon the suggestion of the senator from
Tennessee (Mr. Grundy). When individuals have more money
than they know how to expend, they often squander it foolishly.
The remark applies, perhaps, with still greater force to nations.
When our treasury is overflowing, Congress, who are but mere
trustees for the people, ought to be especially on their guard
against wasteful expenditures of the public money. The surplus can be applied to some good and useful purpose. I am
willing to grant all that may be necessary for the public defence,
but no more. I am therefore pleased that the resolution has
assumed its present form. The true question involved in this
discussion is, on whom ought the responsibility to rest for having
adjourned on the 3d of March last, without providing for the
defence of the country ? There can be no doubt a fearful
responsibility rests somewhere. For my own part, I should
have been willing to leave the decision of this question to our
constituents. I am a man of peace, and dislike the crimination
and recrimination which this discussion must necessarily produce ; but it is in vain to regret what cannot now be avoided.
The friends of the administration have been attacked, and we
must now defend ourselves. I deem it necessary, therefore, to
state the reason why I voted, on the 3d of March last, in favor
of the appropriation of three millions for the defence of the
country, and why I glory in that vote. The language used by

senators in reference to this appropriation has been very strong. It has been denounced as a violation of the Constitution. It has been declared to be such a measure as would not have received the support of the minority, had they believed it could prevail, and that they would be held responsible for it. It has been stigmatized as most unusual—most astonishing—most surprising. And, finally, to cap the climax, it has been proclaimed that the passage of such an appropriation would be virtually to create a dictator, and to surrender the power of the purse and the sword into the hands of the President. I voted for that appropriation under the highest convictions of public duty, and I now intend to defend that vote against all these charges.

"In examining the circumstances which not only justified this appropriation, but rendered it absolutely necessary, I am forced into the discussion of the French question. We have been told, that if we go to war with France, we are the authors of that war. The senator from New Jersey has declared that it will be produced by the boastful vanity of one man, the petulance of another, and the fitful violence of a third. It would not be difficult to conjecture who are the individuals to whom the senator alludes. He has also informed us that, in the event of such a war, the guilt which must rest somewhere will be tremendous. Now, sir, I shall undertake to prove that scarcely an example exists in history of a powerful and independent nation having suffered such wrongs and indignities as we have done from France with so much patience and forbearance. If France should now resort to arms—if our defenceless seacoast should be plundered—if the blood of our citizens should be shed—the responsibility of the Senate, to use the language of the gentleman, will be tremendous. I shall not follow the example of the senator, and say their guilt, because that would be to attribute to them an evil intention, which I believe did not exist.

*   *   *   *   *   *   *

"The justice of our claims upon France are now admitted by

all mankind. Our generosity was equal to their justice. When she was crushed to the dust by Europe in arms, when her cities were garrisoned by a foreign foe, when her independence was trampled under foot, we refused to urge our claims. This was due to our ancient ally. It was due to our grateful remembrance of the days of other years. The testimony of Lafayette conclusively establishes this fact. In the Chamber of Deputies, on the 13th of June, 1833, he declared that we had refused to unite with the enemies of France in urging our claims, in 1814 and 1815 ; and that, if we had done so, these claims would then have been settled. This circumstance will constitute one of the brightest pages in our history.

"Was the sum secured to our injured fellow-citizens by the treaty of the 4th of July, 1831, more than they had a right to demand ? Let the report of our Committee on Foreign Relations, at the last session, answer this question. They concur entirely with the President in the statement he had made in his message, that it was absolutely certain the indemnity fell far short of the actual amount of our just claims, independently of damages and interest for the detention ; and that it was well known at the time that in this respect the settlement involved a sacrifice. But there is now no longer room for any conjecture or doubt upon this subject. The commissioners under the treaty have closed their labors. From the very nature of their constitution it became the interest of every claimant to reduce the other claims as much as possible, so that his own dividend might thus be increased. After a laborious and patient investigation, the claims which have been allowed by the commissioners amount to $9,352,193 47. Each claimant will receive but little more than half his principal, at the end of a quarter of a century, after losing all the interest.

"Why then has this treaty remained without execution on the part of France until this day ? Our Committee on Foreign Relations, at the last session, declared their conviction that the king of France had invariably, on all suitable occasions, manifested an anxious desire faithfully and honestly to fulfill the engagement contracted under his authority and his name. They say that 'the opposition to the execution of the treaty and the payment of our just claims does not proceed from the king's government, but from a majority in the Chamber of Deputies.'

"Now, sir, it is my purpose to contest this opinion, and to show, as I think I can conclusively, that it is not a just inference from the facts ; and here, to prevent all possible misconstruction, either on this side or on the other side of the Atlantic (if by any accident my humble remarks should ever travel to such a distance), permit me to say that I am solely responsible for them myself. These opinions were in a great degree formed while I was in a foreign land, and were there freely expressed upon all suitable occasions. I was then beyond the sphere of party influence, and felt only as an American citizen. Is it not then manifest, to use the language of Mr. Livingston, in his note to the Count de Rigny, on the 3d of August, 1834, that the French government have never appreciated the importance of the subject at its just value? There are two modes in which the king could have manifested this anxious desire faithfully to fulfill the treaty. These are by words and by actions. When a man's words and his actions correspond, you have the highest evidence of his sincerity. Even then he may be a hypocrite in the eyes of that Being before whom the fountains of human action are unveiled. But when a man's words and his actions are at variance ; when he promises and does not perform, or even attempt to perform ; when 'he speaks the word of promise to the ear, and breaks it to the hope,' the whole world will at once pronounce him insincere. If this be true in the transactions of common life, with how much more force does it apply to the intercourse between diplomatists. The deceitfulness of diplomacy has become almost a proverb. In Europe, the talent of overreaching gives the minister the glory of diplomatic skill. The French school has been distinguished in this art. To prove it, I need only mention the name

of Talleyrand. The American school teaches far different lessons. On this our success has in a great degree depended.
The skillful diplomatists of Europe are foiled by the downright
honesty and directness of purpose which have characterized all
our negotiations. Even the established forms of diplomacy
contain much unmeaning language, which is perfectly understood by everybody, and deceives nobody. If ministers have
avowed their sincerity and their ardent desire to execute the
treaty, to deny them on our part would be insulting, and
might lead to the most unpleasant consequences. In forming
an estimate of their intentions, therefore, every wise man will
regard their actions rather than their words. By their deeds
shall they be known. Let us then test the French government
by this touchstone of truth."

Mr. Buchanan here goes into a detailed account of our relations with France, tracing the negotiations between the two
governments step by step up to the time of the delivery of his
speech. After he had concluded this portion of his remarks,
he addressed the Senate in the following strain of indignant
eloquence :

"Sir, at the commencement of the session of Congress, it
became the duty of the President to speak, and what could any
American expect that he would say ? The treaty had been
violated in the first instance by the ministers of the French
king, in neglecting to lay it before the Chambers until after
the first installment was due. It was then twice submitted at
so late a period of the session, that it was impossible for the
Chambers to examine and decide the question before their adjournment. On the last of these occasions, the chairman of
the committee to which the subject was referred had reported
a severe reprimand against the government for not having
sooner presented the bill, and expressed a hope that it might
be presented at an early period of the next session. It was

then rejected by the Chamber of Deputies, and, when the French government had solemnly engaged to hasten the presentation of the rejected law as soon as their Constitution would permit, they prorogued the Chambers to the latest period which custom sanctions, in the very face of the remonstrances of the minister of the United States.   I ask again, sir, before such an array of circumstances, what could any man, what could any American, expect the President would say in his message?   The cup of forbearance had been drained by him to the very dregs.   It was then his duty to speak so as to be heard and to be regarded on the other side of the Atlantic.   If the same spirit which dictated the message, or anything like it, had been manifested by Congress, the money, in my opinion, would ere this have been paid.

"The question was, then, reduced to a single point.   We demanded the execution of a solemn treaty ; it had been refused.   France had promised again to bring the question before the Chambers as soon as possible.   The Chambers were prorogued until the latest day.   The President had every reason to believe that France was trifling with us, and that the treaty would again be rejected.   Is there a senator within the sound of my voice who, if France had finally determined not to pay the money, would have tamely submitted to this violation of national faith?   Not one!

"The late war with Great Britain elevated us in the estimation of the whole world.   In every portion of Europe we have reason to be proud that we are American citizens.   We have paid dearly for the exalted character we now enjoy among the nations, and we ought to preserve it, and transmit it unimpaired to future generations.   To them it will be a most precious inheritance.

"If, after having compelled the weaker nations of the world to pay us indemnities for captures made from our citizens, we should cower before the power of France, and abandon our rights against her, when they had been secured by a solemn

8

treaty, we should be regarded as a mere hector among the nations. The same course which you have pursued towards the weak, you must pursue towards the powerful. If you do not, your name will become a by-word and a proverb.

"But, under all the provocations which the country had received, what is the charcter of that message? Let it be scanned with eagle eyes, and there is nothing in its language at which the most fastidious critic can take offence. It contains an enumeration of our wrongs, in mild and dignified language, and a contingent recommendation of reprisals in case the indemnity should again be rejected by the Chambers. But in this, and in all other respects, it defers entirely to the judgment of Congress, every idea of an intended menace is excluded by the President's express declaration. He says, 'such a measure ought not to be considered by France as a menace. Her pride and power are too well known to expect anything from her fears, and preclude the necessity of the declaration, that nothing partaking of the character of intimidation is intended by us.' I ask, again, is it not forbearing in its language? Is there a single statement in it not founded upon truth? Does it even state the whole truth against France? Are there not strong points omitted?"

Mr. Buchanan then discusses the questions of national defence, its necessity and constitutional bearing, and closes with the following brilliant peroration:

"On the 5th of June, the President had officially sanctioned the explanations which had been made to the French government by Mr. Livingston in his letter of the 25th of April, as he had previously sanctioned those which had been made by the same gentleman in his note of the 29th of January. These were considered by the President amply sufficient to satisfy the susceptible feelings of France. In order to give them full time to produce their effect, and to afford the French ministry an ample opportunity for reflection, he delayed sending any orders to demand the money secured by the treaty until the middle of September. On the 14th of that month, Mr. Barton was instructed to call upon the Duke de Broglie, and request to be informed what were the intentions of the French government in relation to the payment of the money secured by the treaty. He executed these instructions on the 20th of October. The special message has communicated to us the result : 'We will pay the money,' says the Duke de Broglie, 'when the government of the United States is ready on its part to declare to us, by addressing its claim to us officially in writing that it regrets the misunderstanding which has arisen between the two countries ; that this misunderstanding is founded on a mistake ; that it never entered into its intention, to call in question the good faith of the French government, nor to take a menacing attitude towards France ;' and he adds, 'if the government of the United States does not give this assurance, we shall be obliged to think that this misunderstanding is not the result of an error.'

"Is there any American so utterly lost to those generous feelings which love of country should inspire as to purchase five millions with the loss of national honor ? Who for these or any number of millions, would see the venerable man now at the head of our government bowing at the footstool of the throne of Louis Philippe, and like a child prepared to say its lesson, repeating this degrading apology ? First perish the five millions—perish a thousand times the amount. The man whose bosom has been so often bared in the defence of his country will never submit to such degrading terms. His motto has always been death before dishonor.

"Why, then, it may be asked, have I expressed a hope, a belief, that this unfortunate controversy will be amicably terminated, when the two nations are now directly at issue ? I will tell you why. This has been called a mere question of etiquette, and such it is, so far as France is concerned. She has already received every explanation which the most jealous susceptibility ought to demand. These have been voluntarily tendered to her.

"Since the date of the Duke de Broglie's letter to Mr. Pageot on the 17th of June, we have received from the President of the United States his general message at the commencement of the session, and his special message on French affairs. Both these documents disclaim in the strongest terms, any intention to menace France or to impute bad faith to the French government, by the message of December, 1834. Viewing the subject in this light—considering that at the interview with Mr. Barton, the duke could not have known what would be the tone of these documents, I now entertain strong hope that the French government have already reconsidered their determination. If a mediation has been proposed and accepted, I cannot entertain a doubt as to what will be the opinion of the mediator. He ought to say to France, you have already received all the explanations, and these have been voluntarily accorded, which the United States can make without national degradation. With these you ought to be satisfied. With you it is a mere question of etiquette. All the disclaimers which you ought to desire have already been made by the President of the United States. The only question with you now is not one of substance, but merely whether these explanations are in proper form. But in regard to the United States the question is far different. What is with you mere etiquette, is a question of life and death to them. Let the President of the United States make the apology which you have dictated—let him once admit the right of the foreign governments to question his messages to Congress, and to demand explanations of any language at which they may choose to take offence, and our independent existence as a government, to that extent, is virtually destroyed.

"We must remember that France may yield with honor, we never can without disgrace. Will she yield? That is the question. I confess I should have entertained a stronger belief that she would, had she not published the duke's letter to Mr.

Pageat as an appeal to the American people. She must still believe that the people of this country are divided in opinion in regard to the firm maintenance of their rights. In this she will find herself entirely mistaken. But should Congress, at the present session, refuse to sustain the President, by adopting measures of defence—should the precedent of the last session be followed for the present year, then I should entertain the most gloomy forebodings. The Father of his Country has informed us that the mode of preserving peace is to be prepared for war. I firmly believe, therefore, that a unanimous vote of the Senate in favor of the resolutions now before them, to follow to Europe the acceptance of the mediation, would, almost to a certainty, render it successful. It would be an act of the soundest policy, as well as of the highest patriotism. It would prove, not that we intend to menace France, because such an attempt would be ridiculous, but that the American people are unanimous in the assertion of their rights, and have resolved to prepare for the worst. A French fleet is now hovering upon our coasts, and shall we sit still with our overflowing treasury and leave our country defenceless? This will never be said with truth of the American Congress.

"If war should come (which God forbid!)—if France should still persist in her effort to degrade the American people in the person of their chief magistrate, we may appeal to Heaven for the justice of our cause, and look forward with confidence to victory from that Being in whose hands is the destiny of nations."

It is gratifying to know that the decided stand taken by Gen. Jackson on French affairs hastened the settlement of this troublesome question, and secured to our citizens what had so long been their just dues.

Mr. Buchanan took an early and decided stand in favor of specie payments by the general government, instead of depreciable bank paper. Upon this subject he stood side by side with that Ajax of democracy, on the currency question, Mr. Benton. "The evils," said Mr. Buchanan, "which result from a large increase of banking capital to the laboring man, to the manufacturer, and to all classes of society except speculators, were palpable. Banks could make money plenty at one time and scarce at another ; at one moment nominally raise the price of all property beyond its real value, and the next moment reduce it below that standard, and thus prove most ruinous to the best interests of the people. The increase of banking capital was calculated to transfer the wealth and property of the country from the honest, industrious, and unsuspecting classes of society, into the hands of speculators, who knew when to purchase and when to sell." Probably no one element has been a stronger one in Mr. Buchanan's character than his devoted friendship to the laboring classes. Born in the most humble circumstances of life, and always residing among a people who justly consider idleness disgraceful, it is not surprising that he should have been naturally the friend and ally of the producing classes. As a proof of this it is only necessary to state that every measure introduced into Congress during his long membership of that body, which was calculated in any way to benefit them, he advocated ; while every one intended to injure them he opposed.

One of the most prominent subjects before this Congress was the admission of Michigan and Arkansas into the Union. Mr. Buchanan was the northern senator chosen to present the bill admitting Arkansas, and Mr. Benton was selected to present the one admitting Michigan. The subject gave rise to much debate, in all of which Mr. Buchanan bore a distinguished and honorable part. It was objected to Michigan that foreigners or unnaturalized citizens had been allowed to vote in the formation of the Constitution of Michigan. Mr. Buchanan demonstrated that aliens who were residents of the Northwest Territory had a right, under the ordinance of 1787, to exercise the elective franchise.

"The territory ceded by Virginia to the United States," said Mr. B., "was sufficiently extensive for an immense empire. The parties to this compact of cession contemplated that it would form five sovereign States of this Union. At that early period, we had just emerged from our revolutionary struggle, and none of the jealousy was then felt against foreigners, and particularly against Irish foreigners, which now appears to haunt some gentlemen. There had then been no attempts to get up a Native American party in this country. The blood of the gallant Irish had flowed freely upon every battle-field, in defence of the liberties which we now enjoy. Besides, the Senate will well recollect that the ordinance was passed before the adoption of our present Constitution, and whilst the power of naturalization remained with the several States. In some, and perhaps, in all of them, it required so short a residence, and so little trouble to be changed from an alien to a citizen, that the process could be performed without the least difficulty. I repeat that no jealousy whatever then existed against foreigners."

In the course of the same speech, Mr. Buchanan used the following memorable and emphatic language upon a question, which at the present day is a most exciting topic of discussion:

"*The older I grow, the more I am inclined to be what is called 'a State rights man.'* The peace and security of this Union depend upon giving to the Constitution a literal and fair construction, such as would be placed upon it by a plain and intelligent man, and not by ingenious constructions, to increase the powers of this government, and thereby diminish those of the States. The rights of the States, reserved to them by that instrument, ought ever to be held sacred. If, then, the Constitution leaves to them to decide according to their own discretion, unrestricted and unlimited, who shall be electors, it follows as a necessary consequence that they may, if they think proper, confer upon resident aliens the right of voting."

"It is curious to remark," said Mr. Buchanan, in concluding the speech from which the foregoing extracts are taken, "that except in a few instances, the Constitution of the United States has not prescribed that the officers elected or appointed under its authority, shall be citizens ; and we all know, in practice, that the Senate have been constantly in the habit of confirming the nomination of foreigners as consuls of the United States. They have repeatedly done so, I believe, in regard to other officers."

This Congress closed its first session on the 14th of July, 1836. It had been a protracted and important session, as the reader of this and the preceding chapter will not fail to have observed.

CHAPTER XII.

Second Session of Twenty-fourth Congress—Specie Circular—Expunging Resolutions—
Mr. Buchanan's Speech upon them.

THE second session of the twenty-fourth Congress opened on
the 5th of December, 1836. Mr. Buchanan was chosen to the
honorable and responsible position of Chairman of the Committee of Foreign Relations. Associated with him were Messrs.
Clay, of Kentucky ; Tallmadge, of New York ; King, of Georgia, and Rives, of Virginia. The first subject brought before
the Senate was a resolution offered by Mr. Ewing, of Ohio, to
rescind an order made by the Secretary of the Treasury, generally known as the "specie circular." The object of the order
was the laudable one to check speculation in public lands, as
well as the excessive issues of bank paper in the West, and thus
to increase the specie currency of the country. The aim of the
President to accomplish these desirable objects was, however,
represented like almost everything Gen. Jackson did while in
office, as an act of executive tyranny, and a wish on his part to
wield the power of the revenue for his own and his party's
political advantage. The resolution of Mr. Ewing, after being
shorn of most of its objectionable features, and modified so as
to leave the Secretary of the Treasury a discretion in regard to
the matter upon which he assumed to act, passed the Senate.

The principal feature of this session was, however, the adoption of the celebrated "expunging resolution" which Mr. Benton introduced to vindicate the name and honor of Gen. Jackson. With an heroic determination, reminding one of Spartan

8*

valor, the distinguished senator from Missouri had session after session introduced a resolution for expunging from the journal of the Senate the stain which had been affixed upon Gen. Jackson for his removal of the deposits from the United States Bank. No epithet had caused him to waver for a moment in his determination, and for three successive years, through evil and good report, he had each session presented the resolution ; but owing to the majority against the President in the Senate, justice had not been granted him.   He had now, however, been elected the second time, and the people had ratified what the minority of the Senate had so long contended for.   Once more, therefore, did Mr. Benton introduce his long abused resolution. "Solitary and alone," said Mr. Benton, "and amidst the jeers and taunts of my opponents, I put this ball in motion.   The people have taken it up and rolled it forward, and I am no longer anything but a unit in the vast mass which now propels it.   In the name of that mass I speak.   I demand the execution of the edict of the people ; I demand the expurgation of that sentence which the voice of a few Senators, and the power of their confederate, the Bank of the United States, has caused to be placed on the journal of the Senate, and which the voice of millions of freemen has ordered to be expunged from it." The persevering and unyielding determination which Mr. Benton evinced in rendering this act of justice to Gen. Jackson will ever associate his name in the history of our country, side by side with that of " the hero of New Orleans."

He was destined at this session to have the efficient and earnest aid of Mr. Buchanan, in a speech of such masterly power, of rich and graceful eloquence, as has seldom, if ever, been delivered upon the floor of the United States Senate. The reader is requested to notice in the following speech the account of the abuse heaped upon Gen. Jackson for the fearless discharge of his duty.   It was even greater than that bestowed upon Gen. Pierce, at the present day, for the repeal of the unconstitutional Missouri restriction :

Mr. President: After the able and eloquent display of the senator from Kentucky (Mr. Clay), who has just resumed his seat after having so long enchained the attention of his audience, it might be the dictate of prudence for me to remain silent. But I feel too deeply my responsibility as an American senator, not to make the attempt to place before the Senate and the country the reasons, which, in my opinion, will justify the vote which I intend to give this day.

"A more grave and solemn question has rarely, if ever, been submitted to the Senate of the United States, than the one now under discussion. This Senate is now called upon to review its own decision, to rejudge its own justice, and to annihilate its own sentence, deliberately pronounced against the co-ordinate executive branch of this government. On the 28th of March, 1834, the American Senate, in the face of the American people, in the face of the whole world, by a solemn resolution, pronounced the President of the United States to be a violator of the Constitution of his country, of that Constitution which he had solemnly sworn, ' to preserve, protect, and defend.' Whether we consider the exalted character of the tribunal which pronounced this condemnation, or the illustrious object against which it was directed, we ought to feel deeply impressed with the high and lasting importance of the present proceeding. It is in fact, if not in form, the trial of the Senate for having unjustly and unconstitutionally tried and condemned the President ; and their accusers are the American people. In this cause I am one of the judges. In some respects, it is a painful position for me to occupy. It is vain, however, to express unavailing regrets. I must, and shall firmly and sternly do my duty, although in the performance of it, I may wound the feelings of gentlemen whom I respect and esteem ; I shall proceed no further than the occasion demands, and will therefore justify.

" Who was the President of the United States against whom this sentence has been pronounced ? Andrew Jackson—a name which every American mother, after the party strife which agitates us for the present moment shall have passed away will, during all the generations which this Republic is destined to endure, teach her infant to lisp with that of the venerated name of Washington. The one was the founder, the other the preserver, of the liberties of his country.

"If President Jackson has been guilty of violating the Constitution of the United States, let impartial justice take its course. I admit that it is no justification for such a crime, that his long life has been more distinguished by acts of disinterested patriotism than that of any American citizen now living. It is no justification that the honesty of his heart and the purity of his intentions have become proverbial, even amongst his political enemies. It is no justification that in the hour of danger, and in the day of battle, he has been his country's shield. If he has been guilty, let his name be 'damned to everlasting fame' with those of Cæsar and Napoleon.

"If, on the other hand, he is pure and immaculate from the charge, let us be swift to do him justice, and to blot out the foul stigma which the Senate have placed upon his character. If we are not, he may go down to the grave in doubt as to what may be the final judgment of his country. In any event, he must soon retire to the shades of private life. Shall we, then, suffer his official term to expire without first doing him justice? It may be said of me, as it has already been said of other senators, that I am one of the gross adulators of the President. But, sir, I have never said thus much of him whilst he was in the meridian of his power. Now, that his political sun is nearly set, I feel myself at liberty to pour forth my grateful feelings as an American citizen, to a man who has done so much for his country. I have never for myself, either directly or indirectly, solicited office at his hand; and my character must greatly change if I should ever do so from any of his successors If I should bestow upon him the meed of my poor praise, it springs from an impulse far different from that which has been attribnted to the majority on this floor.   I speak as an independent freeman and American senator, and I feel proud now to have the opportunity of raising my voice in his defence.

"On the 28th day of March, 1834, the Senate of the United States resolved 'that the President, in the late executive proceedings in relation to the public revenue, has assumed upon himself authority and power not conferred by the Constitution and laws, but in derogation of both.'

"In discussing this subject, I shall undertake to prove, first, that this resolution is unjust ; secondly, that it is unconstitutional ; and in the last place, that it ought to be expunged from our journals, in the manner proposed by the senator from Missouri (Mr. Benton).   First, then, it is unjust.   On this branch of the subject, I had intended to confine myself to a bare expression of my own decided opinion.   This point has been so often and so ably discussed that it is impossible for me to cast any new light upon it.   But as it is my intention to follow the footsteps of the senator from Kentucky (Mr. Clay) wherever they may lead, I must again tread the ground which has been so often trodden.   As the senator, however, has confined himself to a mere passing reference to the topics which this head presents, I shall, in this particular, follow his example.

"Although the resolution condemning the President is vague and general in its terms, yet we all know that it was founded upon his removal of public deposits from the bank of the United States.   The senator from Kentucky has contended that this act was a violation of law.   And why ?   Because, says he, it is well known that the public money was secure in that institution ; and by its charter the public deposits could not be removed from it, unless under a just apprehension that they were in danger.   Now, sir, I admit that if the President had no right to remove these deposits, except for the sole reason that their safety was in danger, the senator has established his position. But what is the fact ?   Was the government thus restricted by the terms of the bank charter ?   I answer, no.   Such a limitation is nowhere to be found in it. Let me read the sixteenth section, which is the only one relating to the subject. It enacts 'that the deposits of the money of the United States, in places in which the said bank and branches thereof may be established, shall be made in said bank or branches thereof, unless the Secretary of the Treasury shall at any time otherwise order and direct, in which case, the Secretary of the Treasury shall immediately lay before Congress, if in session, and if not, immediately after the commencement of the next session, the reasons of such order or direction.

"Is not the authority thus conferred upon the Secretary of the Treasury as broad and as ample as the English language will admit? Where is the limitation, where the restriction? One might have supposed, from the argument of the senator from Kentucky, that the charter had restricted the Secretary of the Treasury from removing the deposits, unless he believed them to be insecure in the Bank of the United States; but the language of the law itself completely refutes his argument. They were to remain in the Bank of the United States, 'unless the Secretary of the Treasury shall at any time otherwise order and direct.'

"The whole limitation upon the discretion of that officer, was his immediate and direct responsibility to Congress. To us he was bound to render his reasons for removing the deposits. We, and we alone, are constituted the judges as to the sufficiency of these reasons.

"It would be an easy task to prove that the authors of the bank charter acted wisely in not limiting the discretion of the Secretary of the Treasury over the deposits to the single case of their apprehended insecurity. We may imagine many other reasons which would have rendered their removal both wise and expedient. But I forbear, especially as the case now before the Senate presents as striking an illustration of this proposition as I could possibly imagine. Upon what principle, then, do I justify the removal of the deposits?

"The Bank of the United States had determined to apply for

a re-charter at the session of Congress immediately preceding the last presidential election. Preparatory to this application, and whilst it was pending, in the short space of sixteen months, it had increased its loans more than $28,000,000. They rose from forty-two millions to seventy millions between the last of December, 1830, and the 1st of May, 1832. Whilst this boasted regulator of the currency was thus expanding its discounts, all the local banks followed the example. The impulse of self-interest urged them to pursue this course. A delusive property was thus spread over the land. Money everywhere became plenty. The bank was regarded as the beneficent parent, who was pouring her money out into the laps of her children. She thought herself wise and provident in thus rendering herself popular. The re-charter passed both houses of Congress by triumphant majorities. But then came 'the frost, the killing frost.' It was not so easy to propitiate the 'Old Roman.' Although he well knew the power and influence which the bank could exert against him at the then approaching presidential election, he cast such considerations to the winds. He vetoed the bill, and in the most solemn manner, placed himself for trial upon this question before the American people.

"From that moment, the faith of many of his former friends began to grow cold. The bank openly took the field against his re-election. It expended large sums in subsidizing editors, and in circulating pamphlets, and papers, and speeches, throughout the Union, calculated to influence the public mind against the President. I merely glance at these things.

"Let us pause for a single moment, to consider the consequences of such conduct. What right had the bank, as a corporation, to enter the arena of politics for the purpose of defending itself, and attacking the President? Whilst I freely admit that each individual stockholder possessed the same rights, in this respect, as every other American citizen, I pray you to consider what a dangerous precedent the bank has thus estab-

lished.   Our banks now number nearly a thousand, and our
other chartered institutions are almost innumerable.   If all
these corporations are to be justified in using their corporate
funds for the purpose of influencing elections, of elevating their
political friends, and crushing their political foes, our condition
is truly deplorable.   We shall thus introduce into the State a
new, a dangerous, and an alarming power, the effects of which
no man can anticipate.   Watchful jealousy is the price
which a free people must ever pay for their liberties, and this
jealousy should be argus-eyed in watching the political move-
ments of corporations.

"After the bank had been defeated in the presidential election, it adopted a new course of policy.   What it had been
unable to accomplish by making money plenty, it determined it
would wrest from the sufferings of the people by making money
scarce.   Pressure and panic then became its weapons, and with
these it was determined, if possible, to extort a re-charter from
the American people.   It commenced this warfare upon the
interests of the country about the 1st of August, 1833.   In
two short months it decreased its loans more than four millions
of dollars, whilst the deposits of the government with it had
increased, during the same period, two millions and a quarter.
I speak in round numbers.   It was then in the act of reducing
its discounts at the rate of two millions of dollars per month.

"The State banks had expanded their loans with the former
expansion of the Bank of the United states.   It now became
necessary to contract them.   The severest pressure began to
be felt everywhere.   Had the Bank of the United States been
permitted a short time longer to proceed in this course, fortified
as it was with the millions of the government which it held on
deposits, a scene of almost universal bankruptcy and insolvency
must have been presented in our commercial cities.   It thus
became absolutely necessary for the President either to deprive
the bank of the public deposits, as the only means of protecting
the State banks, and, through them, the people from these

impending evils, or calmly to look on and see it spreading ruin throughout the land. It was necessary for him to adopt this policy for the purpose of preventing a universal derangement of the currency, a general sacrifice of property, and, as an inevitable consequence, the re-charter of this institution.

"By the removal of the deposits, he struck a blow against the bank from which it has never since recovered. This was the club of Hercules with which he slew the Hydra. This was the master-stroke by which he prostrated what a large majority of the American people believed to have been a corrupt and a corrupting institution. For this he is not only justified, but deserves the eternal gratitude of his country. For this the Senate have condemned him; but the people of the United States have hailed him as a deliverer.

"It has been said by the senator from Kentucky, that the President, by removing the deposits from the Bank of the United States, united in his own person the power of the purse of the nation with that of the sword. I think it is not difficult to answer this argument. What was to become of the public money in case it had been removed from the Bank of the United States, under its charter, for the cause which the senator himself deems justifiable? Why, sir, it would then have been immediately remitted to the guardianship of those laws under which it had been protected, before the Bank of the United States was called into existence. Such was the present case. In regard to this point, no matter whether the cause of removal were sufficient or not, the moment the deposits were actually removed, they became subject to the pre-existing laws, and not to the arbitrary will of the President.

"The senator from Kentucky has contended that the President violated the Constitution and the laws by dismissing Mr. Duane from office because he would not remove the deposits, and by appointing Mr. Taney to accomplish this purpose. I shall not discuss at any length the power of removal. It is now too late in the day to question it. That the executive possesse this power was decided by the first Congress. It has often since been discussed and decided in the same manner, and it has been exercised by every President of the United States. The President is bound by the Constitution to 'take care that the laws be faithfully executed.' If he cannot remove his executive officers, it is impossible that he can perform this duty. Every inferior officer might set up for himself, might violate the laws of the country, and put him at defiance whilst he would remain perfectly powerless. He could not arrest their career. A foreign minister might be betraying and disgracing the nation abroad, without any power to recall him until the next meeting of the Senate. This construction of the Constitution involves so many dangers, and so many absurdities, that it could not be maintained for a moment, even if there had not been a constant practice against it of almost half a century.

"But it is contended by the senator that the Secretary of the Treasury is a sort of independent power in the State, and is released from the control of the executive. And why? Simply because he is directed by law to make his annual report to Congress, and not to the President. If this position be correct, then it necessarily follows that the executive is released from the obligation of taking care that the numerous and important acts of Congress regulating the fiscal concerns of the country shall be faithfully executed. The Secretary of the Treasury is thus made independent of his control. What would be the position of this officer under such a construction of the Constitution and laws, it would be very difficult to decide. And this wonderful transformation of his character has arisen from the mere circumstance that Congress have by law directed him to make an annual report to them ! No, sir, the executive is responsible to Congress for the faithful execution of the laws ; and if the present or any other President should prove faithless to his high trust, the present senate, notwithstanding all which has been said, would be as ready as their predecessors to inflict condign punishment upon him, in the mode pointed out by the Constitution.

"I have now arrived at the great question of the constitutional power of the Senate to adopt the resolution of March, 1834. It is my firm conviction that the Senate possesses no such power; and it is now my purpose to establish this position. The decision on this point must depend upon a true answer to the question, does this resolution contain any impeachable charge against the President? If it does, I trust I shall demonstrate that the Senate violated its constitutional duty in proceeding to condemn him in this manner. I shall again read the resolution:

" ' *Resolved*, That the President in the late executive proceedings, in relation to the public revenue, has assumed upon himself authority and power not conferred by the Constitution and laws, but in derogation of both.'

" This language is brief and comprehensive. It comes at once to the point. It bears a striking impress of the character of the senator from Kentucky. Does it charge an impeachable offence against the President?

" The fourth section of the second article of the Constitution declares, 'that the President, Vice President, and all civil officers of the United States, shall be removed from office on impeachment for, and conviction of, treason, bribery, or other high crimes or misdemeanors.'

" It has been contended that this condemnatory resolution contains no impeachable offence, because it charges no criminal intention against the President; and I admit that it does not attribute to him any corrupt motive in express words. Is this sufficient to convince the judgment of any impartial man that none such was intended? Let us, for a few moments, examine this proposition. If it be well founded, the Senate may forever hereafter usurp the power of trying, condemning, and destroying any officer of the government, without affording him the slightest opportunity of being heard in his defence. They may thus abuse their power, and prostrate any object of their vengeance. It seems we have now made the discovery that the

Senate are authorized to exert this tremendous power ; that they may thus assume to themselves the office both of accuser and of judge, provided the indictment contains no express allegation of a criminal intention. The President, or any officer of the government, may be denounced by the Senate as a violator of the Constitution of his country, as derelict in the performance of his public duties, provided there be no express imputation of an improper motive. The characters of men whose reputation is dearer to them than their lives may thus be destroyed They may be held up to public execration by the omission of a few formal words. The condemnation of the Senate carries with it such a moral power, that perhaps there is no man in the United States, except Andrew Jackson, who could have resisted its force. No, sir ; such an argument can never command conviction. That which we have no power to do directly, we can never accomplish by indirect means. We cannot by resolution convict a man of an impeachable offence, merely because we may omit the formal words of an impeachment. We cannot regard the substance of things and not the mere form.

"But again, although a criminal intention be not charged in so many words by this resolution, yet its language, even without the attending circumstances, clearly conveys this meaning. The President is charged with having ' assumed upon himself authority and power not conferred by the Constitution and laws, but in derogation of both.' 'Assumed upon himself !' What is the plain, palpable meaning of this phrase, connected with what precedes and follows ? Is it not ' to arrogate,' to ' claim or seize unjustly ?' These are two of the first meanings of the word assume, according to the lexicographers. To assume upon one's self is a mode of expression which is rarely taken in a good sense. As it is used here, I ask if any man of plain, common understanding, after reading this resolution, would ever arrive at the conclusion that any senator voted for it under the impression that the President was innocent of any improper intention, and that he violated the Constitution from mere mistake, and from pure motives? The common sense of mankind revolts at the idea. How can it be contended for a single moment, that you can denounce the President as a man who had 'assumed upon himself' the power of violating the laws and the Constitution of his country, and in the same breath declare that you had not the least intention to criminate him, and that your language was altogether inoffensive. The two propositions are manifestly inconsistent.

"But I go one step further. If we were sitting as a court of impeachment, and the bare proposition were established to our satisfaction, that the President had, in violation of the Constitution and laws, withdrawn the public revenue of the country from the depositary to whose charge Congress had committed it, and assumed the control over it himself, we would be bound to convict him of a high official misdemeanor. Under such circumstances, we should be bound to infer a criminal intention from this illegal and unconstitutional act. Criminal justice could never be administered, society could not exist if the tribunals of the country should not attribute evil motives to illegal and unconstitutional conduct. Omniscience alone can examine the heart. When poor, frail man is placed in the judgment seat, he must infer the intention of the accused from his actions. That 'the tree is known by its fruits,' is an axiom which we have derived from the fountain of all truth. Does a poor, naked, hungry wretch, at this inclement season of the year, take from my pocket a single dollar, the law infers a criminal intent, and he must be convicted and punished as a thief, though he may have been actuated by no other motive than that of saving his wife and children from starvation. And shall a different rule be applied to the President of the United States? Shall it be said of a man elevated to the highest station on earth, for his wisdom, his integrity, and his virtues, with all his constitutional advisers around him, when he violates the Constitution of his country and usurps the control over its entire revenue, that he may successfully defend

himself by declaring that he had done this deed without any
criminal intention? No, sir; in such a case, above all others,
the criminal intention must be inferred from the unconstitutional exercise of high and dangerous powers. The safety of
the Republic demands that the President of the United States
should never shelter himself behind such flimsy pretexts. This
resolution, therefore, although it may not have assumed the
form of an article of impeachment, possesses all the substance.

"It was my fate some years ago to have assisted as a mana-
ger, in behalf of the House of Representatives, in the trial
of an impeachment before this body. It then became my duty
to examine all the precedents in such cases which had occurred
under our government since the adoption of the Federal Constitution. On that occasion I found one which has a strong bearing upon this question. I refer to the case of Judge Pickering.
He was tried and condemned by the Senate upon all the four
articles exhibited against him, although the three first contained no other charge than that of making decisions contrary
to law, in a cause involving a mere question of property, and
then refusing to grant the party injured an appeal from his
decision, to which he was entitled. From the clear violation
of the law in this case, the Senate must have inferred an im-
pure and improper motive.

"If anything further were wanting to prove that the resolution of the Senate contained a criminal and impeachable charge
against the President, it might be demonstrated from all the
circumstances attending the transaction. Whilst this resolution was in progress through the Senate, the Bank of the United
States was employed in producing panic throughout the land.
Much actual suffering was experienced by the people, and,
where that did not exist, they dreaded unknown and awful
calamities. Confidence between man and man was at an end.
There was a fearful pause in the business of the country. We
were then engaged in the most violent party conflict recorded
in our annals. To use the language of the senator from Ken-

tucky, we were in the midst of a revolution. On the one side it was contended that the power over the purse of the nation had been usurped by the President; that in his own person he had united this power with that of the sword, and that the liberties of the people were gone, unless he could be arrested in his mad career. On the other hand, the friends of the President maintained that the removal of the deposits from the Bank of the United States was an act of stern justice to the people, that it was strictly legal and constitutional, that he was impelled to it by the highest and purest principles of patriotism, and that it was the only means of prostrating an institution which threatened the destruction of our dearest rights and liberties. During this terrific conflict public indignation was aroused to such a degree, that the President received a great number of anonymous letters threatening him with assassination, unless he should restore the deposits.

"It was during the pending of this conflict throughout the country, that the senator from Kentucky thought proper, on the 26th of December, 1832, to present his condemnatory resolution to the Senate, and here, sir, permit me to say, that I do not believe there was any corrupt connection between any senator upon this floor and the Bank of the United States. But it was at this inauspicious moment that the resolution was introduced. How was it supported by the senator from Kentucky? He told us that a revolution had already commenced. He told us, that by the 3d of March, 1837, if the progress of innovation should continue, there would be scarcely a vestige remaining of the government and policy, as they had existed prior to the 3d of March, 1829. That in a term of years, a little more than that which was required to establish our liberties, the government would be transformed into an elective monarchy—the worst of all forms of government. He compared the measure adopted by General Jackson with the conduct of the usurping Cæsar, who, after he had overrun Italy in sixty days, and conquered the liberties of his native country,

terrified the tribune, Metellus, who guarded the treasury of the
Roman people, and seized it by open force. He declared that
the President had perpretrated an open, palpable, and daring
usurpation. He concluded by asserting that the premonitory
symptoms of despotism were upon us, and if Congress did not
apply an instantaneous and effectual remedy, the fatal collapse
would soon come on, and we should die—ignobly die—base,
mean, and abject slaves, the scorn and contempt of mankind,
unpitied, unwept, and unmourned. What a spectacle was then
presented in this chamber! We are told, in the reports of the
day, that when he took his seat, there was repeated and loud
applause in the galleries. This, it will be remembered, was the
introductory speech of the senator. In my opinion, it was one
of the ablest and most eloquent of all his able and eloquent
speeches. He was then riding upon the whirlwind and directing the storm. At the time I read it, for I was not then in
the Senate, it reminded me of the able, the vindictive, and the
eloquent appeal of Mr. Burke before the House of Lords, on
the impeachment of Warren Hastings, in which he denounced
that Governor-General as the ravager and oppressor of India,
and the scourge of the millions placed under his authority.

"And yet, we are now told that this resolution did not intend to impute any criminal motive to the President ; that he
was a good old man, though not a good constitutional lawyer,
and that he knew better how to wield the sword than to construe the Constitution."

Mr. Clay here rose to explain. He said, "I never have
said, and never will say, that personally I acquitted the President of any improper intention. I lament that I cannot say it.
But what I did say was, that the act of the Senate of 1834 is
free from the imputation of any criminal motives."

"Sir (said Mr. B.), this avowal is in character with the
frank and manly nature of the senator from Kentucky. It is
no more than what I expected from him. The imputation of
any improper motive to the President has been again and again

disclaimed by other senators upon this floor. The senator from Kentucky has now boldly come out in his true colors, and avows the principles which he held at the time. He acknowledges that he did not acquit the President from improper intentions, when charging him with a violation of the Constitution of his country.

"This trial of the President before the Senate, continued for three months. During this whole period, instead of the evidence which a judicial tribunal ought to receive, exciting memorials, signed by vast numbers of the people, and well calculated to inflame the passions of his judges, were poured in upon the Senate. He was denounced upon this floor by every odious epithet which belongs to tyrants. Finally, the obnoxious resolution was adopted by a vote of the Senate, on the 28th day of March, 1834.

"After the exposition which I have made, can any impartial mind doubt but that this resolution intended to charge against the President a willful and daring violation of the Constitution and the laws? I think not.

"The senator from Kentucky has argued, with his usual power, that the functions of the Senate, acting in a legislative capacity, are not to be restricted, because it is possible that the same question in another form, may come before us judicially. I concur in the truth and justice of this position. We must perform our legislative duties; and if, in the investigation of facts, having legislation distinctly in view, we should incidentally be led to the investigation of criminal charges, it is a necessity imposed upon us by our condition, from which we cannot escape. It results from the varying nature of our duties, and not from our own will. I admit that it would be difficult to mark the precise line which separates our legislative from our judicial functions. I shall not attempt it. In many cases, from necessity, they are in some degree intermingled. The present resolution, however, stands far in advance of this line. It is placed in bold relief, and is clear of all such difficulties. It

9

is a mere marked resolution of censure.   It refers solely to the
past conduct of the President, and condemns it in the strongest
terms, without even proposing any act of legislation by which
the evil may be remedied hereafter.   It was judgment upon the
past alone ; not prevention for the future.   Nay more, the
resolution is so vague and general in its terms, that it is impossible to ascertain from its face the cause of the President's condemnation.   The Senate have resolved that the executive ' has
assumed upon himself authority and power not conferred by the
Constitution and laws, but in derogation of both.'   What is the
specification under this charge ?   Why, that he has acted thus,
' in the late executive proceedings in relation to the public revenue.'   What executive proceedings ?   The resolution leaves
us entirely in the dark upon this subject.   How could any legislation spring from such a resolution ?   It is impossible.   None
such was ever attempted.

" If the resolution had preserved its original phraseology, if
it had condemned the President for dismissing one Secretary of
the Treasury because he would not remove the deposits, and
for appointing his successor to effect this purpose, the senator
might then have contended that the evil was distinctly pointed
out ; and although no legislation was proposed, the remedy
might be applied hereafter.   But he has deprived himself even of
this feeble argument.   He has left us upon an ocean of uncer-
tainty, without a chart or compass.   ' The late executive proceedings in relation to the revenue,' is a phrase of the most
general and indefinite character.   Every senator who voted in
favor of this resolution may have acted upon different principles.
To procure its passage, nothing more was necessary than that
a majority should unite in the conclusion that the President
had violated the Constitution and the laws in some one or
other of his numerous acts in relation to the public revenue.
The views of the senators constituting the majority may have
varied from each other to any conceivable extent ; and yet
they may have united in the final vote.   That this was the fact

to a considerable extent I have always understood. It is utterly impossible either that such a proceeding could ever have been intended to become the basis of legislation, or that legislative action could have ever sprung from such a source.

"I flatter myself, then, I have succeeded in proving that this resolution charged the President with a high official misdemeanor, wholly disconnected from legislation, which, if true, ought to have subjected him to impeachment. This brings me directly to the question, had the Senate any power under the Constitution, to adopt such a resolution? In other words, can the Senate condemn a public officer, by a simple resolution for an offence which would subject him to an impeachment? To state the proposition, is to answer this question in the negative. Dreadful would be the consequences, if we possess and should exercise such a power.

"This body is invested with high and responsible powers, of a legislative, an executive, and a judicial charcter. No person can enter it until he has attained a mature age. Our term of service is longer than that of any other elective functionary. If senators will have it so, it is the most aristocratic branch of our government. For what purpose did the framers of the Constitution confer upon it those varied and important powers, and this long tenure of office? The answer is plain. It was placed in this secure and elevated position, that it might be above the storms of faction which so often inflame the passions of men. It never was intended to be an arena for political gladiators. Until the second session of the third Congress, the Senate always sat with closed doors, except in the single instance when the eligibility of Mr. Gallatin to a seat in the body was the subject under discussion. Of this particular practice, however, I cannot approve. I merely state it to show the intention of those who formed the Constitution. I was informed by one of the most eminent statesmen and senators which this country has ever produced, now no more (the late Mr. King), that for some years after the federal government commenced its operation, the debates of the Senate resembled conversations rather than speeches, and that it originated but few legislative measures. Senators were then critics rather than authors in legislation. Whether its gain in eloquence since it has become a popular assembly, and since the sound of thundering applause has been heard in our galleries at the denunciation of the President, has been an equivalent for its loss in true dignity, may well be doubted. To give this body its just influence with the people, it ought to preserve itself as free as possible from angry political discussions. In the performance of our executive duties—in the notification of treaties and in the confirmation of nominations—the Constitution has connected us with the executive. The efficient and successful administration of the government, therefore, requires that we should move on together in as much harmony as may be consistent with the independent exercise of our respective functions.

" But, above all, we should be the most cautious in guarding our judicial character from suspicion. We constitute the high court of impeachment of this nation, before which every officer of the government may be arraigned. To this tribunal is committed the character of men, whose character is far dearer to them than their lives. We should be the rock standing in the midst of the ocean for the purpose of affording a shelter to the faithful officer from unjust persecution, against which the billows might dash themselves in vain. Whilst we are a terror to evildoers, we should be a praise to those who do well. We should never voluntarily perform any act which might prejudice our judgment, or render us suspected as a judicial tribunal. More especially when the President of the United States is arraigned at the bar of public opinion, for offences which might subject him to an impeachment, we should remain not only chaste but unsuspected. Better, infinitely better, would it be for us not to manifest our feeling, even in a case in which we were morally certain the House of Representatives would not prefer before us articles of impeachment, than to reach the object of our disapprobation by a usurpation of their rights. It is true that when the Senate passed the resolution condemning the President, a majority in the House were of a different opinion. But the next elections might have changed that majority into a minority. The House might then have voted articles of impeachment against the President. Under such circumstances I pray you to consider in what a condition the Senate would have been placed. They had already pre-judged the case. They had already convicted the President, and denounced him to the world as a violator of the Constitution. In criminal prosecutions, even against the greatest malefactor, if a juror has pre-judged the cause, he cannot enter the jury-box. The Senate had rendered itself wholly incompetent in this case, to perform its highest judicial functions. The trial of the President, had articles of impeachment been preferred against him, would have been but a solemn mockery of justice.

"The Constitution of the United States has carefully provided against such an enormous evil, by declaring that 'the House of Representatives shall have the sole power of impeachment,' and 'the Senate shall have the sole power to try all impeachments.' Until the accused is brought before us by the House, it is a manifest violation of our solemn duty to condemn him by a resolution.

"If a court of criminal jurisdiction, without any indictment having been found by a grand jury, without having given the defendant notice to appear, without having afforded him an opportunity of cross-examining the witnesses against him, and making his defence, should resolve that he was guilty of a high crime, and place his conviction upon their records, all mankind would exclaim against the injustice and unconstitutionality of the act. Wherein consists the difference between this case and the condemnation of the President? In nothing, except that such a conviction by the Senate, on account of its exalted character, would fall with tenfold force upon its object. I have often been astonished, notwithstanding the extended and well-deserved popularity of General Jackson, that the moral influence of this condemnation by the Senate had not crushed him. With what tremendous effect might this assumed power of the Senate be used to blast the reputation of any man who might fall under its displeasure. The precedent is extremely dangerous, and the American people have wisely determined to blot it out forever.

"It is painful to reflect what might have been the condition of the country, if at the inauspicious moment of the passage of the resolution against the President, its interests and its honor had rendered it necessary to engage in a foreign war. The fearful consequences of such a condition, at such a moment, must strike every mind. Would the Senate then have confided to the President the necessary power to defend the country? Where could the sinews of war have been found? In what condition was this body at that moment to act upon an important treaty negotiated by the President, or upon any of his nominations? But I forbear to enlarge upon this topic.

"I have now arrived at the last point in this discussion. Do the Senate possess the power, under the Constitution, of expunging the resolution of March, 1834, from their journals, in the manner proposed by the senator from Missouri (Mr. Benton)? I cheerfully admit that we must show that this is not contrary to the Constitution ; for we can never redress one violation of that instrument by committing another. Before I proceed to this branch of the subject, I shall put myself right by a living historical reminiscence. I entered the Senate in December, 1834, fresh from the ranks of the people, without the slightest feeling of hostility against any senator on this floor. I then thought that the resolution of the senator from Missouri was too severe in proposing to expunge. Although I was anxious to record, in strong terms, my entire disapprobation of the resolution of March, 1834, yet I was willing to accomplish this object without doing more violence to the feelings of my

associates on this floor than was absolutely necessary to justify
the President. Actuated by these friendly motives, I exerted
all my little influence with the senator from Missouri, to induce
him to abandon the word expunge, and substitute some others
in its place. I knew that this word was exceedingly obnoxious
to the senators who had voted for the former resolution.
Other friends of his also exerted their influence, and at length
his kindly feelings prevailed, and he consented to abandon that
word, although it was peculiarly dear to him. I speak from
my own knowledge, 'All which I saw, and part of which I
was.'

"The resolution of the senator from Missouri came before
the Senate on the 3d of March, 1835. Under it the resolution
of March, 1834, was 'ordered to be expunged from the journal,'
for reasons appearing on its face, which I need not enumerate.
The senator from Tennessee (Mr. White), moved to amend
the resolution of the senator from Missouri, by striking out the
order to expunge, with the reasons for it, and inserting in their
stead the words 'rescinded, reversed, repealed, and declared to
be null and void.' Some difference of opinion then arose
among the friends of the administration as to the words which
should be substituted in place of the order to expunge. For
the purpose of leaving this question perfectly open, you, sir
(Mr. King, of Alabama, was in the chair), then moved to
amend the original motion of Mr. Benton by striking out the
words 'ordered to be expunged from the journal of the Senate.'
This motion prevailed on the ayes and noes by a vote of thirty-
nine to seven, and amongst the ayes the name of the senator
from Missouri is recorded. The resolution was thus left a
blank in its most essential feature, ready to be filled up as the
Senate might direct. The era of good feeling in regard to the
subject had commenced. It was nipped in the bud, however,
by the senator from Massachusetts (Mr. Webster). Whilst
the resolution was still in blank, he rose in his place, and proclaimed the triumph of the Constitution by the vote to strike out

the word expunge, and then moved to lay the resolution on the table, declaring that he would neither withdraw his motion for friend nor foe. This motion precluded all amendment and all debate. It prevailed by a party vote ; and thus we were left with our resolution a blank. Such was the manner in which the senators in opposition received our advances of courtesy and kindness, in the moment of their strength and our weakness. Had the senator from Massachusetts suffered us to proceed but for five minutes, we should have filled up the blank in the resolution. It would then have assumed a distinct form, and they would never afterwards have heard of the word expunge. We should have been content with the words 'rescinded, reversed, repealed, and declared to be null and void.' But the conduct of the senator from Massachusetts on that occasion, and that of the party with which he acted, roused the indignation of every friend of the administration on this floor. We then determined that the word expunge should never again be surrendered.

"The senator from Kentucky has introduced a precedent from the proceedings of the House of Representatives of Pennsylvania, for the purpose of proving that we have no right to adopt this resolution. To this I can have no possible objection. But I can tell the senator, if I were convinced that I had voted wrong when comparatively a boy, more than twenty years ago, the fear of being termed inconsistent would not now deter me from voting right upon the same question. I do not, however, repent of my vote upon that occasion. I would now vote in the same manner under similar circumstances. I should not vote to expunge, under any circumstances, any proceeding from the journal, by obliterating the record. If I do not prove before I take my seat, that the case in the legislature of Pennsylvania was essentially different from that now before the Senate, I shall agree to be proclaimed inconsistent and time-serving.

"It was my settled conviction, at the commencement of the last session of Congress, that the Senate had *no* power to obliterate their journal.   This was shaken, but not removed, by the argument of the senator from Louisiana (Mr. Porter), who confessedly made the ablest speech on the other side of the question.   The Constitution declares that ' each house shall keep a journal of its proceedings, and from time to time publish the same, excepting such parts as may in their judgment require secrecy.'   What was the position which that senator then attempted to maintain?   In order to prove that we had no power to obliterate or destroy our journals, he thought it necessary to contend that the word ' keep,' as used in the Constitution, means both to record and to preserve.   This appeared to me 'o be a mere begging of the question.

" I shall attempt no definition of the word ' keep.'   At least since the days of Plato, we know that definitions have been dangerous.   Yet, I think that the meaning of the word, as applied to the subject-matter, is so plain, that he who runs may read.   If I direct my agent to keep a journal of his proceedings, and publish the same, my palpable meaning is, that he shall write these proceedings down from day to day, and publish what he has written for general information.   After he has obeyed my commands, after he has kept his journal and published it to the world, he has executed the essential part of the trust confided to him.   What may become of this original manuscript journal afterwards, is a matter of total indifference.   So in regard to the manuscript journal of either House of Congress ; after more than a thousand copies have been printed and published, and distributed over the Union, it is a matter of not the least importance what disposition may be made of them.   They have answered their purpose, and in any practical view become useless.   If they were burnt or otherwise destroyed, it would not be an event of the slightest public consequence.   Such indifference has prevailed upon this subject, that these journals have been considered, in the House of Representatives, as so much waste paper, and, during a period of thirty-four years after the organization of the government, they were actually destroyed. From this circumstance no public or private inconvenience has been or ever can be sustained, because our printed journals are received in evidence in all courts of justice, in the same manner as if the originals were produced.

"The senator from Louisiana has discovered that to 'keep' means both 'to record' and 'to preserve.' But can you give this, or any other word in the English language, two distinct and independent meanings at the same time, as applied to the same subject? I think not. From the imperfection of human language, from the impossibility of having appropriate words to express every idea, the same words, as applied to different subjects, has a variety of significations. As applied to any one subject, it cannot, at the same time, convey two distinct meanings. In the Constitution it must mean either 'to write down' or 'to preserve.' It cannot have both significations.

"Let senators then take their choice. If it signifies 'to write down,' as it unquestionably does, what becomes of the constitutional injunction to preserve? The truth is, that the Constitution has not provided what shall be done with the manuscript journal, after it has served the purposes for which it was called into existence. When it has been published to the people of the United States, for whose use it was ordered to be kept, after it has thus been perpetuated, and they have been furnished with the means of judging of the public conduct of their public servants, it ceases to be an object of the least importance. Whether it be thrown into the garret of the capitol, with other useless lumber, or be destroyed, is a matter of no public interest. It has probably never once been referred to in the history of our government. If it should ever be determined to be a violation of the Constitution to obliterate or destroy this manuscript journal, it must be upon different principles from those which have been urged in this debate. My own impression is, that as the framers of the Constitution have directed us to keep a journal, a constructive duty may be implied from this command, which would forbid us to obliterate or destroy it. Under this impression, I should vote, as I did twenty years ago in the Legislature of Pennsylvania, against any proposition actually to expunge any part of the journal. But, waiving this unprofitable discussion, let us proceed to the real point in controversy.

"Is any such proceeding as that of actually expunging the journal, proposed by the resolution of the senator from Missouri? I answer, no such thing. If the Constitution had, in express terms, directed us to record and to preserve a journal of our proceedings, there is nothing in the resolution now before us which would be inconsistent with such a provision.

"Is the drawing of a black line around the resolution of the Senate of March, 1834, to obliterate or to deface it? On the contrary, is it not to render it more conspicuous, to place it in bold relief, to give it a prominence in the public view beyond any other proceeding of this body in past, and I trust, in all future time? If the argument of senators were, not that we have no power to obliterate, but that the Senate possesses no power to render one portion of the journal more conspicuous than another, it would have had much greater force. Why, sir, by means of this very proceeding, that portion of our journal upon which it operates will be rescued from a slumber which would otherwise have been eternal, and fac-similes of the original resolution without a word or letter defaced, will be circulated over the whole Union.

"But, sir, this resolution also directs, that across the face of the condemnatory resolution, there shall be written by the secretary: 'Expunged by order of the Senate, this   day of   , in the year of our Lord 1837.

"Will this obliterate any part of the original resolution? If it does, the duty of the secretary will be performed in a very bungling manner. No such thing is intended. It would be easy to remove every scruple from every mind upon this subject, by amending the resolution of the senator from Missouri, so as to direct the secretary to perform his duty in such a manner as not to obliterate any part of the condemnatory resolution. Such a direction, however, appears to me to be wholly unnecessary. The nature of the whole proceeding is very plain. We now adopt a resolution expressing our strong reprobation of the original resolution, and for this purpose we use the word 'expunged' as the strongest term which we can apply. We then direct our secretary to draw black lines around it, and place such a reference to our proceedings of this day upon its face, that in all time to come, whoever may inspect this portion of our journal, will be pointed at once to the record of its condemnation. What lawyer has not observed upon the margin of the judgment docket, if the original judgment has been removed to a superior court and there reversed, a minute of such reversal? In our editions of the statutes, have we not all noted the repeal of any of them which may have taken place at a subsequent period? Who ever heard, in the one case or in the other, that this was obliterating or destroying the record or the book? So in this case : we make a mere reference to our future proceedings upon the face of the resolution instead of the margin. Suppose we should only repeal the obnoxious resolution, and direct such a reference to be made upon its face, would any senator contend that this would be an obliteration of the journal?

"But it has been contended that the word expunge is not an appropriate word ; and we have wrested it from its true signification in applying it to the present case. Even if this allegation were correct, the answer would be at hand. You might then convict us of bad taste, but not for violation of the Constitution. On the face of the resolution we have stated distinctly what we mean. We have directed the secretary in what manner he shall understand it, and we have excluded the idea that it is our intention to obliterate or to destroy the journal.

"But I shall contend that the word expunge is the appropriate word, and that there is not another in the English language so precisely adapted to convey our meaning. I shall show from the highest literary and parliamentary authorities, that this word has acquired a signification entirely distinct from that of actual obliteration. Let me proceed immediately to this task. After citing my authorities, I shall proceed with the argument. First, then, for those of a literary character: I read from Crabbe's Synonyms, page 140 (and every senator will admit that this is a work of established reputation), in speaking of the use of the word 'expunge,' the author says: 'When the contents of a book are in part rejected, they are aptly described as being expunged; in this manner the free thinking sects expunge everything from the Bible which does not suit their purpose, or they expunge from their creed what does not humor their passions.' The idea that an actual obliteration was intended in these cases would be manifestly absurd. In the same page there is a quotation from Mr. Burke, to illustrate the meaning of this word. 'I believe,' says he, 'that any person who was of age to take a part in public concerns forty years ago (if the intermediate space were expunged from his memory), could hardly credit his senses when he should hear that an army of two hundred thousand men were kept up on this island. I shall now cite Mr. Jefferson as a literary authority. He has often been referred to on this floor as a standard in politics. For this high authority I am indebted to my friend from Louisiana (Mr. Nicholas). In the original draught of the Declaration of Independence, he uses the word 'expunged' in the following manner: 'Such has been the patient sufferance of these colonies, and such is now the necessity which constrains them to expunge their former systems of government.' Although the word 'alter' was afterwards substituted for 'expunge,' I presume upon the ground that this was too strong a term, yet the change does not detract from the literary authority of the precedent.—*Jefferson's Correspondence, and 1st vol. page 17.*

"I presume that I have shown that the word 'expunge' has

acquired a distinct metaphorical meaning in our literature, which excludes the idea of actual obliteration. If I should proceed one step further, and prove that in legislative proceedings it has acquired the very same signification, I shall then have fully established my position. For this purpose I cite, first, 'the secret proceedings and debates of the Federal Convention.' In page 118 we find the following entries: 'On motion to expunge the clause of the qualification as to age, it was carried —ten States against one.'

"Again : 'On the clause respecting the ineligibility to any other office, it was moved that the words, "by any particular State," be expunged—four States for, five against, and two divided.' See page 119. 'The last blank was filled up with one year, and carried—eight ayes, two noes, one divided.'

" ' Mr. Pinckney moved to expunge the clause—agreed to, nem. con.'

"Again : 'Mr. Butler moved to expunge the clause of the stipends—lost ; seven against, three for, one divided.'

"Again, in page 157 : 'Mr. Pinckney moved that that part of the clause which disqualifies a person from holding an office in the State be expunged, because the first and best characters in a State may thereby be deprived of a seat in the national council.'

" ' Question put to strike out the words moved for, and carried—eight ayes, three noes.'

"It will thus be perceived, that in the proceedings of the very convention which formed the Constitution under which we are now governed, the word 'expunge' was often used in its figurative sense. It will certainly not be asserted, or even intimated, by any senator here, that when these motions to expunge prevailed, the words of the original draught of the Constitution were actually obliterated or defaced. The meaning is palpable. These provisions were merely rejected, not actually blotted out.

"But I shall now produce a precedent precisely in point. It

presents itself in the proceedings of the Senate of Massachusetts, and refers to the famous resolution of that body, adopted
on the 15th day of June, 1813, in relation to the capture of
the British vessel Peacock ; denouncing the late war, and
declaring that it was not becoming in a moral and religious
people to express any approbation of military or naval exploits
which were not immediately connected with the defence of our
sea coast.   Some ten years afterwards, a succeeding Senate of
Massachusetts adopted the following resolution :

"*Resolved*—That the aforesaid resolve of the 15th day of June, A. D.,
1813, and the preamble thereof, be, and the same are hereby expunged
from the journals of the Senate."

"It is self-evident that in this case not the least intention
existed of defacing the old manuscript journal.   The word
'expunge' was used in its figurative signification, just as it is in
the case before us, to express the strongest reprobation of the
former proceeding.   That proceeding was to be expunged solely
by force of the subsequent resolution, and not by any actual
obliteration.   There never was any actual obliteration of the
journal.

"Judging, then, from the highest English authorities, from
the works of celebrated authors and statesmen, and from the
proceedings of legislative bodies, is it not evident that the word
'expunge' has acquired a distinct meaning, altogether inconsistent with any actual obliteration ?

"All that we have heard about defacing and destroying the
journal are mere phantoms, which have been conjured up to
terrify the timid.   We intend no such thing.   We only mean
most strongly to express our conviction that the condemnatory
resolution ought never to have found a place on the journal
If more authorities were wanted, I might refer to the legislature of Virginia.   The present expunging resolution is in exact
conformity with their instructions to their senators.   As a matter of taste, I cannot say that I much admire their plan,

though I entertain no doubt that it is perfectly constitutional. That State is highly literary, and I think I have established that their legislature, when they used the word 'expunge,' without intending thereby to effect an actual obliteration of the journal, justly appreciated the meaning of the language which they employed.

"The word 'expunge' is in my opinion the only one which we could have used clearly and forcibly to accomplish our purpose. Even if it had not been sanctioned by practice as a parliamentary word, we ought ourselves to have first established the precedent. It suits the case precisely. If you rescind, reverse, or repeal a resolution, you thereby admit that it once had constitutional or legal authority. If you declare it to have been null and void from the beginning, this is but the expression of your own opinion that such was the fact. This word 'expunge' acts upon the resolution itself: it at once goes to its origin, and destroys its legal existence, as if it had never been. It does not merely kill, but it annihilates.

"Parliamentary practice has changed the meaning of several other words from their primitive signification in a similar manner with that of the word 'expunge.' The original signification of the word 'rescind,' is 'to cut off.' Usage has made it mean, in reference to a law or resolution, to abrogate or repeal it. We every day hear motions 'to strike out.' What is the literal meaning of this expression? The question may be best answered by asking another, If I were to request you to strike out a line from your letter, and you were willing to comply with my request, what would be your conduct? You would run your pen through it immediately, you would literally strike it out. Yet, what use do we make of this phrase every day in our legislative proceedings? If I make a motion to strike out a section from a bill, and it prevails, the Secretary encloses the printed copy of it in black lines, and makes a note on the margin that it has been stricken out. The original he never touches. Why, then, should not the word 'expunge,' without obliterating the proceedings to which it is directed, signify to destroy, as if it never had existed?

"After all that has been said, I think I need scarcely again recur to the Pennsylvania precedent. It is evident, from the whole of that proceeding, that an actual expunging of the journal was intended, if it had not already been executed. I have no recollection whatever of the circumstances, but I am under a perfect conviction, from the face of the journal, that such was the nature of the case. I should vote now as I did then, after a period of more than twenty years. Both my vote and the motion which I subsequently made upon that occasion, evidently proceeded upon this principle. The question arose in this manner, as it appears from the journal: On the 10th of February, 1816, 'The Speaker informed the House that a constitutional question being involved in a decision by him yesterday, on a motion to expunge certain proceedings from the journal, he was desirous of having the opinion of the House on that decision,' viz.: "that a majority can expunge from the journal proceedings in which the yeas and nays have not been called."' Now, as no trace whatever appears upon the journal of the preceding day, of the motion to which the Speaker refers, it is highly probable, nay, it is almost certain, that the proceedings had been actually expunged before he asked the advice of the House.

"No man feels with more sensibility the necessity which compels him to perform an unkind act towards his brother senators than myself; but we have now arrived at that point when imperious duty demands that we should either adopt this expunging resolution, or abandon it forever. Already much precious time has been employed in its discussion. The moment has arrived when we must act. Senators in the opposition console themselves with the belief that posterity will do them justice, should it be denied to them by the present generation. They place their own names in the one scale and ours in the other, and flatter themselves with the hope, that before that tribunal, at least, their weight will preponderate. For my own part, I am willing to abide the issue. I am willing to be judged for the vote which I shall give to-day, not only by the present, but by the future generation, should my obscure name ever be mentioned in after times. After the passions and prejudices of the present moment shall have subsided, and the impartial historian shall record the proceeding of this day, he will say that the distinguished men who passed the resolution condemning the President, were urged on to the act by a desire to occupy the high places in the government, that an ambition, noble in itself, but not wisely regulated, had obscured their judgment, and impelled them to the adoption of a measure, unjust, illegal, and unconstitutional ; that, in order to vindicate both the Constitution and the President, we were justified in passing this expunging resolution, and thus stamping the former proceeding with our strongest disapprobation.

"I rejoice in the belief that this promises to be one of the last highly exciting questions of the present day. During the period of General Jackson's civil administration, what has he not done for the American people? During this period, he has had more difficult and dangerous questions to settle, both at home and abroad—questions which aroused more intensely the passions of men—than any of his predecessors. They are now all happily ended, except the one which we shall this day bring to a close—

"'And all the clouds that lowered upon our house
In the deep bosom of the ocean buried.'

"The country now enjoys abundant prosperity at home, whilst it is respected and admired by foreign nations. Although the waves may yet be in some agitation from the effect of the storms through which we have passed, yet I think I can perceive the rainbow of peace extending itself across the firmament of heaven.

"Should the next administration pursue the same course of policy with the present ; should it dispense equal justice to all portious and all interests of the Union without sacrificing any ; should it be conducted with prudence and with firmness, and I doubt not but that this will be the case, we shall hereafter enjoy comparative peace and quiet in our day. This will be the precious fruit of the energy, the toils, and the wisdom of the pilot who has conducted us in safety through the storms of his tempestuous administration.

" I am now prepared for the question. I shall vote for this resolution, but not cheerfully. I regret the necessity which exists for passing it, but I believe that imperious duty demands its adoption. If I know my own heart, I can truly say that I am not actuated by any desire to obtain a miserable, petty, personal triumph, either for myself or for the President of the United States over my associates upon this floor.

" I am now ready to record my vote, and thus in the opprobrious language of senators in the opposition, to become one of the executioners of the condemnatory resolution."

Immediately after the delivery of Mr. Buchanan's speech, the vote on the " Expunging Resolution " was taken, and the odious sentence stricken from the record of the Senate. Mr. Benton had the gratification of seeing his labors accomplished, and all the friends of Gen. Jackson were abundantly pleased that he would now retire from the distinguished position he had occupied through a period of unexampled political strife, with honor to himself, and without a blot upon his fair fame. As it may be interesting to know at this day what senators refused this act of justice to President Jackson, now that his administration has been unanimously ratified by the judgment of posterity, we give the vote on this celebrated resolution.

Yeas.—Messrs. Benton, Brown, Buchanan, Dana, Ewing of Illinois, Fulton, Grundy, Hubbard, King of Alabama, Linn, Morris, Nicholas, Niles, Page, Rives, Robinson, Ruggles, Sevier, Strange, Tallmadge, Tipton, Walker, Wall, Wright.—24.

Nays.—Bayard, Black, Calhoun, Clay, Crittenden, Davis, Ewing of Ohio, Hendricks, Kent, Knight, Moore, Prentiss, Preston, Robbins, Southard, Swift, Tomlinson, Webster, White.—19.

The subsequent events of this session were not important. Mr. Buchanan, from the Committee on Foreign Relations, made a report in regard to the state of affairs between our country and Mexico, and as early as this stated that strict justice would require us even then to go to war with that country, but for the present he counselled further forbearance. The session adjourned on the 3d of March, after having at least accomplished one notable and praiseworthy act, the vindication of Gen. Jackson.

CHAPTER XIII.

Mr. Van Buren's Administration—The Extra Session—Mr. Buchanan's Speech on the
Sub-Treasury Bill.

MARTIN VAN BUREN was inaugurated President, and took his
seat as the successor of General Jackson, on the 4th of March,
1837. The financial embarrassment and commercial distress
were if possible even greater than in the revulsion of 1820–21.
The flooding of the country with excessive issues of paper currency had stimulated another of these disastrous periods of general
speculation, which had spread desolation and ruin far and near.
In the midst of the universal distress Mr. Van Buren called an
extra session of Congress, to take some measures to relieve, if
possible, the pressure of the times, and to promote the general
welfare of the country. Among the new members who made
their first appearance at this session was the Hon. Franklin
Pierce, the present chief magistrate ; Clay, Calhoun, Webster,
Benton, Silas Wright, and other prominent names still continued on the senatorial list. Mr. Buchanan occupied the same
place, the chairmanship of the Committee on Foreign Relations,
he had in the previous Congress. Almost the first bill introduced was what is known as the " Sub-Treasury Act." It was
violently opposed, and though it passed the Senate twice it was
both times rejected by the House.

Simple as were the principles of this bill, and as fully as they
are now acknowledged to be right and proper, yet the opposition both in Congress and out of it, which was raised against
the measure, demonstrates what a powerful, temporary excitement can be produced where there is not the slightest reason to

warrant it. Mr. Van Buren wished merely to complete the divorce between bank and state which General Jackson had so nobly inaugurated.   What more simple to effect this than that the government by its own agents should disburse its own revenue, instead of employing banks to do it ?   As long as the government was in any way mixed up with these institutions, it would be charged with almost every financial embarrassment the currency might experience.   The agitation the question caused in politics would be avoided by adopting the simple direct principles of the Constitution, and one more step would have been taken towards returning to the letter and spirit of that instrument.   Mr. Buchanan made a speech of great power and research upon the bill, which is valuable as going into a full explanation of the causes of financial embarrassment in a profound statesmanlike manner, and in presenting a clear conception of the powers of the general government in regard to the question under consideration.   Its great length has compelled us to abridge it, but we trust we have given its most important points.   The following is the opening portion :

Mr. President : It cannot be denied that the commercial and manufacturing classes of our people throughout the Union are now suffering severely under one of those periodical pressures which have so often afflicted the country.   Neither have the agricultural and other interests escaped without injury, although they have not suffered to the same extent.   The exhaustion of the human system does not succeed a high degree of unnatural excitement with more unerring certainty than that a depression in the business of the country must follow excessive speculation.   The one is a law of nature, the other a scarcely less uniform law of trade.   The degree of this depression will always bear an exact proportion to the degree of overaction.   As many degrees as the system has been elevated above the point of healthy action, so many degrees must it sink below, after the effects of the stimulus have passed away.

" What has been the history of the country in this respect ? One of constant vibration. I can speak positively on this subject in regard to the period of time since I came into public life. What has been will be again. The same causes will produce the same effects. We can cherish no reasonable hope of a change unless State legislatures should take a firm and decided stand. The history of the past will become that of the future This year we have sunk to the extreme point of depression. The country is now glutted with foreign merchandise. There will, therefore, be but few importations. All our efforts are now directed towards the payment of our foreign debt. The next year the patient will begin to recruit his exhausted energies. Domestic manufactures will flourish in proportion as foreign goods become scarce. The third year, a fair business will be done. The country will present a flourishing appearance. Property of all descriptions will command a fair price, and we shall glide along smoothly and prosperously. The fourth or the fifth year the era of extravagant speculation will return, again to be succeeded by another depression. At successive periods the best and most enterprising men of the country are crushed. They fall victims at the shrine of the insatiate and insatiable Moloch of extravagant banking. It is an everlasting cycle. The wise man says there is no new thing under the sun, and we are destined, I fear, again and again to pass through the same vicissitudes. The aspect is perpetually changing, but is never new.

" Senators have plumed themselves, and their admirers throughout the country have applauded them as being wonderfully sagacious in their predictions. Their respective partisans are ready to exclaim :

'The spirit of deep prophecy he hath,
Exceeding the nine Sibyls of old Rome ;
What's past and what's to come he can descry.'

" But no deep penetration into futurity was required to make these prophecies. Until existing causes shall be removed, the future must be the counterpart of the past.

"Whence this eternal vicissitude in the business of the country? What is the secret spring of all these calamities? I answer, the spirit of enterprise, so natural to American citizens, excited into furious action by the stimulus of excessive banking. It operates as does the inhaling of oxygen gas upon the human mind, urging it on to every extravagance and to every folly.

"I do not deny that several subordinate circumstances have operated in unison with this grand cause to make the present catastrophe more severe than it otherwise might have been. Still it is the root of all the evil. It is the chief and almost the only source from which the existing distress has flowed.

"I was not a member of this body when the discussion took place of the veto of the bank charter, or the removal of the deposits. Although both these measures received my cordial approbation, yet I refrain purposely from replying at this late period to the remarks which have been made on these subjects. They have already passed into history, and been sanctioned by the public approbation.

"Amongst these subsidiary causes of the existing distress, may be enumerated the destruction of capital by the great fire at New York in December, 1835. The wild speculations in public lands, and in splendid towns and cities upon paper throughout the Western States, which withdrew capital from the commercial cities, where it was most wanted, to portions of the country where it was not required; and the specie circular, if you please, which, however wise it may have been in its origin, ought not, in my opinion, to have been continued in force after it had performed its office and had checked the wild speculations in public lands. I voted in favor of the bill at the last session, which repealed this circular; and, under the same circumstances, I would again act in the same manner. But permit me to say that its effects have been greatly exaggerated.

It did not carry to the West anything approaching the amount of gold and siver which senators have estimated. According to the report of the Secretary of the Treasury, all the specie in all the western deposit banks, including Michigan, but little exceeded four millions of dollars at the date of the suspension of specie payments ; and in the southwestern deposit banks it did not amount to one million two hundred thousand dollars. I shall not stop to inquire how much less gold and silver there would have been in these depositories had the specie circular never existed. Certain it is that the comparatively small amount of specie which came into these banks in consequence of this circulation, could have produced but an inconsiderable effect on the business of our commercial cities, and still less upon the suspension of specie payments.

"These causes may have made the revulsion a little more severe ; but, had they never existed, still it must have come with desolating force.

" Senators have attributed some portions of the existing distress to the act of 1834, regulating the standard of our gold coins. They have not told us, and they cannot tell us, how this act could have produced such an effect. It was no party measure, and upon its passage, there were but few, I believe but seven, votes against it in the Senate. It was a measure of absolute necessity, if we desired that our own gold coins should circulate in this country. Before its passage, a half eagle, as an article of merchandise, was intrinsically worth about five dollars and thirty-three cents in silver, whilst its standard value, as currency, under our laws was only five dollars. It is manifest, therefore, that eagles and half eagles never could have entered into general circulation had it not been for the passage of this act, which is now condemned. It was a mere adjustment of the relative value of gold to silver, according to the standard of other nations, and, if I am not greatly mistaken in my memory, conformed exactly in this particular with the laws of Spain and Portugal.

10

"I have been utterly at a loss to conceive the cause of the hostility of senators to this necessary measure, unless it be from a feeling similar to that which, it is said, made a distinguished gentleman desire to kill every sheep which came in his way. He could feel no personal hostility to these innocent and harmless animals, but was such a violent anti-tariff man that the sight of them always reminded him of our woollen manufactures. Certainly no gentleman can entertain any objection to the eagles and half eagles themselves ; but they may remind senators of the efficient and untiring exertions of the senator from Missouri (Mr. Benton), to introduce a gold currency into circulation. As gold, they may like these coins ; but as Bentonian mint-drops, they are detestable.

"Senators have also contended that the present depressed condition of the country has been produced, in some degree, by the large importations of specie which were encouraged by the administration of General Jackson. I shall not be diverted from my main purpose by answering this objection in detail. Even if their position were correct, which I by no means admit, that more gold and silver had been forced into the country than our necessities demanded, or the fixed laws of trade would have justified, still the effect would have been transient and trifling. It would have immediately flowed back through the channels cf commerce to the place from whence it came, until the par exchange had been restored. This is one of the fixed and invariable laws of trade, from the obligation of which we can never be released.

" The senator from Kentucky (Mr. Clay), in the course of his remarks upon this subject, involved himself in a strange contradiction. At the commencement of his speech, he deprecated, with his usual eloquence and ability, the policy of the past administration in forcing specie into this country, contrary to the laws of trade. Towards the conclusion, when his fancy became excited by the contemplation of the splendid bank of the United States which it was his purpose to establish, he seemed entirely to have changed his opinion. In order to obtain the necessary amount of specie capital, he proposed that some twenty or twenty-five millions of this bank stock should be transmitted to Europe, and sold to foreigners in exchange for gold and silver. It was a violation of the laws of trade, which must recoil upon us, to force a greater amount of specie into the country than our just proportion, for the purpose of putting it into circulation among the people ; but, when the purpose is to furnish a specie capital of twenty or twenty-five millions for a new bank of the United States, then all difficulties vanish from the mind of the gentleman.

"No, sir," said Mr. B., "without the agency of any of these secondary causes, the present distress must have come. It was inevitable as fate. No law of nature is more fixed, than that our over-banking and our over-trading must have produced the disastrous results under which we are now suffering.

"Is there now, in any of our large commercial cities, such an individual as a regular importing or commission merchant ? I mean a merchant who is content to grow rich, as our fathers did, by the successive and regular profits of many years of industry in his own peculiar pursuit. If there be such persons, they are rare. No, sir, all desire to grow rich rapidly. Each takes his chance in the lottery of speculation. Although there may be a hundred chances to one against him, each eagerly intent upon the golden prize, overlooks the intervening rocks and quicksands between him and it, and when he fondly thinks he is about to clutch it, he sinks into bankruptcy and ruin. Such has been the fate of thousands of our most enterprising citizens. It is enough to make one's heart bleed to contemplate the blighted hopes and ruined prospects of those who have fallen victims to the demon of speculation. Many of them have been the most promising, and but for this fatal error, would have become the most useful citizens of our country. Under the influence of this feeling, they not only risk their own all, but often the all of others, which has been confided to them ; not, as I firmly believe, with any deliberate purpose of being dishonest, but in the confident but delusive hope that fortune may smile upon their efforts, and enable them to meet all their responsibilities.

" Far be it from me to utter one word against the profession of the merchant. By their ability and enterprise, our merchants have cast lustre upon the character of our country throughout the world. They are amongst our most useful citizens. They are agents for exchanging our productions with distant nations and among ourselves. Commerce is the handmaid of agriculture and manufactures, and heaven forbid, that I should be the instrument of exciting hostility between them. Again, I am the last man in the country who would crush that spirit of enterprise and of untiring effort which belongs to the American character. It has produced miracles. It has covered every sea with our flag. With a rapidity unexampled in the history of the world, it has converted the wilderness into fruitful fields, and flourishing towns and cities. It has erected splendid improvements of every kind. It has covered, and is covering the face of our vast country with railroads and canals, and has enabled a nation, centuries behind in the start, to surpass all her rivals in the career of internal improvement. If I had the power, I would regulate this spirit. I would limit it within proper bounds. God forbid that I should destroy it.

" It is impossible that manufactures and commerce can flourish to any great degree in this country without the aid of extensive credit ; I would not, therefore, abolish banks if I could. A return to a pure metallic currency is impossible. To make such an attempt would be ruinous as well as absurd. It would at once diminish the nominal value of all property more than fifty per cent., and would, in effect, double the amount of every man's debts. It would enrich creditors at the expense of their debtors, and thus make the rich richer, and the poor poorer.

It would paralyze industry and enterprise.   I would give enterprise wholesome food to feed upon, but would not drive it into
mad speculation, by administering unnatural stimulants.

"What power does this government possess to regulate the
banking system of the country?   None, comparatively none.
It belongs to the States.   We shall soon see whether they will
exert this power in a wise and beneficial manner.   Every
obstacle has been removed from their course, by the general
suspension of specie payments.   But the banks are all-powerful.
Their presidents, their directors, their cashiers, their stockholders, and their agents, pervade our whole society.   They are
spread over the land.   A common interest will unite them in a
solid phalanx, for the purpose of making a common effort.
They will invade our halls of legislation, and exert all the
influence which they may possess with every department of our
State governments, for the purpose of preserving their exorbi
tant privileges.   The people may now establish these institu
tions upon a stable and useful foundation.   The conflict will be
tremendous, and I confess, I tremble for the result.   The weal
or the woe of this country, for many years to come, depends
upon the issue.

"In this crisis, all which the general government can effect
is, in the first place, to withhold its deposits from the banks,
and thus refrain from contributing their funds to swell the
torrent of wild speculation, and, in the second place, to restrain
the extravagance of their credits and issues, in some small
degree, by collecting and disbursing our revenue exclusively in
specie, or in the notes of banks which will pay the balances due
from them in specie, at short intervals.   To accomplish these
two purposes, as well as to render the public revenues more
secure, are the objects of the bill and amendment now before
the Senate.

"The evils of a redundant paper circulation are now manifest to every eye.   It alternately raises and sinks the value of
every man's property.   It makes a beggar of the man to-mor-

row who is indulging in dreams of wealth to-day. It converts the business of society into a mere lottery, whilst those who distribute the prizes are wholly irresponsible to the people. When the collapse comes, as come it must, it casts laborers out of employment, crushes manufactures and merchants, and ruins thousands of honest and industrious citizens. Shall we, then, by our policy, any longer contribute to such fatal results? That is the question.

"The system of extravagant banking benefits no person, exept the shrewd speculator, who knows how to take advantage of the perpetual fluctuation in prices which a redundant paper currency never fails to produce. He sees, in the general causes which operate upon the commercial world, when money is about to be scarce, and when it will become plenty. He studies the run as a gambler does that of the cards. He knows when to buy and when to sell, and thus often realizes a large estate in a few happy ventures. Those who have been initiated into the mysteries of the paper-money market, can thus accumulate rapid fortunes at the expense of their less skillful neighbors.

"The question before the Senate is not, whether we shall divorce the government from the banks; the banks themselves have done that already; the alliance is already dissolved. The question now is, shall we, with all the experience of the past, restore this ill-fated union? No propitious divinities would grace the new nuptials, but the fatal sisters would be there ready again to cut the cord at the first approach of difficulty and danger.

"The senator from Virginia (Mr. Rives) has appealed to us in the name of consistency to support his amendment, but circumstances have entirely changed since we voted for it at the last session. Then the union existed between the banks and the treasury, and his bill prescribed the relative duties of the contracting parties. Now the contract is at an end. The banks have violated its fundamental obligations, and the gov-

ernment is free   The preliminary question now is, shall we
enter into a new alliance?   We must first determine that we
shall, before any question of consistency can arise   Should we
again connect ourselves with the banks, then, and not till then,
can we be called upon to adopt rules regulating the union
The amendment of the senator from Virginia proceeds upon
the assumption that our former relations are to be restored   I
oppose the amendment mainly because I am hostile to this
re-union.   If Congress should first determine to restore the old
relations between the parties, then, and not till then, might
there be some force in an appeal to our consistency.

"We are left, at this moment, entirely free to decide what is
best to be done with the public money.   To use the language
of the Senator from South Carolina (Mr. Calhoun), we have
reached a point from whence we are about to take a new
departure.   But three courses have been, or, in the nature of
things, can be presented for our selection.   We must either
deposit the public money in a bank of the United States, to be
created for that purpose, or restore it to the State banks, or
provide for its safe custody in the hands of our own officers,
without the agency of any bank, State or national.

"And first, in regard to the creation of another bank of the
United States.   It was not my purpose, at this time, to offer
my objections in detail to such an institution.   Even if I had
intended to present my views fully upon this subject, the overwhelming vote of the Senate on Tuesday last, against the
establishment of such a bank, would warn me to forbear.   It
would be labor lost, and time expended in vain.   I shall content myself, therefore, with a few general observations upon
this branch of the subject, and a short reply to some of the
remarks which have been made by the advocates of a new
bank.

"In my opinion, the most alarming dangers which would
result from such an institution, have never yet been presented
in bold relief before the people.   This has arisen from the

unnatural position of that institution towards the government. We have seen it struggling against executive power, and its efforts have been tremendous They would have been irresistible against any other President than Andrew Jackson. As it was, the conflict was of the most portentous character, and shook the Union to its centre. But we have witnessed the exception, not the rule. It is the natural ally, not the enemy of power. Wealth and power necessarily attract each other, and are always ready to rush to each other's embrace. In the language once used by a distinguished orator, now no more (Mr. Randolph), 'Male and female created he them.' Suppose General Jackson and the bank had been in alliance, and not in opposition ; what then might have been the consequences, had he been an enemy to the liberties of his country ? Armed with all the power and all the patronage which belonged to the President of the United States, enjoying unbounded popularity, and wielding the combined wealth of the country, through the agency of this all-powerful bank and its branches, planted in every portion of the Union, can any man say that our liberties would not have been in danger ? All the forms of the Constitution might have remained, the people might still have been flattered with the idea of electing their own officers, but the animating spirit of our free institutions would have departed forever. A secret, an all-pervading influence, would have sapped the foundations of liberty, and made it an empty name. Under such circumstances, a President might always select his successor. But, thank Heaven, the danger has passed away, and I trust forever.

" If any of my friends on this side of the House, who advocate the establishment of a national bank, should be elected President—and if their political principles are to prevail with a majority of the people of this country, that majority could not make a better selection—in what situation shall we be placed ? One of the first measures of the administration would be to establish a magnificent bank of the United States, with a capi-

tal of at least fifty millions of dollars, and with branches
throughout the different States.   A feeling of gratitude towards
their creator would render them subservient to his will.   It
would be their pride and their pleasure to promote his influence
and extend his power.   We should have no more wars between
the bank and the government.   They would move on harmoniously together.   In other days, the time might arrive when
the bank would be used by some bad and aspiring President,
as a powerful instrument to subvert the liberties of his country.

"Even if such a bank could better regulate the currency and
the domestic exchanges of the country than any other instrument, still it would be infinitely better to bear the ills we have
than to endanger the existence or the purity of our free institutions.

"But would such a bank control and regulate the issues of the
State banks? I answer, no. It would not if it could ; it
could not if it would.   In the affairs of human life, if you
expect an agent to restrain and control another, you ought to
render either their interests or their inclinations different and
counteracting.   To accomplish this purpose they must be
'antagonistical' to each other. When such agents are corporations, this is emphatically true.   Peculiarly governed by
self-interest, they feel no enthusiasm unless it be to make large
dividends for their stockholders.   Now, a bank of the United
States would have precisely the same interest with the State
banks in making extravagant loans and issues.   Whenever, in
their estimation, they should extend their accommodations,
without endangering their own security, they would pursue that
course. This is the powerful instinct of self-interest. You
cannot change the fixed laws which govern human nature, by
making men directors and stockholders in the Bank of the
United States.   It is absurd to suppose that a large moneyed
corporation, having in view solely its own interests, will voluntarily become the regulator of the paper currency of a great
nation, and prevent those ruinous contractions and expansions

under which both England and this country have periodically suffered. It would be easy for me to prove, at least to my own satisfaction, that, in point of fact, neither the first nor the last bank of the United States ever did exercise a regular and efficient control over the issues of the State banks. Both the one and the others have thus rushed together, and have together administered to that spirit of over-trading and extravagant speculation which has so often desolated our country. To pursue such a course of illustration would, however, be to revive the old controversy ; to tread the ground which has been so often trodden, and to direct me from that which more essentially belongs to the present question.

" The mistake committed in regard to the deposit banks, was the belief that they would be able and willing to restrain the issues of the other State banks. Fortified with the public deposits, and numerous as they were, they might possibly have done something towards the accomplishment of such a purpose. But, bank like—human nature like—instead of aiming at any such result, the government deposits became the instrument in their hands of still more extravagant credits and circulation. Their objects seemed to be not to restrain, but to give loose reins to the other banks and to themselves, and thereby increase their own profits."

*   *   *   *   *   *   *

Mr. Buchanan having concluded this portion of his subject, then noticed the position Mr. Webster had taken upon the question, and thus referred to that distinguished man :

" What, then, was the senator's main position ? In this I think I cannot be mistaken, I wish to state it distinctly and fairly. He contended that Congress not only possess the power under the Constitution, but that it is their imperative duty to create and furnish for the people of this country a paper currency which shall be at par in all portions of the Union, and everywhere serve as the medium of domestic exchanges. In what particular mode or by what means, this paper currency was to be called into existence, the senator did not explain. On this point he was quite mysterious. He infers the existence of this power from two clauses in the Constitution ; the first, that which confers on Congress the power 'to regulate commerce with foreign nations, and among the several States, and with the Indian tribes ;' and the second, 'to coin money, regulate the value thereof, and of foreign coin, and fix the standard of weights and measures.'"

(Here Mr. Webster also referred Mr. Buchanan to that clause of the Constitution which prohibits the States from coining money or emitting bills of credit.)

"What, in my opinion, constitutes the chief excellence of the senator from Massachusetts, as a public speaker, is the clearness with which he states his propositions, and his power of condensation in maintaining them. When he happens to be in the wrong, these high qualities operate against himself, and render his errors more conspicious. Such was my conviction yesterday, when he undertook the herculean task of deducing the power to create a paper currency, without any limit but the discretion of Congress, from the simple powers of regulating commerce, and coining hard money.

" By the state of the question before the Senate, the gentleman has been driven into a narrow place, and has chosen a position which his great powers will not enable him to maintain. The bill upon your table proposes to keep on deposit, and to transfer the public revenue, where it may be required, without the agency of any bank. If these duties can be successfully performed by the officers of the government, then there can be no pretence for claiming the power to incorporate a national bank from that clause in the Constitution giving Congress the power 'to levy and collect taxes, duties, impost, and excises, and to pay the debt of the United States.' The present bill provided for all these purposes, independently of all banks. There

can, then, be no necessity to create one as a fiscal agent of the
government; and, of consequence, the ancient argument in
favor of its constitutionality falls to the ground. This was its
origin; this was the foundation on which it has formerly rested.
The power to issue notes, and that to regulate the exchanges
of the country, have heretofore been considered as merely incidental to the bank itself, after it had been called into existence
as a necessary fiscal agent of the treasury. These have never
been considered as powers inherent in the government, but as
mere consequences of the regular action of a national banking
institution. Under existing circumstances, the senator is driven
even from these comparatively narrow limits. He disclaims the
idea of advocating, at present, the establishment of a national
bank, hence he has never once, throughout the whole course of
his argument, called to his aid the power 'to levy and collect
taxes.' He has not even mentioned it. He casts this power
into the background, whilst he claims for Congress, from the
other clauses of the Constitution which I have read, the transcendent power of creating a paper currency without limits.

"Let us for a few moments examine his argument. The
framers of the Constitution were sturdy patriots, who, with a
bold but cautious hand, conferred upon the general government
certain enumerated powers. Dreading lest this government
might attempt to usurp other powers which had not been
granted, they have expressly declared that 'the powers not
delegated to the United States by the Constitution, nor prohibited by it to the States, are reserved to the States respectively or to the people.' This caution was absolutely necessary to
prevent astute and subtle lawyers from extending, by forced and
ingenious constructions, the clear and explicit grant of powers
which was traced by the hand of our fathers.' Does the Constitution, then, anywhere expressly confer upon Congress the
power of creating a national paper currency? This is not pretended. But the senator from Massachusetts has found it lurk-
ing under the power 'to regulate commerce with foreign

nations, and among the several States, and with the Indian
tribes.' What is the signification of the word 'regulate?'
Does it mean to create? No, sir. Such a signification would
be to confound the meaning of two of the plainest words in the
English language. You create something new ; you regulate
the action of that which has already been called into existence.
The meaning of the word ' regulate,' as used by the framers of
the Constitution themselves, clearly appears in a subsequent
clause in the instrument. ' Congress shall have power to coin
money, regulate the value thereof, and of foreign coin, and fix
the standard of weights and measures.' To coin money is the
creation of the subject ; after it has been coined, and thus
brought into existence, you regulate the value of it and of
foreign coin. There are no two words in the English language
which have more distinct and precise meanings than to ' create'
and to ' regulate.' The word ' regulate' necessarily presupposes
the previous existence of something to be regulated. Such is
its plain, clear signification in the Constitution. Commerce had
long existed ' with foreign nations and among the several States,
and with the Indian tribes,' previous to the date of the Constitution. Its framers took the subject up as they found it, and
acting upon the existing state of things, they authorized Congress to regulate, or to prescribe rules for conducting this commerce in all future times. To infer, therefore, from this simple
power of regulating commerce, that of creating and issuing a
supply of paper money for the country, strikes me as one of the
most extraordinary propositions which has ever been presented
to the Senate."

It cannot be denied that the above plain, common sense views
of the power of Congress to establish a national bank is so plainly
and so palpably correct, that no arguments renowned as the
senator from Massachusetts was for his logical abilities, could
overthrow them. Mr. Buchanan, in closing this part of his
speech, presented the following very clear statement of the dif-

ference between the political parties of our country. He said :

" Two political schools have existed in this country from the time the Constitution was adopted. The one favored a strict, the other a liberal, construction of that instrument. The one has been jealous of State rights, the other the advocate of federal power. The senator from Massachusetts, if we may judge by his argument upon the present occasion, is far in advance of those who have hitherto gone the farthest in support of federal power. He has made large strides towards consolidation or conservatism. I use these terms with no offensive meaning."

Mr. Buchanan's speech then goes into a discussion as to whether the public deposits ought to be restored to the State banks, and shows that they ought not, because these banks were not and never had been safe depositories of the public money. More than all that, it gave them a capital upon which to make large paper issues, and thus flood the country with means for the speculators to use the government money to injure the laboring classes. These banks, after going on during a period of extravagant expansion, would fail, and " in such cases," said Mr. Buchanan, " what classes of society are most likely to suffer from the explosion ? Who do you suppose, Mr. President, held the notes of the hundred and sixty-five banks, that proved insolvent, between 1811 and 1830 ? Not the shrewd men of business, nor the keen speculator ; because they snuff the danger from afar. It was the honest and industrious classes of society, who are without suspicion, and whose pursuits in life do not render them familiar with the secret history of banking.

" We are now just experiencing another great evil which has resulted from extravagant loans and issues, and consequent suspension of specie payments by banks. The country is now deluged with small notes, vulgarly called shin-plasters. They are of every form and every denomination between five cents and five dollars ; and they are issued by every individual and every corporation who think proper. It is impossible for the poor man to say he will not take them, for there is scarcely any silver change in circulation anywhere. He must receive them for his labor or starve. The paper on which these small notes are printed is often so bad, and they are so inartificially got up, that it is almost impossible to distinguish between the counterfeit and the genuine. To counterfeit then has became a regular business, as it has been carried to a great extent.

"Our currency below five dollars now consists of this combined mass of genuine and counterfeit shin-plasters, and many of the counterfeits are intrinsically of equal value with the genuine. Some are payble in one medium and some in another. Some are on demand, and others have years to run before they reach maturity. The very moment the banks resume specie-payments, this mass of illegal and worthless currency will be rendered entirely useless. It will fall a dead weight in the hands of the holders, and these will be chiefly the very men who are least able to bear the loss. A scene of confusion and distress will then be presented, which I need not describe. Such is one of the effects of extravagant banking."

No one at this day will question the faithfulness of the above picture, and yet we have men who are called great statesmen, who labored, mistakingly we must charitably suppose, to fasten upon the people of this country a policy which would have constantly rendered us liable to the fluctuation and distress which Mr. Buchanan so truthfully, and without any embellishment, describes.

The speech from which we have made the above extracts, then refers to the bill under discussion, showing that it amounted to simply this, that to the duties of the existing officers of government, who already collect the revenue and disburse it, be merely superadded, that of safely keeping and transferring the public money, according to the exigencies of the govern-

ment during the time that must necessarily intervene between
its receipt and disbursement. After going into a detailed
statement of the arguments bearing upon the bill, our indebt-
edness to foreign countries, Mr. Buchanan concluded as follows :

"But, gentlemen allege that the President has committed
another grave error, in stating that the foreign debt contracted
by our citizens was estimated, in March last, at more than
thirty millions of dollars. This estimate, they say, is below
the truth some eighty or ninety millions. If it were, this
would only be, as in the case of the other alleged mistakes, so
much in favor of the President's argument, not against it. But
how do they prove this mistake ? By adding to our actual
foreign debt now due, and payable by the merchants, all foreign
investments in our stocks, and all the permanent loans which
have been made in England to the several States and to corporations. The bare statement of this fact is sufficient. It is
evident the President was not estimating the amount of permanent investments made by foreigners in this country, but the
actual amount of our commercial debt due in March last, which
it was necessary to extinguish before our trade could revive.
This debt may have been thirty-five or forty millions of dollars,
but from the information communicated by the senator from
New York (Mr. Tallmadge), a few days ago, that in the
opinion of the merchants of New York, it was now reduced to
twelve millions of dollars. I should very much doubt whether
it at all exceeded thirty millions in March last.

"How cheering the intelligence that our foreign debt has
been reduced to twelve millions of dollars ! The resources of
our country are so abundant, that this debt must very soon be
extinguished. Our next cotton crop will create a large balance
in our favor. The foreign exchanges will soon no longer be
against us, and then the foreign demand for specie will cease.
All sound banks may then with safety resume specie payments.

They will have nothing to dread, except the want of confidence at home.   This, I fear, has been greatly increased, at least throughout the interior of Pennsylvania, by the refusal of the banks in Philadelphia to meet those of New York, even for the purpose of consulting at what time it was probable specie payments might with safety be resumed.   I have received numerous letters on the subject, which all speak the same language. This refusal, I feel confident, did not arise from any apprehension that these banks were less able to resume specie payments than those of their sister city.

"Mr. Van Buren is not only correct in his statements of fact, but by his message, he has forever put to flight the charge of non-committalism, of want of decision and energy.   He has assumed an attitude of moral grandeur before the American people, and has shown himself worthy to succeed General Jackson.   He has elevated himself much in my own esteem. He has proved equal to the trying occasion.   Even his political enemies who cannot approve the doctrines of the message, admire its decided tone, and the ability with which it sustains what has been called the new experiment.   And why should the sound of new experiments in governments grate so harshly upon the ears of the senator from Massachusetts?   Was not our government itself, at its origin, a new and glorious experiment? Is it not now upon its trial?   If it should continue to work as it has heretofore done, it will at least secure liberty to the human race, and rescue the rights of man, in every clime, from the grasp of tyrants.   Still it is, as yet, but an experiment. For its future success it must depend upon the patriotism and the wisdom of the American people and the government of their choice.   I sincerely believe that the establishment of the agencies which the bill provides, will exert a most happy influence upon the success of our grand experiment, and that it will contribute in no small degree to the prosperous working of our institutions generally.   The message will constitute the touchstone of political parties in this country for years to come, and I shall always be found ready to do battle in support of its doctrines, because their direct tendency is to keep the federal government within its proper limits, and to maintain the reserved rights of the States. To take care of our own money through the agency of our own officers, without the employment of any banks, whether State or national, will, in my opinion, greatly contribute to these happy results ; and, in sustaining this policy, I feel confident I am advocating the true interest and the dearest rights of the people."

Mr. Buchanan's powerful speech was answered both by Mr. Webster of Massachusetts, and Mr. Preston of South Carolina. It was customary then as now, for the public press to give the impression to the country that every democratic speech in Congress was always crushed by the answer of opponents. Mr. Buchanan shortly after the delivery of his speech referring to this peculiarity remarked :

"He had not flattered himself," he said, "that the remarks which he had made some days ago, in answer to the senator from Massachusetts, would have called him out in reply. It has, sir, been already reported over the whole country, by a portion of the newspaper press, that the blows which I aimed at him with a feeble hand, had been repelled by his adamantine armor, without leaving the slightest impression. Besides," said Mr. B., "I have been utterly prostrated, according to the same reports, by the senator from South Carolina (Mr. Preston), and so belabored after I was down, that I can scarcely now be recognized by my most intimate friends. Under those painful circumstances, it affords me a ray of comfort to find that the senator from Massachusetts has deemed my argument worthy of a studied reply. I hope it may not be presumptuous in me to say a few words by way of rejoinder.

"Heaven forbid that I should be forced to lie down in the same bed with the senator from Massachusetts, the senator from South Carolina (Mr. Calhoun), and the Secretary of the Treasury. For a man of peace like myself, the bed of Procrustes would be a mercy compared with such fellowship. Never were there more ill-assorted and heterogeneous materials brought together. If my argument has made the three gentlemen lie down together in the same bed, as the senator has asserted, there let them lie as best they can ; I beg to be excused from becoming a partner with this triple alliance ; conscious that in that event my fate would deserve to be pitied, I shall endeavor to support myself alone."

All the prominent debates at this session took place upon the currency question, and such collateral subjects as district banks, deposit banks, &c. Although the great measure of the session had not been carried yet, the discussion elicited had prepared the way for a measure of a similar character. The extra session, which had commenced on the 5th of September, adjourned on the 16th of October.

CHAPTER XIV.

Expunging Resolution—Relations with Mexico—A New National Bank—Mr. Buchanan's Speech on Pre-emption Rights—The Slavery Question—Resurrection Notes—
The Independent Treasury.

THE first regular session of the twenty-fifth Congress opened
on the 4th of December, 1837. Mr. Buchanan, according to
his usual custom, was in his seat on the first day of the session.
A careful scrutiny of the proceedings of Congress will show
that Mr. Buchanan took a more active part in the business of
the country than any other senator. In the present session,
his name stands as speaking or voting upon more public questions than any other senator. Mr. Clay was considered a very
active member, yet Mr. Buchanan ranks ahead of him in this
respect. Many politicians go to Congress with their heads
filled with a single idea or hobby. Upon this they are always
ready to make a speech or vote, but they take very little, if
any, interest in the ordinary and general business of government. Mr. Buchanan, however, never had any specialties ; he
regarded himself as a senator particularly elected to represent
the great State of Pennsylvania, and bound by the duties he
owed to his constituents and to his country at large, to take
part in all the legislation that came before him, no matter of
how slight importance it might be considered. In this he showed
the jealous watchfulness of the true statesman, who cares for
the interests of even the humblest of the people, and neglects nothing that appertains to their welfare.

Only ten days of the session had elapsed before Mr. Bayard
of Delaware presented a resolution to rescind the former

"expunging resolution," which had been passed by the previous Congress, just as Gen. Jackson was retiring from the chair which he had so nobly filled. Mr. Bayard did not propose to express any opinion upon the propriety of passing the resolution of censure upon Gen. Jackson. He contended, however, that it was wrong to have "expunged" it from the journal, and he announced his resolute determination to set the ball in motion, *à la* Benton, and so keep it until the "expunging resolution" should be repealed ; and he predicted that he should live to see that day arrive. Mr. Buchanan replied to him by saying, "that the honorable member from Delaware must desire a very long existence in this vale of tears if he expected to live until what was asked by the resolution was adopted. The senator has been pleased to say he would not be willing to die so soon. He certainly wished the senator long life and prosperity ; but to remain until his aim were accomplished, would be to render him miserable, unless he feasted on the Medean herb to renovate his youth." And such has proved to be the fact. No man to increase his popularity would be likely now to make a move to replace the stigma upon Gen. Jackson's official conduct which the heated exasperations of momentary party spite put upon it.

The relations of this country with Mexico was again a subject of debate in this session, and again we find Mr. Buchanan, as ever, the resolute defender of his country's honor. In the course of a debate upon this subject, Mr. B. traced the conduct of the Mexican government towards our citizens, showed how American citizens had been forced to leave the country, that the American flag was no protection to them, and that, after being insulted and robbed, no satisfaction or apology was given. When Mr. Clay suggested that in consideration of the deranged state of the currency we had better avoid war, Mr. Buchanan replied that, "if the national honor demanded vindication, he would not be deterred by any such consideration. He for one 'would not consent to see American citizens plundered with impunity.'" It was on this occasion that he uttered that sentence which will be as immortal as the mind that conceived it: "Millions to defend our rights, but not a cent for tribute."

Mr. Clay could not give up entirely his favorite scheme of a United States Bank, and although the institution had only just been fairly crushed by the gigantic exertions of a great man, yet, so intent was he upon some institution of a similar character, that he brought before Congress in May the plan of a national bank, to be located in the city of New York, with a capital of some fifty millions of dollars, with Mr. Albert Gallatin at its head. Mr. Buchanan met the project of the senator from Kentucky at the outset, and said, " that he was rejoiced that the senator had come out in a bold and manly manner, and presented his project of a national bank. The two great parties of the country would now know precisely where they stood. From this day the issue would be fairly formed and distinctly presented to the people. On the one side there was a national bank, with a capital of fifty millions, sustained by the revenues of the government, and enjoying the privilege of having its notes received in payment of the public dues ; whilst on the other, we desired a separation—a friendly separation—of the business of the Treasury from that of all the banks, leaving each of them to its own resources, and to perform its own duties, without danger of being crushed or controlled by a mammoth institution. We wished to part from them in peace, and to remain at peace with them, interposing no obstacles in the way of their healthy and vigorous action. We leave them to be regulated by the States where they belong. He did not fear the final result of such a trial before the American people." And why, we ask, did Mr. Buchanan not fear the result of this question ? We reply, because he had a firm confidence in the judgment and intelligence of the people, the first sentiment in the heart of every true democrat, as it is the first plank in the platform of the party. It is sufficient to say, he was not mistaken.

The pre-emption right of land to actual settlers, is one of the most important to the hardy pioneer, of any measure ever enacted by our government. It has been the foundation of the fortune of many a person who now stands at the head of society, for all the noble qualities that can adorn the human character. A young man with his wife, and scarcely any wordly effects, except it may be a dog and a gun, settles upon the broad prairies of the West, and after having improved a section of the land, and perchance accumulated a part of the money necessary for its purchase, is suddenly surprised in his dreams of a comfortable home by some speculator, who comes along, and purchasing his land, assumes the right to dispossess him and seize upon the fruits of his hard-earned toil. It is strange that there ever were any persons elected to Congress who defended a measure which would allow this. Yet such is the fact. While, however, there were but few who went to this extent, there were many who believed that a distinction ought to be made between our own citizens and the industrious emigrant from the old world, who, after plowing his weary way through thousands of miles of trackless seas like our forefathers, should, when arriving upon the fertile fields of the West, be there subjected to the ruthless sport of the speculator. It is a gratification of no trifling character, that we find Mr. Buchanan at this early day resolutely condemning that spirit of ostracism that would thus place barriers in the way of those who seek a home among us, from having the same opportunity of reaping the rewards of industry, and of enjoying the advantages of equal laws, after they had come so far and braved so many dangers to obtain them. The following short speech delivered by Mr. Buchanan on this subject, in January, 1838, in reply to Mr. Clay, will be responded to by every liberal and true-hearted democrat everywhere :

Mr. Buchanan said that, " It was not his intention to go into any detailed argument upon the question before the Senate.

He would merely state in general terms, the reasons why he should vote for the bill. This he would do not for the purpose of convincing others, but of placing himself in the position which he desired to occupy.

"It had been repeated over and over again in the course of this debate, that the bill before the Senate would confer a bounty upon the actual settlers on the public lands, at the expense of the people of the United States. He denied that it would produce any such effect. These settlers would be compelled to pay the minimum price of one dollar twenty-five cents per acre for their land. Could the government now obtain more for it at public auction, had it remained unsettled? Let the history of the past answer this question. From the 1st of January, 1823, until the present day, averaging all the land sales which had been made, the result was, that we had received two, three, four, five, or at the most, six cents per acre more than what the settlers would be obliged to pay under this bill. Senators had differed in their statements upon this subject, but none of them had contended that the average price upon the whole sales exceeded one dollar and thirty-one cents per acre. The commissioner of the land office states it to have been one dollar and twenty-seven cents and nine-twentieths. The question then was, whether for the prospect, and a hopeless one it was, of obtaining six cents per acre more at public auction, we should attempt to expel the settlers from their lands, and thus by depriving them of a home, inflict the greatest misery and distress upon themselves and their families?

"Mr. B. said that our past experience ought to have taught us that this was a question in which the government had but little, if any, pecuniary interest. It was a question between the actual settler on the one side, and the organized bands of speculators which attended the land sales on the other. It was notorious—it had often been established on this floor—that these speculators, acting in concert, had prevented bidding above the minimum price, and had purchased our most valuable lands at a dollar and a quarter per acre. If the settlers should not obtain these lands at this price, the speculators would. This was the alternative. Turn this question and argue it in whatever mode you might, still we come to the same result. It was a matter of indifference so far as the Treasury was concerned, whether you granted these pre-emptions or not. In either event the government would neither be benefited nor injured. Then he was called upon to decide between the actual settler, who had spent his time and his labor in cutting down the forest and preparing himself a home in the wilderness, and the heartless speculator who might be anxious to deprive these hardy pioneers of the benefit of their toils and to purchase the land which they had improved. He could not hesitate upon that subject. Past experience had rendered it certain that the United States will never receive more for their land than a cent or two per acre above the minimum price ; and for this inconsiderable difference he would not turn off the men who had settled upon our public lands, in order that they might be monopolized at the public sales by speculators. Let the actual settler have ' the first cut,' and sufficient will remain for the companies of speculators who attend the public auctions. He had no doubt that in both these modes of sales there had been frauds ; but he should always lean to that side which would protect the poor man in the possession of the land which he had rendered valuable by the sweat of his brow, rather than in favor of those who had come from a distance to purchase him out of house and home.

"Mr. B. probably should not have said a word upon the subject, had it not been for the amendment which had been offered by the senator from Maryland (Mr. Merrick). This amendment proposed to make an invidious distinction, which had never been made heretofore in our legislation, against foreigners who had settled upon the public lands, and had not been naturalized prior to the first day of December last. Whilst it granted pre-emptions in such cases to our own citizens, it

11

excluded these foreigners. Why had this change been proposed in our settled policy? He had observed with regret that attempts were now extensively making throughout the country, to excite what was called a native American feeling against those who had come from a foreign land to participate in the blessings of our free Constitution. Such a feeling was unjust— it was ungrateful. In the darkest days of the Revolution. who had assisted us in fighting our battles and achieving our independence? Foreigners; yes sir, foreigners. He would not say, for he did not believe that our independence could not have been established without their aid; but he would say the struggle would have been, longer and more doubtful. After the Revolution, immigration had been encouraged by our policy. Throughout the long and bloody wars of Europe which had followed the French revolution, this country had ever been an asylum for the oppressed of all nations. He trusted that at this late day, the Congress of the United States were not about to establish, for the first time, such an odious distinction as that proposed between one of our citizens, who had settled upon the public lands, and his neighbor who had pursued the same course under the faith of your previous policy, merely because that neighbor had not resided long enough within the United States to have become a naturalized citizen. He was himself the son of a naturalized foreigner, and perhaps might feel this distinction the more sensibly on that account. He was glad the yeas and nays had been demanded, that he might record his vote against the principle proposed by the amendment."

*　　*　　*　　*　　*　　*　　*

" Wise and practical statesmen would study the actual condition of the country, and never attempt that which was from its nature morally impossible. We ought to yield with a good grace to circumstances which we could not control. In what situation were we now placed? A very great number of persons had settled upon the public land since the date of the last pre-emption law. They had gone there on the presumption that you would place them upon the same footing with those who had gone before them. You had for years pursued this system, and you had passed no law which indicated any intention of abandoning it. You had thus, to a certain extent, pledged your faith that you would respect the rights which might be acquired in this manner. You were now placed in a condition that you could not draw back even if you would. In that part of Wisconsin, west of Mississippi, called Iowa, there were now more than thirty thousand settlers on the public lands. They had formed themselves into counties, and erected court-houses, and this government had sent them judges. They were now a flourishing and prosperous community, under the protection of your laws. They had cleared away the forests, and erected farm-houses and barns, planted orchards, cultivated the land, and were surrounded by all the necessaries and many of the conveniences of life. Could you now expel such an entire community from their homes? The attempt would be vain. It would cast disgrace upon the government. After an unavailing effort, it would be abandoned. It might be persisted in until civil commotion would be excited, and blood would be shed. At that point it must end. The moral sense of the people of this country would be roused against proceeding any further.

"It is true, that if the whole power of the United States were exerted for such a purpose, we might destroy this happy community, and drive them from their homes; but it would never thus be exerted. It is wise, therefore, to submit at once to a moral necessity which has been imposed upon you in consequence of your own conduct. It is true that you may lose a cent or two per acre on the price of the land; but is such a loss worth mentioning when compared either with the calamities and injustice you would inflict by a rigid adherence to the letter of the law, or with the expense which you would incur by sending an armed force into that country, in a vain attempt to enforce its provisions?

"Mr. B. had been asked by the senator from Kentucky if he would compare the hordes of foreign paupers that are constantly flooding our shores, with the de Kalbs, the Steubens, the Lafayettes, and the Pulaskis of the Revolution? It was easy to ask such a question. He felt a deep and grateful veneration for the memory of these illustrious men. They were leaders of our armies ; but what could they have accomplished without soldiers? Was it not a fact known to the world, that the emigrants from the Emerald Isle—that land of brave hearts and strong arms—had shed their blood freely in the cause of our liberty and independence? It was now both ungrateful and unjust to speak of these people, in the days of our prosperity, as hordes of foreign paupers. Such was not the language applied to them during the revolutionary war, when they constituted a large and effective proportion of our armies.

"The senator had asked if he (Mr. B.) would grant preemptions to the Hessians? It was true, they had fought upon the wrong side, and were not much entitled to our sympathies Still some apology might be made even for them. They were the slaves of despotic power, and they were sold by their masters like cattle, to the British government. They had no will of their own, but were under the most abject subjection to petty princes, who considered themselves, by the grace of God, born to command them. But the condition even of the poor Hessian has since been greatly improved. The principles of liberty, which were sanctified by the American Revolution, are winning their way among every civilized people. In no country have they made greater progress than among the people of Germany. The Hessian of the present day is far different from what his fathers were ; and let me tell senators from the West, that the best settlers they can have amongst them are the Germans. Industrious, honest, and persevering, they make the best farmers of our country, while their firmness of character qualifies them for defending it against any hostile attacks, which may be made by the Indians along our western frontier.

As to the hordes of foreigners of which we had heard, they did not alarm him. Any foreigner from any country under the sun, who, after landing with his family on our Atlantic coast, will make his long and weary way into the forests or prairies west of the Mississippi, and there, by patient toil, establish a settlement upon the public lands, whilst he thus manifests his attachment to our institutions, shows that he is worthy of becoming an American citizen. He furnishes us by his conduct the surest pledge that he will become a citizen the moment the laws of the country permit. In the meantime, so far as my vote is concerned, he shall continue to stand upon the same footing with citizens, and have his quarter section of land at the minimum price."

The exciting question of slavery again came up at the present session upon some resolutions offered by Mr. Calhoun. Mr. Buchanan again stated his position and declared his determination, no matter what were the consequences, to give the South their constitutional right, on this question, and to resist the aggression which was coming from the North. On this occasion, amid the power which the abolitionists were gaining, and while it was yet muttering in the distance, attracting the attention of politicians who always began to think that something might yet be made out of this new British exotic, Mr. Buchanan uttered these memorable words : "I have long since taken my stand, and from it I shall not be driven. I do not desire to maintain myself at home, unless I can do it with a due regard to the rights and safety of the South." In the same speech he said :

"And, if the Union should be dissolved upon the question of slavery, what will be the consequences? An entire non-intercourse between its different parts, mutual jealousies, and implacable wars. The hopes of the friends of liberty, in every clime, would be blasted ; and despotism might regain her empire over the world. I might present in detail the evils which would flow from disunion, but I forbear, I shall no further lift the curtain. The scene would be too painful. The good sense and sound patriotism of the people of the North, when once aroused to the danger, will apply the appropriate remedy. The peaceful influence of public opinion will save the Union.

"The select committee might report a resolution, which would obtain the unanimous vote of the Senate, declaring that neither the Congress of the United States, nor any State, nor any combination of individuals in any State, has any right to interfere with the existence or regulation of slavery in any other State, where it is recognized by law. Even the abolitionists themselves, so far as my knowledge extends, have never denied this principle. It was solemnly announced by the first Congress, and it is most clearly the doctrine of the Constitution, that instrument expressly recognizes the right to hold slaves as property in States where slavery exists. This, then, is not a question of general morality, affecting the consciences of men, but it is a question of constitutional law. When the States became parties to the federal compact, they entered into a solemn agreement that property in slaves should be as inviolable as any other property. Whilst the Constitution endures, no human power, except that of the State within which slavery exists, has any right to interfere with the question. An attempt on the part of any other State, or of Congress, to violate this right, would be a palpable violation of the Constitution. Congress might as well undertake to interfere with slavery under a foreign government, as in any of the States where it now exists. I feel confident that there would not be a single dissenting voice raised in the Senate against the adoption of such a resolution as I have suggested.

"A second resolution might assert the principle that Congress have no right under the Constitution to prohibit the transfer of slaves by a citizen of one State to a citizen of another State, when slavery is recognized by the laws of both. The power " to regulate commerce among the several States," can never be construed into a power to abolish this commerce. Regulation is one thing, destruction another As long as slaves continue to be property under the Constitution. Congress might as well undertake to prohibit the people of Massachusetts from selling their domestic manufactures in South Carolina, as to prohibit the master of a slave in Virginia from disposing of him to his neighbor in North Carolina Both cases rest upon the same principle of constitutional law. The power to regulate does not imply the power to destroy. I believe that such a resolution would encounter no serious opposition in the Senate.

"Again, a third resolution might be adopted in regard to the abolition of slavery in the District of Columbia, which would unite nearly every suffrage in the Senate. This District was ceded to the United States by Virginia and Maryland. At the date of the cession, they were both slaveholding States, and they continue to be so at this day. Does any man suppose for a single moment, that they would have ever made this cession, if they had supposed that Congress would abolish slavery in this District of ten miles square, whilst it existed in their surrounding territories ? So long as it continues in these two States, it would be a violation of the implied faith which we pledged to them by the acceptance of the cession, to convert this very cession into the means of injuring and destroying their peace and security."

A matter of no small importance came before Congress in relation to the old United States Bank. It could not be content to die gracefully and resignedly after it had received its fatal blow, but by disobeying the act of Congress it sought to perpetuate its existence by proxy, and the Pennsylvania Bank of the United States having been recently re-chartered, the old institution, instead of winding up its affairs, as it was bound to do, made an assignment of all its effects and business to the Philadelphia concern. This re-issued the notes of the old bank, and hence the introduction into Congress of a bill to prohibit the circulation of these "resurrection notes" as they were called. Mr. Buchanan made a long and exceedingly able speech upon this bill, in the beginning of which he referred to the chartering of the Pennsylvania Bank of the United States, declaring that whatever might be his opinion in regard to the policy of that measure, he had no right to discuss it upon the floor of the United States Senate. It was a state affair with which Congress had nothing to be.

"As I am on the floor, however," said Mr. Buchanan, "I shall proceed to discuss the merits of the bill now before the Senate. It proposes to inflict a fine not exceeding ten thousand dollars, or imprisonment for not less than one or more than five years, or both such fine and imprisonment at the discretion of the court, upon those who shall be convicted under its provisions. Against whom does it denounce these penalties? Against directors, officers, trustees, or agents of any corporation created by Congress, who, after its term of existence is ended, shall re-issue the dead notes of the defunct corporation, and push them into the circulation of the country, in violation of its original charter. The bill embraces no person, acts upon no person, interferes with no person, except those whose duty it is, under the charter of the old bank, to redeem and cancel the old notes as they are presented for payment, and who, in violation of this duty, send them again into circulation.

" This bill inflicts severe penalties, and before we pass it, we ought to be entirely satisfied, first that the guilt of the individuals who shall violate its provisions is sufficiently aggravated to justify the punishment ; second, that the law will be politic in itself ; and third, that we possess the constitutional power to enact it.

" First, then, as to the nature and aggravation of the offence. The charter of the late Bank of the United States expired by its own limitation, on the 3d of March, 1836. After that day, it could issue no notes, discount no new paper, and exercise none of the usual functions of a bank For two years thereafter, until the 3d of March, 1838, it was merely permitted to use its corporate name and capacity 'for the purpose of suits for the final settlement and liquidation of the affairs and accounts of the corporation, and for the sale and disposition of their estate, real, personal, and mixed, but not for any other purpose, or in any other manner whatsoever.' Congress had granted the bank no power to make a voluntary assignment of its property to any corporation or any individual. On the contrary, the plain meaning of the charter was, that all the affairs of the institution should be wound up by its own president and directors. It received no authority to delegate this important trust to others ; and yet what has it done ? On the 2d day of March, 1836, one day before the charter had expired, this very president and these directors assigned all the property and effects of the old corporation to the Pennsylvania Bank of the United States. On the same day, this latter bank accepted the assignment, and agreed to ' pay, satisfy, and discharge all debts, contracts, and engagements, owing, entered into, or made by this (the old) bank, as the same shall become due and payable, and fulfill and execute all trusts and obligations whatsoever arising from its transactions, or from any of them, so that every creditor or rightful claimant shall be fully satisfied.' By its own agreement it has thus expressly created itself a trustee of the old bank. But this was not necessary to confer upon it that character. By the bare act of accepting the assignment, it became responsible, under the laws of the land, for the performance of all the duties and trusts required by the old charter. Under the circumstances, it cannot make the slightest pretences of any want of notice.

"Having assumed this responsibility, the duty of the new bank was so plain, that it could not have been mistaken. It had a double character to sustain. Under the charter from Pennsylvania, it became a new banking corporation, whilst, under the assignment from the old bank, it became a trustee to wind up the concerns of that institution under the act of Congress. These two characters were in their nature separate and distinct, and never ought to have been blended. For each of these purposes it ought to have kept a separate set of books. Above all, as the privilege of circulating bank notes, and thus creating a paper currency, is that function of a bank which most deeply and vitally affects the community, the new bank ought to have cancelled or destroyed all the notes of the old bank, which it found in its possession on the 4th of March, 1836, and ought to have redeemed the remainder at its counter, as they were demanded by the holders, and then destroyed them. This obligation no senator has attempted to doubt or deny. But what was the course of the bank? It has grossly violated both the old and the new charter. It at once declared independence of both, and appropriated to itself all the notes of the old bank, not only those which were then still in circulation, but those which had been redeemed before it accepted the assignment, and were then lying dead in its vaults. I have now before me the first monthly statement which was ever made by the bank to the Auditor General of Pennsylvania. It is dated on the 2d of April, 1836, and signed, J. Cowperthwaite, acting cashier. In this statement the bank charges itself with 'notes issued,' $36,620,420 16, whilst in its cash account, along with its specie and the notes of State banks, it credits itself with 'notes of the Bank of the United States and offices' on hand, $16,794,713 71. It thus seized these dead notes to the amount of $16,794,713 71, and transformed them into cash, whilst the difference between those on hand and those issued, equal to $19,825,706 45, was the circulation which the new bank boasted it had inherited from the old. It thus, in an instant appropriated to itself, and adopted as its own circulation, all the notes and all the illegal branch drafts of the old bank, which were then in existence. Its boldness was equal to its utter disregard of law. In this first return it not only proclaimed to the legislature and people of Pennsylvania that it had disregarded its trust as assignee of the old bank, by seizing upon the whole of the old circulation, and converting it to its own use, but that it had violated one of the fundamental provisions of its new charter.

"In Pennsylvania, we have for many years past deemed it wise to increase the specie-basis of our paper circulation. We know that, under the universal law of currency small notes, and gold and silver coin of the same denomination, cannot circulate together The one will expel the other Accordingly, it is now long since we prohibited our banks from issuing notes of a less denomination than five dollars. The legislature which re-chartered the bank of the United States, deemed it wise to proceed one step farther in regard to this mammoth institution, and in that opinion I entirely concur. Accordingly, by the sixth fundamental article of its charter, they declare that 'the notes and bills which shall be issued by order of said corporation, or under its authority, shall be binding upon it, and those made payable to order shall be assignable by endorsement, but none shall be issued of a denomination less than ten dollars.'

"Now, it is well known to every senator within the sound of my voice, that a large proportion of these resurrection-notes, as they have been aptly called, which have been issued and re-issued by order of the new bank, are of the denomination of five dollars. Here, then, is a plain, palpable violation, not only of the spirit but of the very letter of its charter. The Senate will perceive that the bank, as if to meet the very case, is not merely prohibited from issuing its own notes, signed by its own president and cashier, of a denomination less than ten dollars, but this prohibition is extended to the notes or bills which shall be issued by its order or under its authority. If I should even be mistaken in this construction of the law, and I believe I am not, it will only follow, that its conduct has not amounted to a legal forfeiture of its charter. In both cases, the violation of the spirit of its charter, and the contravention of the wise policy of the legislature, are equally glaring. ·So entirely did the bank make these dead notes its own peculiar circulation, that until July last, in its monthly return to the Auditor-General of Pennsylvania, the new and the old notes are blended together, without any distinction. In that return we are, for the first time, officially informed that the bank had ever issued any notes of its own

"And here an incident occurs to me which will be an additional proof how lawless is this bank, whenever obedience to its charter interferes in the least degree with its policy. By the tenth fundamental article of that charter, it is required ' to make to the Auditor General monthly returns of its condition, showing the details of its operations, according to the forms of the returns the bank of the United States, now makes to the Secretary of the Treasury of the United States, or according to such form as may be established by law.' From no idle curiosity, but from a desire to ascertain, as far as possible, the condition of the banks of the country, and the amount of their circulation, I requested the Auditor General, during the late special session of Congress in September, to send me the return of the bank for that month. In answer, he informed me, under date of the 22d of September, that the bank had not made any return to his office since the 15th of the preceding May. Thus, from the date of the suspension of specie payments, until some time after the 22d of September last, how long I do not know, a period during which the public mind was most anxious on the subject, the bank put this provision of its charter at defiance. Whether it thus omitted its duty, because at the date of the suspension of specie payments it had less than a million and a half of specie in its vaults, I shall not pretend to determine. If this were the reason, I have no doubt that it sent to the Auditor General all the intermediate monthly returns on the 2d of October, 1837, because at that period it had increased its gold and silver to more than three millions of dollars.

"In order to illustrate the enormity of the offence now proposed to be punished, senators have instituted several comparisons. No case which they have imagined equals the offence as it actually exists. Would it not, says one gentleman, be a flagrant breach of trust for an executor intrusted with the settlement of his testator's estate, to re-issue, and again put in circulation for his own benefit, the bills of exchange or promissory notes which he had found among the papers of the deceased, and which had been paid and extinguished in his lifetime? I answer, that it would. But, in that case, the imposition upon the community would necessarily be limited, whilst the means of detection would be ample. The same may be observed in regard to the case of the trustee, which has been suggested. What comparison do these cases bear to that of the conduct of the bank? The amount of its re-issues of these dead notes of its testator, is many millions. Their circulation is co-extensive with the Union, and there is no possible means of detection. No man who receives this paper can tell whether it belongs to that class which the new bank originally found dead in its vaults, or to that which it has since redeemed and re-issued, in violation of law, or to that which has remained circulating lawfully in the community, and has never been redeemed since the old charter expired. There is no earmark upon these notes. It is impossible to distinguish those which have been illegally re-issued from the remainder.

"I can imagine but one case which would present anything like a parallel to the conduct of the bank. In October last, we authorized the issue of $10,000,000 of treasury notes, and directed that when they were received in payment of the public dues, they should not be re-issued, but be cancelled. Now, suppose the Secretary of the Treasury had happened to be the president of a bank in this district, and, in that character, had re-issued these dead treasury notes, which he ought to have cancelled, and again put them into circulation, in violation of the law, then a case would exist which might be compared with that now before the Senate. If such a case should ever occur, would not the secretary at once be impeached ; and is there a senator upon this floor who would not pronounce him guilty ? The pecuniary injury to the United States might be greater in the supposed than in the actual case, but the degree of moral guilt would be the same.

"Whether it be politic to pass this law is a more doubtful question. Judging from past experience, the bank may openly violate its provisions with impunity. It can easily evade them by sending packages of these old notes to the South and South-west, by its agents, there to be re-issued by banks or individuals in its confidence. There is one fact, however, from which I am encouraged to hope that this law may prove effectual. No man on this floor has attempted to justify, or even to palliate, the conduct of the bank. Its best friends have not dared to utter a single word in its defence against this charge. The moral influence of their silence, and the open condemnation of its conduct by some of them, may induce the bank to obey the law.

"I now approach the question, do Congress possess power under the Constitution to pass this bill? In other words, have we power to restrain the trustees of our own bank from re-issuing the old notes of that institution, which have already been redeemed, and ought to be destroyed? Can there be a doubt of the existence of this power? The bare statement of the question seems to me sufficient to remove every difficulty. It is almost too plain for argument. I should be glad if any gentleman would even prove this power to be doubtful. Then even I should refrain from its exercise. I am a State rights man, and in favor of a strict construction of the Constitution. The older I grow, and the more experience I acquire, the more deeply rooted does this doctrine become in my mind. I consider a strict construction of the Constitution necessary not only to the harmony which ought to exist between the Federal and State governments, but to the perpetuation of the Union. I shall exercise no power which I do not consider clear. I call upon gentlemen, therefore, to break their determined silence upon this subject, and convince me even that the existence of the power is doubtful. If they do, I pledge myself to vote against the passage of the bill.

"If this power could only be maintained by some of the arguments advanced by the friends of the bill in the early part of this discussion, it never should receive my vote. Principles were then avowed scarcely less dangerous and unsound than the principle on which the senator from Vermont (Mr. Prentiss) insists that the friends of the bill must claim this power. He contends that it does not exist at all, unless it be under that construction of the Constitution advocated by his friend from Massachusetts (Mr. Webster), which would give to Congress power over the whole paper currency of the country, under the coining and commercial powers of the Constitution. The senator from Connecticut (Mr. Niles) was the first in this debate who presented in bold relief the principles on which this bill can securely rest.

"Neither shall I dodge the question, as some senators have done, by taking shelter under the pretext that it is a question for the judiciary to decide whether the general language of the bill be applicable to the officers of the Bank of the United States, under the Pennsylvania charter. We all know that it was intended to embrace these. Indeed, it was their conduct, and that alone, which called this bill into existence. It is true that the provisions of the bill extend to all corporations created by Congress; but it is equally certain that had it not been intended to apply to the Bank of the United States, it would have been confined in express terms to the District of Columbia, where alone corporations now exist under the authority of Congress. Away with all such subterfuges; I will have none of them.

"Suppose, sir, that at any time within the period of two years thus allowed by the charter to the president and directors to make up its affairs, these officers, created under your own authority, had attempted to throw thirty millions of dollars of their dead paper money again into circulation, would you have had no power to pass a law to prevent and to punish such an atrocious fraud? Would you have been compelled to look on and patiently submit to such a violation of the charter which you had granted? Have you created an institution and expressly limited its term of existence which you cannot destroy after that term has expired? This would indeed be a political hydra, which must exist forever, without any Hercules to destroy it. It you possess no power to restrain the circulation of the notes of the old bank, they may continue to circulate for ever, in defiance of the power which called them into existence. You have created that which you have no power to destroy, although the law which gave it birth limited the term of its existence. Will any senator contend that during these two years allowed by the charter for winding up the concerns of the bank, we possessed no power to restrain its president and directors from re-issuing these old notes? There is no man on this floor bold enough to advance such a doctrine. This point being conceded, the power to pass the present bill follows as a necessary consequence.

"If the president and directors of the old bank could not evade our authority, the next question is, whether by assigning the property of the corporation to a trustee the day before the charter expired, and delivering up to him the old notes which ought to have been cancelled, they were able to cut this trustee loose from the obligations which had been imposed upon them by the charter, and from the authority of Congress. Vain and impotent indeed would this government be, if its authority could be set at naught by such a shallow contrivance. No, sir; the fountain cannot ascend beyond its source. The assignee in such a case is not released from any obligation which the assignor assumed by accepting the original charter. In regard to Congress, the trustee stands in the same situation with the president and directors of the old bank. We have

the same power to compel him to wind up the concerns of the
bank according to the charter, that we might have exercised
against those from whom he accepted the assignment. The
question is too plain for argument."

Mr. Buchanan at this point in his speech went into a very
able argument to show the causes of the suspension of specie
payments by the banks of the country. He also noticed the
charge that had been made that the democratic party were opposed to all banks, and in favor of a pure metallic currency.
He denied this, and again stated that all they wanted was to
separate the business of the government from that of the banks,
not to render them hostile to each other. "Until that propitious day shall arrive," said Mr. Buchanan, "we shall be forever agitated by the connection of the currency with our miserable party politics. Political panics, political pressures,
charges against the government for exercising an improper influence over the banks, and charges against the banks for interfering in the politics of the country; all, all which have kept us
in a state of constant agitation for the last seven years, will
continue to exist, and will be brought into action upon every
successive election of President and Vice-President." In concluding this truly great speech, Mr. Buchanan said—

"In conclusion, permit me to remark, that the people of the
United States have abundant cause for the deepest gratitude
towards that great and glorious man now in retirement, for
preventing the re-charter of the Bank of the United States.
He is emphatically the man of the age, and has left a deeper
and more enduring impress upon it than any individual of our
country. Still, in regard to the bank, he performed but half
his work. For its completion we are indebted to the president
of the bank. Had the bank confined itself, after it had accepted the charter from Pennsylvania, to its mere banking and
financial operations—had it exerted its power to regulate the

domestic exchanges of the country—and above all, had it taken the lead in the resumption of specie payments, a new bank, Phœnix-like, might have arisen from the ashes of the old. That danger, from present appearances, has now passed away. The open defiance of Congress by the bank, the laws of the country over and over again violated—its repeated atttempts to interfere in the party politics of the day—all, all have taught the danger of such a vast moneyed corporation. Mr. Biddle has finished the work which General Jackson only commenced.

"Not one particle of personal hostility towards that gentleman has been mingled in my discussion of the question. On the contrary, as a private gentleman, I respect him , and my personal intercourse with him, though not frequent, has been of the most agreeable character. I am always ready to do justice to his great and varied talents. I have spoken of the public conduct of the bank over which he presides, with the freedom and boldness which I shall always exercise in the performance of my public duties. It is the president of the bank, not the man, that I have assailed. It is the nature of the institution, over which he presides, that has made him what he is. Like all other men, he must yield to his destiny. The possession of such vast and unlimited power, continued for a long period of years, would have turned the head of almost any other man, and have driven him to as great excesses.

"In vain you may talk to me about paper restrictions in the charter of a bank of sufficient magnitude to be able to crush the other banks of the country. When did a vast moneyed monopoly ever regard the law, if any great interest of its own stood in the way? It will then violate its charter, and its own power will secure it immunity. It well knows that in its destruction the ruin of hundreds of thousands would be involved, and therefore it can do almost what it pleases. The history of the bank·for several years past has been one continued history of violated laws, and of attempts to interfere in the politics of the country. Create another bank, and place any other man at its hand, and the result will be the same. Such an institution will always hereafter prove too strong for the government; because we cannot again expect to see, at least in our day, another Andrew Jackson in the presidential chair On the other hand, should such a bank, wielding the moneyed power of the country, form an alliance with the political power, and that is the natural position of the parties, their combined influence will govern the Union, and liberty might become an empty name."

This speech of Mr. Buchanan was probably one of the most effective he ever delivered. It hit a deadly blow at Mr. Clay's favorite scheme of a new national bank ; and scarcely had Mr. Buchanan taken his seat before Mr. C. sprung to his feet, and replied in one of his most happy impromptu efforts. After Mr. Clay had concluded, Mr. Buchanan immediately returned the compliment in a good-natured, graceful rejoinder, and said " he had never enjoyed many triumphs, and therefore he prized the more the one he had won this day. He had forced the honorable senator from Kentucky (Mr. Clay) to break that determined silence that had hitherto sealed his lips on the subject of this bill. Thus," said Mr. B., " I have adorned my brow with a solitary sprig of laurel. Not one word was he to utter upon the present occasion. This he had announced publicly. (Mr. Clay dissented) I thought," resumed Mr. B., " that he had announced the other day his determination not to debate the question, and stated the reason therefor. (Mr. Clay explained.) Well," said Mr. Buchanan, " the senator *did* intend to address the Senate on the subject, and the only sprig of laurel which I ever expected to win from him has already withered. Immediately after I had taken my seat he sprung to his feet, and has made one of his best speeches, for it belongs to the character of his mind to make his ablest efforts with the least preparation. I will venture to say that he had not intended to make the speech when he entered the Senate chamber this morning. (Mr. Clay admitted this to be the fact.) Then," said Mr. Buchanan, "I have succeeded, and my sprig of laurel is again green." Mr. Buchanan continued at some length in reply to Mr. Clay, defending the bill under consideration, and predicting that the embarrassment in financial affairs under which they were then laboring would soon be dispelled. "Even at the risk of being called a false prophet," said Mr. B., "I can prophesy nothing but good."

The Independent Treasury Bill came before Congress at this session, and to Mr. Buchanan is the country indebted for the idea upon which our present admirable system of disbursing the revenue is founded. He was earnestly desirous of completing the separation of the banks from the government, and although he had been defeated at the extra session upon the Sub-treasury Bill, yet he felt it the duty of Congress to devise some plan to meet the proposed requirements. Some friends of the administration began to falter, and to fear they were carrying things too far. Not so Mr. Buchanan. With a clear conception of the application of democratic truth to this question, he determined never to cease until the measure was accomplished. He was destined, however, to be defeated at this session, though eventually he had the satisfaction to see the principle he advocated triumphant; and it now stands the law of the land, with not a person who dares to raise his voice for its repeal. Such is one of the beneficent conquests that the democratic party has achieved. Mr. Buchanan declared that the adoption of the measure would bring quiet and harmony to the country upon the question of the currency. And who shall say that he was mistaken? Has not experience, the only true test of all principles, proved the accuracy of his prediction, and thus placed upon the brow of James Buchanan the civic wreath of that far-seeing and profound statesmanship, which comprehends, as if by unerring intuition, the wants of his country and the interests of the people?

CHAPTER XV.

Twenty-fifth Congress—The Last Session—Interference of Federal Officers in Elections
—Mr. Buchanan's Speech.

THE third, or second regular session of the Twenty-fifth Congress commenced on the 3d of December, 1838. A number of important matters were discussed, among which were the graduation of the prices of the public lands, our civil and diplomatic policy, the Maine Boundary question, and the interference of federal officers in elections, in all of which Mr. Buchanan took an active and leading part. His great speech of this session was upon the latter bill. Probably there never was an act introduced into Congress which contained so much of the spirit of ancient federalism as this measure to prevent, as it was termed, the interference of the federal officers in elections. Mr. Buchanan met it with his most indignant condemnation. He had never favored a single measure for the oppression of any class or portion of the people, neither did he believe that because a man accepted a trifling office from the government, he should, on that account, be deprived of the freedom of speech, which belongs as an inalienable right to every American citizen. It seems strange that such a measure, one that embraced all the odious features of the old sedition law, could have been proposed in the Senate of the United .States only fifteen years ago, and advocated by leading senators. Yet such is the fact. Mr. Buchanan made in opposition to it one of the best speeches of his life. He showed in this effort the same instinctive regard for equal rights, which has

been the distinguishing feature of his whole political career.
We make copious extracts from this eloquent and triumphan
vindication of the right of each and every citizen to express hi,
opinions in regard to the affairs of the government to which he
owes allegiance. The following extract gives the openinr
portion :

"MR. PRESIDENT : The question raised for discussion by the
bill now before the Senate, is very simple in its character. This
bill proposes to punish, by a fine of five hundred dollars—the
one moiety payable to the informer, and the other to the United
States—and by a perpetual disability to hold office under the
United States, any officer of this government below the rank
of a district attorney, who 'shall by word, message, or writing, or in any other manner whatsoever, endeavor to persuade
any elector to give, or dissuade any elector from giving, his
vote for the choice of any person to be elector of President
and Vice-President of the United States, or to be a senator
or representative in Congress, or to be a governor or lieutenant-
governor, or senator or representative within any State of the
Union, or for the choice of any person to serve in any public
office established by the law of any of the States.' The officers
of the United States against whom the penalties of this bill are
denounced, consist of marshals and their deputies, postmasters
and their deputies, receivers and registers of land offices and
their deputies and clerks, surveyors general of the public lands
and their deputies and assistants, collectors, surveyors, naval
officers, weighers, gaugers, appraisers, or other officers or persons concerned or employed in the charging, collecting, levying,
or managing the customs or any branch thereof ; and engineers,
officers, or agents, employed or concerned in the execution or
superintendence of any of the public works.

"The senator from Kentucky (Mr. Crittenden) before he
commenced his remarks, moved to amend the bill by striking
from it the pecuniary penalty and perpetual disability against

these officers, and substituting in their stead, the penalty of a removal from office by the President, upon the production of evidence satisfactory to him that any of them had been guilty of the offence.

"Now, for myself (said Mr. B), I shall not vote for this amendment. I will not take advantage of the amiable weakness of my friend from Kentucky, in yielding to the solicitation of others that which his own judgment approved. I will more especially not give such a vote because the proposed amendment makes no change in the principle of the bill. There is a beautiful harmony and consistency in its provisions as it came fresh from its author which ought to be preserved. I shall not assist in marrying any of its fair proportions. Let it remain in its perfect original form, and let his friends upon this floor come up to the baptismal font and act as its sponsors, and let its avowed principles be recognized as the established doctrines of the political church to which they are all devoted. No sir, no ; if a village postmaster should dare to exercise the freedom of speech, guaranteed to him by an antiquated instrument, called the Constitution of the United States, and have the audacity 'to endeavor to persuade any elector' to vote for Martin Van Buren, or what would be a much more aggravated offence, dissuade any good whig from voting for the other distinguished senator from Kentucky (Mr. Clay), a mere forfeiture of his office would bear no just proportion to the enormity of the crime. Let such a daring criminal be fined five hundred dollars; let him be disqualified forever from holding any office under the government; and let him be pointed at as a man of blasted reputation all the days of his life. With honest Dogberry in the play of 'Much ado about Nothing,' I pronounce the offence to be 'flat burglary as ever was committed.''

"There is another reason why I shall vote against the amendment. An issue has been fairly made between the senator from Kentucky and my friend from New Jersey (Mr. Wall), who, from what we have heard in the course of this debate, has but a few shattered planks left on which he can escape from a total shipwreck of his fair fame. In mercy to him I would not remove any of them. Let him have a chance for his life. He has dared to make a report against the bill in its original form, as it was referred to the committee of which he is the chairman, and for this cause has encountered all the withering denunciations of the senators from Kentucky and Virginia (Messrs. Crittenden and Rives). In justice to him, the aspect of the question should not now be changed. Let us, then, have the bill, the whole bill, and nothing but the bill, against which his report is directed.

"It would seem almost unnecessary to discuss the question, whether this bill be constitutional or not, as the senator from Kentucky, throughout the whole course of his argument, never once attempted to point to any clause of the Constitution on which it could be supported. It is true that he did cite some precedents in our legislation, which he supposes to have a bearing on the subject, but which I shall undertake to prove, hereafter, are wholly inapplicable. The senator from Virginia (Mr. Rives), has gone further into the argument, and has attempted to prove that this bill is constitutional. At the proper time, I shall endeavor to furnish a proper answer to his remarks. By-the-bye, this Constitution is a terrible bugbear. Whilst a member of the other house, I once heard an old gentleman exclaim, when it was cited against one of his favorite measures, "what a vast deal of good it prevents us from doing!" After this bill shall have passed, it will be a bugbear no longer, so far as the freedom of speech or the press is concerned. It will not, then, alarm even political children.

"The gentlemen have a precedent for their bill. Yes, sir, they have a precedent in the sedition law, but it does not go far enough for their purpose. That law, which is the only true precedent on which this bill can be founded, and on which alone it can be sustained, permitted every man to write and to publish what he pleases concerning public men and public measures, and only held him responsible in case his charges should prove to be false. But this bill is a gag-law. It goes to the fountain. It prohibits the officer not only from writing, but from speaking anything good, bad, or indifferent, whether true or false, on any subject whatever, which may affect any pending election from that of a President down to a constable. It has a much broader sweep than the sedition law, which did not interfere with the liberty of speech, however, much it may have abridged the freedom of the press. Indeed, among the more enlightened despotisms of Europe, I know not one which prohibits the freedom of speech on all public subjects ; it is only in free and enlightened America that we propose actually to insert the gag. The sedition law was bad enough, God knows, but it extended only to the use of the pen, not to that of the tongue. There is, therefore, no parallel between the two cases.

"Had it not been for the existence of the sedition law, I should have supposed it to be impossible that there could have been two opinions in regard to the utter unconstitutionality of this bill. The Constitution, in language so plain as to leave no room for misconstruction, declares, that ' Congress shall make no law abridging the freedom of speech, or of the press.' The rule is universal. There is no exception. The bill proposes not only to abridge, but utterly to destroy, the freedom of speech and of the press ; to interdict their use altogether to the enumerated officers on all questions touching the election of any officer of the Federal or State government. A plain man would naturally suppose that, barely to state the contradiction between the Constitution and this bill was to decide the question. Not so ; an ingenious and astute lawyer, in favor of a liberal construction of that instrument, can, by inference and ingenuity, confer powers upon Congress in direct violation both of its letter and its spirit, and of which its framers never once dreamed. Such was the power to pass the sedition law. That law engrafted one limitation upon the freedom of the press. It in effect, changed the meaning of the general terms, ' Congress

12

shall make no law abridging the freedom of speech or of the press,' and excepted from their operation any law which might be passed to punish libels against the President, the government, or either house of Congress. The present bill, in principle at least, proceeds much farther. It excepts from the general prohibition of the Constitution the power of punishing all persons holding offices under the government of the United States, who shall dare either to speak or to write at all on questions which may affect the result of any election. This interpolation must be inserted, before gentlemen can show any power to pass the present bill. They cannot advance one step in their argument without it. This Constitution can never be construed according to the meaning of its framers, but by men of plain, well informed, and practical judgment. Common sense is its best expounder. Ingenious men, disposed to raise one implication upon another in favor of federal power, and to make each previous precedent a foundation on which to proceed another step in the march towards consolidation, may soon make it mean anything or nothing. The liberties of this country can only be preserved by a strict construction of the enumerated powers granted by the States to Congress.

" Before I proceed further in my argument against the constitutionality of this bill, it will be proper that I should develop some of its latent beauties. I desire to delineate a little more precisely its character—to present some of its striking features, and to show what it is in principle, and what it will prove to be in practice.

" There are twenty-six sovereign States in this confederacy, united by a federal compact, called the Constitution of the United States. Each individual elector in this country sustains two distinct characters. He is a citizen of some one of the States, and he is also a citizen of the United States. He is bound to perform the duties of a good citizen both towards his own State and towards the United States. Now, what does this bill propose ? In the older States of this confederacy, all the federal officers which we have in the interior are postmasters. It is true that at our ports of entry there are customhouse officers, but in Pennsylvania for example, from the Schuylkill to the Ohio and to Lake Erie, our people scarcely feel their connection with the general government except through the medium of the Post-office Department. These postmasters are very numerous. They are planted in every village and at every cross road. They are agents for disseminating information throughout the country. I might probably say that in nine instances out of ten the office is scarcely worth holding, on account of its pecuniary emoluments. In most cases, the postmaster accepts it for the accommodation of his neighbors. Now this postmaster is generally a man of property and of character, having a deep stake in the community, and in the faithful administration and execution of the laws. Two candidates are presented to the people for office, say that of a justice of the peace. If one of these village postmasters should, in the exercise of his unquestionable rights as a citizen of Penn sylvania, advise his neighbor to vote for one of these candidates, and against the other, this bill dooms him to a fine of five hundred dollars, and to a perpetual disqualification from ever holding any office under the government of the United States. No matter whether the merits which he may have ascribed to one of the candidates be true as holy writ, and the delinquencies which he may have charged against the other may be susceptible of the clearest proof, this will not arrest the vengeance of the bill. He is doomed to remain mute, although his dearest interests may be involved, or incur its penalties. A gag is to be put into his mouth, and he is to be punished if he dare to express a preference for one candidate over the other ; and let me tell the gentleman, these postmasters hold all sorts of political opinions. In my own State a considerable proportion of their numbers are whigs and anti-masons, opposed to the present administration. I might cite other examples to depict the enormity of this bill, but I consider it wholly unnecessary. I might ascend from the justice of the peace or the constable, through all the gradations of elective office, State and Federal, to the President of the United States, and show that at each ascending grade, the violation of the rights of the citizen becomes more and more outrageous. I might enumerate the weighers and the gaugers, and the other proscribed classes of inferior office-holders, and paint the mad and wanton injustice which this bill would inflict upon them. But enough."

Mr. Buchanan here went on to show that any man who would accept office upon such terms, would forfeit all self-respect, and become at once a fit tool for corruption and despotism. That it would be degrading to American freemen, and a degradation to which they would not submit. It would also, he said, raise troops of informers and eavesdroppers to catch every incautious word dropped by a postmaster or other official, in order to find grounds for his punishment.

"But," said Mr. Buchanan, "there is another remark which I desire to make on this branch of the subject. Whenever you attempt to violate the plain letter and spirit of the Constitution, a thousand evils, of which you have never dreamed, present themselves in the perspective. This law can alone be executed by the courts of the United States. Where are they situated? In the large States, such as Pennsylvania and Virginia, they are held at great distances from each other. A postmaster in either of these States, the income of whose office does not exceed fifty dollars per annum, may be dragged from home, a distance of one hundred and fifty or two hundred miles, to stand his trial under this bill, before a federal court. The expense would be enormous, whilst he is obliged to appear before a tribunal far from the place where his character and that of his prosecutor are known and appreciated. Under such circumstances, he would almost be certain to become the victim of the common informer, under this most unjust and unconstitutional law. He would either be convicted, or compelled to buy his peace at almost any price.

"In conferring the powers enumerated in the Constitution on the federal government, the States expressly reserved to themselves respectively, or to their people, all the powers not delegated by it to the United States, or prohibited by it to the States. Now, I would ask the senator from Kentucky when, or where, or how has the State of Pennsylvania surrendered to Congress the right of depriving any of her citizens who may accept office under the general government, of the freedom of speech or of the press? Where is it declared by the Constitution, either in express terms, or from what clause can it be fairly inferred, that Congress may make a forfeiture of the best of all political rights, an indispensable condition of office? Each one of the people of Pennsylvania, under her constitution and laws, is secured in the inalienable right of speaking his thoughts. The State, as well as each individual citizen, has the deepest interest in the preservation of this right. I ask the gentleman to lay his finger on the clause of the Constitution by which it has been surrendered. Where is it declared, or from what can it be inferred, that because the States have yielded to the federal government their citizens to execute public trusts under the general government, that therefore they have yielded the rights of those citizens to express their opinions freely concerning public men and public measures? The proposition appears to me to be full of absurdity. In regard to the qualifications of electors, the States have granted no power whatever to the United States. This subject they have expressly reserved from federal control. The legislatures of the States, and they alone, under the Constitution, possess the power of prescribing the qualifications of the electors of members of the House of Representatives in Congress. They have reserved the same power themselves in regard to voters for the choice of electors of President and Vice-president. What then does this bill attempt? To separate two things which reason and the

Almighty himself have united beyond all power of separation.
You might as well attempt, by arbitrary laws, to separate
human life from the power of breathing the vital air, as to
detach the elective franchise from freedom of thought, of
speech, and of the press. In this atmosphere alone can it live,
and move, and have its being. To speak his thoughts is every
free elector's inalienable right. Freedom of speech and of the
press are both the sword and the shield of our republican institutions. To declare that when the citizens of a State accept
office from the general government, they thereby forfeit this
right to express an opinion in relation to the public concerns of
their own State and of the nation, is palpable tyranny. In the
language referred to in the report, 'it puts bridles into their
mouths and saddles upon their backs,' and degrades them from
the rank of a reasoning animal. The English precedent of the
senator was wiser, much wiser, in depriving these officers of the
right of suffrage altogether. It does not attempt to separate,
by the power of man, two things which Heaven itself has indis-
solubly united.

"If, therefore, the Constitution contained no express provision whatever, prohibiting Congress from passing any law
abridging the freedom of speech or of the press, I think I have
shown conclusively, that the power to pass this bill could not
be inferred from any of the express grants of power. But the
Constitution is not silent on the subject. Before its adoption
by the State, it was dreaded by the jealous patriots of the day,
that the federal government might usurp the liberties of the
people by attacking the liberty of speech and of the press.
They, therefore, insisted upon the insertion of an express provision, as an amendment, which, in all time to come, would prevent Congress from interfering with these inestimable rights.
The amendment to which I have often referred, was adopted,
and these rights were expressly excepted from the powers of
the federal government ; and yet in the very face of this express negative of federal power, we find the senator from Ken-

tucky coming forward with his bill, declaring direct war against any exercise of the freedom of speech and of the press by those citizens of the United States who happen to be office-holders under the general government. But, says the senator from Virginia, Congress possess and have exercised the unquestionable power of creating offices under the Constitution, and they may, therefore, annex to the holding of these offices such a condition as that prescribed by the bill, or rather the amendment of the senator from Kentucky. Now, sir, what is this but to say that Congress may declare that any citizen of Pennsylvania who accepts a federal office, shall take it upon condition that it shall be forfeited the moment he exercises the dearest political right guaranteed to him and every other citizen by the Constitution of the United States. Can Congress impose any such condition upon an office? If they can, they can repeal the most solemn provision of the Constitution, and render it a dead letter in regard to every person in the employment of the general government. All mankind may then speak and publish what they please, except those individuals who have been selected, I hope generally, for their integrity and ability, to execute the important public trusts of the country.

* * * * * * *

"But I do not mean even to rest the Constitutional question here. From the very nature of the Constitution itself, two great political parties must ever exist in this country. You may call them by what names you will; their principles must ever continue to be the same. The one dreading federal power, will ever be friendly to a strict construction of the powers delegated to the federal government and to State rights. The other, equally dreading federal weakness, will ever advocate such a liberal construction of the Constitution as will confer upon the general government as much power as possible, consistently with a free interpretation of the terms of the instrument. The one party is alarmed at the danger of consolidation, the other at that of disunion. In the days of the elder

Adams the party friendly to a liberal construction of the Constitution got into power. And what did they do? Among other things, in the very face of that clause of the Constitution which prohibited Congress from passing any law abridging the freedom of speech or of the press, they passed the sedition law. What were its provisions? It punished false, scandalous, and malicious libels against the government of the United States, either House of Congress or the President, by a fine not exceeding two thousand dollars and imprisonment not exceeding two years.

*   *   *   *   *   *   *

" The Constitution had declared that ' Congress shall pass no law abridging the freedom of speech or of the press.' Its framers well knew that, under the laws of each of the States composing this Union, libels were punishable. They, therefore, left the character of all officers created under the Constitution and laws of the United States to be protected by the laws of the several States They were afraid to give this government any authority over libels, lest the colossal power might be wielded against the liberty of the press. Congress were, therefore, prohibited from passing any law upon the subject, whether good or bad. It was not merely because the law was unjust in itself, though it was bad enough, Heaven knows, that the indignant republicans of that day rose against it, but it was because it violated the Constitution. It expired by its own limitation, in March, 1801, but not until it had utterly prostrated the political party which gave it birth.

*   *   *   *   *   *   *

" The federalists of that day honestly believed that the government should be strengthened at the centre, and that the pulsations of the heart were not powerful enough to extend a wholesome circulation to the extremities. They, therefore, used every effort to enlarge the powers of the federal government by construction. This was the touchstone which then divided parties, and which will continue to divide them until, which God forbid, the government itself shall cease to exist.

*　　*　　*　　*　　*　　*　　*

"And yet this bill is supported by my friend from Virginia, who, to use his own language, 'has been imbued with the principles of democracy and a regard for State rights from his earliest youth.' If such a charge should ever be made against him hereafter, his speech and his vote in favor of this bill will acquit him before any court in Christendom where the truth may be given in evidence. I yet trust he may never vote for its passage.

"Every measure of this kind betrays a want of confidence in the intelligence and patriotism of the American people. It is founded on a distrust of their judgment and integrity. Do you suppose that when a man is appointed a collector or a postmaster he acquires any more influence over the people than he had before? No, sir ; on the contrary, his influence is often diminished instead of being increased. The people of this country are abundantly capable of judging whether he is most influenced by love of country or love of office. If they should determine that his motives are purely mercenary for supporting a political party, this will destroy his influence. If he be a noisy, violent, and meddling politician, he will do the administration under which he has been appointed much more harm than good. Let me assure gentlemen that the people are able to take care of themselves. They do not require the interposition of Congress to prevent them from being deceived and led astray by the influence of office-holders. Whilst this is my fixed opinion, I think the number of federal officers ought to be strictly limited to the actual necessities of the government. Pursue this course, and my life for it, all the land officers, and postmasters, and weighers and gaugers which you shall spread abroad over the country, can never influence the people to betray their own cause. For my own part, I entertain the most perfect confidence in their intelligence as well as integrity.

* * * * * * *

"And here I hope the senator from Kentucky will pardon me for suggesting to him an amendment to his bill. He has, I think, made one or two mistakes in the classification of his officers, though, in general, it is sufficiently perfect. The principle would seem to have been to separate what may be called the aristocracy of office-holders from the plebeians. Those of the elevated class are still permitted to enjoy the freedom of speech and of the press, whilst the hard working operatives among them are denied this privilege. The heads of departments and bureaus, the officers of the army and navy, the superintendents and officers of our mints, and the district attorneys are not affected by the bill. These gentlemen are privileged by their elevation. They are too high to be reached by its provisions. Who, then, ought to care whether weighers and gaugers, and village postmasters, and hard-handed draymen, and such inferior people, shall be permitted to express their thoughts on public affairs? I would suggest, however, that the collectors of our principal seaports, the marshals of our extensive judicial districts, and the postmasters in our principal cities, receive compensation sufficient to enable them to figure in 'good society.' They ought to rank with the district attorneys, and should be elevated from the plebeian to the patrician rank of office-holders. They ought to be allowed the freedom of speech and of the press. As to the subordinate officers, they are not worth the trouble of a thought.

"To be sure there is one palpable absurdity on the face of the bill. Its avowed purpose is to prevent office-holders from exercising an influence in elections. Why, then, except from its operation all those office-holders who from their station in society can exercise the most extensive influence, and confine its provisions to the humbler, but not less meritorious class, whose opinions can have but a limited influence over their fellow men ? The District Attorney, for example, is excepted, the very man of all others who, from his position and talents, has the best opportunity of exerting an extensive influence. He may ride over his district, and make political speeches to secure the election of his favorite candidate. He is too high a mark for the gentleman's bill. But if the subordinates of the custom-house, or the petty postmaster at the cross-roads, with an income of fifty dollars per annum, shall dare even in private conversation, to persuade an elector to vote for or against any candidate, he is to be punished by a fine of five hundred dollars, and a perpetual disability to hold any office under the government. Was there ever a bill more unequal or more unjust ?

"Now, sir, I might here with great propriety, and very much to the relief both of my audience and myself, leave this subject ; but there are still some other observations which I conceive it to be my duty to add to what I have already said. Most of them will be elicited by the very strong remarks of my friend from Virginia. For I trust that I may still be permitted to call him by that name.

"He and I entered the House of Representatives almost together. I believe he came into it but two years after myself. We soon formed a mutual friendship, which has ever since, I may say, on my part, with great sincerity, continued to exist. We fought shoulder to shoulder, and his great powers were united with my feeble efforts in prostrating the administration of the younger Adams. General Jackson came into power, and, during the whole period of that administration, he was the steady, unwavering supporter of all its leading measures except the specie circular and his advocacy of the currency bill ; and, on that bill, I stood by him, in opposition to the administration. Whilst this man of destiny was in power—this man of the lion heart, whose will the whigs declared was law, and whose roaring terrified all the other beasts of the forest, and subdued them into silence—where was then the senator from Virginia ? He was our chosen champion in the fight. Whilst General Jackson was exerting all this tremendous influence, and marshalling all his trained bands of office-holders to do his bidding, according to the language of the opposition, these denunciations had no terrors for the senator from Virginia. Never in my life did I perform a duty of friendship with greater ardor than when, on one occasion, I came to his rescue from an unjust attack made against him by the Whigs, in relation to a part of his conduct whilst minister in France. After holding out so long together, ought he not at least to have parted from us in peace, and bade us a kind adieu? In abandoning our camp, why did he shoot Parthian arrows behind him? In taking leave of us, I hope not forever, is it not too hard for us to hear ourselves denounced by the gentleman in the language which he has used? He is amazed and bewildered with the scenes passing before him. Whither, he asks, will the mad dominion of party carry us? His mind is filled with despondency as to the fate of his country. Shall we emulate the servility of the Senate and people of Rome? You already have your Prætorian bands in this city. I might quote from his speech other phrases of a similar character, but these are sufficient. I do not believe that any of these expressions were aimed at me personally, yet they strike me with the mass of my political friends, and I feel bound to give them a passing notice.   *   *   *   *   *

Not long previous to the time of the delivery of this speech, M. de Tocqueville had been in this country, and had published, on his return to Europe, a work upon " Democracy in America," a curious compound of sagacity and obtuseness of a great mind, naturally acute and expansive, but so bound up in the habitudes of European ideas, that the simple truths of democracy to him were, like the gospel to the Greeks—foolishness. This work of his had been frequently cited in the course of debate, and Mr. Buchanan had exposed some of his errors. In referring to the subject, he said ·

"I may truly say, that I have never met any Frenchman or Englishman who could understand the complicated relations existing between our Federal and State governments, in this respect, De Tocqueville has not succeeded much better than the rest. I am disposed to quarrel with him for one thing, and that is, that he is opposed to the doctrines of the Virginia and Kentucky resolutions. He is one of those old federalists, in the true acceptance of that term, who believe that the powers of the general government are not sufficiently strong to protect it from the encroachments of the States. Hence one great object of his book is to prove that this government is becoming weaker and weaker, whilst that of the States is growing stronger and stronger ; and although he does not think the time near, yet the final catastrophe must be, that it will be dissolved by its own weakness, and the people, at length tired of the perpetual struggles of liberty, will finally seek repose in the arms of despotism. This result, in his opinion, is not to be brought about by the strength, but by the weakness of the federal government. I might adduce many quotations to this effect from his book, but I shall trouble the Senate with but a few. He says, in summing up a long chapter on this subject, ' I am strangely mistaken if the federal government of the United States be not constantly losing strength, retiring gradually from public affairs, and narrowing its circle of action more and more. It is naturally feeble, but it now abandons even its pretensions to strength. On the other hand, I thought I remarked a more lively sense of independence, and a more decided attachment to provincial government, in the States. The Union is to subsist, but to subsist as a shadow ; it is to be strong in certain cases, and weak in all others ; in time of warfare it is to be able to concentrate all the forces of the nation, and all the resources of the country in its hands, and in time of peace, its existence is to be scarcely perceptible, as if this alternate debility and vigor were natural or possible.'

"'I do not foresee anything for the present which may be

able to check this general impulse of public opinion; the causes in which it originated do not cease to operate with the same effect. The change will therefore go on, and it may be predicted that, unless some extraordinary event occurs, the government of the Union will grow weaker and weaker every day.'

"Again : 'So far is the federal government from acquiring strength, and from threatening the sovereignty of the States as it grows older, that I maintain it to be growing weaker and weaker, and that the sovereignty of the Union alone is in danger.' And again : 'It may, however, be foreseen, even now, that when the Americans lose their republican institutions, they will speedily arrive at a despotic government, without a long interval of limited monarchy.'

"Speaking of the power of the President, he says, 'Hitherto, no citizen has shown any disposition to expose his honor or his life, in order to become the President of the United States, because the power of that office is temporary, limited, and subordinate. The prize of fortune must be great, to encourage adventurers in so desperate a game. No candidate has as yet been able to arouse the dangerous enthusiasm or the passionate sympathies of the people in his favor, for the very simple reason, that when he is at the head of the government he has but little power, but little wealth, and but little glory to share amongst his friends, and his influence in the State is too small for the success or the ruin of a faction to depend upon the elevation of an individual to power.'

"Now, if this greater than Montesquieu, is to be believed, and his authority is to be relied upon by the senator from Virginia, whence his terror and alarm lest the power of the President might be strengthened by the influence of the lower class of federal office-holders at the elections ? Why should they be deprived of the freedom of speech and of the press, upon the principle that the power of Mr. Van Buren is dangerous to the liberties of his country ? The gentleman's lauded authority is entirely against his own position."

Mr. Buchanan, however, went on to explain that he differed altogether from M. de Tocqueville, and apprehended no such weakness as he pointed out ; on the contrary, he believed the executive and federal government would always be strong enough to exercise its legitimate powers. It will be seen that what De Tocqueville supposed was our weakness, is actually our strength. To be "strong in certain cases, and weak in all others" was just the idea which the founders of our system of government had in view. To be strong in the enforcement of all powers delegated to it by the States, but weak in all things pertaining to State rights, is just the point and pith of our federal Constitution, the bulwark of our Union, and the support of all our most cherished institutions ; yet, the great European writer on democracy could not understand such profound simplicity !

In the course of the same debate, England was again, as it is often now, held up as a model for America. Mr. Buchanan did not, however, feel disposed to go to such a source for guidance. In reference to some remarks that Mr. Rives of Virginia had made, he said :

"I agree with him, that we are indebted for several of our most valuable institutions to our British ancestors. We have derived from them the principles of liberty established and consecrated by Magna-Charta, the trial by jury, the petition of right, the habeas corpus act, and the revolution of 1688. And yet, notwithstanding all this, I should be very unwilling to make the British government a model for our legislation in republican America. Look at its effect in practice. Is it a government which sheds its benign influence, like the dews of heaven, upon all its subjects? Or is it not a government, where the rights of the many are sacrificed to promote the interest of the few? The landed aristocracy have controlled the election of a majority of the members of the House of Commons, and they, themselves, compose the House of Lords. The main scope and principal object of their legislation was to promote the great landed interest, that of the large manufacturers, and the fund-holders of a national debt, amounting to more than seven hundred and fifty millions sterling. In order to accomplish these purposes, it became necessary to oppress the poor. Where is the country beneath the sun, in which pauperism prevails to such a fearful extent? Is it not known to the whole world, that the wages both of agricultural and manufacturing labor are reduced to the very lowest point necessary to sustain human existence? Look at Ireland, the fairest land I have ever seen. Her laboring population is confined to the potatoe. Rarely, indeed, do they enjoy either the wheat or the beef which their country produces in such plentiful abundance. It is chiefly sent abroad for foreign consumption.

"The people of England are now struggling to make their institutions more free, and, I trust in God, they may succeed; yet, their whole system is artificial, and without breaking it down altogether, I do not perceive how the condition of the mass of the people can be much ameliorated. In the present state of the world, no friend of the human race ought, probably, to desire its immediate destruction. We ought to regard it rather as a beacon to warn us than as a model for our imitation. We ought never, like England, to raise up by legislation any great interests or monopolies, to oppress the people, which we cannot put down without crushing the government itself. Such is now the condition of that country. I am no admirer of the British Constitution, either in church or state, as it at present exists. I desire not a splendid government for this country."

In concluding his speech, Mr. Buchanan defined his last position upon the bill. He said:

"I will tell the senator from Kentucky how far I am willing to proceed with him in punishing public officers. If a postmaster will abuse his franking privilege, as I know to my sorrow has been done in some instances, by converting it into the means of flooding the surrounding country with base libels in the form of electioneering pamphlets and handbills, let such an officer be instantly dismissed and punished. If any district-attorney should either favor or oppress debtors to government, for the purpose of promoting the interest of his party, he ought to share a similar fate. So, if a collector will grant privileges in the execution of his office to one importer, which he denies to another, in order to subserve the views of his party, he ought to be dismissed from office, and punished for his offence. I would not tolerate any such official misconduct. But whilst a man faithfully and impartially discharges all the duties of his office, let him not be punished for expressing his opinion in regard to the merits or demerits of any candidate. Above all, let us not violate the Constitution, in order to punish an officer.

"The senator from Virginia has of late appealed to us often to arise above mere party, and to go for our country. Such appeals are not calculated to produce any deep impression on my mind, because, in supporting my party, I honestly believe I am in the best manner promoting the interest of my country. I am, but I trust not servilely, a party man. I support the present President, not because I think him the wisest or best man alive, but because he is the faithful and able representative of my principles. As long as he shall continue to maintain these principles, he shall receive my cordial support, but not one moment longer. I do not oppose my friends on this side of the house because I entertain unkind feelings towards them personally. On the contrary, I esteem and respect many of them highly. It is against the political principles of which they are the exponents that I make war.

"I support the President because he is in favor of a strict and limited construction of the Constitution, according to the true spirit of the Virginia and Kentucky resolutions. I firmly believe that if the government is to remain powerful and permanent, it can only be by never assuming doubtful powers, which must necessarily bring it into collision with the States. It is not difficult to foresee what would be the termination of such a career of usurpation of the rights of the States.

"I oppose the whig party because, according to their reading of the Constitution, Congress possess, and they ought to exercise, powers which would endanger the rights of the States, and the liberties of the people. Such a free construction of the Constitution as can derive from the simple power 'to levy and collect taxes,' that of creating a national bank, appears to me to be fraught with imminent danger to the country. I am opposed to the party so liberal in their construction of the Constitution, as to infer the existence of a power in the federal government to create and circulate a paper currency for the whole Union, from the clause which merely authorizes Congress 'to regulate commerce with foreign nations, and among the several States, and with the Indian tribes.' Such constructions would establish precedents which might call into existence other alien and sedition laws, and it is such a construction which has given birth to the bill now before the Senate, denying the freedom of speech and of the press to a respectable portion of our citizens."

This speech of Mr. Buchanan effectually settled this federal measure, for such it unquestionably was, though advocated by one or two who had always hitherto been true to democratic ideas. It shows how even the clearest mind may sometimes get befogged upon plain democratic doctrines. Thus it has ever been. Many noble democratic leaders have had a vivid conception of the application of democratic principles to some questions, but have failed to see it in regard to others. Our own day exhibits some melancholy examples of the truth of this statement; but it is a satisfaction to know, that if a few armor-bearers have fainted and fallen by the way, others have arisen to take their places, and above all, the great earnest heart of the democratic masses has remained unperverted and true.

The other speeches made by Mr. Buchanan at this session were of far less national importance though embracing a discussion of some of our most important public interests. As the foregoing speech, however, was made upon a question that involved a radical departure from fundamental law, we have thought it most important of any, for it shows how sternly and resolutely he has always maintained democratic principles, and how senseless are the accusations of his enemies, that he was ever the advocate of those opprobrious doctrines which have made the otherwise respectable name of federal, a term of odium and reproach. This long and stormy Congress was brought to a close on the 4th of March, 1839, and although it had not completed the principal measure Mr. Van Buren had in view—the independent treasury system, yet it had laid the foundation for it, and paved the way for a final divorcement of bank and State.

CHAPTER XVI.

The Twenty-sixth Congress — The Independent Treasury — Mr. Buchanan's great Speech—His reply to Hon. John Davis.

THE twenty-sixth Congress, the last under Mr. Van Buren's administration, commenced its first session on the 2d of December, 1839. It was a protracted and important session, and did not close its labors until the 18th of July, 1840. Early in December, Hon. Silas Wright gave notice of a bill "to more effectually secure the public money in the hands of the officers and agents of the government," and which is subsantially the independent treasury system now in existence. This was a call to combat between the forces of the old federal bank system, and the advocates of separating the government from all connections with such institutions. Silas Wright was the recognized leader of the measure of the administration on the floor of the Senate. The contest was a most desperate one. It was the expiring effort of a giant monster—the death struggle of the alliance between the government and the banks. At this day it is perfectly astonishing to read the disasters predicted from the passage of this measure, even by men who have great reputations as shrewd statesmen. The country at the time was, no doubt, in a most unfortunate financial condition, the effects of a period of paper currency expansion never before equalled in the history of our country. The measure advocated by the democratic party was just the one to prevent the recurrence of such a catastrophe ; yet the bill was fought against by its enemies with a resistance that can scarcely be imagined. Even after it had passed, and nothing remained but the form of agreeing to its title, its opponents pursued the beneficent act as if it were a malignant virus which, after it had entered the public system, could produce only disease and death. A member of the House from Pennsylvania proposed to entitle the bill an act " to reduce the value of property, the products of the farmer, and the wages of labor ; to destroy the indebted portions of the community, and to place the treasury of the nation in the hands of the President." Mr. Clay declared that " the certain tendency of the measure would be to reduce prices ;" and all pictured only ruin, devastation and destruction to every business and occupation in society. Undaunted, however, amid the storm that surrounded them, that important bill was sustained by the democratic members, and finally passed the Senate by a vote of 24 to 18, and the House by a majority of 124 to 107. The final result, however, was not reached until the 30th of June, when the presidential election of 1840 began to assume the enthusiastic spirit, which finally turned a victory into a rout.

Mr. Buchanan's great speech upon the Independent Treasury Bill was delivered in reply to Mr. Clay, on the 22d of January, 1840. Like all of his efforts, it was able, dignified, and profound. It contains, without doubt, the best synopsis of the science of political economy, the relation between capital and labor, that has ever been presented by any American states-man. Most assuredly it has never been surpassed, and we believe not equalled. Mr. Buchanan, at the time of the delivery of this speech, had been familiar with the policy of our government for twenty years ; he had passed through financial revulsions before ; he had studied the effect of extravagant bank expansions, and could place his finger upon the errors of the past, and, like a skillful mariner, direct how to avoid the shoals and quicksands that might lie in the future. What makes his views of more importance, is the fact that time has proved their accuracy. The speech, however, is so long, and goes so much into financial and commercial details that we have not thought it interesting to give it entire, especially as he delivered a shorter one immediately after, in reply to the Hon. John Davis, of Massachusetts, which contains, in a much more condensed form, all the facts and arguments of the first one. We cannot, however, refrain from giving the following extract from the main speech, in which he explains the disastrous effects of extravagant bank expansions upon all the multifarious interests of society. After showing what evils this course had produced in England, he said :

"But why need we resort to foreign nations for illustrations of the truth of this position, when it has been brought home to the actual knowledge of every man within this country ? Have we not all learned by bitter experience, that when our periodical expansions commence, the price of all property begins to rise ? It goes on increasing with the increasing expansions, until the bubble bursts, and then bank accommodations and bank issues are contracted, the amount of property is reduced, and prices fall to their former level. This is the history of our own country, and we all know it. A certain amount of currency is necessary to represent the entire exchangeable property of a country, and if this amount should be greatly increased without a corresponding increase in the exchangeable productions of the country, the only consequence would be a great enhancement in nominal prices. I say nominal, because this increased price will not enable the man who receives it to purchase more real property, or more of the necessaries and luxuries of life than he could have done before.

"Let me now recur to the proposition with which I commenced ; and I will repeat that I do not pretend to mathematical accuracy in the illustration which I shall present. The United States carry on a trade with Germany and France, the former a hard money country, and the latter approaching it so nearly as to have no bank notes in circulation under the denomination of five hundred francs, or nearly one hundred dollars. On the contrary, the United States is emphatically a paper money country, having eight hundred banks of issue, all of them emitting notes of a denomination as low as five dollars, and most of them one, two, and three dollar notes. For every dollar of gold and silver in the vaults of these banks, they issue three, four, five, and some of them as high as ten and even fifteen dollars of paper. This produces a vast but ever changing expansion of the currency, and a consequent increase of the prices of all articles, the value of which is not regulated by the foreign demand above the prices of similar articles in Germany and France. At particular stages of our expansions, we might, with justice, apply the principle which I have stated to our trade with these countries, and assert that, from the great redundancy of our currency, articles are manufactured in France and Germany for half their actual cost in this country. Let me present an example. In Germany, where the currency is purely metallic, and the cost of everything is reduced to a hard money standard, a piece of broadcloth can be manufactured for fifty dollars, the manufacture of which in our country, from the expansion of our paper currency, would cost one hundred dollars. What is the consequence?. The foreign French or German manufacturer imports his cloth into our country, and sells it for one hundred dollars. Does not every person perceive that the redundancy of our currency is equal to one hundred per cent. in favor of the foreign manufacturer? No tariff of protection, unless it amounted to prohibition, could counteract this advantage in favor of foreign manufacturers. I would to Heaven that I could arouse the attention of every manufacturer in the nation to this important subject.

"The foreign manufacturer will not receive our bank notes in payment. He will take nothing home except gold and silver, or bills of exchange, which are equivalent. He does not expend this money here, where he would be compelled to support his family, and to purchase his labor and materials at the same rate of prices which he receives for his manufactures. On the contrary, he goes home, purchases his labor, his wool and all other articles which enter into manufacture, at half their cost in this country, and again returns to inundate us with foreign woollens, and to ruin our domestic manufactures. I might cite many other examples ; but this I trust will be sufficient to draw public attention to the subject. This depreciation of our currency is, therefore, equivalent to a direct protection granted to the foreign over the domestic manufacturer. It is impossible that our manufacturers should be able to sustain such an unequal competition.

"Sir, I solemnly believe that if we could but reduce this inflated paper bubble to anything like reasonable dimensions, New England would become the most prosperous manufacturing country that the sun ever shone upon. Why cannot we manufacture goods, and especially cotton goods, which will go into successful competition with British manufactures in foreign markets ? Have we not the necessary capital ? Have we not the industry ? Have we not the machinery ? And, above all, are not our skill, energy, and enterprise proverbial throughout the world ? Land is also cheaper here than in any other country on the face of the earth. We possess every advantage which Providence can bestow upon us for the manufacture of cotton ; but they are all counteracted by the folly of man. The raw material costs us less than it does the English, because this is an article the price of which depends upon foreign markets, and is not regulated by our own inflated currency. We, therefore, save the freight of cotton across the Atlantic, and that of the manufactured article on its return here. What is the reason that, with all these advantages, and with the prospective duties which our laws afford to the domestic manufacturer of cotton, we cannot obtain exclusive possession of the home market, and successfully contend for the markets of the world ? It is simply because we manufacture at the nominal prices of our own inflated currency, and are compelled to sell at the real prices of other nations. Reduce our nominal to the real standard of prices throughout the world, and you cover our country with blessings and benefits. I wish to Heaven I could speak in a voice loud enough to be heard throughout New England; because if the attention of the manufacturers could once be directed to the subject, their own intelligence and native sagacity would show them how injuriously they are affected by our bloated banking and credit system, and would enable them to apply the proper corrective.

"We are also charged by the senator from Kentucky with a desire to reduce the wages of the poor man's labor. We have been often termed Agrarians on our side of the house. It is something new under the sun to hear the senator and his friends attribute to us a desire to elevate the wealthy manufacturer at the expense of the laboring man and the mechanic. From my soul I respect the laboring man. Labor is the foundation of the wealth of every country; and the free laborers of the North deserve respect both for their probity and their intelligence. Heaven forbid that I should do them wrong! Of all the countries on the earth, we ought to have the most consideration for the laboring man. From the very nature of our institutions, the wheel of fortune is constantly revolving and producing such mutations in property, that the wealthy man of to-day may become the poor laborer of to-morrow. Truly, wealth often takes to itself wings and flies away. A large fortune rarely lasts beyond the third generation, even if it endure so long. We must all know instances of individuals obliged to labor for their daily bread whose grandfathers were men of fortune. The regular process of society would almost seem to consist of the efforts of one class to dissipate the fortunes which they have inherited, whilst another class, by their industry and economy, are regularly rising to wealth. We have all, therefore, a common interest, as it is our common duty, to protect the rights of the laboring man; and if I believed for a moment that this bill would prove injurious to him, it should meet my unqualified opposition.

"Although the bill will not have as great an influence as I

13

could desire, yet, as far as it goes, it will benefit the laboring man as much, and probably more, than any other class of society. What is it he ought most to desire? Constant employment, regular wages, and uniform, reasonable prices for the necessaries and comforts of life which he requires. Now, sir, what has been his condition under our system of expansions and contractions? He has suffered more by them than any other class of society. The rate of his wages is fixed and known; and they are the last to rise with the increasing expansion, and the first to fall when the corresponding revulsion occurs. He still continues to receive his dollar per day, whilst the price of every article which he consumes is rapidly rising. He is at length made to feel that, although he nominally earns as much, or even more than he did formerly, yet, from the increased price of all the necessaries of life, he cannot support his family. Hence, the strikes for higher wages, and the uneasy and excited feelings which have at different periods existed among the laboring classes. But the expansion at length reaches the exploding point, and what does the laboring man now suffer? He is for a season thrown out of employment altogether. Our manufactures are suspended; our public works are stopped; our private enterprises are abandoned; and whilst others are able to weather the storm, he can scarcely procure the means of bare subsistence.

"Again, sir, who do you suppose held the greatest part of the worthless paper of the one hundred and sixty-five broken banks to which I have referred? Certainly it was not the keen and wary speculator, who snuffs danger from afar. If you were to make the search, you will find more broken bank notes in the cottages of the laboring poor than anywhere else. And these miserable shinplasters, where are they? After the revolution of 1837, laborers were glad to obtain employment on any terms; and they often received it upon the express condition that they should accept this worthless trash in payment. Sir, an entire suppression of all bank notes of a lower denomination than the value of one week's wages of the laboring man, is absolutely necessary for his protection. He ought always to receive his wages in gold and silver. Of all men on the earth, the laborer is most interested in having a sound and stable currency.

"The sound state of the currency will have another most happy effect upon the laboring man. He will receive his wages in gold and silver; and this will induce him to lay up, for future use, such a portion of them as he can spare, after satisfying his immediate wants. This he will not do at present, because he knows not whether the trash which he is now compelled to receive as money, will continue to be of any value a week or a month hereafter. A knowledge of this fact tends to banish economy from his dwelling, and induces him to expend all his wages as rapidly as possible, lest they may become worthless on his hands.

"Sir, the laboring classes understand this subject perfectly. It is the hard-handed and firm-fisted men of the country on whom we must rely in the day of danger, who are the most friendly to the passage of this bill. It is they who are the most ardently in favor of infusing into the currency of the country a very large amount of the precious metals."

No one at this day will pretend to question the accuracy of the above remarks. Indeed, they evince a political sagacity, amid the delusions of the time on the currency question, so industriously maintained by those interested in banks, that does infinite credit to the statesmanship of Mr. Buchanan. It is not too much to say that this manly and able defence of the rights of the laboring classes has saved thousands, yes, hundreds of thousands of dollars to the men who earn their living by the sweat of their brows. And not these classes alone have been benefited, but every business man has reaped innumerable blessings, in the uniformity and healthful activity which the adoption of the principles Mr. Buchanan advocated with so much earnestness and ability, has secured to every department of industrial, manufacturing or mercantile pursuits. But how has Mr. Buchanan been repaid for this defence of the interests of his country? No reasonable man would suspect from the foregoing extract we have given from his great speech in answer to Mr. Clay, that Mr. Buchanan was not advocating the interests of the laboring man. Yet, upon this, Mr. John Davis, of Massachusetts, founded a speech of a most unjust and unfair character, charging Mr. Buchanan with being in favor of low wages, and from this have the many newspaper slanders on this subject originated. It is this speech in reply to Mr. Davis which we now give, and a more searching and indignant exposition of the meanness of an opponent in putting words in the mouth of his adversary, we have never encountered :

"Mr. President : I rise to perform a painful, but imperious duty, which I owe to myself. The speech which I lately delivered in favor of the independent treasury bill, has been made the subject of criticism and censure in another part of this capitol ; under what rule of order, I confess I cannot comprehend. In some portions of the country, at public meetings, and in the public press, I have been denounced as the enemy of the laboring man, and have been charged with a desire to reduce his wages, and depress his condition to that of the degraded serfs of the European despotisms. Sentiments have been attributed to me, which I never uttered, and which my soul abhors. I repeat what I declared in that speech, that if I could believe for a moment that the independent treasury bill would prove injurious to the laboring man, it would meet my unqualified opposition.

"I had intended to embrace the first opportunity which presented of doing myself justice upon this subject. Business called me away, and I was absent whilst the senator from Kentucky (Mr. Crittenden) addressed the Senate on the resolutions now before it. I understood that he had referred to the wages of labor, in no offensive terms to me, however, but in such a manner as to have presented the opportunity which I so much desired. When the senator from New York (Mr. Tallmadge) afterwards alluded to the same subject, the debate had assumed a personal character, and I was not the man to interfere against him in such a contest. He had said nothing which could excite a disposition on my part to pursue such a course.

"Had I obtained the floor at any time during the last week, my explanation would have been short and simple. The means, and the only means, by which it was alleged that I had sought to reduce the wages of labor to the standard of the hard money despotisms of Europe, was, by the introduction of an exclusive metallic currency into this country. Now, to such a radical change in our currency, I have forever been opposed. I have avowed my opposition repeatedly upon this floor and elsewhere, and never more distinctly, than in my late speech in favor of the independent treasury bill. My motto has always been to reform, not to destroy the banks ; and I have endeavored to prove—with what success I must leave the public to judge—that such a radical reform in these institutions as would prevent violent expansions and contractions of the currency, and thus enable them always to redeem their notes in specie, would prove eminently beneficial to all classes of society, but more especially to the laboring man.

"On Saturday evening last, a message was sent me by a friend, requesting me to examine the published speech of the senator from Massachusetts (Mr. Davis) and suggesting that it contained an erroneous statement of the arguments which I had used in favor of the independent treasury bill. I examined his speech in the 'National Intelligencer,' having never read it before, and I confess it struck me with the utmost astonishment. I found that, throughout, he had attributed to me arguments in favor of the bill which I never used—nay, more, that the objections of the bill, which I had endeavored to combat, had been imputed to me as the very arguments which I urged in its favor.

" I shall proceed to make some remarks upon his speech. In performing this duty, it is my sole purpose to justify myself, without feeling the slightest disposition to do him injury.

" In my remarks, I urged the passage of the independent treasury bill, because it would separate the banks from the government, and would render the money of the people always secure, and always ready to promote their prosperity in peace, and to defend them in war. Great as are the advantages, direct and indirect, which the country will derive from the passage of this bill, I knew that it could accomplish little or nothing towards reforming our paper currency, or retaining the banks within safe limits. This opinion I have declared upon all occasions, and never more emphatically than in my late speech. I stated that the additional demand for gold and silver which it might create, would not exceed five millions of dollars per annum, according to the President's estimate, and that although this might compel the banks to keep more specie in their vaults in proportion to their circulation and deposits, yet that it would prove but a very inadequate restraint upon excessive banking. Nay, more ; I plumed myself upon the fact that I had been the first to suggest the amendment requiring the holders of treasury drafts to present them for payment to the depositors, with as little delay as possible, for the express purpose of saving the banks from the injury which might be inflicted upon them by locking up a large surplus of revenue in gold and silver, in the vaults of the depositories, and I endeavored to prove, not only by my own argument, but by the authority of one of the most distinguished financiers that history has ever produced, that the bank never could be injured by the adoption of the independent treasury bill, unless in the event of a large surplus revenue, which would not probably soon occur. I also stated that it would thus become their interest, as it already was that of the rest of the community, to prevent the accumulation of such a surplus. In referring to the blessings which would flow to the laboring man from the existence of a sound mixed currency, whose basis should be gold and silver, I expressly declared that the bill would exercise no great influence in producing this desirable result.

"Again, in speaking of the effect which this measure would produce in reducing the amount of our imports—a consummation devoutly desired by all—what was my argument? That the bill would, in some degree, especially after June, 1842, diminish our imports; because we should then have a system of cash duties, which would operate as an encouragement to our domestic manufactures.

"One of the great objects of my speech was to answer the objections which had been urged against the independent treasury bill, by proving that it would not injuriously influence the business of the country in the manner which had been predicted by its enemies, and especially that it would produce little or no effect upon the sound and solvent banks of the country. I thought I had succeeded. It certainly never entered into my conception that any person on the face of the earth could so far have mistaken my meaning as to attribute to me arguments in favor of the bill, as directly opposite to those which I urged as darkness is to light.

"You may judge, then, Mr. President, of my astonishment, when, in the very second paragraph of the speech of the senator from Massachusetts, I read the following sentence:

"'The senator from Mississippi (Mr. Walker) with his usual acknowledged ability, and the distinguished senator from Pennsylvania (Mr. Buchanan) following in his track, have advanced the propositions that the embarrassments and distress with which the country has been grievously afflicted for several years past, and which now paralyze all its energies, are imputable to the pernicious influence of bank paper, that this bill (the Independent Treasury bill) contains the necessary corrective, as it will check importations of foreign goods, suppress what they call the credit system, and by restoring a specie currency, reduce the wages of labor and the value of property. This is the character given to the measure by its friends ; and alarming as the doctrines are, I am gratified that they are frankly avowed.'

"Now, sir, I openly declare in the face of the Senate and the world, not only that no such doctrines were ever avowed by me, but that these remarks of the senator are palpable, I will not say intentional, misrepresentations both of the letter and spirit of my speech.

"What, sir ! to attribute to me the remark, that this bill, by applying the necessary corrective to the pernicious influence of bank paper, 'and by thus restoring a specie currency' will produce the disastrous consequences which he has enumerated, when a considerable portion of my argument was devoted to prove that the bill would produce no injurious effect whatever upon the sound and solvent banks of the country ! Nay, more, that it would exert but a very trifling influence, indeed, if any, even in restraining within safe limits their loans and issues. Now, sir, it may be very ingenious, but it is certainly not very fair, to put into the mouth of a friend of the bill, as arguments in its favor, the strongest objections which have been urged against it by its enemies. These would be so many admissions of its fatal consequences, and they would be the stronger when converted into arguments in its favor by one of its friends. Against the whole interest of my remarks—against my express and reiterated declarations, both upon this and former occasions, that I was no friend to an exclusive hard money currency, but was in favor of well regulated State banks, how could the sena tor be so far mistaken as to sit down and deliberately write that I had urged in favor of this bill, that it would restore a specie currency, and thereby reduce the wages of labor and the value of property ? I leave it for him to answer the question according to his own sense of justice towards a brother senator who had never done him harm.

"But the senator does not stop here. Throughout his whole speech he imputes to me the use of such arguments in favor of the bill as I have stated, and dwells upon them at length— arguments which if I had ever used, would prove conclusively that I was an enemy of the bill which I professed to advocate, and that scarcely even in disguise. This is the light in which he presents me before the world. Towards the conclusion of his speech, he caps the climax. He says:

" 'To follow out the case, I have supposed: The income of every man except the exporter, is to be reduced one half in the value of wages and property, while all foreign merchandise will cost the same, which will obviously, in effect, double the price, as it will take twice the amount of labor, or twice the amount of the products of labor, to purchase it.'

" I do not ascribe this power to the bill, but it is enough for me that its friends do. What response will the farmers, mechanics, manufacturers, and laborers make to such a flagitious proposition?

" And all this, the senator says in a professed reply to me. He thus charges me with having ascribed to the Independent Treasury bill the power of reducing the income of every man in the country, 'one half in the value of wages and property.' Had I contended in favor of any such power, well might the senator have said, it was 'a flagitious proposition.' He would almost have been justified in the use of a term so harsh and unparliamentary.

" Self-respect, as well as the respect which I owe to the Senate, restrains me from giving such a contradiction to this allegation as it deserves. It would surely not be deemed improper, however, in me, if I were to turn to the senator, and apply the epithet which he himself has applied to the proposition he imputes to me, and were to declare that such an imputation was a 'flagitious' misrepresentation of my remarks.

" So far from imagining that the Independent Treasury bill would restore to the country a metallic currency, I believed that it would exercise but a slight influence in restraining the excesses of the banking system. Other and much more efficient

17*

remedies must be adopted by the several States to restrain the excesses, and thus to prevent future suspensions. In my remarks, I stated distinctly what legislation would, I thought, be required to accomplish this purpose. In the first place I observed that the banks ought to be compelled to keep in their vaults a certain fair proportion of specie compared with their circulation and deposits, or in other words, a certain proportion of immediate specie means, to meet their immediate responsibilities. 2d. That the foundation of a specie basis for our paper currency should be laid, by prohibiting the circulation of bank-notes, at the first, under the denomination of ten, and afterwards, under that of twenty dollars. 3d. That the amount of bank dividends should be limited. 4th. And above all, that upon the occurrence of another suspension, the doors of the bank should be closed at once, and their affairs placed in the hands of commissioners. A certainty that such must be the inevitable effect of another suspension, would do more to prevent it than any other cause. To reform, and not to destroy, was my avowed motto. I know that the existence of banks, and the circulation of bank-paper, are so identified with the habits of our people, that they cannot be abolished, even if this were desirable.

"Such a reform in the banking system, as I have indicated, would benefit every class of society, but above all others, the man who makes his living by the sweat of his brow. The object at which I aimed by these reforms was not a pure metallic currency, but a currency of a mixed character ; the paper portion of it always convertible into gold and silver, and subject to as little fluctuation in amount as the regular business of the country would admit. Of all reforms, this is what the mechanic and the laboring man ought most to desire. It would produce steady prices and steady employment, and, under its influence the country would march steadily on in its career of prosperity, without suffering from the ruinous expansions, and contractions, and explosions which we have endured during the last twenty years. What is most essential to the prosperity of the mechanic and laboring man? Constant employment, steady and fair wages, with uniform prices for the necessaries and comforts of life which he must purchase, and payment for his labor in a sound currency.

"Let us, in these particulars, compare the present condition of the laboring man under the banking system which now exists, with what it would be under such reforms as I have indicated. And first, in regard to constant employment. What is the effect of the present system of bank expansions, and contractions, and revulsions, in this particular? Is it not absolutely certain, has not experience demonstrated, that under such a system, constant employment is rendered impossible? It is true, that during the short period whilst the bubble is expanding, and the banks are increasing their loans and their issues, labor of every kind finds employment. Then buildings of all sorts are erected, manufactures are established, and the mason, and other mechanics are in demand. Public works are prosecuted, and afford employment to an immense number of laborers. The tradesman of every description then finds customers, because the amount of paper in circulation produces a delusive appearance of prosperity, and promotes a spirit of extravagance. But, sir, under this system the storm is sure to succeed the sunshine, the explosion is certain to follow the expansion—and when it comes, and we are now suffering under it—what is then the condition of the mechanic and the laboring man? Buildings of every kind cease, manufactories are closed, public works are suspended, and the laboring classes are thrown out of employment altogether. It is enough to make one's heart bleed to reflect upon their sufferings, particularly in our large cities, during the past winter. In many instances the question with them has not been what amount of wages they could earn, but whether they could procure any employment which would save them and their families from starvation. If our State legislatures, which alone possess the power, would but regulate our bloated credit system wisely, by restraining the banks within safe limits, our country would then be permitted to proceed with regular strides, and the laboring men would suffer none of these evils because he would receive constant employment.

" In the second place, what is the effect of the present system upon the wages of labor, and upon the price of the necessaries and comforts of life ? It cannot be denied that that country is the most prosperous where labor commands the greatest reward ; but this not for one year merely, not for that short period of time when our bloated credit system is most expanded, but for a succession of years, for all time. Permanence in the rate of wages is indispensable to the prosperity of the laboring man. He ought to be able to look forward with confidence to the future, to calculate upon being able to rear and educate his family by the sweat of his brow, and to make them respectable and useful citizens. In this respect, what is the condition of the laboring man under our present system ? Whilst he suffers more under it than any other member of society, he derives from it the fewest advantages. It is a principle of political economy confirmed by experience, that whilst the paper currency is expanding, the price of everything else increases more rapidly than the wages of labor. They are the last to rise with the expansion, and the first to fall with the contraction of the currency. The price of a day's or of a month's labor of any kind, the price of a hat, of a pair of boots, of a pound of leather, of all articles of furniture ; in short, of manual and mechanical labor generally, is fixed and known to the whole community. The purchaser complains when these fixed prices are enhanced, and the mechanic or laborer, in order to retain his customers, cannot and does not raise his price until he is compelled to do so by absolute necessity. His meat, his flour, his potatoes, clothing for himself and family, mount up to an extravagant price long before his compensation is increased. It was formerly supposed that the productions of meat and flour were so vast in our extended and highly favored land, that a monopoly of them would be impossible. The experience of the last two or three years has proved the contrary. The banks, instead of giving credit in small sums to honest men, who would have used the money wisely in promoting their own welfare, and as a necessary consequence, that of the community, have loaned it to monopolists, to enable them to raise the price of the necessaries of life to the consumer. Have we not all learned that a million of dollars have been advanced by them to an individual for the purpose of enabling him to monopolize the sale of all the beef consumed in our eastern cities? Do we not all know that this effort proved successful during the last year in raising the price of this necessary of life to twelve and sixteen cents, and even higher, per pound. Now, sir, although the wages of the laboring man were then nominally high, what was his condition? He could not afford to go into the market and purchase beef for his family. If his wages increased with the increasing expansion of our credit system, aggravated in its effects by the immense sales of State bonds of Europe, still the prices of all the necessaries of life rose in a greater proportion, and he was not benefited. I might mention also, the vast monopoly of pork, produced by a combination of individuals, extending from Boston to Cincinnati, which, by means of bank facilities, succeeded in raising the price of that necessary of life to an enormous pitch. What then did the laborer gain, even at the time of the greatest expansion? Nothing—literally nothing. The laborers were a suffering class even in the midst of all this delusive prosperity. Instead of being able to lay by anything for the present day of adversity, which was a necessary consequence of the system, the laborer was even then scarcely able to maintain himself and his family. His condition has been terrible during the past winter. In view of these facts, I said—

" ' All other circumstances being equal, I agree with the sena tor from Kentucky that that country is most prosperous when labor commands the highest wages. I do not, however, mean by the terms "highest wages" the greatest nominal amount During the revolutionary war, one day's work commanded a hundred dollars of continental paper ; but this would scarcely have purchased a breakfast. The more proper expression would be to say, that that country is most prosperous where labor commands the greatest reward—where one day's labor will procure, not the greatest nominal amount of a depreciated currency, but most of the necessaries and comforts of life. If, therefore, you should, in some degree, reduce the nominal price paid for labor, by reducing the amount of your bank issues within reasonable and safe limits, and establishing a metallic basis for your paper circulation, would this injure the laborer ? Certainly not ; because the price of all .the necessaries and comforts of life are reduced in the same proportion, and he will be able to purchase more of them for one dollar in a. sound state of the currency, than he could have done in the days of extravagant expansion for a dollar and a quarter. So far from injuring, it will greatly benefit the laboring man. It will insure to him constant employment, and regular prices, paid in a sound currency, which of all things he ought most to desire ; and it will save him from being involved in ruin by a recurrence of those periodical expansions and contractions of the currency, which have hitherto convulsed the country.'

" Now, sir, is not my meaning clearly expressed in this para· graph ? I contended that it would not injure but greatly bene fit the laboring man, to prevent the violent and ruinous expan· sions and contractions to which our currency was incident, and by judicious bank reform, to place it on a settled basis. If this were done, what would be the consequence ? That, if the laboring man could not receive as great a nominal amount for his labor as he did 'in the days of extravagant expansion,' which must always, under our present system, be of short duration, he would be indemnified, and far more than indemnified, by the constant employment, the regular wages, and the uniform and more moderate prices of the necessaries and comforts of life, which a more stable currency would produce. Can this proposition be controverted? I think not; it is too plain for argument. Mark, me, sir; I desire to produce this happy result not by establishing a pure metallic currency, but by reducing the amount of your bank issues within reasonable and safe limits and establishing a metallic basis for your paper circulation. The idea plainly expressed is, that it is better, much better, for the laboring man, as well as for every other class of society, except the speculator, that the business of the country should be placed upon that fixed and permanent foundation which would be laid by establishing such a bank reform as would render it certain that bank notes should be always convertible into gold and silver.

"And yet this plain and simple exposition of my views has been seized upon by those who desired to make political capital out of their perversion; and it has been represented far and wide, that it was my desire to reduce wages down to the prices received by the miserable serfs and laborers of European despotisms. I shall most cheerfully leave the public to decide between me and my traducers. The senator from Massachusetts, after having attributed to me the intention of reducing the wages of labor to the hard money standard, through the agency of the Independent Treasury Bill, has added, as an appendix to his speech, a statement made by the senator from Maryland (Mr. Merrick), of the prices of labor in these hard money despotisms; and it is thus left to be inferred that I am in favor of reducing the honest and independent laborer of this glorious and free country to the same degraded condition. The senator ought to know that there is too much intelligence among the laboring classes in this highly favored land, to be led astray by such representations.

Payment of wages in a sound currency. Under the present unrestricted banking system this is entirely out of the question. Nothing can ever produce this effect, except the absolute prohibition of the issue and circulation of small notes As long as bank notes exist of denominations so low as to render it possible to make them the medium of payment for a day's or a week's labor, so long will the laboring man be compelled to accept the very worst of these notes for his wages. Unless it may be at periods of the highest expansion, when labor is in the very greatest demand, notes of doubtful credit will always be forced upon him. This was emphatically the case after the explosion of the banks in 1837. He could then procure nothing for his work, but the miserable shinplaster-currency with which the country was inundated. This he would not lay by for a rainy day, because he did not know at what moment it might become altogether worthless on his hands. The effect of it was to destroy all habits of economy. Besides, as a class, laborers suffer more from counterfeit and broken bank-notes than any other class of society. In order to afford the laborer the necessary protection against these evils, he ought always to be paid, and would from necessity always be paid, in gold and silver, if the issue and circulation of small notes were entirely prohibited.

"Thus, it will be perceived, that without the imposition of wholesome restrictions upon the banks, the laboring man can never expect to receive either constant employment or steady and fair wages, paid in a sound currency ; or to pay uniform prices for the necessaries and comforts of life, which he is obliged to purchase. Under our present system everything is in a state of constant fluctuation and change. Prices are high to-day, low to-morrow. Labor is in demand to-day, there is no employment to-morrow. There is no stability, no uniformity under our present system. Of all men, laborers are the most interested in such a wise regulation of the banking system by the States, as would prevent the violent expansions and contractions in the currency, and the consequent suspensions of specie payments under which we have been suffering.

" Why, sir, under our present system, we endure the evils both of an exclusive hard money currency and a bloated paper system, without experiencing the benefits of either. The one is the inevitable consequence of the other. At the present moment, we have reached a point of depression in the currency which the senator from South Carolina (Mr. Calhoun), considers as low, or lower, than the hard money standard. Here we are without credit, because no man for the prosecution of his necessary business, can procure a loan from the banks. They are now in that state of exhaustion which is the inevitable consequence of their former highly excited action. The case which senators supposed might exist should we suddenly adopt a hard money currency, exists already. It is now fact, and not fancy. The man who purchased a property but one year ago, in the days of the highest expansion, for two thousand dollars, and paid half the purchase-money upon it, could at this moment of depression, scarcely sell it for the remaining one thousand dollars. This is one of the greatest evils of our present ever-changing system ; but, such things must recur and recur again for ever, unless some efficient remedy shall be applied."

This triumphant reply to the special pleading and sophistry of Mr. Davis, was not the last compliment Mr. Buchanan paid that individual for his attack upon him. The matter would not have been of so much consequence, had it not been that it was just previous to a presidential election, and the charge of the administration being in favor of " low wages," was likely to be used with some advantage as an electioneering cry in the contest. Mr. Davis, in his reply to Mr. Buchanan, insisted upon the most unreasonable and outrageous interpretation to his remarks. The enemies to the Independent Treasury had used as their principal argument against it, " that it would reduce the wages of labor." The answer to this was, " no, it will *not* have such an effect. It will give labor a much better reward than formerly, but should, perchance, the *nominal* standard of wages be reduced below what it is when everything, as during a bank expansion, is at speculative prices, still the *real* reward of labor will not be reduced. This is the argument on both sides in a nutshell, and yet because the friends of the administration allowed that prices of all things would be less when there were no bank-expansions than when there were, they were charged with being in favor of "low wages."

Mr. Buchanan showed that the laboring man was never benefited by extravagant speculation. Said Mr. B., " It brings to him nothing but unmitigated evil, because the increased prices which he is compelled to pay for the necessaries and comforts of life, counterbalance, and more than counterbalance, this advantage. What he desires is regularity and stability in the business of the country." But what made the offence of Mr. Davis more palpable and condemnatory, was the fact, that after Mr. Buchanan had replied and disavowed any such sentiments as had been attributed to him, he refused to make the *amende honorable*, and still continued his pettifogging play upon words. Referring to this, in his last reply to Mr. Davis, Mr. Buchanan, who rarely becomes excited, and must be very grossly wronged before he would speak in terms of denunciation of any one, said : " But when the senator thought proper to treat my complaints with scorn and contempt, which he said they deserved, I believed it to be a duty which I owed to myself to hurl back his defiance, and he may make the most of it."

The good use to which it was supposed this wholesale fabrication could be put in the coming presidential election was doubtless the reason which induced the opponents of the administration to adhere to it so tenaciously. The cry doubtless did have some effect, and it is a lamentable evidence of the malevolence of party spirit that although the independent treasury upon which Mr. Buchanan's arguments were founded has been ten years in operation, and every one of his positions have been ratified by time and experience, yet there are now found, unfortunately for the credit of human nature, persons who give this slander either a direct or partial endorsement.

And here it is but proper to refer to Mr. Buchanan's conduct while smarting under the gross wrong which had been done him by Mr. Davis. While most men would have denounced Mr. Davis in language such as his conduct really deserved. Mr. Buchanan remembering his place and position, and that the Senate was not the arena for personalities, avoided all severe denunciations. The strongest remark of a personal character which he indulged in was to say "that Mr. Davis was unworthy of the courtesy which one gentleman owes to another," and continued Mr. Buchanan, "I ask the pardon of every other member of the Senate for using such an expression." Considering the character of the assault upon him, this language may be considered unusually mild. Mr. Buchanan was always a resolute opponent of every thing like personality in the Senate, considering and justly, too, that individuals who are privileged by law, and have only their honor to restrain them in their language, should be the last to abuse that freedom of speech granted to them for the good of their country and the safety of its institutions.

We have now given an account of the principal debate of this session, but it comprises only a small portion of the actual discussion which occurred. Besides the speeches which Mr. Buchanan delivered on the Independent Treasury bill, he took part in an animated debate upon the circulation of small notes, the expenditures of the government, etc. The stormy session, however, came to a close upon the 30th of June in the midst of the most remarkable presidential contest that our country has ever experienced. When the next session of this Congress assembled on the 7th of December, 1840, the whirlwind had spent its force; the misrepresentations and abuse of the democracy which had been accumulating for years, had effected their pur-

pose.   General Harrison had been elected and the democratic
party was temporarily prostrated, not by the strength of its
foes, but paradoxical as it may seem, by the very weakness of its
enemies.

The second session of the twenty-sixth Congress was not an
important one.   The democracy were confounded but not dismayed ; astonished but not overcome, confident that it was
but a freak of the popular will which "the sober second
thought," as Mr. Buchanan announced in the early part of the
session, would soon set right.   The most important bill brought
up at this session was the proscription desired to be applied
to foreigners in regard to the pre-emption right to public lands.
Mr. Buchanan was again compelled to come to the rescue.   He
said, " he could not understand the opposition which had been
manifested in certain quarters to foreigners, who sought a
refuge and a home in our country.   Had they not materially
assisted in achieving our independence ?   In the days of the
revolution no such jealousy was felt towards the brave Irishmen, Frenchmen, and Germans, who side by side with our natural citizens had fought the battles of liberty.   On the contrary
he had no doubt, it was from a grateful sense of their services,
that it had ever been the settled policy of our government to
allow them to purchase our vacant lands upon the same terms
with American citizens."

The well known fact, however, that the next Congress was
whig, prevented any important legislation by the party now in
power.   The democrats were more anxious to see the inauguration of the measures of the new administration than to present
any of their own.   Hence the debates usually run either into
a review of the past or speculations in regard to the future.
There was a man whom Mr. Buchanan never would hear aspersed
without coming to his rescue.   The day had not then passed
when men hoped to make something by attacking Gen. Jackson.   In reply to some remarks by a distinguished senator, Mr.
Buchanan said : " Gen. Jackson has now retired to the hermi-

tage, and may perhaps live to have the judgment of posterity as it were passed upon him. He was an able, sagacious and truly patriotic man ; and I now say that those of us, if there be any such, who shall survive during a quarter of a century longer, will live to see the day when Jackson's name and fame shall be cherished alike by persons of all political parties." Mr. Buchanan was only mistaken in one thing, his prediction has become true much sooner than he anticipated.

This Congress was brought to a close with 4th of March, 1841, when Gen. Harrison was duly inaugurated President of the United States.

CHAPTER XVII

An **Extra** Session of Congress called—Death of Gen. Harrison—Accession of John Tyler—The Fiscal Bank—The Fiscal Corporation—Mr. Buchanan's Speeches on these Measures—Mr. Clay's Reply—Mr. Buchanan's Rejoinder.

ALMOST immediately after the accession of Gen. Harrison to the Presidential chair, he issued a proclamation convoking Congres, to meet in the extra session on the 31st day of May ensuing. Before, however, that period arrived, death had removed him from the scene of his duties, and for the first time in our history a President had deceased during the term of his office. Mr. John Tyler, who had been elected Vice President, according to the Constitution, now became acting Chief Magistrate. The decree which had already gone forth for an extra session was not annulled by Gen. Harrison's successor, and accordingly Congress convened on the day designated. Among the names on the roll of the Senate at this session, were those of Franklin Pierce, Rufus Choate, Silas Wright, W. C. Rives, John C. Calhoun, Henry Clay, and Thomas H. Benton. In the House were Robert C. Winthrop, John Quincy Adams, Millard Fillmore, Henry A. Wise, Fernando Wood, Aaron Ward, Linn Boyd, and Wm. O. Butler.

The very first measure the new party introduced was a bill for the repeal of the Independent Treasury. This was the special object of hatred, as it stood in the way of the establishment of a national bank, a brilliant scheme for which Mr. Clay already had in preparation. Nothing could resist the proposed repeal, for a triumphant majority in both houses of Congress demanded it. The democracy resisted it with all their might, but the effort was as useless as their exertions to re-elect Mr. Van Buren had been powerless. It was, indeed, a dark day. Were all the beneficent reforms which Gen. Jackson had labored so long to accomplish to be swept away in a moment? Were the banks and the government which had been united by Hamilton, and divorced by Jackson and Van Buren to be reunited, and a new national bank be formed even before the injurious effects of the old one h d passed away? It did seem, indeed, that the severe labors of twelve long years were thus to be rendered useless in one short session. But such was not the fact. What has been called the treachery of John Tyler by some, and his patriotism by others, prevented these disastrous results.

Mr. Clay, in the early part of the session, presented his plan of a "Fiscal Bank." In detail it was somewhat different from former national banks, though in principle no wise dissimilar. As Mr. Silas Wright had been the chosen champion of the democracy in presenting and carrying through the Independent Treasury bill, so was Mr. Buchanan honored with a like position in combating upon the floor of the Senate the great measure upon which Mr. Clay had staked we may almost say the existence of his party and his reputation as a statesman. No one will deny that Mr. Buchanan did not have a bold, a skillful and powerful antagonist. But he was as honorable, as bold, and as chivalric in victory as resigned in defeat. Whatever may be said of the old whig party, it had noble and honorable leaders, who despised personalities, and who, if fall they must, would do so on the field of manly warfare. The names of Clay and Webster will ever be the synonyms of all that was dignified in debate, noble in spirit or generous in personal conduct. To the democracy they were "foemen worthy of their steel." The whole range of parliamentary debates scarcely furnishes a parallel to the conduct of Mr. Clay in this, in more than one respect, extraordinary session. For years he had been contend-

ing for the establishment of a national bank, and no one will
dare to ascribe to him any improper motives as an excuse for
his conduct.   He undoubtedly sincerely believed that such an
institution would be an important and valuable agent in the
financial transactions of the government.   He looked to the
success of Gen. Harrison as the realization of his hopes.   His
brilliant imagination had pictured to itself his dream as already
accomplished, and when his favorite measure had been sanctioned by Congress, lo ! it was arrested by the power of one
man, and that man the chosen elect of his own party !   Could
anything be imagined more chafing to the feelings of a man
honest in his desires to serve his country ?   Yet no ungentle-
manly harshness, no unparliamentary language escaped the lips
of this great man, but in the very period of chagrin and morti-
fication he made a speech, unequalled for wit and humor.

Mr. Buchanan's great speech on the Fiscal Bank was delivered on the 7th day of July, 1841.   We regret that the limits
of this volume will not permit us to give it in full.   We shall
be compelled to confine ourselves to a few extracts from it, and
give instead the greater part of his reply to Mr. Archer of Virginia, where he presents the arguments of his main speech in a
less detailed form.   In noticing the constitutional power to pass
the bill he said :

" The principle of constitutional construction which would
here deduce the power to establish a bank of the United States
from the source where it is said to exist, would break down all
the barriers erected by our fathers between federal and State
authority.   If you can infer this power from the simple power
of taxation in the Constitution, I ask what other power which
you may desire to exercise may not be inferred from that of
some other clause ?   An ingenious man might thus fasten any
power which Congress or the President may desire to exercise,
on some one of the express grants contained in the Constitution.
But the incident cannot transcend its principle—the stream

cannot ascend higher than the fountain ; and upon the mere power of levying the taxes necessary to support an economical government, you can never erect a vast corporation to overshadow the whole land, and, if not in form, yet in substance, to change the character of all our institutions. Never, never can you fairly infer the existence of the power to create a bank from that of the power to levy and collect taxes."

Mr. Buchanan, after going into a detailed explanation of the institution proposed to be established, summed up its principal features as follows :

" Then sir, that is the real government bank ; the directors controlled by the government, the greater portion of the stock held by the government, the surplus profits, if any, given to the government, and the most profitable business of the bank founded on the use of the money of the government. And why should such a charter have been offered to Congress by the secretary of the treasury department ? I shall not say that it was concocted there for the express purpose of erecting a mere engine or instrument of political power ; but if Talleyrand himself had been a great financier as he was a diplomatist, he could not have desired a charter more completely adapted to effect this purpose than the bill now before us presents. The influence of this machine, located at Washington under the eye of the government, will be felt everywhere throughout the Union."

One argument used in favor of a national bank was, that other nations had these institutions. In reply to this, Mr. Buchanan eloquently remarked :

" Sir, other nations have emperors and kings, and titles of nobility, and established churches, as well as national banks ; but is that any reason why the people of the United States should abandon their republican principles and imitate those

14

foreign forms of government? Although the senator from Kentucky (Mr. Clay) may not, and I believe does not, desire such a change, yet he may virtually accomplish it much sooner than he anticipates. If he can create this great national bank, and ally it with the government in Washington city, on terms of the closest intimacy, if he can thus concentrate the money power here, and render its interest identical with that of the political power, he may succeed in establishing for this country, not a monarchy, but the very worst form of government with which mankind has ever been cursed. A hereditary aristocracy has acquired this infamous pre-eminence, but the government of a moneyed aristocracy would, if possible, be still worse. From interest and from habit, a landed aristocracy has always cherished some feelings of kindness for the people; but an upstart moneyed aristocracy has no heart to feel for them, no desire to promote their welfare. It looks upon mankind as mere laboring machines for its own benefit. It never indulges in those kindly and Christian sympathies, which make us feel that all men are alike created in the image of their Maker, and are brethren. This is a kind of government that may be established by an intimate union of the political with the money power. We may approach nearer to the government of the old world by establishing this bank than the senator or any of his friends imagine. If this should be the case, corruption will insinuate itself into the sinews and nerves, and very vitals of the body politic. The people will still attend the elections, and be flattered with the idea that they still enjoy all their liberties, while a secret, controlling, all-pervading influence would direct their conduct. The corpse of a free government would then only remain, whilst the animating spirit had fled forever. But I do not myself indulge in these gloomy forebodings. I am not afraid that this bank will ever be established; and if ever it should, the people of this country will pursue it with a steady vigilance, which will never tire until they accomplish its destruction."

Such was the concluding portion of Mr. Buchanan's speech upon the " Fiscal Bank." The arguments he had presented were unanswerable, but the decree had gone forth, and the bill was passed. Mr. Tyler, however, threw himself in the way of its becoming a law, and interposed the executive veto. Then a new and similar measure was devised, called the Fiscal Corporation, and upon that Mr. Buchanan delivered the following able speech, in reply to Mr. Archer, of Virginia :

" The senator from Virginia concluded his remarks by telling us that the whig party had done a great deal at this extra session. I admit they have done much, and they have done one thing for which the country ought to be grateful—they have *done for* themselves (a laugh). The gentleman quoted to us, on the subject of our abstractions, a couplet from Hudibras ; but he stopped with the two first lines. Let me supply the couplet immediately following, which the senator did not quote, but which I think, applies quite as well to the pretended difference between the present bill and that which the President has returned to us with his veto :

> ' What mighty difference can there be
> 'Twixt tweedle-dum and tweedle-dee ?'

" Before I conclude, I think I shall be able to show, that if the President would have deserved the condemnation of all honest men, had he approved the bill to establish a fiscal bank ; having rejected that, he will deserve not only the condemnation, but the contempt and ridicule of all mankind if he shall sign the bill to create this ' fiscal corporation.' But, while I express this opinion, I do not desire or intend to say anything which shall wound the feelings of my honorable friend from Virginia (Mr. Archer), for I can in all truth and sincerity declare, that if there is such a thing in the entire world of politics as an honest man (and I doubt not there are many), I believe my friend is that man. I think, indeed, that he has by

some means got himself involved in a strange delusion ; but if
he has changed his opinion, I am certainly not to blame for
not changing mine.

"I desire to say a few things concerning this bank, before
execution shall have been done upon it either by the President
or the Senate ; for I believe no human being anticipates that
such a thing as the present bill will ever become the law of the
land. I believe further, that if all hearts here could be
searched, it would be found that this bill is not what gentlemen
on either side desire.

"A word or two as to the constitutional argument of the
senator from Virginia. If I rightly apprehend the position he
took, his character as a State rights man is gone forever. The
senator from South Carolina (Mr. Calhoun) need now no longer
apprehend anything from the senator's competing with him for
the palm. He has avowed himself a consolidationist, and one
of the most thorough-going of the sect. The senator says that
the government of the United States has a right to purchase
bills of exchange ; that it may, if it pleases, instead of ' wagon-
ing ' the specie (to use the senator's phrase) to the head waters
of the Missouri or Mississippi, purchase a bill which will accomplish the same purpose. Undoubtedly it may; though in practice, this is rarely, if ever, done. There is not the least difficulty in the government's transferring its funds to our extreme
western frontier ; because even the very Indians will accept a
government bill drawn on New York, and would prefer it to
specie, knowing that it can be sold at a premium anywhere in
the far west for gold and silver. As the next step in his argument, the senator tells us that it is perfectly incontrovertible
that, having the right over a part, the government must have a
right over the whole ; that if it possesses the power, it possesses the whole power ; that a constitutional power cannot be
broken into fragments ; but if the power be given at all, the
whole power must be given. And so, because government may
purchase a bill of exchange to discharge its obligations on the

western frontier, it can therefore set up a bank of exchange,
with a capital of fifty millions of dollars, and confer on it the
power of dealing in bills, not only for the purposes of government, but for the use of all the people of this country ! A proposition like this needs only to be stated. The men who
framed the Constitution of the United States were jealous of
federal power, and they dealt it out to Congress with a parsi-
monious hand. What do they say in the Constitution ? Anything which gives the slightest sanction to the senator's doctrine ? Not at all.. The power to transfer the public funds
from one part of the country to another, by bills of exchange, is
palpable. Nobody denies it. But that it should follow, as a
necessary inference, that it has power to deal in exchange to
every extent ; to buy and sell foreign bills between this country
and Europe, and bills between State and State, in which it has
no interest, is a position such as I never heard, in all my life,
from the greatest and most avowed consolidationist. Why, at
this rate, an ingenious expositor may make the Constitution
mean anything or nothing. But there is no foundation for any
construction or inference in the case. The United States may
confessedly buy and sell bills of exchange as a means of transferring its funds ; this it has done uninterruptedly and without
objection, for the past fifty years. But before my astute and
very ingenious friend from Virginia made the discovery, I
believe it never was dreamed of that such a simple power as
this laid a foundation for the erection of our immense bank of
exchange.

       *   *   *   *   *   *

   " There is a striking difference between the two bills (the
Fiscal Bank and the Fiscal Corporation). The former bill
went on the presumption that members of Congress are men of
mortal mould ; that they possess the same passions and the
same frailties as other men ; that they are neither better nor
worse than their fellow citizens ; and that, as depended upon
the vote of the two Houses of Congress whether proceedings

should be instituted to forfeit its charter in case it were violated, they ought not to have any accommodations from the bank, lest they might thus be swerved from their integrity of purpose. This, to be sure, was a very severe restriction, because gentlemen may desire, like some of their predecessors, to form another congressional land company, and it might be very convenient to obtain money on kiteflying bills, as some of their predecessors had done. Under similar circumstances, it would certainly be a very convenient matter for a member of Congress to fly a kite as far as Baltimore for ten or twenty thousand dollars, and no doubt he would find the bank extremely accommodating. Another advantage is, that if he should not be able to pay at maturity, there is not the least danger that he will be ever publicly exposed. I believe it is a rule in love never to kiss and tell, and this rule has been most pertinaciously observed by the old corrupt and rotten Bank of the United States. If that bank accommodated members of Congress—and we know it did, to an immense amount—it has always refused to give up their names. The tears and the groans of the widows and orphans whom it has ruined have ascended to heaven, and accused its directors. These directors have been changed again and again, but still they have kept the secret. No resolves and no efforts of this body, or of the other House, have ever been able to extort it from them. There is among the secret arcana of that bank a document known by the name of the ' suspended list,' which, if ever published, would give the information ; but every human being who has had access to that paper, has most religiously kept the secret. If they had not, it may be that men who now hold their heads very high, and who occupy distinguished stations in the State, would be covered with shame, and humbled in the very dust. Could that list be procured, it is at least possible that we might learn how bank accommodations can be paid off by the transfer of lots in lithographed paper cities, and valueless western lands. Happily under this bill these golden opportunities will again be afforded, and the wind will again prove fair for members of Congress to fly their kites as well as other men.

"And here let me point out something of the working of this new patent machine. Why, sir, to use a western phrase, 'it will go without greasing,' there will be no manner of difficulty in the way. The borrower in Philadelphia will, as I told you, draw his bill on some far remote city in another State—such as Camden, and when his bill is due, his bona fide correspondent in Camden can draw back on him just such another on Philadelphia, and thus, without discounting a single promissory note, the bank can lend more money and make more profit than if its discounting power were without restriction. I was really astonished to hear the gentleman from Virginia (Mr. Archer) assert, whilst he denounced the power of discount as being so immense and dangerous, and so utterly inadmissible, that this other power of dealing in exchanges was the most benign, the most beneficent, and the most felicitous power that ever was devised by man and that a bill which conferred it should, as a matter of course, unite in its favor the vote of all the Whig party. Then there is the city of New York and Jersey city. If the honorable senator should, at any time, want a loan, he has only to fly his kite across the Hudson river, and he can readily be accommodated."

Mr. Archer—"I never drew a bill which had one character and asserted another."

"Yes, but when you establish a bank of such a character as this, you must expect that such consequences will follow. A bank from which all restrictions are taken away, and at whose counter the whole speculating world is invited to borrow—from such a bank, what else can you expect? It will loan money on bills of exchange, instead of loaning on promissory notes, and for my soul, I cannot perceive any essential difference between the two modes. The only effect in thus changing the form will be to induce men to commit fraud. Instead of draw--

ing on real funds, they will draw bills on places where they have nothing to answer them. They will thus make their loans, and the bank make its profits, with this only difference—that they have to pay a little more for their money, while the bank will receive a larger interest, in the name of a premium, than the law would allow it to take on the discount of a promissory note. I can see that some cities—and cities of great business, too—will derive little benefit from this bill. Buffalo, for example, and Pittsburgh, will both be in a ' bad fix,' for Buffalo cannot draw on New York ; nor Pittsburgh on Philadelphia, and why ? Because under this wise bill, two cities in the same State cannot draw on each other. I cannot imagine how the merchants who conduct the immense flour and other business of Buffalo will be able to obtain accommodations, unless, indeed, they resort to flying kites to the Canada shore, and they present foreign bills to the bank for discount. Cincinnati will be well off, because Newport is just across the river, and the drawer and the acceptor will be almost within hail of each other. This machine, such as I have described it, will regulate the price of every commodity in the country, and it will be done by this kite-flying process.

*   *   *   *   *   *

" And now I have one word to say on the late presidential veto, and then I shall have done. It has been said that John Tyler was bound by the fidelity which he owed to his party to approve the bill for a fiscal bank. I deny it altogether, and say that, if he had approved that bill, he would have deserved to be denounced as a self-destroyer, as false to the whole course of his past life, false to every principle of honor, and false to the sacred obligation of his oath to support the Constitution. He had declared, again and again, that such a bank was unconstitutional, and yet he is denounced because he did not render himself infamous by an utter disregard of that instrument. The President had but one righteous course before him, and had he taken any other, it would not only have blasted his own character, but it would have fixed a blot on the history of his country to all future generations. How was he committed to sign a bill which he believed to be unconstitutional? What was the history of the Harrisburgh convention? —and it will be remembered that I do not live far from that celebrated place. How was that convention composed? It contained, I admit, many men of the highest responsibility, but in a political view, it was made up 'of all nations, and people, and kindred, and tongues.' 'Black spirits and white, blue spirits and grey,' all mingled their counsels there, to attain a single end—an available candidate for the Presidency. In this they succeeded; and the result was, to turn Mr. Van Buren out, and put themselves in. The infidel philosopher Volney, in his celebrated 'Ruins of Empires,' presents us with an imaginary picture of an assemblage, in which all the religious sects of the earth were collected together, and engaged in defending their respective creeds; and such a confusion ensued as might put to shame that at the tower of Babel. Just so would it have been at Harrisburg, if they had attempted to discuss any political principles. There was the abolitionist, ready to call down fire from Heaven to annihilate slavery from the face of the earth; and side by side with him sat the honorable and high-spirited Southern slaveholder. There was the anti-mason, whose motto was, 'destruction to all secret societies,' mingling in sweet communion with the bank director, who, with the fidelity of a vestal, had preserved the secrets of his prison-house. There was the consolidationist, holding, as my friend from Virginia does, that the mere power to buy a bill of exchange, vested in Congress the power to create an exchange bank; while hand and hand with him we might see the tight-laced strict constructionist, who will not allow the government power to do anything. In that one motley assembly were to be seen all colors and all shades of political opinion From absolute necessity, not from choice, they were compelled to abstain from making any public declaration of their prin

14*

ciples.   Now, if John Tyler had a right to infer anything from
the proceedings of that body, it was that he would be at liberty
to oppose a bank of the United States.   Certain leaders of that
convention were, it is true, in favor of a bank ; but, while the
convention, as a body, selected well known anti-bank men as
their chosen candidates for the Presidency and Vice-Presidency,
were those candidates to infer that they must change all their
opinions and become bank men ?   Sir, I deplored the death of
General Harrison, from the deep respect I entertained for his
name and character, however much I may have differed from
his political principles.   But General Harrison was, par excellence, an anti-bank man.   All his public declarations, up to the
very moment of the election, established this fact.   Nay, more,
we who have been denounced as the loco-foco, barn-burning,
agrarian portion of our party, because we assert the constitutional right to repeal a public corporation intrusted with the
sovereign power of managing the finances of the country, when
the public interest demands it, may claim him as a brother in
the faith ; for when a resolution was introduced in the House,
in 1819, to repeal at a single blow the charter of the late
bank, he voted in its favor ; and as to John Tyler, he has so
often declared himself against a Bank of the United States,
that there is no need I should specially refer any gentleman
to his opinion on that subject.   There they both were, holding
these opinions, and having only avowed them ; and it is utterly
impossible that the members of this convention should have been
ignorant of the fact.   The convention, then, made no avowal
of its principles, and what was the voice of the people ?   I can
truly say that, during the whole election campaign, I never saw
one single resolution in favor of a national bank, which had
been passed by any whig meeting in any part of the country.

     *   *   *   *   *   *   *

"I say that President Tyler could not have done otherwise
than veto that bill, if he wished to preserve his character as an

honest man. He must have done it from necessity, if not from choice. He could not have approved and signed that bill without exhibiting to the American people the disgraceful spectacle of a high public officer contradicting all the professions of his past life, and giving the lie to all his own often-avowed principles. A rumor exists, we have been told on this floor, that the veto was given against the unanimous opinion of the cabinet. And suppose it was, who is responsible to the people of the United States for conducting the government? Is it not the President? Undoubtedly he ought to consult the opinions of the cabinet; but if he and his cabinet cannot agree in sentiment, which is to yield—the cabinet or the President? Certainly, according to the theory of our government, it is the cabinet. I was glad to find in the official organ of the administration, such good old-fashioned democratic doctrine as I saw there a few days since. It is true I was not, to every extent, in favor of 'the mint;' but I would say, in behalf of the article to which I refer, that it is one of the best I have ever read, and one that would not disgrace the palmiest day of the democratic administration. If the President cannot agree with his cabinet, or if the cabinet cannot agree with the President, I do not say what ought to be the consquences. I have no feeling on the subject; it matters nothing to me who are in, and who are out of office.

"The senator from Kentucky tells us that he never said President Tyler ought to have resigned, but only that resignation was one of the alternatives before him. A President resign! A President who had been but three months in power resign his place! Why, sir, this is almost a moral impossibility, so deeply is the love of power rooted in the human breast. No President will ever think of doing any such thing. In the whole range of history, I recollect but two memorable instances of the kind; one was that of the Roman emperor Diocletian, and the other of the emperor Charles V. The Roman emperor, you know, went to raising cabbages, as Mr. Van Buren is now doing ; and Charles buried himself before he was dead—a very fit emblem of the condition of a President who should resign his office, that he might suffer a bill for the fiscal bank to become a law."

The happy conclusion of Mr. Buchanan's speech caused much merriment, and he resumed his seat amid a general laugh. Mr. Clay immediately rose and replied, and in opening, referred pleasantly to Mr. Buchanan's attempt at wit, and advised the senator from Pennsylvania, with his permission, that his appropriate province was logic or grave debate, rather than wit. Mr. Clay said, however, he trusted he would be excused if he should happen while up, to catch by contagion, somewhat of the same vein. Mr. Clay then made the following humorous speech, descriptive of a reported interview between some of the democratic members of Congress and President Tyler, convulsing, as he proceeded, the Senate with laughter :

"An honorable senator from New Hampshire (Mr. Woodbury) proposed, some days ago, a resolution of inquiry into certain disturbances which are said to have occurred at the presidential mansion on the night of the memorable 16th of August last. If any such proceedings did occur, they were certainly very wrong and highly culpable. The chief magistrate, whoever he may be, should be treated by every good citizen with all becoming respect, if not for his personal character, on account of the exalted office which he holds for and from the people ; and I will here say that I read with great pleasure the acts and resolutions of an early meeting, promptly held by the orderly and respectable citizens of this metropolis, in reference to, and in condemnation of, these disturbances. But, if the resolution had been adopted, I had intended to move for the appointment of a select committee, and that the honorable senator from New Hampshire himself should be placed at the head of it, with a majority of his friends, and will tell you why,

Mr. President. I did hear that about eight or nine o'clock, on the same night of the famous 16th of August, there was an irruption on the President's house, of the whole loco-foco party in Congress, and I did not know but that the alleged disorder might have grown out of, or had some connection with that fact. (A laugh.) I understand that the whole party were there. No spectacle I am sure could have been more supremely amusing and ridiculous. If I could have been in a position in which, without being seen, I could have witnessed that most extraordinary reunion, I should have had an enjoyment which no dramatic performance could possibly communicate. I think that I can now see the principal dramatis personæ who figured in the scene.— There stood the grave and distinguished senator from South Carolina."

Mr. Calhoun here rose, and earnestly insisted on explaining ; but Mr. Clay refused to be interrupted or to yield the floor.

Mr. Clay : "There I say, I can imagine stood the senator from South Carolina—tall, careworn, with furrowed brow, haggard, and intensely gazing, looking as if he were discussing the last and newest abstraction which sprung from metaphysician's brain, and muttering to himself, in half-uttered sounds : 'This is indeed a real crisis !' (Loud laughter.) Then there was the senator from Alabama (Mr. King) standing upright and gracefully, as if he were ready to settle in the most authoritative manner any question of order or of etiquette that might possibly arise between the high assembled parties on that new and unprecedented occasion. Not far off stood the honorable senators from Arkansas and from Missouri (Mr. Sévier and Mr. Benton) the latter looking at the senator from South Carolina, with an indignant curl on his lip and scorn in his eye, and pointing his finger with contempt towards that senator (Mr. Calhoun) whilst he said, or rather seemed to say : 'He call himself a statesman ! why, he has never even produced a decent humbug !'" (Shouts of laughter.)

Mr. Benton here interposed by saying that the senator from Missouri was not there.

Mr Clay: " I stand corrected ; I was only imagining what you would have said if you had been there. (Renewed laughter.) Then there stood the senator from Georgia (Mr. Cuthbert) conning over in his mind on what point he should make his next attack upon the senator from Kentucky. (Laughter.) On yonder ottoman reclined the other senator from Missouri on my left (Mr. Linn) indulging, with smiles on his face, in pleasing meditations on the rise, growth and future power of his new colony of Oregon. The honorable senator from Pennsylvania (Mr. Buchanan) I presume stood forward as spokesman for his whole party, and, although I cannot pretend to imitate his well known eloquence, I beg leave to make an humble essay towards what I presume to have been the kind of speech delivered by him on that August occasion :

" ' May it please your Excellency : A number of your present political friends, late your political opponents, in company with myself, have come to deposit at your excellency's feet the evidences of our loyalty and devotion ; and they have done me the honor to make me the organ of their sentiments and feelings. We are here more particularly to present to your excellency our_grateful and most cordial congratulations on your rescue of the country from a flagrant and alarming violation of the Constitution, by the creation of a bank of the United States ; and also our profound acknowledgments for the veto, by which you have illustrated the wisdom of your administration, and so greatly honored yourself. And we would dwell particularly on the unanswerable reasons and cogent arguments with which the notification of the act to the legislature has been accompanied. We had been, ourselves, struggling for days and weeks to arrest the passage of the bill, and to prevent the creation of the monster to which it gives birth. We have expended all our logic, exerted all our ability, employed all our eloquence ; but in spite of all our utmost efforts the

friends of your excellency in the Senate and House of Representatives proved too strong for us. And we have now come
most heartily to thank your excellency that you have accomplished for us that against your friends which we with our
most strenuous exertions were unable to achieve.' (Roars of
laughter.)

" I hope the senator will view with indulgence this effort to
represent him, although I am but too sensible how far it falls
short of the merits of the original. At all events he will feel
that there is not a greater error than was committed by the
stenographer of the 'Intelligencer' the other day, when he
put into my mouth a part of the honorable senator's speech.
(Laughter.) I hope the honorable senators in the other side
of the chamber will pardon me for having conceived it possible
that, amidst the popping of champagne, the intoxication of
their joy, the extasy of their glorification, they might have
been the parties who created a disturbance of which they never
could have been guilty had they waited for their 'sober second
thoughts.' (Laughter, loud and long.) I have no doubt the very
learned ex-Secretary of the Treasury, who conducted that department with such distinguished ability, and such happy results
to the country, and now has such a profound abhorrence of all
the taxes on tea and coffee, though, in his official reports, he so
distinctly recommended them, would if appointed chairman of
the committee, have conducted the investigation with that industry which so eminently distinguishes him, and would have
favored the Senate with a report, marked with all his accustomed precision and ability, and with the most perfect lucid
clearness."

When Mr. Clay had concluded, Mr. Buchanan rose and re-
joined in the following graceful and eloquent speech :

"The senator has informed me that I do not succeed in
attempts at wit, and in this he is, doubtless, correct. I am a

plain man, and speak right on that which I have to say. I think i can, with equal justice, return his compliment. If I do not succeed at wit, he as rarely succeeds in argument. Argument is as little his province as wit is mine. He is eloquent, as we all know, and sagacious, and besides, he is the very best drill-officer that ever disciplined any party ; but, in regard to sound logic, or what he denominates 'abstractions,' he is not very famous.

"The honorable senator has, with great power of humor, and much felicity of description, drawn for us a picture of the scene which he supposes to have been presented at the President's house on the ever memorable evening of the riot. It was a happy effort ; but unfortunately, it was but a fancy-sketch, at least, or as far as I am concerned. I was not there at all upon the occasion. But, I ask, what scenes were enacted on that eventful night at this end of the avenue ? The senator would have no cause to complain, if I should attempt, in humble imitation of him, to present a picture, true to the life, of the proceedings of himself and his friends amidst the dark and lowering clouds of that never-to-be-forgotten night, a caucus assembled in one of the apartments of this gloomy building, and sat in melancholy conclave, deploring the unhappy fate of the whig party. Some rose and advocated vengeance ; 'their voice was still for war.' Others, more moderate, sought to repress the ardent zeal of their fiery compatriots, and advised to peace and prudence. It was finally concluded that, instead of making open war upon Captain Tyler, they should resort to stratagem, and, in the elegant language of one of their number, that they should endeavor 'to head' him. The question was earnestly debated by what means they could best accomplish this purpose, and it was resolved to try the effect of the 'fiscality' now before us. Unfortunately for the success of the scheme, "Captain Tyler' was forewarned and forearmed, by means of a private and confidential letter, addressed by mistake to a Virginia Coffee-House. It is by means like this, that 'enterprises of great pith and moment' often fail. But so desperately intent are the whig party still on the creation of a bank, that one of my friends on this side of the house told me that a bank they would have, though its exchanges should be made in bacon hams, and its currency be small potatoes. (A laugh.)

"The senator has often lauded to the very echo the Macedonian phalanx, as he terms them, in the other house, and proposed their example as worthy of our imitation. Now, sir, I should never have made any reference upon this floor to the proceedings in that house (which is contrary to all parliamentary rule), had I not been driven to it by the previous remarks of the senator. Before heaven, I believe that the conduct of that phalanx, of which the senator seems so proud, forebodes the destruction of the liberties of this country, unless the sovereign people should frown it down forever. If the representatives of fifty thousand freemen can be deprived of the right of speech by arbitrary rules prescribed by a tyrannical majority, and the people of the United States should tamely submit to such a violation of their liberties in the persons of their representatives, then they will deserve to be slaves. Let it once be fully known throughout the country that those whom the people have selected to represent their sentiments and their interests in the other branch of Congress have been prevented from expressing their opinions, and have even been denied the poor privilege of recording their votes on questions of the last importance ; and then, if their constituents should silently acquiesce in this usurpation, we shall be subjected to the same tyranny with that imposed upon France by Napoleon, when he organized his silent Legislative Council. I did not believe that the House of Representatives had been reduced to any such condition, until I read the able letter upon the subject, of a member from South Carolina (Mr. Rhett). With that letter in my hand, I would go into any congressional district of this Union, and, humble as I am, I should feel confident of obtaining the unanimous voice of the people in condemnation of such proceedings as it describes. This question soars far above all mere party distinctions. It is one upon the decision of which depends the efficient existence of our representative republican form of government.

"The present bill to establish fiscal corporation was hurried through the House with the celerity, and so far as the democracy was concerned, with the silence of despotism. No democrat had an opportunity of raising his voice against it. Under the new rules in existence there, the majority had predetermined that it should pass that body within two days from the commencement of the discussion. At first, indeed, the determination was, that it should pass the first day ; but this was too great an outrage, and the mover was graciously pleased to extend the time one day longer. Whilst the bill was in Committee of the Whole, it so happened that in the struggle for the floor, no democratic member succeeded in obtaining it ; and at the destined hour of four in the afternoon of the second day, the committee rose and all further debate was arrested by the previous question. The voice of that great party in this country, to which I am proud to belong, was, therefore, never heard through any of their representatives in the House against this odious measure. Not even one brief hour, the limit prescribed by the majority to each speaker, was granted to any democratic member.

"But the democracy of the land are not only deprived of the liberty of speech in the persons of their representatives, but these representatives are even denied the right of recording their vote on the ayes and noes, for or against any amendment to any bill, unless the majority please to grant them this permission. Under the rule, the ayes and noes cannot be demanded in Committee of the Whole. Every amendment offered there, which is disagreeable to the majority, is voted down without any responsibility of the representative to his constituents, because the names of the voters are not recorded on the journal; and it is impossible to renew any such amendment after the bill has been reported to the House, because at that very instant the gag of the previous question is applied, which cuts off all debate and every amendment not sanctioned by the committee. And this is the bright, the glorious example which the senator from Kentucky has so often proposed for the imitation of the Senate of the United States! But enough of this.

"The senator, with his usual tact and skill, has seized upon a playful remark of mine in reply to my friend from Virginia (Mr. Archer), over the way, that, although I did not know at present what might be the opinions of Mr. Tyler, yet, I hoped this might not long be the case. Upon this feeble foundation, the senator, with that commanding eloquence which is ever ready, has indulged himself in declaring that John Tyler would be guilty of the most atrocious treason, should he be willing to desert his own party, and ally himself with the democracy; and in that event, he has expressed the confident belief that we would be too honorable to receive him into our ranks. Now, sir, if the avowed opinions of Mr. Tyler's whole life be, as they are, in diametrical opposition to those of the senator, what course is he to pursue? Must he abandon his long cherished principles merely because they are identical with those of the democratic party? And is he to be denounced as a traitor for this mere coincidence of opinion? This would, indeed, be unjust vengeance. No man of the democratic party, to my knowledge, either expects or desires office or power at his hands. I will tell the honorable senator, however, what we do intend, although we have studiously kept ourselves aloof from all interference with the President, and from every attempt to influence his conduct. So far as his measures shall be in conformity with our principles, we shall give them a cordial and zealous support. Should the senator, in utter violation, as we believe, of the Constitution, again attempt to establish a National Bank, with the privilege of spreading its branches throughout the Union, and thus, by concentrating the money power, to corrupt the land ; and should the President again and again conscientiously veto such a dangerous measure, we shall be ever ready to yield him our support in a cause so righteous. Whatever the senator may think of us, we shall cheer him on in the path of duty with, ' Well done, good and faithful servant, you have redeemed your country from an institution in deadly hostility both to the spirit and letter of our form of government ; and will the whigs charge him with treason for this ? The idea of falsehood is always involved in that of treason, and they never can succeed in branding a man as a traitor for adhering to the well-known principles of his whole life.

"The senator expects that President Tyler will approve this bill. If he does, he will then render himself forever infamous. His name will be the scorn and ridicule of one party, and the contempt of the other. No, he will never do it ; destiny has left him but one course to pursue as an honest man, and that is to go straight ahead, and fearlessly perform his duty. He cannot now turn back without disgrace and dishonor. If he shall pursue this course, a vast majority of the American people of all political parties will award to him the merit of having sacrificed all his personal feelings, and encountered the frowns of many of his ancient friends, from a sacred regard to the Constitution and welfare of his country. This will be his reward. He will then stand forever in a niche of the temple of fame, associated with those pure and exalted patriots which have sacrificed all selfish considerations to save the country.

"As for our party, we want neither patronage nor power, from John Tyler. We shall give him a liberal and manly support whenever we believe he deserves it. Let all the offices and all the honors be given, with our hearty consent, to those who elected him.

"When I rose in reply, I had intended to reciprocate the kindness of the senator, and make a speech to the whig caucus for him, as he has done to the President for me. It was my purpose to have presented to the Senate a faint imitation of what I conjecture he must have said on that night of sorrow and gloom. I think I know the senator well enough to imagine just such a speech as he must have made upon that occasion. But I forbear it ; it must have been both eloquent and efficient ; for I believe, in my soul, that no other drill-officer in existence could have reanimated his dispirited and scattered forces, and again brought them up to the charge in solid column to sustain such a thing as this 'fiscal corporation.' "

The fiscal corporation passed both houses of Congress but unfortunately for the success of Mr. Clay's policy it shared the same fate with the executive as the first bill.

At this session the celebrated case of Alexander McLeod came before Congress, and was discussed with great spirit and animation. The circumstances are generally known, but we were briefly recapitulate them. In 1837 a rebellion or revolution was commenced in Canada having for its object a separation of that country from England. An American vessel, the Caroline, had been accused of carrying provisions and arms to the insurgents. This report had excited a determination on the part of the English officers to destroy it, but they did not choose to wait if perchance they might detect the Caroline on their territory in unlawful trade, but resolved to attack and destroy her, upon American soil. One Captain Drew of the British army it appears gave notice, " that upon a certain night he wanted fifty or sixty desperate fellows to follow him to the devil." At all events while the steamer Caroline was lying at her dock on the American shore she was boarded by a gang of outlaws who killed one man and then towing the steamer out in the stream sent her over Niagara Falls. Some time after this, one Alexander McLeod came in the State of New York and boasted that he had been one of the number engaged in the murder on board the Caroline and in the destruction of the ves sel. He was arrested upon the charge of murder, and while in custody therefor, a demand was made upon our government by England for him. Mr. B. took ground against yielding to this demand, contending that if the man were actually guilty he should be tried and condemned according to the laws of the State where the crime was committed. After concluding this portion of a speech of great power upon this case, he ended·by an admirable *résumé* of the law of nations as bearing upon the question as follows :

"I shall now offer a few remarks on the question of public law involved in this case, and then close what I have to say. I sincerely believe the administration of Mr. Van Buren was perfectly correct on this doctrine, as laid down by Mr. Forsyth. If I had found any authority to induce me to entertain a doubt on that point, I would refer to it most freely. I now undertake to say that the only circumstance which has produced confusion and doubts in the minds of well informed men on this subject is, that they do not make the proper distinction between a state of national war and national peace. If a nation be at war, the command of the sovereign power to invade the territory of its enemy, and do battle there against any hostile force, always justifies the troops thus engaged.

"When any of the invaders are seized, they are considered as prisoners of war, and as having done nothing, but what the laws of war justified them in doing. In such a case they can never be held to answer, criminally in the courts of the invaded country. That is clear. The invasion of an enemy's territory is one of the rights of war, and, in all its necessary consequences, is justified by the laws of war. But there are offences committed even in open war, which the express command of the offender's sovereign will not shield from exemplary punishment. I will give, gentlemen, an example. A spy will be hung, if caught, even though he acted under the express command of his sovereign. We might cite the case of the unfortunate Major Andre. He was arrested on his return from an interview with Arnold, and his life being in danger, the British commander (Sir Henry Clinton I believe) made an effort to save him, by taking upon himself the responsibility of the act. But although he had crossed our lines whilst the two nations were in a state of open and flagrant war, in obedience to instructions from his commander in chief, yet Washington, notwithstanding, rightfully hung him as a spy.

"Now, let me tell whoever shall answer me (if, indeed any gentleman will condescend to notice what I have said, for it seems, we on this side of the House, are to do all the speaking, and they all the voting), that whilst all the modern authorities concur in declaring that the law of nations protects individuals when obeying the orders of their sovereign, during a state of open and flagrant war, whether it has been solemnly declared or not, and whether it be general or partial, yet these authorities proceed no farther. But, to decide correctly on the application of this principle in the case before us, we must recollect that the two belligerents here were England on the one hand and her insurgent subjects on the other, and that the United States were a neutral power in perfect peace with England. But what is the rule in regard to nations at peace with each other? This is the question. As between such nations, does the command of an inferior officer of the one, to individuals to violate the sovereignty of the other, and commit murder and arson, if afterwards recognized by the supreme authority, prevent the nation whose laws have been outraged from punishing the offenders? Under such circumstances, what is the law of nations? The doctrine is laid down in Vattel, an author admitted to be of the highest authority on questions of international law ; and the very question 'totidem verbis' which arises in this case, is in his book stated and decided. He admits that the lawful commands of a legitimate government, whether to its troops or other citizens, protects them from individual responsibility for hostile acts done in obedience to such commands, whilst in a state of open war.   In such a case, a prisoner of war is never to be subjected to the criminal jurisdiction of the country within which he has been arrested.   But what is the law of nations in regard to criminal offences committed by the citizens or subjects of one power, with the sovereignty of and jurisdiction of another, they being at peace with each other, even if these criminal acts should be recognized and justified by the offender's sovereign?   This is the case of capture and destruction of the Caroline.   The subject is treated of by Vattel, under the head ' of the concern a nation may have in the actions of her citizens,' book 6, chap. ii., page 161.   I shall read sections 73, 74 and 75.

"'However, as it is impossible,' says the author, 'for the best regulated state, or for the most vigilant and absolute sovereign, to model at his pleasure all the actions of his subjects, and to confine them on every occasion to the most exact obedience, it would be unjust to impute to the nation or the sovereign every fault committed by the citizens. We ought not, then, to say in general that we have received an injury from a nation, because we have received it from one of its members.'

"'But if a nation or its chief approves and ratifies the act of the individual, it then becomes a public concern, and the injured party is then to consider the nation as the real author of the injury, of which the citizen was perhaps only the instrument.'

"'If the offended state has in her power the individual who has done the injury, she may without scruple, bring him to justice and punish him.   If he has escaped, and returned to his own country, she ought to apply to his sovereign to have justice done in the case.'

"Can any thing in the world be clearer?   The author puts the case distinctly.   The nation injured ought not to impute to the sovereign of a friendly nation the acts of its individual citizens, but if such friendly sovereign shall recognize the act as his own, it then becomes a national concern. But does such a recognition wash away the guilt of the offender, and release him from the punishment due to his offence under the jurisdiction of the country whose laws he has violated? Let Vattel answer this question. He says: 'If the offended state has in her power the individual who has done the injury, she may, without scruple, bring him to justice and punish him.' There is the direct, plain and palpable authority; and, here permit me to add, that I think I can prove, that according to sound reason, the principle is correct, and that the question would now be so decided by our courts, even if the law of nations had been silent on the subject. This not only is, but ought to be, the principle of public law.

"Mr. Webster, in his letter to Mr. Cox, of the 24th of April, tells the British minister that the line of frontier which separates the United States from her Britannic Majesty's North American Provinces 'is long enough to divide the whole of Europe into halves.'

"This is true enough. Now by admitting the doctrine of Vattel to be incorrect and unfounded, on what consequences are we forced? I beg senators to consider this question. The line which separates us from the British Provinces is a line long enough to divide Europe into halves. Heaven knows I have no desire to see a rebellion in Canada, or the Canadian Provinces annexed to the United States; but no event in futurity is more certain than that those provinces are destined to be ultimately separated from the British Empire. Let a civil war come, and 'et every McNab who shall then have any command in the British possessions along this long line be permitted to send a military expedition into the territory of the United States, whenever he shall believe or pretend that it will aid in defending the royal authority against those who are resisting it, and war between Great Britain and the United States becomes

15

inevitable. A British subject marauding under the orders of his superior officer on this side of the line, is seized in the very act. Well, what is to be done? I suppose we are to wait until we can ascertain whether his government chooses to recognize his hostile or criminal act, before we can inflict the punishment which he deserves for violating our laws. If it should recognize his act, the jail door is immediately to be thrown open, the offender, it may be murderer, takes his flight to Canada, and we must settle the question with the British government. Such is the doctrine advanced by the British government and our Secretary of State. This principle would, as I say, lead us inevitably into war with that power. What can be done in a state of war? In that case, the laws of war provide that persons invading our territory who are captured, shall be considered and treated as prisoners of war. But while the two countries continued at peace, a man taken in the flagrant act of invasion and violence, cannot be made a prisoner of war. McLeod, however, is not to be treated on this principle, and punished under our laws if he be guilty, lest we should offend the majesty of England. The laws of New York are to be nullified, and the murderer is to run at large.

" But if the principle laid down by Vattel be sound and true, all difficulty at once vanishes. If such an offender be caught in the perpetration of a criminal act, he is then punished for his crime. Let him be tried for it at least, and then, if there are any mitigating circumstances in his case, for the sake of good neighborhood, let him escape. There will then be no danger of war from this cause. Let me suppose a case. Suppose Colonel Allen McNab should take it into his head that there exists in the United States a conspiracy against the British government, and should believe that he could unravel the whole plot by seizing on the United States mail in its passage from New York to Buffalo—he places himself at the head of a party, comes over the line, and seizes and robs the mail ; but in the act he is overpowered and arrested, and he is indicted before a criminal court of the United States. Will it be maintained, if the British government should say, We recognize the act of McNab in robbing your mail, as we have already recognized that of his burning your steamboat and killing your citizens, that Mr. Webster would be justified in directing a nolle prosequi to be entered in his favor, and thus suffer him to go free?

"I do not say that the British government would act in this manner, but I put the case as a fair illustration of the argument. There was one case in which something very like this might have happened, and it was even thought probable that it would happen. It was reported that an expedition had been planned to seize the person of McLeod, and to carry him off to Canada; and I believe that a very distinguished and a gallant general in the United States service (Gen. Scott)—an officer for whom, in common with his fellow-citizens, I cherish the highest respect and regard—went, in company with the Attorney General, to Lockport; and it was conjectured that he had received orders to hold McLeod and defend the Lockport jail against any incursion of Sir Allen McNab or any other person.

"Suppose now that such an expedition had been set on foot, that it had succeeded, and that McLeod had been seized and carried off in triumph, the two nations being still in profound peace. The rescue of a prisoner is high criminal offence. What would have been done with McNab if he had voluntarily come within our jurisdiction and been arrested? If he could be indicted, and tried, and punished before the British government should have time to recognize his act—very well. But if not, then, at the moment of such recognition, he would be no longer responsible, and must forthwith be set free. The principle of Vattel rightly understood, absolutely secures the territorial sovereignty of nations in time of peace by permitting them to punish all invasions of it in their own criminal courts, and his doctrine is eminently calculated to preserve peace among all nations. War has its own laws, which are never to be extended to the intercourse between nations at peace.

" The principle assumed in Mr. Fox's letter is well calculated for the benefit of powerful nations against their weaker neighbors. (But in saying this I do no not mean to admit that we are a weak nation in comparison with England. We do not, indeed, wish to go to war with her, yet I am confident in the belief that whatever we might suffer during the early period of such a contest would be amply compensated by our success before we reached the end of it.) But let me present an example :

" Let us suppose that the empire of Russia has by her side a conterminous nation, which is comparatively weak. A Russian colonel, during the season of profound peace, passes over the boundary, and commits some criminal act against the citizens of the weaker nation. They succeed, however, in seizing his person, and are about to punish him according to the provisions of their own laws. But immediately the Russian double-headed black eagle makes its appearance, a Russian officer says to the authorities of the weaker nation, ' stop, take off your hands ; you shall not vindicate your laws and sovereignty. We assume this man's crime as a national act.' What is the consequence ? The rule for which Britain contends will in this case compel the injured nation, though the weaker, to declare war in the first instance against her stronger neighbor. But she will not do it ; she will not become the actor, from the consciousness of her weakness and the instinct of self-preservation. This principle, if established, will enable the strong to insult the weak with impunity. But take the principle as laid down by Vattel. The weaker nation defends the majesty of her own laws by punishing the Russian subject who had violated them ; and, if war is to ensue, Russia must assume the responsibility of declaring it, in the face of the world, and in an unjust cause, against the nation whom she has injured. It is said that one great purpose of the laws of nations is to protect the weak against the strong, and never was this tendency more happily illustrated than by this very principle of Vattel for which I am contending.

" I, therefore, believe that the Secretary of State was as far wrong in his view of international law as in his haste to appease the British government, in the face of a direct threat, by his instructions to Mr. Crittenden. The communication of these instructions to that government, we know, had the desired effect. They went out immediately to England, and no sooner were they known on that side of the water than in a moment all was calm and tranquil. The storm portending war passed away, and tranquil peace once more returned and smiled over the scene. Sir, the British government must have been hard-hearted, indeed, if a perusal of these instructions did not soften them, and afford them the most ample satisfaction. This amiable temper will never even be ruffled in the slightest degree by the perusal of Mr. Webster's letter to Mr. Fox, written six weeks afterwards. The matter had all been virtually ended before its date.

" In the views I have now expressed I may be wrong ; but as an American senator, without any feeling on my part, but such as I think every American senator ought to cherish, I am constrained to say, that I cannot approve of the course pursued by the Secretary of State in this matter ; while at the same time, I hope and trust that no other occasion may arise to demand from me a similar criticism on the official conduct of that gentleman. "

The difficulty between our government and England on this question, which threatened a rupture between the two countries, was happily terminated in the acquittal of MacLeod, by the court at Lockport before which he was tried. This excited and important session of Congress closed on the 13th of September, 1841.

CHAPTER XVIII.

Second Session of the Twenty-seventh Congress—The Veto Power—Mr. Buchanan's Speech in Reply to Mr. Clay—The Board of Exchequer—Mr. Buchanan's Speech—Mr. Clay's Retirement from the Senate—Third Session of the Twenty-seventh Congress—The Webster Treaty.

NOT three months elapsed after the adjournment of the extra session of Congress, before the first regular session of the twenty-seventh Congress convened, on the 6th of December, 1841. Mr. Clay introduced some resolutions to restrict the veto power. Mr. Buchanan did not agree with Mr. C. that the presidential prerogative of a veto upon bills passed by Congress, was a dangerous power granted to the executive. On the contrary, he believed that the provision in the Constitution, making it the duty of the President to return all bills he did not approve to Congress with his objections, was a safeguard against hasty and inconsiderate legislation, and that the wise framers of our organic law had inserted it from the most patriotic considerations of the public good. On the 2d of February, 1842, Mr. Buchanan made an elaborate reply to Mr. Clay upon his proposition, reviewing our whole system of government, and showing the relations that existed between its parts. This logical and profound speech embraces valuable principles of political economy, and shows with what attention Mr. Buchanan has studied the fundamental laws and maxims of civil government. After showing that the veto power bore no analogy to tyrannical or despotic power, he said :

" This system of self-imposed restraints is a necessary element of our social condition. Every wise and virtuous man adopts the resolutions by which he regulates his conduct, for the purpose of counteracting the evil propensities of his nature, and preventing him from yielding under the impulses of sudden and strong temptation. Is such a man the less free, the less independent because he choses to submit to these self-imposed restraints? In like manner, is the majority of the people less free and less independent because it has chosen to impose constitutional restrictions upon itself and its representatives? Is this any abridgement of popular liberty? The true philosophy of republican government, as the history of the world has demonstrated, consists in the establishment of such counteracting powers—powers always created by the people themselves—as shall render it morally certain that no law can be passed by their servants which shall not be in accordance with their will, and calculated to promote their good.

"It is for this reason that a Senate has been established in every State of the Union to control the House of Representatives; and I presume there is now scarcely an individual in the country who is not convinced of its necessity. Fifty years ago, opinions were much divided upon this subject, and nothing but experience has settled the question. In France, the National Assembly, although they retained the king, rejected a senate as aristocratic, and our own Franklin was opposed to it. He thought that the popular branch was alone necessary to reflect the will of the people, and that a senate would be but a mere encumbrance. His influence prevailed in the convention which formed the first Constitution for Pennsylvania, and we had no senate. The doctor's argument against it was contained in one of his homely but striking illustrations : 'Why,' said he, 'will you place a horse in front of a cart to draw it forward, and another behind to pull it back ?' Experience, which is the wisest teacher, has demonstrated the fallacy of this and all other similar arguments ; and public opinion is now unanimous on the subject. Where is the man who does not now feel that the control of a senate is necessary to restrain and modify the action of the popular branch ?

"All the beauty and harmony and order of the universe arise from counteracting influences. When its great author, in the beginning, gave the planets their projective impulse, they would have rushed in a straight line through the realms of boundless space, had he not restrained them within their prescribed orbits by the counteracting influence of gravitation. All the valuable inventions in mechanics consist in blending simple powers together so as to restrain and regulate the action of each other. Restraint—restraint—not that imposed by arbitrary and irresponsible power, but by the people themselves, in their own written constitutions, is the great law which has rendered democratic representative government so successful in these latter times. The best security which the people can have against abuses of trust by their public servants, is to ordain that it shall be the duty of one class of them to watch and restrain another. Sir, this federal government, in its legislative attributes, is nothing but a system of restraints from beginning to end. In order to enact any bill into a law, it must be passed by the representatives of the people in the House, and also by the representatives of the sovereign States in the Senate, where, as I have observed before, it may be defeated by senators from States containing but one-fourth of the population of the country. After it has undergone these two ordeals, it must yet be subjected to that of the executive, as the tribune of the whole people, for his approbation. If he should exercise his veto power, it cannot become a law unless it be passed by a majority of two-thirds of both houses. These are the mutual restraints which the people have imposed on their public servants, to preserve their own rights and those of the States from rash, hasty and impolitic legislation. No treaty with a foreign power can be binding upon the people of this country unless it shall receive the assent of the President and two-thirds of the Senate, and this is the restraint which the people have imposed on the treaty making power."

After referring to instances where the rights of the States might be broken down if the veto power were abolished, he continued :

"But let me suppose another case of a much more dangerous character. In the southern States, which compose the weaker portion of the Union, a species of property exists which is now attracting the attention of the whole civilized world. These States never would have become parties to the Union, had not their rights in this property been secured by the federal Constitution. Foreign and domestic fanatics—some from the belief that they are doing God's service, and others from a desire to divide and destroy this glorious Republic—have conspired to emancipate the southern slaves. On this question, the people of the South, beyond the limits of their own States, stand alone and unsupported by any power on earth, except that of the northern democracy. These fanatical philanthropists are now conducting a crusade over the whole world, and are endeavoring to concentrate the public opinion of all mankind against the right of property. Suppose they should ever influence a majority in both Houses of Congress to pass a law, not to abolish this property—for that would be too palpable a violation of the Constitution—but to render it of no value, under the letter, but against the spirit, of some of the powers granted ; will any lover of his country say that the President ought not to possess the power of arresting such an act by his veto, until the solemn decision of the people should be known on this question, involving the life or death of the Union ? We, sir, of the non-slaveholding States, entered the Union upon the express condition that this property should be protected. Whatever may be our own private opinions in regard to slavery in

15*

the abstract, ought we to hazard all the blessings of our free institutions—our Union and our strength—in such a crusade against our brethren of the South ? Ought we to jeopard every political right we hold dear for the sake of enabling these fanatics to invade southern rights, and render that fair portion of our common inheritance a scene of servile war, rapine and murder ? Shall we apply the torch to the magnificent temple of human liberty which our forefathers reared at the price of their blood and treasure, and permit all we hold dear to perish in the conflagration ? I trust not.

"It is possible, that at some future day, the majority in Congress may attempt, by indirect means, to emancipate the slaves of the South. There is no knowing through what channel the ever-active spirit of fanaticism may seek to accomplish its object. The attempt may be made through the taxing power, or some other express power granted by the Constitution. God only knows how it may be made. It is hard to say what means fanaticism may not adopt to accomplish its purpose. Do we feel so secure, in this hour of peril from abroad and peril at home, as to be willing to prostrate any of the barriers which the Constitution has reared against hasty and dangerous legislation ? No, sir, never was the value of the veto power more manifest than at the present moment. For the weaker portion of the Union, whose constitutional rights are now assailed with such violence, to think of abandoning this safeguard, would be almost suicidal. It is my solemn conviction, that there never was a wiser or more beautiful adaptation of theory to practice in any government than that which requires a majority of two-thirds in both houses of Congress to pass an act returned by the President with his objections, under all the high responsibilities which he owes to his country.

" Sir, ours is a glorious Constitution. Let us venerate it ; let us stand by it as the work of great and good men, unsurpassed in the history of any age or nation. Let us not assail it rashly with our invading hands, but honor it as the fountain of our prosperity and power. Let us protect it as the only system of government which could have rendered us what we are in half a century, and enable us to take the front rank among the nations of the earth. In my opinion, it is the only form of government which can preserve the blessings of liberty and prosperity to the people, and at the same time secure the rights and sovereignty of the States. Sir, the great mass of the people are unwilling that it shall be changed, although the senator from Kentucky, to whom I cannot, and will not, attribute any but patriotic motives, has brought himself to believe that a change is necessary, especially in the veto power, I must differ from him entirely, convinced that his opinions on this subject are based upon fallacious theories of the nature of our institutions. This view of his opinions is strengthened by his declarations the other day as to the illimitable rights of the majority in Congress. On that point, he differs essentially from the framers of the Constitution. They believed that the people of the different States had rights which might be violated by such a majority, and the veto power was one of the modes which they devised for preventing these rights from being invaded."

Mr. Buchanan then noticed the argument of Mr. Clay, that the veto power gave the President undue influence over Congress, and by that means brought many supporters to his administration. Mr. Buchanan answered this objection, by asking how many friends Mr. Tyler had obtained by his vetoes, and how much power he had secured by the entire patronage of the administration. He closed his speech showing how trifling was the danger of the abuse of the veto power, compared with the evils certain to follow its abolishment, and expressed his hope that it might be perpetual. This important feature of our Constitution certainly never had a more powerful defence than Mr. Buchanan gave it, and it will, probably, be a long time before it will require another vindication.

After the disastrous failures of the "Fiscal Bank" and the "Fiscal Corporation," Mr. Tyler himself recommended a scheme for managing the financial business of the government, to be called "A Board of Exchequer." The plan was somewhat different from that of a National Bank, but it embraced the principle which the democracy had always contended against, that of using the people's money as capital upon which to make bank issues by the government, and, of course, it met with their determined hostility. Indeed, it seemed to be forsaken by all. It never was even called up for consideration in the House. In the Senate it was referred to the Committee of Finance, where it duly expired. Mr. Buchanan, however, made a speech upon it on a motion to refer the subject to a select committee. Many of the arguments are so similar to those which he used in former bills of the same kind, most of which we have already given, that it is unnecessary to repeat them.

During this session Mr. Clay presented his resignation, and retired from Congress. He delivered a valedictory of much feeling and great eloquence, and sought in the shades of private life that retirement, which he had so long desired. A combination of circumstances had defeated all his leading measures, and he had been taunted with trying to be a dictator, because of the energy and perseverance he had exhibited in endeavoring to carry them out. "That my nature is warm," said Mr. Clay, "my temper ardent, my disposition in the public service enthusiastic, I am ready to own. But those who suppose they have seen any proof of dictation in my conduct, have only mistaken that ardor for what I at least supposed to be patriotic exertions for fulfilling the wishes by which I hold this seat : they having mistaken the one for the other." Mr. Clay had, however, at least one consolation : if Mr. Tyler obtained the power of the government, he retained the affections of the great whig party, and died in its embrace ! No one at this day will be likely to accuse Mr. Clay of dictation. The charge was the result of temporary party asperities, and never received any support from Mr. Buchanan, who always regarded Mr. Clay as a man of the most earnest and sincere patriotism. If he made mistakes upon some public questions, it was but what all men in this fallible world are liable to do. At all events, his heart was always for his country, and upon questions now at issue he assumed a stand that placed himself and Mr. Buchanan on the same platform, nobly battling against sectional strife and disunion.

Mr. Buchanan was uncommonly active at this session in his participation in public questions, yet we are only enabled to refer to his most prominent speeches. The reader may judge of the attention he gave to the public service, by the fact that he voted or addressed the Senate more than one hundred and seventy different times. It was a long, arduous and trying session, of nearly nine months' duration.

The third and last session of the twenty-seventh Congress convened on the 5th of December, 1842. There were no bills of great national importance brought before it, but an interesting debate is incorporated in the proceedings of this Congress, which took place in executive session before the adjournment on the 30th of August previous, upon the British treaty negotiated by Mr. Webster and Lord Ashburton, in settlement of our Northeast boundary line. It was believed by many persons, and is still so regarded by some, that Mr. Webster made too great concessions to the demands of England in the settlement of that question. Indeed if any person will look at a map upon which is marked the boundary as designated by the treaty of 1783, and that settled upon by the Webster treaty, he will be struck with the valuable advantages England has derived from the latter. She now has the unobstructed right of the valley of the St. John's River, and a military road directly through it from the province of New Brunswick to Quebec. It may be said that the territory is mostly sterile and not worth contending for, but if it really belonged to us our rights are never so valueless as to be given up upon demand, no matter of how little importance in an intrinsic point of view they may be. Mr Buchanan made a long and well considered speech upon the treaty, taking grounds against its ratification in the form in which it was presented to the Senate.

Amongst the objections which he urged against the treaty, was that it did not settle other matters of dispute then existing between England and our government, indeed, the absence of a firm declaration of our rights, Mr. Buchanan con tended would embarrass future negotiations, and particularly any that might become necessary for the settlement of our north-west boundary. The twenty-seventh Congress expired by constitutional limitation, on the 3d of March, 1843, after three exciting, important, but to the party that had rolled on a whirlwind into power, very unsatisfactory sessions.

CHAPTER XIX.

The Twenty-Eighth Congress—Territorial Government in Oregon—Annexation of Texas —Election of James K. Polk.

THE twenty-eighth Congress, the last under Mr. Tyler's administration, convened at its first session on the 4th of December, 1843.   The most important subjects of discussion were the organization of a territorial government for Oregon, and the annexation of Texas.   Mr. Buchanan took an early and decided stand in favor of extending to the far-off settlements on the Pacific, all the advantages which our laws could furnish.

In his speech on this subject, he takes the following prophetic and brilliant survey of the destiny of this country :

The senator from New Jersey (Mr. Miller) believes that a hundred years must roll around before the valley of the Mississippi will have a population equal in density to that of some of the older States of the Union ; and for fifty years, at least, our people should not pass beyond their present limits.   And in this connection he has introduced the Texas question.   In regard to that question, all I have now to say is, 'that sufficient unto the day is the evil thereof.'   I have no opinion to express at this time on the subject.   But this I believe : Providence has given to the American people a great and glorious mission to perform, even that of extending the blessings of Christianity and civil and religious liberty over the whole North American continent.   Within less than fifty years from this moment, there will exist one hundred millions of free Americans between the Atlantic and the Pacific oceans.   This will be a glorious specta-

cle to behold ; the distant contemplation of it warms and ex-
pands the bosom.   The honorable senator seems to suppose
that it is impossible to love our country with the same ardor
when its limits are so widely extended.   I cannot agree with
him in this opinion.   I believe an American citizen will, if possible, more ardently love his country, and be more proud of its
power and glory, when it shall be stretched out from sea to sea,
than when it was confined to a narrow strip between the Atlantic
and the Alleghanies.   The Almighty has implanted in the very
nature of our people that spirit of progress, and that desire to
roam abroad, and seek new homes, and new fields of enterprise,
which characterises them above all other nations, ancient or
modern, which have ever existed.   This spirit cannot be repress-
ed.   It is idle to talk of it.   You might as well attempt to
arrest the stars in their courses through heaven.   The same
Divine power has given impulse to both.   What, sir ! prevent
the American people from crossing the Rocky Mountains.   You
might as well command Niagara not to flow.   We must fulfill
our destiny.   The question presented by the senator from New
Jersey is, whether we shall vainly attempt to interpose obstacles to our own progress, and passively yield up the exercise of
our rights beyond the mountains, on the consideration that it is
impolitic for us ever to colonize Oregon.   To such a question
I shall give no answer.   But, says he, it would be expensive to
the treasury to extend to Oregon a territorial government.   No
matter what may be the expense, the thing will eventually be
done ; and it cannot be prevented, though it may be delayed
for a season."

Mr. Buchanan was one of the earliest, most consistent, and
steady advocates of the annexation of Texas, and in his
speech defending the policy of this act, he took a survey of
the varied interests upon which it would have an influence,
which probably does more to give his mind the stamp of enlarged statesmanship, than any other speech he ever delivered.

If anything were wanting to show that his remarks exhibited that profound knowledge of human affairs which enables great minds to grasp the future with all the confidence of reality, it is that time has affixed the seal of confirmation to their correctness. In opening his speech upon this important subject, he said:

"Mr. President: The present is a question of transcendent importance. For weal or for woe—for good or for evil, it is more momentous than any question which has been before the Senate since my connection with public affairs. To confine the consequences of our decision to the present generation would be to take a narrow and contracted view of the subject. The life of a great nation is not to be numbered by the few and fleeting years which limit the period of man's existence. The life of such a nation must be counted by centuries and not by years! 'Nations unborn and ages yet behind' will be deeply affected in their moral, political, and social relations, by the final determination of this question. Shall Texas become a part of our glorious confederacy; shall she be bone of our bone and flesh of our flesh; or shall she become our dangerous and hostile rival? Shall our future history and that of hers diverge more and more from the present point, and exhibit those mutual jealousies and wars, which, according to the history of the world, have ever been the misfortune of neighboring and rival nations; or shall their history be blended together in peace and harmony? These are the alternatives between which we must decide. I do not mean, by these remarks, merely to refer to the vote of the Senate, which will be recorded to-day upon the treaty; but to that ultimate and final decision of the question, which must be made within a brief period." * * * * *

Mr. Buchanan went fully into all the questions bearing on the policy of annexation. He observed that Texas would be an important security and advantage to our southwestern frontier; that England would be enabled to make with her commercial treaties which would injure the general welfare of the Union, while her annexation to us would greatly increase our internal commerce, extend the market for our domestic manufactures, and preserve to the United States one of the finest cotton-growing countries of the earth.

"Whilst the annexation of Texas," said Mr. Buchanan, "would afford that security to the southern and southwestern slave States, which they have a right to demand, it would, in some respects, operate prejudicially upon their immediate pecuniary interests; but to the middle and western, and more especially to the New England States, it would, in my opinion, be a source of unmixed prosperity. It would extend their commerce, promote their manufactures, and increase their wealth. The New England States resisted, with all their power, the acquisition of Louisiana; and I ask what would those States have been at this day without that territory? They will also resist the annexation of Texas with similar energy; although, after it has been acquired, it is they who will reap the chief pecuniary advantages from the acquisition."

Mr. Buchanan closed his speech by urging immediate action, and stated that had Mr. Jefferson delayed one month in his acquisition of Louisiana, that valuable and fertile territory would not have been obtained probably without an expensive and bloody war. The annexation was now before the Senate in the form of a treaty, and not receiving the constitutional majority, it failed of being ratified. The final result, however, was not changed, in fact postponed for only a few months. The present session adjourned on the 17th of June, 1844, and the next one convened on the 2d of December following. Then the annexation of Texas came up in the form of a joint resolution. The election of James K. Polk had been accomplished;

the annexation of Texas had been an issue before the people, and favorably received, and the democracy were again coming into power. All these things combining rendered the annexation of Texas a certainty. The present Congress, therefore, made a virtue of necessity, and just before Mr. Tyler retired from office, received Texas into the American Union upon a joint resolution. It may be remarked that Mr. Buchanan was the only member of the Committee on Foreign Relations in the Senate to whom the subject was referred, who reported favorably upon the admission. The vote upon the annexation of Texas completed Mr. Buchanan's senatorial career, and it will ever be an honor to him, that he crowned his ten years of devotion to the interests of his country in the highest branch of its legislative body, by an act so important and valuable in its results.

CHAPTER XX.

Mr. Buchanan as Secretary of State—The War with Mexico—The Oregon Boundary Negotiation—Treaty with Mexico—The Acquisition of California—The Irish Revolution of 1848—Mr. Buchanan's Denial of British Demands.

THE campaign of 1844, placed James K. Polk in the presidential chair. The annexation of Texas had been disposed of, but there were other questions of great importance still undecided, which if not managed with decision and energy, might involve a sacrifice of our rights. Our relations with Great Britain and Mexico were in a very unsettled state, and Mr. Polk, justly considering that he needed a statesman of tried ability and of unflinching patriotism to fill the important post, the head of the State Department, and considering also the respect due to the eminent man who had been the hero in so many a hard fought democratic battle, then in retirement at the Hermitage, felt it his duty to consult him in regard to the disposition of the portfolio of his chief cabinet appointment. It was an honor, therefore, to Mr. Buchanan, but one of which he was justly deserving, that that man of profound sagacity and of pure patriotism designated him as the proper person to occupy this responsible position. Mr. Buchanan being thus invited to accept the chair of the Secretary of State in Mr. Polk's cabinet, resigned his position as senator from Pennsylvania, a place he had for ten years filled with so much honor to himself and so much acceptance to his constituents, and entered upon the duties of his new office.

It would be quite impossible in the limits of this volume to give anything like a detail of the various and important papers which it became his duty to prepare while connected with the State department. It might be almost enough to say that he occupied the chief position in that cabinet which conducted the brilliant campaign in Mexico, and which first planted the stars and stripes in California. A brief *résumé*, however, of Mr. Buchanan's acts while Secretary of State, will be necessary, in order to show how much the country is indebted to him for the valuable acquisitions of a new territory which has in fact almost changed the face of modern society. The gold of California has been to this era what the mines of Mexico and Peru were to Europe when Spain, by the brilliancy of her achievements, was the leading nation of the world in all those daring and adventurous enterprises which for so many years linked the name of Castilian with all that was enthusiastic and bold. Had not the foresight of such statesmen seen beyond the limits of the present hour, California might have fallen into the hands of England, and the glorious future which will enable us eventually to clasp the trade both of the East and the West Indies as ours, would have been obscured, perhaps forever.

The first negotiation which demanded the attention of Mr. Buchanan after he assumed the duties of his office, was the settlement of our northwestern, or Oregon boundary. Mr. B. had long held the firm opinion that our title to that territory was clear and indisputable up to the parallel of 54° 40 minutes. Upon commencing the duties of his office, however, he found several embarrassments in his way which were not easily obviated. It will be recollected that he took strong ground against the ratification of Mr. Webster's treaty with Lord Ashburton in 1842, and one of the reasons he then gave for his course was, that the adoption of the treaty would embarrass negotiations in regard to the Oregon boundary. Little did he think at the time that upon his shoulders would fall this embarrassment. There was still another difficulty which the administration of Mr. Polk experienced. The negotiations had been commenced under Mr. Tyler, who had offered to settle the line on the parallel of 49° north latitude, and this offer could not be withdrawn abruptly ; indeed courtesy demanded that the new administration should renew it. After reviewing our title to Oregon, in his first protocol to Mr. Pakenham, the British minister, Mr. Buchanan says :

"In view of these facts, the President has determined to pursue the present negotiation to its conclusion upon the principle of compromise in which it was commenced, and to make one more effort to adjust this long pending controversy. In this determination, he trusts that the British government will recognize his sincere and anxious desire to cultivate the most friendly relations between the two countries, and to manifest to the world that he is actuated by a spirit of moderation. He has therefore instructed the undersigned again to propose to the government of Great Britain that the Oregon territory shall be divided between the two countries by the forty-ninth parallel of north latitude from the Rocky Mountains to the Pacific Ocean ; offering at the same time to make free to Great Britain any port or ports on Vancouver's Island which the British government may desire. He trusts that Great Britain may receive this proposition in the friendly spirit by which it was dictated, and that it may prove the stable foundation of lasting peace and harmony between the two countries."

The protocol from which this extract is taken was dated July 12th, 1845. It went over the grounds in dispute, briefly recapitulating the main points of the controversy. Mr. Pakenham replied to it on the 29th of the same month, declining in a somewhat hasty manner the offer. Mr. Buchanan did not reply until the 30th of August ; but when he did, it was in a letter of great historical accuracy, carefully and even technically elaborated, and with such a firm and decided spirit animating it from beginning to end, that the British government were convinced that it would not do to trifle further with Mr.

Polk's administration. In closing this long, able, and argumentative historical paper, Mr. Buchanan says :

"Such a proposition as that which has been made never would have been authorized by the President had this been a new question. Before his accession to office he found the present negotiation pending. It had been instituted in the principle and with the spirit of compromise. Its object, as avowed by the negotiators, was not to demand the whole territory in dispute for either country, but in the language of the first protocol, 'to treat of the respective claims of the two countries to Oregon territory, with a view to establish a permanent boundary between them westward of the Rocky Mountains to the Pacific Ocean.' Placed in this position, and considering that Presidents Monroe and Adams had on former occasions offered to divide the territory in dispute, by the forty-ninth parallel of latitude, he felt it to be his duty not abruptly to arrest the negotiation, but so far to yield his own opinion as once more to make a similar offer. Not only respect for the conduct of his predecessors, but a sincere and anxious desire to promote peace and harmony between the two countries, influenced him to pursue this course. The Oregon question presents the only intervening cloud which intercepts the prospect of a long career of mutual friendship and beneficial commerce between the two nations, and this cloud he desires to remove.

"These are the reasons which actuated the President to offer a proposition so liberal to Great Britain. And how has this proposition been received by the British plenipotentiary ? It has been rejected without even a reference to his own government. Nay, even more. The British plenipotentiary, to use his own language, 'trusts' that the American plenipotentiary will be prepared to offer some other proposal for the settlement of the Oregon question, more consistent with fairness and equity, and with the reasonable expectations of the British government. Under such circumstances, the undersigned is in structed by the President to say, that he owes it to his country and a just appreciation of her title to the Oregon territory, to withdraw the proposition to the British government which had been made under his direction ; and it is hereby accordingly withdrawn.' In taking this necessary step, the President still cherishes the hope that this long pending controversy may yet be finally adjusted in such a manner as not to disturb the peace or interrupt the harmony now so happily subsisting between the two nations."

This decidedly spirited and even indignant reception of Mr. Pakenham's note convinced the British government that the United States were determined to maintain their rights, and not long after it came forward itself with the proposal to settle the boundary as Mr. Polk had at first offered. This it declared to be its ultimatum. Here was a dilemma. For the President not to accept a proposition which he once offered himself, would seem like going to war merely on a point of etiquette, yet to accept it would not be in accordance with his own views or those of his cabinet. The Senate, however, was in session, and as this is a part of the treaty making power of our government, Mr. Polk wisely resolved to submit the *projet* of the treaty to that body, and take its advice on the subject. The offer of Great Britain was therefore sent to the Senate, where, after due deliberation, a resolution was passed, advising Mr. Polk to accept the proposition. Thus, at length ended the famous Oregon controversy, which had been suddenly terminated doubtless solely by the decided stand which Mr. Buchanan had taken in asserting our rights and in rejecting at the very outset anything like trifling in the negotiation.

The management of the negotiation connected with the Mexican war, was, however, the most intricate in its details, as it was the most important in its results of any that came before Mr. Buchanan while a member of Mr. Polk's cabinet. The forbearance we had exercised towards Mexico had been construed by that power into pusillanimity, perhaps, even cowardice. Like a degenerated family, vanity had usurped the place of the courage and bravery of its ancestors, and it had the hardihood even to attack Americans upon American soil. It is needless to say that the descendants of a Washington and a Hancock never so nobly vindicated their patriotism and bravery. Congress authorized the acceptance of a volunteer force of ten thousand men, and no less than fifty thousand offered their services. The delicacy in selecting from the number eager to enroll themselves in defence of the rights of their country was exceedingly embarrassing, and it is doubtful whether some slight feeling may not exist even yet among the rejected against Mr. Buchanan and other members of Mr. Polk's cabinet, because they were compelled to deny them the privilege of engaging in the fight !

Constant negotiations, however, were kept up with Mexico, and repeated offers made to bring the difficulties to a termination, but she would not submit until her people saw the stars and stripes waving from the halls of the Montezumas. During the whole of the protracted and tedious negotiation, which finally resulted in a peace both honorable and advantageous to our country, Mr. Buchanan displayed a degree of consummate statesmanship which demonstrated his appreciation of the wants and interests of his nation. In his letter of instruction to Hon. John Slidell, minister to Mexico, he said :

" The nations of the continent of America have interests peculiar to themselves. Their free forms of government are altogether different from the monarchical institutions of Europe. The interest and independence of these sister nations require that they should establish and maintain an American system of policy for their own protection and security, entirely distinct from that which has so long prevailed in Europe. To tolerate any interference on the part of European sovereigns with controversies in America ; to permit them to apply the worn out dogma of the balance of power to the free States on this con-

16

tinent ; and above all, to suffer them to establish new colonies
of their own, intermingled with our free republics, would be to
make to the same extent a voluntary sacrifice of our independence. These truths ought everywhere throughout the continent
of America to be pressed upon the public mind. If therefore in
the course of your negotiations with Mexico that government
should propose the mediation or guarantee of any European
power, you are to reject the proposition without hesitation.
The United States will never afford, by their conduct, the
slightest pretext for any interference in that quarter in American
concerns. Separated as we are from the Old World by a vast
ocean, and still further removed from it by the nature of our
republican institutions, the march of free governments on this
continent must not be trammelled by the intrigues and selfish
interests of European powers. Liberty here must be allowed
to work out its natural results ; and these, ere long, will astonish the world. Neither is it for the interests of those powers
to plant colonies on this continent. No settlement of the kind
can exist long. The expansive energy of our free institutions
must soon spread over them. The colonists themselves will
break from the mother country to become free and independent States. Any European nation which should plant a
new colony on this continent, would thereby sow the seeds
of troubles and uproars, the injury from which even to her
own interests, would far outweigh all the advantages which
she could possibly promise herself from any such establish
ment."

It seems every true American and real lover of liberty
and free institutions will instinctively respond to the noble
sentiments contained in this extract. Mr. Buchanan's mind
appears to grasp the entire destiny of this continent, and to
see it in the distant future as the spot where mankind shall
live in harmony with their created adaptations, and be "redeemed, regenerated, and disenthralled" from the corruption,

degradation, and misery which royal tyrants have imposed upon them.

Another important discussion which occurred during Mr. Buchanan's secretaryship was one with the British government in regard to American citizens said to have been engaged in the Irish revolution of 1848. England claimed the right to try individuals for treason to her own government who were duly naturalized citizens of ours—in a word it was her old impressment doctrine of once a British subject always a British subject. The controversy arose in the following manner. Two gentlemen, Messrs. Bergen and Ryan, had expressed themselves in this country as warmly sympathizing with the cause of Ireland, and while on a visit to that country were arrested solely for the utterance of their opinions in this country. It is almost needless to say that an act so high-handed and outrageous received from Mr. Buchanan the attention it deserved. In a letter of instruction to Mr. Bancroft then minister to England he says :

" Whenever the occasion may require it, you will resist the the British doctrine of perpetual allegiance and maintain the American principle that British native-born subjects, after they have been naturalized under our laws, are, to all intents and purposes, as much American citizens, and entitled to the same degree of protection, as though they had been born in the United States."

Mr. Bancroft in accordance with these instructions addressed a letter to Lord Palmerston denying the right of the British government, under the circumstances, to arrest Messrs. Bergen and Ryan, and the effect of this decided action on the part of our government was the liberation of the two gentlemen from custody.

At few periods of our history have there been so many or important interests at stake both at home and abroad as during the four years that Mr. Buchanan continued in Mr. Polk's cabinet. An empire was added to our own domain. The country was safely and honorably conducted through the first foreign war, of any importance, in which we had ever been involved. Our relations with England had been adjusted in a manner satisfactory to our citizens, and while the thrones of Europe had tottered to their very foundations, the basis of the only free government on earth had been strengthened, and its position made more honorable in the sight of the world. The light of our beneficent example had shed its rays over the Atlantic where, as silent as the light of Heaven in its influence, yet as powerful as a thunderbolt in its effect, it is yet destined to awake the slumbering energies of the people, and nerve them to inflict upon their oppressors the just vengeance with which a retributive Providence as surely punishes the sins of nations as of individuals.

When Mr. Buchanan left the State department our country was at peace, both at home and abroad. Our territory had been enlarged, and our commerce extended. Not long after, untold riches were flowing into the country, prosperity was everywhere visible, our cities were growing with unexampled rapidity, the fertile prairies of the West were being intersected with railroads, and dotted with villages, and an impulse had been universally given to business, which no one can deny was directly owing to the statesmanlike foresight that had opened California to the adventurous spirit of American genius and enterprise.

CHAPTER XXI.

Ten years in the Senate—A Review of Mr. Buchanan's Senatorial Life—His Position on the Bank Question—As a Friend of Gen. Jackson—The true Test of Statesmanship—The Slavery Question—The Proscription of Foreigners—Mr. Buchanan's Four Years as Secretary of State.

AND here it may be interesting to review briefly the career of Mr. Buchanan— a career, which, for consistency of principle or for devotion to the public interests, finds no superior in the whole range of American statesmen. He entered the Senate when Clay, Webster, Calhoun, and Wright were the mighty intellects which swayed that body, and he immediately took rank among them as a debater, whose blows, if not so brilliant in style, were even more effectual in execution. There is one feature of Mr. Buchanan's speeches which is very remarkable. It is the absence of all display, of all attempts to benefit his cause by any of those adventitious aids which oratory furnishes. He never, even in argument or style, attempts the *ad captandum vulgus*, but with a firm reliance on the power of plain, outspoken truth, he appeals to the common sense rather than to the fancy or imagination. Even where almost every person might be excused for indulging in rhetorical metaphors, Mr. Buchanan adheres strictly to plain, yet graceful and elegant language. There is no sign of a desire to catch the breath of temporary applause, but firm, dignified, and impressive in advancing his opinions, as he is resolute and energetic in maintaining them, he presents by his urbanity in debate, and purity of patriotism, the model of an American senator.

When he entered the Senate in 1834, the great battle that

prostrated what would have undoubtedly grown into a moneyed aristocracy had been victoriously fought. The discussion and settlement of the policy of the general government in regard to the currency question, is one of the most interesting and instructive in the whole history of our existence as a nation. It had to contend against precedents. Some of the very founders of our government had approved a National Bank, and it was difficult, and sometimes almost impossible, to get before the people the circumstances and facts connected with such approval. The democracy were in favor of letting banks, like all other institutions, take care of themselves without assistance or alliance with the general government. They wished to keep the federal government where it belonged ; confined to the few plainly delegated powers given it by the Constitution, and leave each State to manage all its financial, business and domestic regulations, without being under the influence of a central power, which might almost at any moment become a consolidated oligarchy. It is an agreeable reflection that their views have now been so generally acquiesced in.

And here we have the touchstone that has always divided political parties in this country. No matter what may be the particular question, be it banks, commerce, or negro slavery, this is the rock upon which they split. The democracy from the days of Jefferson, as fast as the different questions of public policy have been made issues before the people, have resolutely contended for a strict construction of the Constitution. From the day that Mr. Buchanan entered public life until the present, he has approved this policy ; at least, after a careful perusal of the congressional record we have not observed a single vote of his upon questions where the issue was involved antagonistic to this position. He has thus shown a devotion to correct principles which endears him to every friend of our system of government.

And more : in every question before the Senate, he always

espoused the cause of his country, as contradistinguished from that spirit of timidity which General Jackson used to declare would always produce war. No man who understands Mr. Buchanan's character will suspect him of anything like blustering or bravado. Nor would he appeal to the sword in the settlement of national disputes, except in the direst emergency, and then it would be with the reluctance of a judge who is compelled to sentence a criminal to death in order to vindicate the law. Upon questions where our dearest rights, nay, even our existence as an independent nation is concerned, Mr. Buchanan has always shown that intrepid spirit, which distinguishes every man worthy to bear the name of American. But in questions of etiquette, or where no important interest is involved, he has always exhibited that generosity and forbearance, which a great nation, justly proud of its strength and confident of its resources, can afford to exercise.

No one feature in his life or character is more decided than his respect and admiration for General Jackson. He was among the first to observe the capacity of that distinguished man for the office of Chief Magistrate, and from the very start was his firm and unwavering friend. His speech upon the "Expunging Resolution" was a vindication of the character of that much maligned man, which will ever rank with the best delivered upon the floor of the United States Senate. In that effort there was something to awaken his feelings, indeed there was a pardonable degree of indignation in which he might be allowed to indulge. A great and patriotic man had been assailed, without the means of defence being afforded him, and one, indeed, who, by his acts, had conferred, as he believed, great blessings upon his country.

Upon all public questions Mr. Buchanan was awarded a leading part. We find him the senator chosen to present the Constitution for the admission of Arkansas, the champion of democracy in the debate with Mr. Clay upon the bank question, and for several years the head of the most important committee of the Senate, that on Foreign Relations. In all these positions he acquitted himself to the entire satisfaction of his friends. Upholding the doctrines of a correct public policy with an earnestness which showed his own sincerity, and with an ability which gave evidence of his capacity even for higher and more important duties. Upon our relations with Mexico he early took a stand which was at last found necessary to be adopted in order to vindicate our rights. To him are we indebted for the negotiations that have added to our country the untold wealth of California, and indeed, this result could have been secured only by a man who could stretch his gaze beyond the narrow bounds of a petty statesmanship. Upon the question of the annexation of Texas, we see the same evidence of expanded views, and the same grasp of intellect which has ever rendered real statesmen even greater benefactors to posterity than to the periods in which they lived. But Mr. Buchanan needs no eulogy. His acts, after all, are the points upon which he must stand or fall. These are the rigid evidences which determine whether a man is a statesman or not. The reputation that a person may acquire in life may be merely adventitious, and will pass away as a dream before the inexorable justice of history. The newspapers of the day may create a fame which will last for even years, but posterity will judge of men by the advantages they have conferred upon it, and by their ideas which live and breathe as the sentiments of the people after they are gone. If therefore we may judge of the capacity of statesmen by the results, and, as it were, by the judgment of posterity, we submit that justice has not heretofore been done to Mr. Buchanan and those who acted with him in the great battle on the currency question. Nor would we disparage either Messrs. Clay or Webster. They were both men of that giant mould and undoubted patriotism which we may not soon expect to see again. They were noble leaders—a Cicero and Demosthenes— honorable in conflict, generous to a fault, and when at last defeated, none turned to them with more heartfelt sympathy than the democracy, who honored their talents, respected their patriotism, admired their manly bearing, and only regretted the misfortune that had compelled them to oppose where it would have been a pleasure to agree, and to condemn where it would have been a satisfaction to have admired.

It is a singular coincidence that Mr. Buchanan should have been brought up before the people of the United States for their suffrages at the very time when the two most prominent features of his public life are just now the exciting questions in issue. It seems as if he had been reserved for the occasion. We are confident no man has ever opposed with more determination the spirit that would proscribe persons on account of their birth-place or religion, or that unfortunate and deplorable delusion which has arrayed so many under the banner of sectionalism, than Mr. Buchanan. We have shown by his speeches how early and how earnest were his protests against both of these sentiments. He took his stand upon the great doctrine of equal rights, and nobly declared, when speaking in reference to the slavery agitation, " I do not wish to sustain myself at home unless I can do it by granting to the South her constitutional rights." He had too much patriotism to desire to make capital out of a feeling which he knew would injure and perhaps destroy his country. Every inducement that ambition might hold out as a temptation to him was disregarded, and he resolved, as did Clay and Webster, that if overwhelmed by the cloud that was gathering in the North, it should be while clinging to the Constitution. It is but reasonable to suppose that the firm stand which Mr. Buchanan took upon this question has been one of the reasons why the grand old democratic State of Pennsylvania has been put down as invincible, against any force which faction can bring against her. There she stands as a barrier to the waves of Northern delusion, saying, " thus far thou shalt go and no farther." It is a worthy tribute of her devotion to the Constitution and the laws

16*

that in this the darkest hour of our history as a government, when men have had the hardihood to combine upon narrow sectional issues, when they have trampled under foot the name, the advice, and even the memory of Washington, that her favorite son should be chosen as the standard-bearer in the contest between nationality and sectionalism, between those who love the Union as it is and those who have been laboring for years with a spirit almost fiendish to produce estrangement and alienation between citizens of a common country, whose interests are identical, and whose destiny is the same.

The position which Mr. Buchanan assumed in regard to the policy of our government towards foreigners, was taken, like that of the slavery question, long before there was any political party founded upon it. To make distinctions in regard to religious creed or birth-place would be to follow the European idea of castes or classes in society, and be a great departure from the fundamental principles of our system.

We find him, therefore, in the Senate opposing those who would allow speculators to turn off from government lands the hardy foreign emigrant who had braved a thousand dangers to find in this New World a land where for once he could breathe freely the native air of a freeman, and be relieved of all those odious statutes of favoritism and class legislation which had oppressed him in the Old World, and bound him down in the chains of slavery. Every true man will applaud him for this noble position. Indeed, himself the son of such a settler, he would have been not only recreant to his duty as a democrat, but to his affection as a son, had he so soon forgotten the generous policy of the administration of Washington and Jefferson, and refused that boon to others which had been granted to his own father.

No man can peruse Mr. Buchanan's career as senator in Congress, and as Secretary of State, without being forcibly struck with the vast and important advantages he has conferred upon his country. There is not a prominent act of that fourteen years' devotion to the public service which is not now acknowledged as right by men of all parties, and so fundamentally settled is the policy of our government, that no one now purposes to disturb one of them. Time has given a triumphant vindication of the soundness of his judgment, of the correctness of his statesmanship, and of the purity of his patriotism. In the great and exciting question now at issue, which has absorbed all others, and brought upon a common platform those who have heretofore seen reasons to differ on other subjects, his record is so consistent that even his enemies do not for a moment question it. Always firm in his political views, but moderate and conciliatory in expressing them, he is just the man whom all delight to honor, though they may have been heretofore compelled to differ with him in his political views and opinions. Next to a firm friend is an honorable opponent ; and that Mr. Buchanan has always sustained the latter character, whether on the floor of the Senate, or in the chair of the Secretary of State, no one will attempt to deny.

In referring to the latter position, it is only necessary to say that the acquisition of California completely overshadows all the other valuable and important acts of Mr. Polk's administration. To Mr. Buchanan belongs the greatest honor of this achievement, and our empire on the Pacific will and must ever trace its origin to the wise foresight, superior statesmanship, and commanding talents of James Buchanan.

CHAPTER XXII.

Mr. Buchanan in private life—Opposition to the Wilmot Proviso—Approval of the Compromise Measures—Mr. Buchanan's position in 1852—Mission to England—The Enlistment Question—The Clayton-Bulwer Treaty—The Ostend Meeting—Mr. Buchanan's return to the United States—His reception.

AFTER the retirement of Mr. Buchanan from Mr. Polk's cabinet, in 1849, upon the election of General Taylor, he gladly sought that rest and quiet in private life, which a long and uninterrupted devotion to the public service rendered agreeable as well as desirable. He had never sought public honors. Taken up at an early age by his neighbors, and placed in public life, he had there acquitted himself with such honesty, devotion, and singleness of purpose, that ever afterwards, step by step, his preferment came naturally, just as in this free country it should come, by the spontaneous acts of the people. He was placed in the Senate by the universal demand of his State, and continued there for the same reason. He was sent by General Jackson to Russia without the least solicitation of himself or his friends. He was called from the Senate to Mr. Polk's cabinet, solely because he possessed qualifications for the position which were not excelled, if equalled, by any democratic statesman. Having thus never sought public office, he could retire to private life with a pleasure unknown to those who are pleased with official stations.

Mr. Buchanan was not, however, an uninterested spectator of events. He could not but feel an interest in his country, and especially through that stormy time which finally resulted in the compromises of 1850. The acquisition of new territory

had again started up the old agitation of the power of the
general government to interfere with the *status* of the negro in
the common territories of the Union.   That unconstitutional
dogma known as the Wilmot Proviso, was introduced as a bone
of contention, and was seized by the anti-slavery agitators with
great eagerness.   For a period it obscured even the vision of
many good democrats, who did not see the noxious principles
it contained, and that the right to pass such an edict would
involve still more alarming and more dangerous powers.   The
constitutional democracy opposed this doctrine, Mr. Buchanan
being among the first to raise his voice in opposition to it.   He
proposed as a settlement the basis of the act of 1820, and
that the Missouri line be extended to the Pacific.

This proposition was contained in his celebrated "Harvest
Home Letter," but it was universally condemned by the anti-
slavery agitators of the North.   When the same proposition
was introduced into the Senate, which body it passed, it was
voted down in the House of Representatives by northern men,
of abolition proclivities.   By this act they forced upon the country that terrible agitation which finally compelled all true
patriots to unite for a common defence.   Mr. Clay had retired
to the quiet shades of Ashland, to pass the sunset of his life in
meditation and repose, but hearing the angry voices of sectional
strife, he rushed again to the Senate, and there, with Mr. Webster, Gen. Cass, and others whose names which will live forever
in our history, they passed the Compromise Measures of 1850,
which were accepted by union men everywhere.   However, much
we may differ upon banks, tariffs, and other measures, the language of these men was, all good and true men can agree upon
this question.   In establishing these compromise measures, they
acknowledged the principles now incorporated in the Kansas-
Nebraska bill, and upon these principles the union men of all
parties agreed.   Yet when it became necessary to apply this
fundamental principle of government in the territorial bills of
Nebraska and Kansas, an agitation again commenced which has

had no parallel in our history. The very men who in 1848 had rejected the Missouri line as a basis of settlement—who had declared that it was an infamous measure, and that if it was right to leave the question of negro slavery south of this line to the people, it was right to grant them the same privilege north of it, now denounced their own principles, and declared themselves in favor of that once infamous measure, the Missouri restriction ! Political inconsistency could go no further.

After the passage of the Compromise Measures of 1850, Mr. Buchanan was among the first to endorse them, and to spread throughout his State a sound public sentiment in their favor. In a letter to a meeting held at Philadelphia, he said that the Missouri restriction had " passed away." All remember how the authors of these measures were assailed. Many of the political friends of Webster and Clay denounced them without mercy. No epithet was too severe to be applied to them, and even Mr. Webster was denied the privilege of speaking in Faneuil Hall, in defence of an act, demanded by the Constitution of his country ! The firm stand taken by such patriots as Clay, Webster, Cass, and Buchanan, however, finally quieted the storm.

And was it not a noble and a sublime sight ? For years they had been opponents upon nearly all prominent public questions, but when a subject came up which involved the safety of their country, they cast to the winds all thoughts of personal ambition, and shoulder to shoulder fought against the surging tide of sectionalism. Nothing more is necessary to establish their patriotic love of country, or their devotion to its best interests. This coincidence of opinion among these great men is just now worthy of remembrance, for if the opposing leaders could thus so cordially unite, there is no reason why their friends may not lay aside every recollection of past party contests, and come up to the defence of their country and its Constitution, against a spirit which would ruin the one and destroy the other.

The following copious extracts from a letter written by Mr.

Buchanan, in November, 1850, when invited to attend a meeting in Philadelphia, give his opinions freely and frankly on the Compromise Measures of 1850 :

"I now say that the platform of our blessed Union is strong enough and broad enough to sustain all true-hearted Americans. It is an elevated—it is a glorious platform on which the down-trodden nations of the earth gaze with hope and desire, with admiration and astonishment. Our Union is the star of the West, whose genial and steadily increasing influence will at last, should we remain an united people, dispel the gloom of despotism from the ancient nations of the world. Its moral power will prove to be more potent than millions of armed mercenaries. And shall this glorious star set in darkness before it has accomplished half its mission? Heaven forbid! Let us all exclaim with the heroic Jackson, 'The Union must and shall be preserved.'

"And what a Union has this been! The history of the human race presents no parallel to it. The bit of striped bunting which was to be swept from the ocean by a British navy, according to the predictions of a British statesman, previous to the war of 1812, is now displayed on every sea, and in every port of the habitable globe. Our glorious stars and stripes, the flag of our country, now protects Americans in every clime. 'I am a Roman citizen!' was once the proud exclamation which everywhere shielded an ancient Roman from insult and injustice. 'I am an American citizen!' is now an exclamation of almost equal potency throughout the civilized world. This is a tribute due to the power and resources of these thirty-one United States. In a just cause, we may defy the world in arms. We have lately presented a spectacle which has astonished the greatest captain of the age. At the call of their country, an irresistible host of armed men, and men, too, skilled in the use of arms, sprung up like the soldiers of Cadmus, from the mountains and valleys of our confederacy. The struggle among

them was not who should remain at home, but who should
enjoy the privilege of enduring the dangers and privations of a
foreign war, in defence of their country's rights. Heaven forbid
that the question of slavery should ever prove to be the stone
thrown into their midst by Cadmus, to make them turn their
arms against each other, and die in mutual conflict.

*   *   *   *   *   *

" The common sufferings and common glories of the past, the
prosperity of the present, and the brilliant hopes of the future,
must impress every patriotic heart with deep love and devotion
for the Union. Who that is now a citizen of this vast Republic, extending from the St. Lawrence to the Rio Grande, and
from the Atlantic to the Pacific, does not shudder at the idea
of being transformed into a citizen of one of its broken, jealous,
and hostile fragments ? What patriot had not rather shed the
last drop of his blood, than see the thirty-one brilliant stars,
which now float proudly upon her country's flag, rudely torn
from the national banner, and scattered in confusion over the
face of the earth ?

" Rest assured that all the patriotic emotions of every true-
hearted Pennsylvanian, in favor of the Union and Constitution,
are shared by the southern people. What battle field has
not been illustrated by their gallant deeds ; and when in our
history, have they ever shrunk from sacrifices and sufferings in
the cause of their country ? What, then, means the muttering
thunder which we hear from the South ? The signs of the
times are truly portentous. Whilst many in the South openly
advocate the cause of secession and union, a large majority, as
I firmly believe, still fondly cling to the Union, awaiting with
deep anxiety the action of the North on the compromise lately
effected in Congress. Should this be disregarded and nullified by
the citizens of the North, the southern people may become united,
and then farewell, a long farewell to our blessed Union. I am no
alarmist ; but a brave and wise man looks danger steadily in
the face. This is the best means of avoiding it. I am deeply

impressed with the conviction that the North neither sufficiently understands nor appreciates the danger. For my own part, I have been steadily watching its progress for the last fifteen years. During that period I have often sounded the alarm ; but my feeble warnings have been disregarded. I now solemnly declare as the deliberate conviction of my judgment, that two things are necessary to preserve this Union from danger :

" ' 1. Agitation in the North on the subject of southern slavery must be rebuked and put down by a strong and enlightened public opinion.

" ' 2. The Fugitive Slave Law must be enforced in its spirit.'

" On each of these points I shall offer a few observations.

" Those are greatly mistaken who suppose that the tempest that is now raging in the South has been raised solely by the acts or omissions of the present Congress. The minds of the southern people have been gradually prepared for this explosion by the events of the last fifteen years. Much and devotedly as they love the Union, many of them are now taught to believe that the peace of their own firesides, and the securities of their families, cannot be preserved without separation from us. The crusade of the Abolitionists against their domestic peace and security commenced in 1835. General Jackson, in his annual message to Congress, in December of that year, speaks of it in the following emphatic language : 'I must also invite your attention to the painful excitement produced in the South by attempts to circulate through the mails inflammatory appeals, addressed to the passions of the slaves, in prints and various sorts of publications, calculated to stimulate them to insurrection, and produce all the horrors of a servile war.'

" From that period the agitation in the North against southern slavery has been incessant, by means of the press, of State Legislatures, of State and County Conventions, Abolition lectures, and every other method which fanatics and demagogues could devise. The time of Congress has been wasted in violent harangues on the subject of slavery. Inflammatory appeals have been sent forth from this central point throughout the country, the inevitable effect of which has been to create geographical parties, so much dreaded by the Father of his Country, and to estrange the northern and southern divisions of the Union from each other.

"Before the Wilmot Proviso was interposed, the abolition of slavery in the District of Columbia had been the chief theme of agitation. Petitions for this purpose, by thousands, from men, women and children, poured into Congress, session after session. The rights and the wishes of the owners of slaves within the District, were boldly disregarded. Slavery was denounced as a national disgrace, which the laws of God and the laws of men ought to abolish, cost what it might. It mattered not to the fanatics that the abolition of slavery in the District would convert it into a citadel, in the midst of two slaveholding States, from which the abolitionist could securely scatter arrows, firebrands and death, all around. It mattered not with them that the abolition of slavery in the District would be a violation of the spirit of the Constitution and of the implied faith pledged to Maryland and Virginia, because the whole world knows that those States would never have ceded it to the Union, had they imagined it could ever be converted by Congress into a place from which their domestic peace and security might be assailed by fanatics and Abolitionists. Nay, the Abolitionists went even still further. They agitated for the purpose of abolishing slavery in the forts, arsenals and navy yards which the Southern States had ceded to the Union, under the Constitution, for the protection and defence of the country.

"Thus stood the question when the Wilmot Proviso was interposed, to add fuel to the flame, and to excite the southern people to madness.

*   *   *   *   *   *   *

"It would be the extreme of dangerous infatuation to suppose that the Union was not then in serious danger. Had the Wilmot Proviso become a law, or had slavery been abolished in the District of Columbia, nothing short of a special interposition of Divine Providence could have prevented the secession of most, if not all the slaveholding States.

"It was from this great and glorious old Commonwealth, rightly demonstrated the ' Keystone of the Arch,' that the first ray of light emanated to dispel the gloom. She stands now as the days-man, between the North and the South, and can lay her hand on either party, and say, thus far shalt thou go, and no farther. The wisdom, moderation and firmness of her people, calculate her eminently to act as the just and equitable umpire between the extremes.

"It was the vote in our State House of Representatives, refusing to consider the instructing resolutions in favor of the Wilmot Proviso, which first cheered the heart of every patriot in the land. This was speedily followed by a vote of the House of Representatives at Washington, nailing the Wilmot Proviso itself to the table. And here I ought not to forget the great meeting held in Philadelphia on the birth-day of the Father of his Country, in favor of the Union, which gave a happy and irresistible impulse to public opinion throughout the State, and I may add throughout the Union.

" The honor of the South has been saved by the Compromise. The Wilmot Proviso is for ever dead, and slavery will never be abolished in the District of Columbia whilst it continues to exist in Maryland. The receding storm in the South still continues to dash with violence, but it will gradually subside, should agitation cease in the North. All that is necessary for us to do 'is to execute the Fugitive Slave Law,' and to let the southern people alone, suffering them to manage their own domestic concerns in their own way. *   *   *   *

"2. I shall proceed to present to you some views upon the subject of the much misrepresented Fugitive Slave Law. It is now evident, from all the signs of the times, that this is destined to become the principal subject of agitation at the present session of Congress, and to take the place of the Wilmot Proviso. Its total repeal or its material modification will henceforward be the battle cry of the agitators of the North.

"And what is the character of this law? It was passed to carry into execution a plain, clear, and mandatory provision of the Constitution, requiring that fugitive slaves, who fly from service in one State to another, shall be delivered up to their masters. The provision is so explicit that he who runs may read. No commentary can present it in a stronger light than the plain words of the Constitution. It is a well-known historical fact, that without this provision, the Constitution itself could never have existed. How could this have been otherwise? Is it possible for a moment to believe that the slave States would have formed a union with the free States, if under it their slaves, by simply escaping across the boundary which separates them, would acquire all the rights of freemen? This would have been to offer an irresistible temptation to all the slaves of the South to precipitate themselves upon the North. The Federal Constitution, therefore, recognizes in the clearest and most emphatic terms, the property in slaves, and protects this property by prohibiting any State, into which a slave might escape, from discharging him from slavery, and by requiring that he shall be delivered up to his master.

      *   *   *   *   *   *   *

"The two principal objections urged against the Fugitive Slave Law are, that it will promote kidnapping, and that it does not provide a trial by jury for the fugitive in the State to which he has escaped.

"The very same reasons may be urged, with equal force, against the act of 1793; and yet it existed for more than half a century without encountering any such objections.

"In regard to kidnapping, the fears of the agitators are altogether groundless. The law requires that the fugitive shall be taken before the judge or commissioner. They must there prove, to the satisfaction of the magistrate, the identity of the fugitive, that he is the master's property, and has escaped from his service. Now, I ask, would a kidnapper ever undertake such a task? Would he suborn witnesses to commit perjury and expose himself to detection before the judge or commissioner, and in the presence of the argus eyes of a non-slaveholding community, whose feelings will always be in favor of the slave? No, never. The kidnapper seizes his victim in the silence of the night, or in a remote and obscure place, and hurries him away. He does not expose himself to the public gaze. He will never bring the unfortunate object of his rapacity before a commissioner or a judge. Indeed, I have no recollection of having heard or read of a case in which a free man was kidnapped under the forms of law, during the whole period of more than half a century, since the act of 1793 was passed.

    *   *   *   *   *   *   *

"The Union cannot long endure, if it be bound together only by paper bonds. It can be firmly cemented alone by the affections of the people of different States for each other. Would to Heaven that the spirit of mutual forbearance and brotherly love which presided at its birth, could once more be restored to bless the land! Upon opening a volume, a few days since, my eyes caught a resolution of a Convention of the Counties of Maryland, assembled at Annapolis, in June, 1774, in consequence of the passage by the British Parliament, of the Boston Port Bill, which provided for opening a subscription 'in the several counties of the Province, for an immediate collection for the relief of the distressed inhabitants of Boston, now cruelly deprived of the means of procuring subsistence for themselves and families by the operation of the said act of blocking up their harbor.' Would that the spirit of fraternal affection which dictated this noble resolution, and which actuated all the conduct of our revolutionary fathers, might return to bless and reanimate the bosoms of their descendants!

This would render our Union indissoluble. It would be the living soul infusing itself into the Constitution and inspiring it with irresistible energy."

When the Baltimore Convention of 1852 met, a large number of Mr. Buchanan's friends desired to put him in nomination for the Presidency. According to his usual course during his whole life, he would do nothing to interfere with the pure and free expression of public opinion, perfectly satisfied with whatever the result might be. After a warm contention, our present Chief Magistrate was selected as the standard-bearer in that campaign, and no one gave him a more generous or hearty support than Mr. Buchanan. During the contest he stood in the van of the democratic ranks in Pennsylvania, encouraging the democracy to fight on and fight ever for the main tenance of their time-honored principles.

The following remarkable passages from his speech delivered to a mass meeting of the democracy of Western Pennsylvania, on the 7th of October, 1852, at Greensburg, Westmoreland County, are so characteristic of the man and his opinions that we do not hesitate to copy them. Remember that, at no time did he ever yield a jot or tittle to sectionalism. He was against it instinctively, and from the start. He said :

" From my soul, I abhor the practice of mingling up religion with politics. The doctrine of all our constitutions, both Federal and State, is, that every man has an indefeasible right to worship his God according to the dictates of his own conscience. He is both a bigot and a tyrant, who would interfere with that sacred right. When a candidate is before the people for office, the inquiry ought never even to be made, what form of religious faith he possesses ; but only, in the language of Mr. Jefferson, 'Is he honest, is he capable ?'

" 'Democratic Americans !' What a name for a Native American party ! When all the records of our past history prove that American democrats have ever opened wide their arms to receive foreigners flying from oppression in their native land, and have always bestowed upon them the rights of American citizens, after a brief period of residence in this country. The democratic party have always gloried in this policy, and its fruits have been to increase our population and our power with unexampled rapidity, and to furnish our country with vast numbers of industrious, patriotic and useful citizens. Surely the name of 'Democratic Americans' was an unfortunate designation for the Native American party.

"The Native American party, an 'American excellence,' and the glory of its foundership, belongs to George Washington! No, fellow-citizens, the American people will rise up with one accord to vindicate the memory of that illustrious man from such an imputation. As long as the recent memory of our revolutionary struggle remained vividly impressed on the hearts of our countrymen, no such party could have ever existed. The recollection of Montgomery, Lafayette, De Kalb, Kosciusko, and a long list of foreigners, both officers and soldiers, who freely shed their blood to secure our liberties, would have rendered such ingratitude impossible. Our revolutionary army was filled with the brave and patriotic natives of their lands; and George Washington was their commander-in-chief. Would he have ever closed the door against the admission of foreigners to the rights of American citizens? Let his acts speak for themselves. So early as the 26th of March, 1790, General Washington, as President of the United States, approved the first law which ever passed Congress on the subject of naturalization; and this only required a residence of two years, previous to the adoption of a foreigner as an American citizen. On the 29th January, 1795, the term of residence was extended by Congress to five years, and thus it remained throughout General Washington's administration, and until after the accession of John Adams to the Presidency. In his administration, which will ever be known in history as the reign of terror, as the era of alien and sedition laws, an act was passed on the 18th of June, 1798, which prohibited any foreigner from becoming a citizen until after a residence of fourteen years, and this is the law, or else, perpetual exclusion, which General Scott preferred, and which the Native American party now desire to restore.

"The Presidential election of 1800 secured the ascendency of the democratic party, and under the administration of Thomas Jefferson, its great apostle, on the 14th of April, 1802, the term of residence previous to naturalization was restored to five years, what it had been under General Washington, and where it has ever since remained. No, fellow-citizens, the father of his country was never a 'Native American.' This 'American excellence' never belonged to him."

Speaking of the Fugitive Slave Law, Mr. Buchanan said :

"It is a law founded both upon the letter and the spirit of the Constitution, and a similar law has existed on our statute books ever since the administration of George Washington. History teaches us that but for the provision in favor of fugitive slaves, our present Constitution never would have existed. Think ye that the South will ever tamely surrender the Fugitive Slave Law to northern fanatics and abolitionists ?

"And now, fellow-citizens, what a glorious party the Democratic party has ever been ! Man is but the being of a summer's day, whilst principles are eternal. The generations of mortals, one after the other, rise and sink, and are forgotten, but the principles of democracy, which we have inherited from our revolutionary fathers, will endure to bless mankind throughout all generations. Is there any democrat within the sound of my voice, is there any democrat throughout the broad limits of good and great old democratic Pennsylvania, who will abandon these sacred principles for the sake of following in the train of a military conqueror, and shouting for the hero of Lundy's Lane, Cerro Gordo, and Chapultepec."

After the campaign, President Pierce tendered to Mr. Buchanan the mission to the court of St. James. For a number of years the position of minister to Great Britain has been growing in importance. The intimate commercial and other relations existing between the two countries are of themselves enough to demand the attention of a tried statesman and a prudent man, but when we add to this the constant liability there is of the rising of political questions of great and enduring importance, we may well consider the mission to England only second to that of the position of the President. Certainly Mr. Pierce did a very popular act when he tendered this place to Mr. Buchanan. Our business and mercantile men felt that the relations of peace between the two countries were in the hands of a man of steadiness of character, who would do nothing to involve us in an unnecessary war, while all classes had confidence that he would not barter away any real interest of our country, or tamely submit to anything that would involve national dishonor.

As it happened while he held this responsible position, two questions did arise which have required the most consummate tact for their proper management. To these Mr. Buchanan brought a degree of diplomatic ability which would have inscribed his name, had it not been there before, among the most skillful negotiators. It is sufficient to say, that thus far the United States have decidedly the best of both points in dispute. The dismissal of Mr. Crampton, the British minister, was placed upon grounds so self-evident, that even England has not dared to cavil at them. The various dispatches of Mr. Buchanan have been so recently published, that they are fresh in everyone's mind. They are direct and explicit, and without the usual evasiveness which characterizes diplomacy. Indeed, the direct American plainness and honesty of Mr. Buchanan's diplomatic papers exceedingly puzzle the old school of European tricksters. They are not accustomed to such downright frankness.

17

The management of the Central American question has, however, been the principal subject to which his attention was directed while a minister to Great Britain. To him are we indebted for the unravelling of that curious piece of diplomatic patch-work, called by way of courtesy the Clayton-Bulwer treaty, an instrument so profound that it puzzles even its authors. Such confidence did Mr. Pierce and the cabinet have in Mr. Buchanan's eminent ability to manage the whole affair connected with our rights in Central America, that on the 12th of August, 1853, shortly after his arrival in England, the President "considering his (Mr. Buchanan's) intimate knowledge of the subject in all its bearings," transmitted to him full power to conclude a treaty with Great Britain in relation to the Central American questions. A correspondence was accordingly commenced between Mr. Buchanan and Lord Clarendon, for the purpose of ascertaining if possible the exact difference which existed between the two countries in regard to the construction of the Clayton-Bulwer treaty. This negotiation was interrupted by the Russian war, and the delicacy which Mr. Buchanan naturally and justly felt in pushing a prompt reply to his communications while England was engaged in a foreign contest. At length, after Mr. Buchanan had intimated a desire to be relieved from the onerous duties of his mission, Mr. Marcy addressed him, stating his earnest desire that the question might be brought to a distinct issue before Mr. Buchanan should retire from his mission. "The negotiation," said Mr. Marcy emphatically, "cannot be committed to any one who so well understands the subject in all its bearings as you do, or who can so ably sustain and carry out the views of the United States." This opinion, flattering as it is to Mr. Buchanan, is no more nor less than the simple truth. For thirty years he has studied with care and attention the position of affairs in that portion of our continent, and the remark is a most just one, that no statesman in this country "so well understands the subject."

In accordance, therefore, with the urgent request o the President, Mr. Buchanan made another effort to bring Lord Clarendon to the discussion of the question. In a note to him, Mr. Buchanan very pointedly and urgently says, "the President has directed the undersigned, before retiring fro n his mission, to request from the British government a statement of the positions which it has determined to maintain in regard to the Bay Islands, the territory between the Sibun and Sarstoon, as well as the Belize settlement and the Mosquito protectorate. The long delay in asking for this information has proceeded from the President's reluctance to manifest any impatience on this important subject whilst the attention of her majesty's government was engaged by the war with Russia. But as more than a year has already elapsed since the termination of the discussion on these subjects, and as the first session of the new Congress is speedily approaching, the President does not feel that he would be justified in any longer delay."

The first detailed statement of the positions of our government was submitted by Mr. Buchanan to Lord Clarendon January 6th, 1854. The reply of Lord C. is dated on the 2d of May following, to which Mr. Buchanan replied on the 22d of July, in a long and elaborate history of all the points in dispute. It is impossible to give anything like even the points of this unanswerable vindication of our rights in Central America, yet we cannot refrain from presenting the following short extract, which after all gives the pith of the absurd pretensions of the British government. After citing the article in the treaty in dispute, Mr. Buchanan asks :

"What, then, is the fair construction of the article ? It embraces two objects. 1. It declares that neither of the parties shall ever acquire any exclusive control over the ship canal to be constructed between the Atlantic and the Pacific, by the route of the river San Juan de Nicaragua, and that neither of them shall ever erect or maintain any fortifications command-

ing the same or in the vicinity thereof.   In regard to this stipu-
lation, no disagreement is known to exist between the parties.
But the article proceeds further in its mutually self-denying
policy, and in the second place, declares that neither of the
parties will ' occupy, or fortify, or colonize, or assume, or exercise any dominion over Nicaragua, Costa Rica, the Mosquito
coast, or any part of Central America.'

  " We now reach the true point.   Does this language require
that Great Britain shall withdraw from her existing possessions
in Central America, including ' the Mosquito coast ?'   The language peculiarly applicable to this coast will find a more appropriate place in a subsequent portion of these remarks.

  " If any individual enters into a solemn and explicit agreement that he will not ' occupy ' any given tract of country then
actually occupied by him, can any proposition be clearer, than
that he is bound by his agreement to withdraw from such occupancy ?   Were this not the case, these words would have no
meaning, and the agreement would become a mere nullity.
Nay more, in its effect it would amount to a confirmation of
the party in the possession of that very territory which he had
bound himself not to occupy, and would practically be equivalent to an agreement that he should remain in possession—a
contradiction in terms.   It is difficult to comment on language
which appears so plain, or to offer arguments to prove that the
meaning of words is not directly opposite to their well-known
signification.

  " And yet the British government consider that the convention interferes with none of their existing possessions in Central
America ; that it is entirely prospective in its nature, and
merely prohibits them from making new acquisitions.   If this
be the case, then it amounts to a recognition of their rights, on
the part of the American government, to all the possessions
which they already hold, whilst the United States have bound
themselves by the very same instrument, never, under any circumstances, to acquire the possession of a foot of territory in

Central America. The mutuality of the convention would thus be entirely destroyed ; and whilst Great Britain may continue to hold nearly the whole eastern coast of Central America, the United States have abandoned the right for all future time to acquire any territory, or to receive into the American Union any of the States in that portion of their own continent. This self-imposed prohibition was the great objection to the treaty in the United States at the time of its conclusion, and was powerfully urged by some of the best men in the country. Had it then been imagined that whilst it prohibited the United States from acquiring territory, under any possible circumstances, in a portion of America through which their thoroughfares to California and Oregon must pass, the convention, at the same time, permitted Great Britain to remain in the occupancy of all her existing possessions in that region, Mr. Buchanan expresses the confident conviction that there would not have been a single vote in the American Senate in favor of its ratification. In every discussion it was taken for granted that the convention required Great Britain to withdraw from these possessions, and thus place the parties upon an exact equality in Central America. Upon this construction of the convention there was quite as great an unanimity of opinion as existed in the House of Lords, that the convention with Spain of 1786 required Great Britain to withdraw from the Mosquito protectorate."

Lord Clarendon, in the course of his statement, referred, in a somewhat sneering manner, to the Monroe doctrine, and characterized it as merely the " dictum of its distinguished author." Mr. Buchanan replied that " did the occasion require, he would cheerfully undertake the task of justifying the wisdom and policy of the Monroe doctrine, in reference to the nations of Europe, as well as to those on the American continent." Mr. Buchanan closes his statement as follows :

" But no matter what may be the nature of the British claim

to the country between the Sibun and the Sarstoon, the observation already made in reference to the Bay Islands and the Mosquito coast must be reiterated, that the great question does not turn upon the validity of this claim previous to the convention of 1850, but upon the facts that Great Britain has bound herself by this convention not to occupy any part of Central America, nor to exercise dominion over it ; and that the territory in question is within Central America, even under the most limited construction of these words. In regard to Belize proper, confined within its legitimate boundaries, under the treaties of 1783 and 1786, and limited to the usufruct specified in these treaties, it is necessary to say but a few words. The government of the United States will not, for the present, insist upon the withdrawal .of Great Britain from this settlement, provided all the other questions between the two governments concerning Central America can be amicably adjusted. It has been influenced to pursue this course partly by the declaration of Mr. Clayton on the 4th of July, 1850, but mainly in consequence of the extension of the license granted by Mexico to Great Britain, under the treaty of 1826, which that republic has yet taken no steps to terminate.

"It is, however, distinctly to be understood, that the government of the United States acknowledge no claim of Great Britain within Belize, except the temporary 'liberty of making use of the wood of the different kinds, the fruits, and other produce in their natural state,' fully recognizing that the former 'Spanish sovereignty over the country' now belongs either to Guatemala or Mexico.

"In conclusion, the government of the United States most cordially and earnestly unite in the desire expressed by 'her majesty's government, not only to maintain the convention of 1850 intact, but to consolidate and strengthen it by strengthening and consolidating the friendly relations which it was calculated to cement and perpetuate.' Under these mutual feelings, it is deeply to be regretted that the two governments entertain opinions so widely different in regard to its true effect and meaning."

This protocol has certainly so reviewed the whole question in dispute, that it has left but little for his successor to do, except to adhere to the positions already established. Unfortunately, Mr. Buchanan did not have the satisfaction to see this matter arranged before he left England, and it yet remains to be seen what course the British government will take in the matter.

While Mr. Buchanan was in England, the relations of our country with Cuba became very much disturbed, by a difficulty in regard to the steamer Black Warrior. The constant fear that has existed, of a revolution in that unhappy island, was also increased by various developments, and under all the circumstances, the President determined to follow the course adopted by his predecessors in office, and make an effort to purchase Cuba of Spain. Mr. Soulé, our minister to the Spanish government, was specially charged with conducting the negotiation. But as England and France were more or less connected, or rather assumed to connect themselves with whatever disposition Spain might make of Cuba, the President thought it highly important that our ministers to each of these countries should meet at some specified place, and come to a general understanding in regard to the policy to be pursued in order that there might be uniformity of action. This recommendation of the President gave rise to what has been known as the "Ostend Conference," a meeting merely for the familiar interchange of views, between Mr. Buchanan as minister to England, Mr. Mason as minister to France, and Mr. Soulé as minister to Spain. They met first at Ostend, in Belgium, and then at Aix la Chapelle, in Prussia. As the document drawn up by the ministers, containing their views on the question, and presented to the President, has been much maligned and misrepresented, we give it entire. It will be seen that, so far as Mr. Buchanan is con-

cerned, the views do not differ from those he presented to
the public, in his speech on the Panama question, in 1824, and
that no action is either thought of, suggested, or recommended,
except in case Cuba comes under the influence of a foreign
power, or seriously endangers the peace and security of our own
country. The ministers' report is as follows :

"There has been a full and unreserved interchange of views
and sentiments between us, which we are most happy to inform
you, has resulted in a cordial coincidence of opinion on the grave
and important subjects submitted to our consideration.

"We have arrived at the conclusion, and are thoroughly convinced that an immediate and earnest effort ought to be made
by the government of the United States to purchase Cuba from
Spain at any price for which it can be obtained, not exceeding
the sum of ———— dollars.

"The proposal should, in our opinion, be made in such a manner as to be presented through the necessary diplomatic forms
to the Supreme Constituent Cortes about to be assembled. On
this momentous question, in which the people both of Spain and
the United States are so deeply interested, all our proceedings
ought to be open, frank, and public. They should be of
such a character as to challenge the approbation of the
world.

"We firmly believe, that in the progress of human events,
the time has arrived when the vital interests of Spain are as
seriously involved in the sale, as those of the United States in
the purchase of the island ; and that the transaction will prove
equally honorable to both nations.

"Under these circumstances, we cannot anticipate a failure,
unless possibly through the malign influence of foreign powers,
who possess no right whatever to interfere in the matter.

"We proceed to state some of the reasons which have
brought us to the conclusion ; and for the sake of clearness, we
shall specify them under two distinct heads.

" *First*—The United States ought, if practicable, to purchase Cuba with as little delay as possible.

" *Second*—The probability is great that the government and Cortes of Spain will prove willing to sell it, because this would essentially promote the highest and best interests of the Spanish people.

"The first—It must be clear to every reflecting mind, that from the peculiarity of its geographical position, and the considerations attendant on it, Cuba is as necessary to the North American Republic, as any of its present members, and that it belongs naturally to that great family of States, of which the Union is the providential nursery.

" From its locality, it commands the mouth of the Mississippi, and the immense annually increasing trade, which must seek this avenue to the ocean. On the numerous navigable streams, measuring an aggregate course of some 30,000 miles, which disembogue themselves through this magnificent river, into the Gulf of Mexico, the increase of the population during the last ten years amounts to more than that of the entire Union, at the time Louisiana was annexed to it.

"The natural and main outlet to the products of this entire population, the highway of their direct intercourse with the Atlantic and the Pacific States, can never be secure, but must ever be endangered while Cuba is a dependency of a distinct power, in whose possession it has proved to be a source of constant annoyance and embarrassment to their interests.

" Indeed, the Union can never enjoy repose, nor possess reliable security, as long as Cuba is not embraced within its boundaries.

Its immediate acquisition by our government is of paramount importance, and we cannot doubt but that it is a consummation devoutly wished for by its inhabitants.

"The intercourse which its proximity to our coasts begets and encourages between the citizens of the United States, has, in the progress of time, so united their interests, and blended

17*

their fortunes, that they now look upon each other as if they were one people, and had but one destiny.

"Considerations exist which render delay in the acquisition of this island exceedingly dangerous to the United States.

"The system of immigration and labor lately organized within its limits, and the tyranny and oppression which characterize its immediate rulers, threaten an insurrection at every moment, which may result in direful consequences to the American people.

"Cuba has thus become to us an unceasing danger, and a permanent cause of anxiety and alarm.

"But we need not enlarge on these topics. It can scarcely be apprehended that foreign powers, in violation of international law, would interpose their influence with Spain, to prevent our acquisition of the island. Its inhabitants are now suffering under the worst of all possible governments—that of absolute despotism, delegated by a distant power to irresponsible agents, who are changed at short intervals, and who are tempted to improve the brief opportunity thus afforded to accumulate fortunes by the basest means.

"As long as this system shall endure, humanity may in vain demand the suppression of the African slave-trade in the island. This is rendered impossible while that infamous traffic remains an irresistible temptation and a source of immense profit to needy and avaricious officials, who, to attain their end, scruple not to trample the most sacred principles under foot.

"The Spanish government at home may be well disposed, but experience has proved that it cannot control these remote depositories of its power.

"Besides, the commercial nations of the world cannot fail to perceive and appreciate the great advantages which would result to their people from a dissolution of the forced and unnatural connection between Spain and Cuba, and the annexation of the latter to the United States. The trade of England and France with Cuba would, in that event, assume at once an important and profitable character, and rapidly extend with the increasing population and prosperity of the island.

"But if the United States and every commercial nation be benefited by this transfer, the interests of Spain would also be greatly and essentially promoted. She cannot but see that such a sum of money as we are willing to pay for the island would effect in the development of her vast natural resources.

"Two-thirds of this sum, if employed in the construction of a system of railroads, would ultimately prove a source of greater wealth to the Spanish people than that opened to their vision by Cortes. Their prosperity would date from the ratification of th treaty of cession. France has already constructed continuous nes of railroads from Havre, Marseilles, Valenciennes, and Strasbourg, *via* Paris to the Spanish frontier, and anxiously aw its the day when Spain shall find herself in a condition to ext d these roads through her northern provinces to Madrid, Sevi e, Cadiz, Malaga, and the frontier of Portugal.

"This object once accomplished, Spain would become a centre of attraction for the travelling world, and secure a permanent and profitable market for her various productions. Her fields, under the stimulus given to industry by remunerating prices, would teem with cereal grain, and her vineyards would bring forth a vastly increased quantity of choice wines. Spain would speedily become what a bountiful Providence intended she should be—one of the first nations of continental Europe, rich, powerful, and contented.

"Whilst two-thirds of the price of the island would be ample for the completion of her most important public improvements, she might, with the remaining forty (million) thousands, satisfy the demands now pressing so heavily upon her credit, and create a sinking fund which would gradually relieve her from the overwhelming debt now paralyzing her energies.

"Such is her present wretched financial condition, that her best bonds are sold upon her own bourse, at about one-third of their par value, whilst another class on which she pays no interest have but a nominal value, and are quoted at about one sixth of the amount for which they were issued.

"Besides, these latter are held principally by British creditors who may, from day to day, obtain the effective interposition of their own government for the purpose of coercing payment. Intimations to that effect have been already thrown out from high quarters, and unless some new source of revenue shall enable Spain to provide for such exigencies, it is not improbable that they may be realized.

"Should Spain reject the present golden opportunity for developing her resources, and removing her present financial embarrassments, it may never again return.

"Cuba, in her palmiest days, never yielded her exchequer, after deducting the expenses of its government, a clear annual income of more than a million and a half of dollars. These expenses have increased to such a degree as to leave a deficit chargeable on the treasury of Spain to the amount of six hundred thousand dollars.

"In a pecuniary point of view, therefore, the island is an encumbrance instead of a source of profit to the mother country.

"Under no probable circumstances can Cuba ever yield to Spain one per cent. on the large amount which the United States are willing to pay for its acquisition.

"But Spain is in imminent danger of losing Cuba without remuneration.

"Extreme oppression, it is now universally admitted, justifies any people in endeavoring to relieve themselves from the yoke of their oppressors.

"The sufferings which the corrupt, arbitrary, and unrelenting, local administration necessarily entails upon the inhabitants of Cuba, cannot fail to stimulate and keep alive that spirit of resistance and revolution against Spain which has of late years been so often manifested. In this condition of affairs, it is vain to expect that the sympathies of the people of the United States will not be warmly enlisted in favor of their oppressed neighbors.

"We know that the President is justly inflexible in his determination to execute the neutrality laws, but should the Cubans themselves rise in revolt against the oppression which they suffer, no human power could prevent citizens of the United States, and liberal-minded men of other countries, from rushing to their assistance.

" Besides, the present is an age of adventure, in which restless and daring spirits abound in every portion of the world. It is not improbable, therefore, that Cuba may be wrested from Spain by a successful revolution, and in that event, she will not only lose the island, but the price which we are now willing to pay for it—a price far beyond what was ever paid by any one people to another for any province.

" It may, also, be here remarked, that the settlement of this vexed question, by the cession of Cuba to the United States, would forever prevent the dangerous complications between nations to which it may otherwise give birth.

"It is certain that, should the Cubans themselves organize an insurrection against the Spanish government, and should other independent nations come to the aid of Spain in the contest, no human power could, in our opinion, prevent the people and government of the United States from taking part in such civil war, in support of their neighbors and friends.

" But if Spain, deaf to the voice of her own interest, and actuated by stubborn pride and a false sense of honor, should refuse to sell Cuba to the United States, then the question will arise, what ought to be the course of the American government under such circumstances ?

" Self-preservation is the first law of nature with States, as well as with individuals. All nations have at different periods acted upon this maxim. Although it has been made the pretext for committing flagrant injustice, as in the partition of Poland and other similar cases which history records, yet the prin-

ciple itself, though often abused, has always been recog
nized.

"The United States have never acquired a foot of territory
except by fair purchase, or, as in the case of Texas, upon the
free and voluntary application of the people of that independent
State, who desired to blend their destinies with our own.

"Even our acquisitions from Mexico are no exception to the
rule, because, although we might have claimed them by the
right of conquest, in a just way, yet we purchased them for
what was then considered by both parties a full and ample
equivalent. Our past history forbids that we should acquire
the Island of Cuba without the consent of Spain, unless justified
by the great law of self-preservation. We must, in any event,
preserve our own conscious rectitude and our own self-respect.
Whilst pursuing this course, we can afford to disregard the cen-
sures of the world to which we have been so often and so unjustly exposed. After we shall have offered Spain a price for
Cuba far beyond its present value, and this shall have been
refused, it will then be time to consider the question, does Cuba,
in the possession of Spain, seriously endanger our internal peace
and the existence of our cherished Union? Should this question be answered in the affirmative, then by every law, human
and divine, we shall be justified in wresting it from Spain, if we
possess the power. And this upon the very same principle that
would justify an individual in tearing down the burning house
of his neighbor, if there were no other means of preventing the
flames from destroying his own home. Under such circumstances we ought neither to count the cost nor regard the odds
which Spain might enlist against us. We forbear to enter into
the question whether the present condition of the island would
justify such a measure. We should, however, be recreant to our
duty, be unworthy of our gallant forefathers, and commit base
treason against our posterity, should we permit Cuba to be
Africanized and become a second St. Domingo, with all its
attendant horrors to the white race, and suffer the flames to

extend to our neighboring shores, seriously to endanger, or actually to consume the fair fabric of our Union. We fear that the course and current of events are rapidly tending towards such a catastrophe. We, however, hope for the best, though we ought certainly to be prepared for the worst.

"We forbear also to investigate the present condition of the question at issue between the United States and Spain. A long series of injuries to our people have been committed in Cuba by Spanish officials, and are unredressed ; but recently a most flagrant outrage on the rights of American citizens and on the flag of the United States was perpetrated in the harbor of Havana, under circumstances which, without immediate redress, would have justified a resort to measures of war in vindication of national honor. That outrage is not only unatoned, but the Spanish Government has deliberately sanctioned the acts of its subordinates, and assumed the responsibility attaching to them. Nothing could more impressively teach us the danger to which those peaceful relations it has ever been the policy of the United States to cherish with foreign nations are constantly exposed, than the circumstances of that case—situated as Spain and the United States are, the latter having forborne to resort to extreme measures. But this course cannot, with due regard to their own dignity as an independent nation, continue. And our recommendations now submitted are dictated by the firm belief that the cession of Cuba to the United States, with stipulations as beneficial to Spain as those suggested, is the only effectual mode of settling all past differences, and of securing the two countries against future collisions. We have already witnessed the happy results for both countries which followed a similar arrangement in regard to Florida."

Mr. Buchanan returned to his native country on the 23d of April last. His course had been watched with intense anxiety by his fellow citizens, and when the Common Council of New

York city determined, without respect of party, to unite in giving him a public reception, it but expressed the general impulse of gratefulness to him for his distinguished services. The following preamble and resolution were unanimously passed by the city authorities.

"Whereas, Mr. Buchanan's patriotic, dignified and able course as representative of his country at the British Court, and especially the judgment and ability displayed in conducting the recent negotiations with Great Britain, have commanded the admiration and approval of the American people, and whereas, the respect entertained by our citizens, without distinction of party, for his exalted character and commanding talents as evinced in a long career of conspicuous public service, ought to find a fitting expression in their representatives in the Common Council, therefore, be it

Resolved, That a select committee of five be appointed to receive the Hon. James Buchanan, on his arrival at this port, as the guest of this city, and tender to him the hospitalities thereof."

The reception which Mr. Buchanan experienced was cordial and enthusiastic. When he landed from the steamer, a dense crowd of persons surrounded the carriage, and cheer upon cheer attested the deep and earnest affection which the people always bestow upon a faithful public servant. Mr. Buchanan, while stopping in New York, was visited by a large number of persons of all political parties, who congratulated him upon the successful manner in which he had conducted our foreign relations. A public dinner was tendered him by the corporation, but Mr. Buchanan politely but decidedly declined it. He did not wish any display or ostentation. He would be happy to see his fellow-citizens in a familiar manner, but he did not desire to indulge in any feasting or parade. Accordingly, the next day after his arrival, he repaired to the Governor's room in the City Hall, where hundreds and thousands gratified an honorable desire in clasping the hand of one who had in so distinguished a manner sustained and added to the honor of his country abroad.

A brief speech delivered by Mr. Buchanan from the balcony of the Everett House, where he stopped, to a large crowd of persons who had assembled to serenade him, is so full of earnest feeling, that we give the principal portion. He said:

"Friends and Fellow-citizens: I can scarcely describe the emotions I feel at the present moment, in view of the vast crowd of my fellow-citizens of the great commercial emporium of the Union. I have been for years abroad in a foreign land, and I like the noise of the democracy! My heart responds to the acclamations of the noble citizens of this favored country. I have been abroad in other lands; I have witnessed arbitrary power; I have contemplated the people of other countries; but there is no country under God's heavens where a man feels to his fellow-man, except in the United States. If you could feel how despotism looks on; how jealous the despotic powers of the world are of our glorious institutions, you would cherish the Constitution and Union to your hearts, next to your belief in the Christian religion—the Bible for Heaven and the Constitution of your country for earth."

These noble sentiments were received with enthusiastic applause. Indeed, wherever Mr. Buchanan went he was greeted with the warmest affection. He left the city after only two days' sojourn, and hastened homeward. Everywhere on the line of his travel, he was received with the utmost enthusiasm. He was taken entirely by surprise, and so humble and modest was he in the estimate of his own performances, that he could not account for the popular feeling. At his place of residence, Lancaster, however, he was destined to be more than surprised. It seemed as if the entire population, men, women, and children, had turned out to welcome him home. He could undergo the attentions of strangers, but when he saw his neighbors *en masse*, those whom he had lived among for forty years, assembled, and disputing, as it were, who should be the first to express their gratification for his safe return, he was overwhelmed. He attempted to address them, but for a time his feelings overcame his power of utterance, and a tear testified more deeply than the greatest eloquence how sensibly he was affected by the cordial greeting which was so spontaneously extended to him. After the reception was over, Mr. Buchanan sought his quiet home, Wheatland, about a mile-and-a-half west of the city of Lancaster, where he has since remained.

It is difficult, in these days of political misrepresentation, to convince people that every man who is a candidate for the Presidency is not engaged in a deep laid scheme for his own preferment. Yet Mr. Buchanan has not only been entirely guiltless of any such acts, but he was even surprised at the general feeling in his favor. When informed by some of his friends that the country had been looking with anxiety for his return, "For my return!" said Mr. Buchanan in real surprise, "Why should any interest be taken in me?" "Because," they replied, "your consistent and candid position upon all public questions have inspired all with confidence in you." "Well, said Mr. Buchanan, "I certainly have not sought it. I have simply endeavored to do my duty." These facts afford the key to the whole subject. A man who, with honesty of purpose, strives to do his duty, does not take into consideration the effect of his conduct; while the people, with that natural instinct which always responds to purity of intention, take up such a man, and bestow upon him honors that he did not expect, and is surprised to receive. In this way has Mr. Buchanan been placed so prominently before the American people.

CHAPTER XXIII

Mr. Buchanan brought forward for the Presidency—His Nomination at Cincinnati—
The National Democratic Platform—Letter of the Committee officially announcing
the Nomination—Mr. Buchanan's Reply.

Long before Mr. Buchanan returned from Europe a large and
influential portion of his political friends in different parts of
the Union brought forward his name as a candidate for the
Presidency.   The democratic convention of his own State held
at Harrisburg on the 4th of March, 1856, had also presented
his name prominently to the public. All acknowledge the right
of Pennsylvania as the democratic banner State to make a
claim upon the party, and especially should she be heeded when
she presented a name at once so acceptable to her own citizens
as well as to the people of the United States.   The time and
circumstances seemed to conspire to force Mr. Buchanan
upon the attention of the public.   Never since the formation
of our government had a more formidable agitation been conceived, or been conducted upon such systematic principles. He
was known to combine in his character, what is rarely ever
found united in the same person ; a mind always capable of taking an expanded and progressive view of public questions, and
at the same time preserve that healthful degree of conservatism which checks excesses, guides events within the bound of
reason, and in fact sustains that healthful progress of society
which is as equally removed from rashness as from the dead
calm of inactivity. Then too he was looked upon as a citizen
in every emergency—one to whom the country could look with

confidence. He had also arrived at that age in life when the experience of the statesman had ripened into the wisdom of the sage, and when he could have no inducement to act from any impulse of popularity. All these qualifications particularly recommended him for the present emergency, and as his name seemed to be the demand of the people, as it appeared to come up from the very heart of the masses, even those who personally preferred other eminent statesmen, sacrificed their wishes to the people's choice.

In this connection it is proper to refer to Mr. Buchanan's action in this matter.   We can assert upon the best authority that from the very first to the last Mr. Buchanan has utterly refused to do anything whatever, either by word or deed, request or suggestion, in order to procure the nomination for the Presidency.   Could every private letter he has penned to his most intimate friends be laid before the public, all would be firmly convinced that James Buchanan has had no agency in urging in any way his own nomination. He proudly abstained from even expressing any desire for its accomplishment.   In truth he knew too much of the anxieties and difficulties of public stations, and had gone beyond that period of life when ambition may tempt men " to rush in where angels fear to tread."   He had long been deliberately convinced that the Presidency was above all others an office which should not become an object for the scramble of public men.   What action there was in his favor was the spontaneous moving of the people in their primary organizations.

Such was the state of affairs when the Democratic National Convention met at Cincinnati on the 2d day of June.   It is unnecessary to go into the details of that meeting.   It was the only political convention held this year composed of men from every State and District in this broad Union.   It was a noble, a grand, a sublime sight.   In the midst of the controversies of their opponents, divided and sub-divided into antagonistic organizations, some so sectional in their ideas that they would make war upon even the immortal Washington were he now alive, here was a body of men coming up from every town and hamlet in our glorious confederacy, and harmoniously working together for their country's good. There has seldom, if ever, met at any National Convention a body of such good and true men, and who felt so fully the responsibilities of their positions. This is attested by reliable and worthy persons, who were present, and who noted the fact of so much order, sobriety and dignity, considering the immense crowd and the usual circumstances of excitement attending such a convention. In stating the result of this convention it is only necessary to say that Mr. Buchanan was unanimously nominated on the seventeenth ballot, amid the most tumultuous cheering. As the news spread, the booming of cannon caught up the expiring cheers and prolonged the sound, until from the North to the South, from the East to the West the joyful responses had been received that James Buchanan was as unanimously accepted by the party, as he had been by the convention.

As it may often be necessary to refer to this volume during the campaign, we give below the platform of the National Democratic party as adopted at Cincinnati :

PLATFORM OF THE NATIONAL DEMOCRATIC CONVENTION, 1856.

" *Resolved*, That the American democracy place their trust in the intelligence, the patriotism and the discriminating justice of the American people.

" *Resolved*, That we regard this as a distinctive feature of political creed, which we are proud to maintain before the world as the great moral element in a form of government springing from and upheld by the popular will ; and we contrast it with the creed and practice of federalism, under whatever name or form, which seeks to palsy the will of the constituent, and which conceives no imposture too monstrous for the popular credulity.

" *Resolved*, therefore, That entertaining these views, the democratic party of this Union, through their delegates assembled in a general convention, coming together in a spirit of concord, of devotion to the doctrines and faith of a free represented government, and appealing to their fellow citizens for the rectitude of their intentions, renew and re-assert before the American people, the declarations of the principles avowed by them when, on former occasions, in general convention, they have presented their candidate for the popular suffrages.

" 1. That the federal government is one of limited power, derived solely from the Constitution ; and the grants of power made therein ought to be strictly construed by all the departments and agents of the government ; and that it is inexpedient and dangerous to exercise doubtful constitutional powers.

" 2. That the Constitution does not confer upon the general government the power to commence and carry on a general system of internal improvement.

" 3. That the Constitution does not confer authority upon the federal government, directly or indirectly, to assume the debts of the several States, contracted for local and internal improvements, or other State purposes ; nor would such assumption be just or expedient.

" 4. That justice and sound policy forbid the federal government to foster one branch of industry to the detriment of any other, or to cherish the interests of one portion to the injury of another portion of our common country ; that every citizen and every section of the country has a right to demand and insist upon an equality of rights and privileges, and to complete and ample protection of persons and property from domestic violence or foreign aggression.

" 5. That it is the duty of every branch of the government to enforce and practise the most rigid economy in conducting our public affairs, and that no more revenue ought to be raised than is required to defray the necessary expenses of the government, and for the gradual, but certain extinction of the public debt.

" 6. That the proceeds of the public lands ought to be sacredly applied to the national objects specified in the Constitution ; and that we are opposed to any law for the distribution of such proceeds among the States, as alike inexpedient in policy and repugnant to the Constitution.

" 7. That Congress has no power to charter a national bank ; that we believe such an institution one of deadly hostility to the best interests of the country, dangerous to our republican institutions and the liberties of the people, and calculated to place the business of the country within the control of a concentrated money power, and above the laws and the will of the people ; and that the results of democratic legislation in this and all other financial measures upon which issues have been made between the two political parties of the country, have demonstrated to candid and practical men of all parties, their soundness, safety, and utility, in all business pursuits.

" 8. That the separation of the moneys of the government from banking institutions is indispensable for the safety of the funds of the government and the rights of the people.

" 9. That we are decidedly opposed to taking from the President the qualified veto power, by which he is enabled, under restrictions and responsibilities amply sufficient to guard the public interests, to suspend the passage of a bill whose merits cannot secure the approval of two thirds of the Senate and House of Representatives, until the judgment of the people can be obtained thereon, and which saved the American people from the corrupt and tyrannical domination of the Bank of the United States, and from a corrupting system of general internal improvements.

" 10. That the liberal principles embodied by Jefferson in the Declaration of Independence, and sanctioned in the Constitution, which makes ours the land of liberty, and the asylum of the oppressed of every nation, have ever been cardinal principles in the democratic faith, and every attempt to abridge the privilege of becoming citizens and the owners of soil among us, ought to be resisted with the same spirit which swept the alien and sedition laws from our statute books

" And *whereas*, Since the foregoing declaration was uniformly adopted by our predecessors in national conventions, an adverse political and religious test has been secretly organized by a party claiming to be exclusively American, it is proper that the American democracy should clearly define its relations thereto, and declare its determined opposition to all secret political societies by whatever name they may be called.

" *Resolved*, That the foundation of this union of States having been laid in, and its prosperity, expansion and pre-eminent example in free government, built upon entire freedom in matters of religious concernment, and no respect of person in regard to rank or place of birth ; no party can justly be deemed national, constitutional, or in accordance with American principles, which bases its exclusive organization upon religious opinions and accidental birth-place. And hence a political crusade in the nineteenth century, and in the United States of America, against catholics and foreign born, is neither justified by the past history or the future prospects of the country, nor in unison with the spirit of toleration and enlarged freedom which peculiarly distinguishes the American system of popular government.

" *Resolved*, That we reiterate with renewed energy of purpose, the well-considered declarations of former conventions upon the sectional issue of domestic slavery, and concerning the reserved rights of the States :

" 1. That Congress has no power under the Constitution to interfere with or control the domestic institutions of the several States, and that such States are the sole and proper judges of everything appertaining to their own affairs, not prohibited by the Constitution ; that all efforts of the Abolitionists or others, made to induce Congress to interfere with questions of slavery o- to take incipient steps in relation thereto, are calculated to lead to the most alarming and dangerous consequences ; and that all such efforts have an inevitable tendency to diminish the happiness of the people, and endanger the stability and permanency of the Union, and ought not to be countenanced by any friend of our political institutions.

" 2. That the foregoing proposition covers, and was intended to embrace the whole subject of slavery agitation in Congress ; and therefore, the democratic party of the Union, standing on this national platform, will abide by and adhere to a faithful execution of the acts known as the Compromise Measures, settled by the Congress of 1850 ; ' the act of reclaiming fugitives from service or labor,' included ; which act being designed to carry out an express provision of the Constitution, cannot with fidelity thereto be repealed, or so changed as to destroy or impair its efficiency.

" 3. That the democratic party will resist all attempts at renewing, in Congress or out of it, the agitation of the slavery question, under whatever shape or color the attempt may be made.

" 4. That the democratic party will faithfully abide by and uphold the principles laid down in the Kentucky and Virginia resolutions of 1798, and in the report of Mr. Madison to the Virginia Legislature in 1799 ; that it adopts those principles as constituting one of the main foundations of its political creed, and is resolved to carry them out in their obvious meaning and import.

" And that we may more distinctly meet the issue on which a sectional party, subsisting exclusively on slavery agitation, now relies to test the fidelity of the people, North and South, to the Constitution and the Union—

" *Resolved*, That claiming fellowship with, and desiring the co-operation of all who regard the preservation of the Union under the Constitution as the paramount issue—and repudiating all sectional parties and platforms concerning domestic slavery

18

which seek to embroil the States and incite to treason and armed resistance to law in the territories ; and whose avowed purposes, if consummated, must end in civil war and disunion— the American democracy recognize and adopt the principles contained in the organic laws, establishing the territories of Kansas and Nebraska, as embodying the only sound and safe solution of the 'slavery question' upon which the great national idea of the people of this whole country can repose in its determined conservatism of the Union—*non-interference by Congress with slavery in State and Territory, or in the District of Columbia.*

" 2. That this was the basis of the compromises of 1850— confirmed by both the Democratic and Whig parties in national conventions—ratified by the people in the election of 1852.— and rightly applied to the organization of territories in 1854

" 3. That by the uniform application of this democratic principle to the organization of Territories, and the admission of new States, with or without domestic slavery, as they may elect—the equal rights of all the States will be preserved intact—the original compacts of the Constitution maintained inviolate—and the perpetuity and expansion of this Union insured to its utmost capacity of embracing, in peace and harmony, every future American State that may be constituted or annexed, with a republican form of government.

" *Resolved*, That we recognize the right of the people of all the Territories, including Kansas and Nebraska, acting through the legally and fairly expressed will of a majority of actual residents ; and whenever the number of their inhabitants justifies it, to form a Constitution, with or without domestic slavery, and be admitted into the Union upon terms of perfect equality with the other States.

" *Resolved*, finally, That in view of the condition of popular institutions in the Old World (and the dangerous tendencies of sectional agitation, combined with the attempt to enforce civil and religious disabilities against the rights of acquiring and enjoying citizenship in our own land)—a high and sacred duty is devolved with increased responsibility upon the democratic party of this country, as the party of the Union, to uphold and maintain the rights of every State, and thereby the Union of the States ; and to sustain and advance among us Constitutional liberty, by continuing to resist all monopolies and exclusive legislation for the benefit of the few at the expense of the many, and by a vigilant and constant adherence to those principles and compromises of the Constitution, which are broad enough and strong enough to embrace and uphold the Union as it was, the Union as it is, and the Union as it shall be, in the full expansion of the energies and capacity of this great and progressive people.

" [All of the above was adopted unanimously by the Convention.]

" 1. *Resolved*, That there are questions connected with the foreign policy of this country, which are inferior to no domestic question whatever. The time has come for the people of the United States to declare themselves in favor of free seas and progressive free trade throughout the world, and, by solemn manifestations, to place their moral influence at the side of their successful example.

" [Adopted, 234 to 26. Georgia, Maryland, Delaware, and North Carolina voted no.]

" 2. *Resolved*, That our geographical and political position with reference to the other States of this continent, no less than the interests of our commerce and the development of our growing power, requires that we should hold as sacred the principles involved in the Monroe doctrine ; their bearing and import admit of no misconstruction ; they should be applied with unbending rigidity.

" [Adopted, 239 to 23.]

" 3. *Resolved*, That the great highway which nature, as well as the assent of the States most immediately interested in its maintenance, has marked out for a free communication between the Atlantic and Pacific oceans, constitutes one of the most important achievements realized by the spirit of modern times, and the unconquerable energy of our people. That result should be secured by a timely and efficient exertion of the control which we have the right to claim over it, and no power on earth should be suffered to impede or clog its progress by any interference with the relations it may suit our policy to establish between our government and the governments of the States within whose dominions it lies. We can, under no circumstances, surrender our preponderance in the adjustment of all questions arising out of it.

[Adopted, 199 to 56. Maine 1, Connecticut 2, Virginia, Maryland, and Rhode Island formed the principal nays.]

" 4. That in view of so commanding an interest, the people of the United States cannot but sympathize with the efforts which are being made by the people of Central America to regenerate that portion of the continent which covers the passage across the interoceanic Isthmus.

[Adopted, 221 to 38. Rhode Island, Delaware, Maryland, South Carolina, and Kentucky voted nay.]

" 5. *Resolved*, That the democratic party will expect of the next administration that every proper effort be made to insure our ascendency in the Gulf of Mexico, and to maintain a permanent protection to the great outlets through which are emptied into its waters the products raised out of the soil, and the commodities created by the industry of the people of our Western valleys, and of the Union at large.

[Adopted, 229 to 30—last nearly as on previous one.]

" A resolution was introduced and passed, though not adopted as a part of the platform, declaring it to be the duty of the general government, so far as the Constitution will permit, to aid in the construction of a safe overland route between the Atlantic and the Pacific coasts."

A committee was appointed to wait upon Mr. Buchanan and

inform him officially of his nomination. These gentlemen repaired personally to Lancaster, and there presented to Mr. Buchanan the following letter ·

" LANCASTER, June 13, 1856.

"SIR: The National Convention of the democratic party, which assembled at Cincinnati on the first Monday in June, unanimously nominated you as a candidate for the office of President of the United States.

" We have been directed by the convention to convey to you this intelligence, and to request you, in their name, to accept the nomination for the exalted trust which the chief magistracy of the Union imposes.

" The convention, founding their action upon the time-honored principles of the democratic party, have announced their views in relation to the chief questions which engage the public mind ; and, while adhering to the truths of the past, have manifested the policy of the present in a series of resolutions, to which we invoke your attention.

" The convention feel assured, in tendering to you this signal proof of the respect and esteem of your countrymen, that they truly reflect the opinion which the people of the United States entertain of your eminent character and distinguished public services. They cherish a profound conviction that your elevation to the first office in the Republic will give a moral guarantee to the country that the true principles of the Constitution will be asserted and maintained ; that the public tranquillity will be established ; that the tumults of factions will be stilled ; that our domestic industry will flourish ; that our foreign affairs will be conducted with such wisdom and firmness as to assure the prosperity of the people at home, while the interests and honor of our country are wisely but inflexibly maintained in our intercourse with other nations ; and, especially, that your public experience and the confidence of your countrymen will enable you to give effect to democratic principles, so as to render indissoluble the strong bonds of mutual interest and national glory which unite our confederacy and secure the prosperity of our people.

"While we offer to the country our sincere congratulations upon the fortunate auspices of the future, we tender to you, personally, the assurances of the respect and esteem of your fellow-citizens,

> "John E. Ward,
> "W. A. Richardson,
> "Harry Hibbard,
> "W. B. Lawrence,
> "A. G. Brown,
> "Jno. L. Manning,
> "John Forsyth,
> "W. Preston,
> "J. Randolph Tucker,
> "Horatio Seymour

"Hon. James Buchanan.

The reply of Mr. Buchanan is characterized with his usual frankness and clearness, and places in a prominent light all the established traits of his character.

Wheatland (*near Lancaster*), *June* 16, 1856.

"Gentlemen : I have the honor to acknowledge the receipt of your communication of the 13th instant, informing me officially of my nomination by the Democratic National Convention, recently held at Cincinnati, as the democratic candidate for the office of President of the United States. I shall not attempt to express the grateful feelings which I entertain towards my democratic fellow-citizens for having deemed me worthy of this, the highest political honor on earth—an honor such as the people of no other country have the power to bestow. Deeply sensible of the vast and varied responsibility attached to the station, especially at the present crisis of our affairs, I have carefully refrained from seeking the nomination either by word or by deed. Now that it has been offered by the democratic party, I accept it with diffidence in my own abilities, but with an humble trust that, in the event of my election, I may be enabled to discharge my duty in such a manner as to allay domestic strife, preserve peace and friendship with foreign nations, and promote the best interests of the republic.

"In accepting the nomination, I need scarcely say that I accept in the same spirit the resolutions constituting the platform of principles erected by the convention. To this platform I intend to confine myself throughout the canvass, believing that I have no right, as the candidate of the democratic party, by answering interrogatories, to present new and different issues before the people.

"It will not be expected that in this answer I should specially refer to the subject of each of the resolutions, and I shall, therefore, confine myself to the two topics now most prominently before the people.

"And, in the first place, I cordially concur in the sentiments expressed by the convention on the subject of civil and religious liberty. No party founded on religious or political intolerance towards one class of American citizens, whether born in our own or in a foreign land, can long continue to exist in this country. We are all equal before God and the Constitution; and the dark spirit of despotism and bigotry which would create odious distinctions among our fellow-citizens will be speedily rebuked by a free and enlightened public opinion.

"The agitation of the question of domestic slavery has too long distracted and divided the people of this Union and alienated their affections from each other. This agitation has assumed many forms since its commencement, but it now seems to be directed chiefly to the territories; and, judging from its present character, I think we may safely anticipate that it is rapidly approaching a 'finality.' The recent legislation of Congress respecting domestic slavery, derived, as it has been, from the original and pure fountain of legitimate political power, the will of the majority, promises ere long to allay the dangerous excitement. This legislation is founded upon principles as ancient as free government itself, and, in accordance with them, has simply declared that the people of a territory, like those of a State, shall decide for themselves whether slavery shall or shall not exist within their limits.

"The Nebraska-Kansas act does no more than give the force of law to this elementary principle of self-government, declaring it to be 'the true intent and meaning of this act not to legislate slavery into any Territory or State, nor to exclude it therefrom, but to leave the people thereof perfectly free to form and regulate their domestic institutions in their own way, subject only to the Constitution of the United States." This principle will surely not be controverted by any individual of any party professing devotion to popular government. Besides, how vain and illusory would any other principle prove in practice in regard to the Territories! This is apparent from the fact admitted by all, that, after a Territory shall have entered the Union and become a State, no Constitutional power would then exist which could prevent it from either abolishing or establishing slavery, as the case may be, according to its sovereign will and pleasure.

"Most happy would it be for the country if this long agitation were at an end. During its whole progress it has produced no practical good to any human being, whilst it has been the source of great and dangerous evils. It has alienated and estranged one portion of the Union from the other, and has even seriously threatened its very existence. To my own personal knowledge, it has produced the impression among foreign nations that our great and glorious confederacy is in constant danger of dissolution. This does us serious injury, because acknowledged power and stability always command respect among nations, and are among the best securities against unjust aggression, and in favor of the maintenance of honorable peace.

"May we not hope that it is the mission of the democratic party, now the only surviving conservative party of the country, ere long to overthrow all sectional parties, and restore the peace, friendship, and mutual confidence which prevailed in the good old time among the different members of the confederacy? Its character is strictly national, and it therefore asserts no principle for the guidance of the federal government which is not adopted and sustained by its members in each and every State. For this reason it is the same determined foe of all geographical parties, so much and so justly dreaded by the Father of his Country. From its very nature it must continue to exist so long as there is a Constitution and a Union to preserve. A conviction of these truths has induced many of the purest, the ablest, and most independent of our former opponents, who have differed from us in times gone by upon old and extinct party issues, to come into our ranks and devote themselves with us to the cause of the Constitution and the Union. Under these circumstances, I most cheerfully pledge myself, should the nomination of the convention be ratified by the people, that all the power and influence Constitutionally possessed by the Executive shall be exerted, in a firm but conciliatory spirit, during the single term I shall remain in office, to restore the same harmony among the sister States which prevailed before this apple of discord, in the form of slavery agitation, had been cast into their midst. Let the members of the family abstain from intermeddling with the exclusive domestic concerns of each other, and cordially unite on the basis of perfect equality among themselves, in promoting the great national objects of common interest to all, and the good work will be instantly accomplished.

"In regard to our foreign policy, to which you have referred in your communication, it is quite impossible for any human fore-knowledge to prescribe positive rules in advance to regulate the conduct of a future administration in all the exigencies which may arise in our various and ever-changing relations with foreign powers. The federal government must, of necessity, exercise a sound discretion in dealing with international questions as they may occur ; but this under the strict responsibility which the executive must always feel to the people of the United States, and the judgment of posterity. You will, therefore, excuse me for not entering into particulars ; whilst I heartily concur with you in the general sentiment, that our foreign affairs ought to be conducted with such wisdom and firmness, as to assure the prosperity of the people at home, whilst the interests and honor of our country are wisely, but inflexibly, maintained abroad. Our foreign policy ought ever to be based upon the principle of doing justice to all nations, and requiring justice from them in return ; and from this principle I shall never depart.

"Should I be placed in the executive chair, I shall use my best exertions to cultivate peace and friendship with all nations, believing this to be our highest policy, as well as our most imperative duty ; but, at the same time, I shall never forget that in case the necessity should arise, which I do not now apprehend, our national rights and national honor must be preserved at all hazards and at any sacrifice.

"Firmly convinced that a special Providence governs the affairs of nations, let us humbly implore His continued blessing upon our country, and that He may avert from us the punishment we justly deserve for being discontented and ungrateful while enjoying privileges above all nations, under such a constitution and such a Union as has never been vouchsafed to any other people.

"Yours, very respectfully,

"JAMES BUCHANAN."

Hon. JOHN E. WARD, W. A. RICHARDSON, HARRY HIBBARD, W. B. LAWRENCE, A. G. BROWN, JOHN L. MANNING, JOHN FORSYTH, W. PRESTON, J. RANDOLPH TUCKER, and HORATIO SEYMOUR, Committee, &c.

CHAPTER XXIV.

Mr. Buchanan at Home.

HAVING in the preceding chapters given a brief review of some of the more prominent events in Mr. Buchanan's life, as well as the more important of his many public services, it is no more than right to close this volume with some reference to his personal character. To a certain extent the private relations of any man who is presented to the people of the United States to receive their suffrages for the highest office in their gift, is a fair and proper subject of inquiry. "Upon private integrity," said the illustrious Washington, "rests all the safeguards of public virtue." The people have, therefore, undoubtedly the right to inquire whether the candidate before them possess those qualities both of mind and heart, which will confer honor even upon the exalted office to which he may be elected, and give, at the same time, a guarantee that public truth will flow legitimately from private integrity. It is no exaggeration to say, that Mr. Buchanan is a model of all that is praiseworthy or admirable in the character of a public man His has been a life of thorough discipline, of rigid and careful culture, and, guided by those simple methodical habits, which were imbibed in early life, at the feet of a devoted mother, it is not surprising that they have been the foundation of a character at once graceful in its parts and symmetrical in it complete proportions.

One of the strongest traits in Mr. Buchanan' personal life, is the hold he has upon the affections of the people among

whom he resides. His political enemies have represented him
as cold and distant in his manners. There never was a more
unfounded statement. The writer of this has been among his
friends and neighbors, and conversed unreservedly with all he
met, and the universal voice was that for genial, and warm-
hearted friendship he has no equal. This feeling is not confined to any class of the population, but all, rich and poor,
unite in the same expression. In one respect, perhaps, Mr.
Buchanan may not meet the expectations of some. He is not
of that facile, ever-changing mould, capable of adapting himself to any and every individual he meets, and conquering their
friendship by addressing their vanity. To such persons, friendship is but a name. To individuals like Mr. Buchanan, it is
an affection founded upon an acquaintance which ripens into
confidence. All who meet him are at once convinced of the
kindness of his disposition, and the sincerity of his heart. There
is an entire absence of display, no ostentation or formality ; but
accustomed to mingle freely with all classes of society, he instinctively rejects everything that looks like pride or fashion.

In this respect, he is an index of the people among whom
he resides. Probably there is no agricultural population of
equal wealth in our country which has retained so many habits
of rural simplicity, as that of the county of Lancaster, in Pennsylvania. It has resisted with success the follies of fashionable
life which naturally radiate from our large seaboard towns, and
in the whole city of Lancaster, a place of some seventeen
thousand inhabitants, there is less fashion and display to be
found than in one small New England village. The church
of the Presbyterian denomination, which Mr. Buchanan regularly
attends, is a structure so limited in size, and so plain and
unpretending in appearance, that it would shock the sensibili-
ties of the majority of metropolitan church goers.

Mr. Buchanan's equanimity of mind is one of the most
admirable, as it is one of the most prominent, features of his
character. His natural disposition is exceedingly buoyant, and

as years have gradually crept over him, silvering his locks with the frosts of age, the original tendency of his mind has not been perverted, only modified, and at this day he presents that joyous spectacle where the freshness of youth is united to the calmness and maturity of age. It is believed there is no instance during the whole course of Mr. Buchanan's public life where his equanimity of temper was seriously disturbed. At all times and under all circumstances, he has been enabled to bring to the consideration of questions a mind free from that species of insanity, where passion usurps the place of reason. It has been noted with what dignity he repelled the outrageous attack made upon him by John Davis of Massachusetts. Few men would have borne themselves through such a provoking assault, without losing that command of their temper which a proper respect for one's place and position requires, but which it is almost impossible, under great provocation, to exercise. Upon another occasion Mr. Clay indulged, in the course of some remarks, in a reference to the charge of " low wages " in such a manner as to cast a reflection upon Mr. Buchanan. When he had concluded Mr. Buchanan rose with his usual dignity and deliberation and said, "he had listened with his usual gratification to the reply of the distinguished senator from Kentucky, with the exception of a single remark. I refer to his allusion to the electioneering slang of the late contest on the subject of low wages. That remark was wholly unworthy of that senator, and I intend to answer it as it deserves."

Mr. Clay observing that Mr. Buchanan had taken his remark in a serious manner, interrupted him and begged to be permitted to explain. He expressly disclaimed any offensive purpose in his remark, and declared "that it was meant only as a playful allusion and not intended to wound the feelings of the senator in the least." Mr. Buchanan replied, "I am entirely satisfied and am glad we are friends again." This disavowal on the part of Mr. Clay of any respect for the charge of John Davis, as a serious one against Mr. Buchanan, was exactly in accordance with Mr Clay's well known generosity of character, and should shame all at the present day who have the hardihood to revive the exploded slander.   It is by such evenness of temper and entire self-possession as we have referred to in the foregoing instances, that Mr. Buchanan has been enabled to pass a long public life without, it is believed, having a single personal enemy among his political opponents.

The equanimity of Mr. Buchanan's temper is only equalled by the generosity of his disposition.   Did it not seem like parading before the public, deeds whose sincere benevolence has made them almost sacred, we might specify numerous instances where his unostentatious charity has been conspicuous.   Such a course, we feel confident, would be as distasteful to him as it might seem obtrusive to the public.

> " The secret pleasure of a generous act
> Is the great mind's great bribe."

To show, however, what his neighbors think of him in this respect, we give the following quotation from a newspaper published in the place of his residence, and coming as it does from a political opponent, and since his nomination for the presidency, it cannot be suspected of any partiality.   The editor says :

" We knew Mr. Buchanan as one of our most respected fellow citizens—a gentleman of unblemished personal integrity, and unusually agreeable manners in his social intercourse with all classes.   We knew him as a friend of the poor—as a perpetual benefactor of the poor widows of this city, who, when the piercing blasts of each successive winter brought shrieks of cold, and hunger, and want, in the frail tenements of Poverty, could apply to the 'Buchanan Relief Donation' for their annual supply of wood, and sitting down with their orphaned children in the cheerful warmth of a blazing fire, lift their hearts in silent gratitude to God, and teach their little ones to bless the name of James Buchanan.   As a citizen, a neighbor, a friend—in a word, as simply James Buchanan, we yielded to no man in the measure of our respect and esteem."

The "Buchanan Relief Donation" referred to, consists of a fund of several thousand dollars invested by him a number of years since, for purposes indicated in the foregoing extract. If, as Byron asserts,

> "The drying up a single tear has more
> Of honest fame than shedding seas of gore,"

then most assuredly has Mr. Buchanan attained it.

The following extract from a private letter from a gentleman at Washington, written since the nomination, gives such a graphic picture of Mr. Buchanan at home, that we make no apology for introducing it here :

"While at Lancaster, on professional business, I called at his residence, a mile and a half from the city, to see Mr. Buchanan, with whom I had been somewhat acquainted from his entrance into the U. S. Senate, in 1835. I found him at Wheatland, once a large farm noted for its yield of the cereal which conferred its name, now by subdivisions in passing through several generations, reduced to some thirty acres. He occupies an ancient, but spacious, brick dwelling surrounded by a beautiful grove, planted by an early owner. The cultivation is limited to a large garden and a few acres of wheat and oats, while a cow is in full possession of the most beautiful hickory grove I ever saw. I found Mr. B. in his library, the largest room in his house, which is well filled with books, and very neatly and appropriately fitted up with furniture of Pennsylvania oak. He receives his company with a courtesy and simplicity that make every one feel at his ease, though he never appears undignified. His conversation has a peculiar charm, because he uses, as Mr. Calhoun did, common and plain language to communicate his thoughts. He never confounds you with language, or words

you do not understand, nor does he attempt to dazzle by striking expressions or applying pungent epithets. His, is the clear
explicit language of every day life, and which is most befitting
all stations.

"Everything about him indicated that he loves order and
quiet, and that the tendency of his mind is in favor of utility.
There is nothing gaudy or frivolous to be found in his house.
Its furniture is plain, substantial, and appropriate to its place
and uses. His affection for his friends is manifested in all
parts of his house. I was much gratified in finding in his
library a likeness of the late Vice-President King, whom he
loved (and who did not?) He declared that he was the purest
public man that he ever knew, and that during his intimate
acquaintance of thirty years he had never known him to perform
a selfish act. Mr. B.'s tastes are of the most simple kind, and
he lives, like his neighbors, without attempting foolish ostentation or wearisome display. His uniform frugality has crowned
his latter years with a liberal competence, never contaminated
by parsimony. Poverty and affliction never solicited of him in
vain. He has always been liberal and charitable. He is now
about sixty-five years of age and has never married. His family
consists of himself and niece, whose education has been mainly
under his direction, and who accompanied him during his late
mission to England, and whose knowledge and sense, derived
from books, study and reflection, peculiarly qualify her to grace
and cheer the fireside of the Sage of Wheatland.

"Mr. Buchanan is very frank with his friends, and is always
ready to avail himself of their suggestions, when appropriate.
I was much struck with the attachment of his old neighbors
and friends, and indeed of all Pennsylvanians, to him personally. I saw no man in Lancaster, who was not his devoted
friend. You would be surprised to learn the large number who
voluntarily tell you of his numerous acts of kindness to them,
or their parents, relatives or neighbors. His old clients are
universally attached to him, and many speak of his **gratuitons**

professional services, in fighting the battles of the poor. A stranger would suppose that the entire population were his friends. During a stay of two days, at his house, I found him thronged with company, from early morning till a late hour in the evening, who came to congratulate him upon his safe return from Europe, and triumphant nomination. The numerous calls from the Pennsylvania farmers seemed to afford him great pleasure. There was an earnest sincerity manifested by them, that touched the heart. This deep feeling of attachment was strikingly illustrated when I was present. A Kentucky drover had been to Philadelphia, and sold his cattle to a city dealer. When the business was closed, the latter came with the former to Lancaster, a distance of seventy miles, apparently for the sole purpose of congratulating Mr. Buchanan, and introducing his western friend. I was told of other as striking instances of attachment.

"I saw many prominent whigs at his house, and others on the way, who openly avowed their intention to vote for Mr. Buchanan. The reasons for so doing, were, either personal attachment, or an avowed strong desire to repress all agitation and action tending to disunion, and a wish to restore national harmony and quiet. They seemed to be confident that his election would produce this desirable result. Some referred to our foreign affairs, and expressed the opinion that his experience, wisdom and prudence would keep them from falling into confusion, or resulting in contention or stain upon national honor.

"Mr. Buchanan is a large, muscular man, who enjoys the most perfect health, and is capable of enduring as much labor as a young man. During the time I was with him, I heard of no subject of conversation, with which he was not familiar. He was early distinguished as a sound lawyer. Ten years' service in the House, and ten in the Senate, made him familiar with the legislation and policy of the country. Three years service in Russia and three years in England, as Minister, and four in the State department, as Secretary, made him more familiar with our foreign relations than any other living man. From this you will readily believe that it is a treat to converse with him on diplomatic as well as other subjects, and that those who spend much time with him, depart greatly wiser than they came. He instructs without making one feel that he does so, and you regret when he is called off from the subject in hand. Had the state of my own business permitted, I should have been but too happy to have enjoyed his hospitality and society for a much longer period and to have profited by conversation with one so well qualified to impart wisdom and knowledge.

"Like General Jackson, he seems to have nothing to conceal. He remarked, that the time was when he was anxious to be elected President, but years, and the loss of those who had served long with him in public life, and who would have rendered him the needed support, had changed his feelings upon the subject. He had now been made a candidate without an effort of his own, and he felt bound to submit to the wishes of his friends, and therefore consented to become the representative of their principles and wishes. When referring to the fact that all who entered public life with him had left the stage, and he was left alone, he seemed deeply affected. A new generation had sprung up around him, to many of whom he was much attached, but they had not been his companions in arms in the political conflicts of his early life. But the sons of his early friends had demanded his services, and he had no right to refuse. He inquired, with emphasis, ' why should I, after forty years spent in the turmoil and excitement of public life, wish to leave my quiet home, and assume the responsibilities and cares incident to the presidency ? A sense of duty alone has induced me to accept the nomination. They tell me that the use of my name will still the agitated waters, restore public harmony, by banishing sectionalism, and remove all apprehension of disunion. For these objects I would not only surrender my own ease and comfort, but cheerfully lay down my life. Considerations like these have imposed upon me the duty of yielding to the wishes

of those who must know what the public good requires.' I
could not doubt he spoke what he strongly felt. It made a
deep impression upon my mind. I shall long remember this
visit, and whatever may be the future course of his political
fortunes, I shall never cease to admire and venerate the Union-
loving sage of Wheatland."

Such is the man now presented to the American people for
their suffrages. In the sunset of an honorable life, with his
eye yet undimmed, and his natural force unabated, he is
brought forward by the spontaneous voice of his countrymen.
Said the great Edmund Burke, " When bad men combine, good
men should unite ;" and without stopping to inquire whether
those who have combined on sectional issues are bad or not,
certainly their success can only add fuel to the present flame
of unholy strife. All good and reasonable men must therefore
be convinced that the peace, prosperity, and safety of twenty
millions of the happiest, freest, and most advanced white men,
with their noble structure of republican government, cemented
by the blood, the sufferings, and treasures of their ancestors,
should not be sacrificed—nay, not even jeopardized for the supposed interests of three millions of the African race, who,
whatever may be their present condition, are certainly better
off than any other three million of their own race of which we
have any knowledge.

This Union, with its inestimable blessings, its patriotic associations, its trial of the capacity of man for self-government, is
so invaluable to the cause of suffering humanity throughout the
world, that should the American people, with sacrilegious hand,
tear down this noble temple of liberty, they would deserve,
as they would undoubtedly receive, the just contempt and execration of posterity. To restore peace to our already distracted
country, to unite once more the bonds of fraternal feeling
between all sections, and in the language of the immortal
Washington, "to frown indignantly upon the first dawning of

every attempt to alienate any portion of our country from the rest," we cannot but believe that an overwhelming majority, North as well as South, will insist upon placing in the presidential chair, the consistent statesman, the pure patriot, and the honest man, JAMES BUCHANAN.

CHAPTER XXV.

ADDITIONAL.

The Progress of the Election—The Issues Involved—The Final Result—The Election of Mr. Buchanan—The Rejoicings of the Democracy—The Inauguration Ceremonies—The Inaugural Address—Sketches of the Cabinet Officers.

The foregoing chapters were written and published in the early part of the month of July immediately subsequent to Mr. Buchanan's nomination for President, and it is a source of satisfaction that the confidence felt and expressed therein in relation to his election, have received an emphatic confirmation in the voice of the people of the United States. There have been but few presidential elections in the history of our government where greater efforts were made by all parties to secure the triumph. The democracy entered the contest under more than ordinary disadvantages. The repeal of the Missouri Restriction had been so immediately followed by the difficulties in the territory of Kansas, that it was very plausible to charge the responsibility of them solely upon the party which had removed it. For this reason the justice or injustice of this restriction was, in a great measure, lost sight of, and ingenious stump orators, opposing the election of Mr. Buchanan, preferred to dwell in pathetic terms upon the reputed "outrages" in that territory, rather than to discuss the right of excluding a portion of their fellow-citizens from the common domain of the Union, unless they dissolved certain social relations with which the Federal Government has no right to interfere, much less abolish. The entire non-interference by Congress with the *status* of negroes, or in other words, with the social or legal relations of the white and black races, whether in State or Territory, was the great and principal issue of the late campaign. This, though in a somewhat different phraseology, was clearly enunciated in the Democratic platform.

It was perceived, however, in the early part of the canvass, that the real issue was to be avoided as much as possible, and the "evils of slavery," "the wrongs of Kansas," and "the aggressions of the South," were to be the principal texts from which to preach to the northern people. Two parties entered the field as opponents of the Democracy ; one had nominated Millard Fillmore, and the other John C. Frémont, as competitors of Mr. Buchanan. Mr. Fillmore had already served as President with honor to himself and with much satisfaction to many of his countrymen. He had, however, since the close of his official term, adopted the peculiar doctrines of the "American" party, and thus alienated from him many of his old adherents. Mr. Frémont was, however, a new man upon the political field, and with a considerable dash of romance in his life, he attracted even in his personal character more than ordinary attention. Supported, too, by powerful and influential presses, and receiving the endorsement of many men of well-known integrity and ability, it was soon perceived that he was destined to be an opponent of no ordinary strength.

During the early part of the canvass the tide of public opinion seemed to be strongly in favor of the so-called Republican party throughout all the Northern States. The August elections in Maine and Iowa were really disheartening to the Democrats. Their opponents were more than usually confident, and used almost superhuman exertions to effect the election of their candidate. It was soon perceived, however, by all who possessed any degree of political sagacity, that the State of Pennsylvania, the home of Mr. Buchanan, was to be the great, indeed, the decisive battle-ground. Never before had the Democracy of that honored State such immense and overwhelming questions confided to their decision. Mr. Jefferson has somewhere prophetically observed, " Let Virginia stand firm and Pennsylvania remain true to the Democracy, then will our liberties be safe, and our Union perpetual." The remark seemed to have been made with reference to just such a contingency as was now presented. At all events, all parties felt that upon the result in Pennsylvania depended the whole issue of the contest, and hence the most extraordinary efforts were made to defeat the Democrats at the October election. The friends of Mr. Fillmore were very strong in the State, while the peculiar principles of " Republicanism " had met with but an indifferent reception. A successful effort, however, was made to combine both of these parties in the support of the same ticket for State officers, and they, therefore, entered the contest flushed with hope and confident of victory. Defeats in other quarters had not, however, dismayed the " unterrified " democracy. As Virginia had given the first check to Know Nothingism under the lead of the gallant Wise, the honor remained for Pennsylvania to stem the torrent of abolition delusion, and disunion, with the name of her favorite son, James Buchanan, for the rallying cry. The victory in the one case was no less complete than in the other. While there was a dash of chivalry in the first, characteristic of the descendants of the Cavaliers, there was also the steady intrepidity and cool courage in the latter which ever distinguishes the German element. It is sufficient to say, that notwithstanding the union of all parties opposed to the Democracy, their ticket was elected by a handsome majority of nearly three thousand. The result was hailed everywhere throughout the Union by Democrats with the most enthusiastic rejoicing. Poets celebrated it in verse, and orators were never tired of talking about it on the stump. It revived the spirits of the Democracy, and infused new courage into the wavering lines. It was felt that the crisis, which all had been watching with almost breathless anxiety and attention, had passed. Patriots breathed freer, and all who felt in any way alarmed at the portents of the times were sensibly relieved. From that moment the battle was decided, for though much remained to be done, the democracy marched on afterwards to a confident victory. Their opponents felt that there was but little chance of defeating Mr. Buchanan. His name had proved a tower of strength in Pennsylvania, and scattered all the vain imaginations which his opponents had ever conceived.

Indiana and Ohio, which also held their State elections at the same time, did nobly. In the former State the Hon. A. P. Willard had been nominated for Governor, and canvassing the State personally, and taking bold and logical ground on the prominent questions involved in the canvass, he had rolled up a majority at once complimentary to himself and honorable to his State. In Ohio the majority on the State ticket for the "Republicans" was much less than they had confidently been claiming, while the Democrats had secured no less than eight congressmen out of twenty-one, in a delegation that had been wholly against them. They had also gained five members of Congress in Indiana and eleven in Pennsylvania. Thus at one stroke, the moral effect of a victory had not only been secured, but the next House of Representatives would be favorable to the incoming Democratic President.

Only two weeks, however, of precious time now remained for the Democracy to close up their columns and prepare for the final struggle of the fourth of November. If the reverses of October had staggered their opponents, they had not dismayed them or caused them to relax their efforts. It was indispensably necessary for the Democrats to carry Pennsylvania, and one other Northern State, even if they secured all the Southern ones, in order to elect Mr. Buchanan. It was, however, by no means certain that the South would vote in an undivided phalanx. Maryland had been looked upon from the first as one of the doubtful States, and fears were felt of Louisiana and Kentucky. If Maryland should vote for Mr. Fillmore then Mr. Buchanan, besides the remaining electoral votes of the South, would require Pennsylvania and Indiana, or in the event of losing the latter, both New Jersey and California, in order to elect him.

It may be safely said that the Democrats did more active work during the two weeks preceding the day of the presidential election than for any four or six weeks of any other part of the canvass. Everybody who could speak was on the stump. Meetings were held every night in the large cities, while the country was equally alive with the excitement of the strife. The important day at length arrived and the great decision was to be made, when, if we use the language of the "Republicans," the question of "freedom" or "slavery" was to be settled. On that day over four millions of citizens were to exercise the noble, yet natural prerogative of sovereignty, and from Maine to Texas, from the Atlantic to the Pacific, from ocean to ocean, and from the great lakes on the north to the broad gulfs on the south, the silent, yet tremendous ballot was

"To execute a freeman's will."

The decision was another evidence of the confidence to be reposed in the honest masses of the country—another proof of the capacity of man for self-government. Large bodies of men may be deluded, a temporary excitement may even cause the masses to err for a time, but the ultimate decision of the will of the entire people is correct. The news of Mr. Buchanan's election was received with more than ordinary rejoicings. It was generally felt, that at least, danger had been avoided, and the safety of the Union perpetuated.

The result, at all events, was such as to satisfy the democracy. They had been nearly overwhelmed in most of the Northern States; but Pennsylvania, New Jersey, Indiana, Illinois, and California, stood nobly by the banner, which was

19

unfortunately forsaken by some old democratic states. Maryland alone, of all her southern sisters, had refused her vote to Mr. Buchanan. She followed, solitary and alone, the fortunes of Mr. Fillmore. Mr. Frémont had secured the votes of all the Northern States, excepting those we have mentioned, as having gone for Mr. Buchanan, making his electoral vote 114. Mr. Buchanan received 174, and Mr. Fillmore 8. Thus was the long, and exciting contest decided—thus ended one of the most remarkable presidental elections which has ever occurred in the history of our country. To the Democratic party it was an auspicious event, while to the country it was undoubtedly one of infinite moment. The party had returned to its old and excellent rule of electing its first class men to the chief magistracy, while the country had a president in whose honesty, integrity, and patriotism all could confide. There can be no doubt that the personal character of Mr. Buchanan, his unblemished integrity, and solid, private worth contributed in a great measure to decide the contest. He was regarded as an eminently safe man for the position, and one of whom, in all respects, the country might feel justly proud. We might point the hereditary rulers of the world, indeed the whole "divine race of kings," with their lordly titles, to him, and say, "Behold the moral and intellectual accomplishments, the noble, physical proportions—in a word, all that goes to make up the perfect man, and see how far you fall short of our republican President, whose proudest title is, that he is the servant of the people!"

The result of the election, if closely scanned, presents many facts which arrest attention. The total vote the different candidates received in the Northern States was as follows:— Mr. Buchanan, 1.224,750; Mr. Frémont, 1,340,618; and Mr. Fillmore, 393,530. The vote of Mr. Frémont was, therefore, 115,868 over that of Mr. Buchanan. If we recollect, however, that the regular abolitionists gave their votes to Mr. Frémont, we can readily see where this majority came from.

In 1852 John P. Hale received, as the candidate of this party, 157,685 votes.

If this vote had been given to the regular candidate of the party in 1856, as it was in 1852, Mr. Frémont would have had less votes in the north than Mr. Buchanan, showing that Mr. Frémont is entitled to his complimentary northern majority entirely to the partiality of those who openly declare their fixed determination to wage an unrelenting sectional strife. If we add the vote of Mr. Fillmore in the North, which, so far as it relates to the question of negro "slavery," must, at all events, be considered as a condemnation of the doctrines of Mr. Frémont, we have, even with the figures as they now stand, an emphatic majority against him in the Northern States of 277,662. Notwithstanding the supposed falling off of the democratic strength, Mr. Buchanan received more votes in the North than have ever before been given to any democratic president, he having 68,237 more than Mr. Pierce in 1852. In the Southern States Mr. Buchanan received not less than 650,000 votes; Mr. Fillmore about 500,000; and Mr. Frémont 1,194. If we add those votes of Mr. Buchanan and Mr. Fillmore in the South, to the majority against Mr. Frémont in the North, taking out his vote in the South, we have a sweeping majority of 1,426,468 citizens of these United States protesting against the "anti-slavery" principles as enunciated in the "Republican" platform. The total number of votes cast in the entire confederacy was over 4,000,000. This is, however, but a very brief glance at many of the interesting phases which a careful study of the figures of the late election present. It might be shown by tracing localities, that "Republicanism" is mainly confined to New England and to portions of our country, settled principally by those who have emigrated therefrom. Indeed, it can be proved very conclusively, that wherever there exists little or no practical knowledge of the negro character and habits, there, does abolitionism, or the various intermediate shades of opinion which more or less approach it, flourish and prosper.   While in Southern Pennsylvania, Ohio, Indiana, and Illinois, upon the very borders of the "slave" States, there is little or none of it to be found.

Immediately after the result of the election was known, there was much speculation as to what would be the policy of Mr. Buchanan's administration.   Nearly all parties were inclined to the opinion that it would be conservative, and calculated, as far as possible, to harmonize the asperities which the severe political agitation through which the country had just passed, had provoked.   These ideas were foreshadowed by Mr. Buchanan himself, shortly after the 4th of November, in an address which he delivered to the students of Franklin and Marshall College, at Lancaster, who paid him a visit.   On this occasion, Mr. Buchanan remarked, substantially, that the objects of his administration would be to destroy any sectional party, no matter where it existed, whether in the North or in the South, and to restore, if possible, that national, fraternal feeling between the different States that had existed during the days of the fathers of our Republic.   With this exception, Mr. Buchanan kept his own counsels until the day of his inauguration.   Even in the formation of his cabinet the most ingenious newspaper correspondents were not able to give so authentic intelligence concerning who were to compose it, that they did not have to correct themselves the day after the "exclusive information" had been published.

The last session of the thirty-fourth Congress opened on the 1st of December.   The message of Mr. Pierce was remarkable for its decided tone, and for the severe animadversions it contained upon the political principles of the "Republican" party. It, of course provoked a long and excited discussion, and it was many weeks before the legitimate business of the people was much attended to.   The "Republicans" repudiated the ultra principles of sectionalism and abolitionism, with which they were charged, and claimed only as their distinctive creed the fixed determination not to allow the negro to be held in so-called slavery in any future state or territory of the Union. On the 26th of January, while Congress was in session, Mr. Buchanan made a short trip to Washington, in order to enjoy a free and unrestrained interview with his political friends; and thus, doubtless, to prepare himself for the construction of his cabinet, in such a manner as to harmonize all conflicting interests, as far as such a course would not interfere with the public welfare. He remained but a few days, when he returned to Wheatland, where he continued until Monday, the second day of March. On this day, at eight o'clock in the morning, he started in a special train for Baltimore. His old friends and neighbors turned out with unwonted enthusiasm; and, amid the ringing of bells and the firing of cannon, Mr. Buchanan, who, forty-five years before, came among them a poor, friendless boy, left them to preside over the destinies, all things considered, of the greatest nation on the globe. Every demonstration of respect attended him during the entire progress of his journey. The city council of Baltimore gave him a worthy reception, and every arrangement had been made in Washington to render his inauguration one of the most imposing that had ever taken place. The arrangements for the ceremonies were those usually adopted upon such occasions, though more than an ordinary number of the citizen soldiery from various portions of the Union, under the command of General John A. Quitman, of Mississippi, so gratefully remembered by his countrymen for his gallant services in Mexico, contributed to the *éclat* of the proceedings. At one o'clock, P. M., Ex-president Pierce and the President elect, entered the Senate-chamber and proceeded with the Senators, Members of the Supreme Court, the Foreign Ministers, Heads of the Departments, etc., to the east front of the Capitol, where the inauguration ceremonies were conducted. The crowd assembled here was immense, and as soon as the enthusiasm which greeted the appearance of Mr. Buchanan had subsided, he delivered the following address.

MR. BUCHANAN'S INAUGURAL.

" FELLOW-CITIZENS : I appear before you this day to take the solemn oath ' that I will faithfully execute the office of the President of the United States, and will, to the best of my ability, preserve, protect, and defend the Constitution of the United States.'

" In entering upon this great office, I must humbly invoke the God of our fathers for wisdom and firmness to execute its high and responsible duties in such a manner as to restore harmony and ancient friendship among the people of the several States, and to preserve our free institutions throughout many generations. Convinced that I owe my election to the inherent love for the Constitution and the Union which still animates the hearts of the American people, let me earnestly ask their powerful support in sustaining all just measures calculated to perpetuate these, the richest political blessings which Heaven has ever bestowed upon any nation. Having determined not to become a candidate for re-election, I shall have no motive to influence my conduct in administering the government except the desire ably and faithfully to serve my country, and to live in the grateful memory of my countrymen.

" We have recently passed through a presidential contest in which the passions of our fellow-citizens were excited to the highest degree by questions of deep and vital importance; but when the people proclaimed their will, the tempest at once subsided, and all was calm.

" The voice of the majority, speaking in the manner prescribed by the Constitution, was heard, and instant submission followed.   Our own country could alone have exhibited so grand and striking a spectacle of the capacity of man for self-government.

" What a happy conception, then, was it for Congress to apply this simple rule—that the will of the majority shall

shall govern—to the settlement of the question of domestic
slavery in the Territories! Congress is neither 'to legislate
slavery into any Territory or State, nor to exclude it therefrom; but to leave the people thereof perfectly free to form
and regulate their domestic institutions in their own way, subject only to the Constitution of the United States.' As a
natural consequence, Congress has, also, prescribed that when
the Territory of Kansas shall be admitted as a State, it 'shall
be received into the Union, with or without slavery, as their
constitution may prescribe at the time of their admission.'

" A difference of opinion has arisen in regard to the point
of time when the people of a Territory shall decide this question for themselves.

" This is, happily, a matter of but little practical importance. Besides, it is a judicial question, which legitimately
belongs to the Supreme Court of the United States, before
whom it is now pending, and will, it is understood, be speedily
and finally settled. To their decision, in common with all
good citizens, I shall cheerfully submit, whatever this may be,
though it has ever been my individual opinion that, under the
Nebraska-Kansas act, the appropriate period will be when the
number of actual residents in the Territory shall justify the
formation of a constitution with a view to its admission as a
State into the Union. But be this as it may, it is the imperative and indispensable duty of the government of the United
States to secure to every resident inhabitant the free and independent expression of his opinion by his vote. This sacred
right of each individual must be preserved. That being
accomplished, nothing can be fairer than to leave the people
of a Territory free from all foreign interference, to decide
their own destiny for themselves, subject only to the Constitution of the United States.

" The whole territorial question being thus settled upon the
principle of popular sovereignty—a principle as ancient as
free government itself—everything of a practical nature has

been decided. No other question remains for adjustment, because all agree that, under the Constitution, slavery in the States is beyond the reach of any human power, except that of the respective States themselves wherein it exists. May we not, then hope, that the long agitation on this subject is approaching its end, and that the geographical parties to which it has given birth, so much dreaded by the Father of his Country, will speedily become extinct? Most happy will it be for the country when the public mind shall be diverted from this question to others of more pressing and practical importance. Throughout the whole progress of this agitation, which has scarcely known any intermission for more than twenty years, whilst it has been productive of no positive good to any human being, it has been the prolific source of great evils to the master, to the slave, and to the whole country. It has alienated and estranged the people of the sister States from each other, and has even seriously endangered the very existence of. the Union. Nor has the danger yet entirely ceased. Under our system, there is a remedy for all mere political evils in the sound sense and sober judgment of the people. Time is a great corrective. Political subjects which but a few years ago excited and exasperated the public mind, have passed away, and are now nearly forgotten. But this question of domestic slavery is of far graver importance than any mere political question, because, should the agitation continue, it may eventually endanger the personal safety of a large portion of our countrymen where the institution exists. In that event, no form of government, however admirable in itself, and however productive of material benefits, can compensate for the loss of peace and domestic security around the family altar. Let every Union-loving man, therefore, exert his best influence to suppress this agitation, which, since the recent legislation of Congress, is without any legitimate object.

"It is an evil omen of the times that men have undertaken to calculate the mere material value of the Union. Reasoned estimates have been presented of the pecuniary profits and local advantages which would result to different States and sections from its dissolution, and of the comparative injuries which such an event would inflict on other States and sections Even descending to this low and narrow view of the mighty question, all such calculations are at fault. The bare reference to a single consideration will be conclusive on this point. We at present enjoy a free trade throughout our extensive and expanding country, such as the world has never witnessed. This trade is conducted on railroads and canals—on noble rivers and arms of the sea—which bind together the North and the South, the East and the West of our Confederacy. Annihilate this trade, arrest its free progress by the geographical lines of jealous and hostile States, and you destroy the prosperity and onward march of the whole and every part, and involve all in one common ruin. But such considerations, important as they are in themselves, sink into insignificance when we reflect on the terrific evils which would result from disunion to every portion of the Confederacy—to the North not more than to the South, to the East not more than to the West. These I shall not attempt to portray; because I feel an humble confidence that the kind Providence which inspired our fathers with wisdom to frame the most perfect form of government and union ever devised by man will not suffer it to perish until it shall have been peacefully instrumental, by its example, in the extension of civil and religious liberty throughout the world.

"Next in importance to the maintenance of the Constitution and the Union is the duty of preserving the government free from the taint, or even the suspicion, of corruption. Public virtue is the vital spirit of republics; and history proves that when this has decayed, and the love of money has usurped its place, although the forms of free government may remain for a season, the substance has departed for ever.

"Our present financial condition is without a parallel in

19*

history. No nation has ever before been embarrassed from too large a surplus in its treasury. This almost necessarily gives birth to extravagant legislation. It produces wild schemes of expenditure, and begets a race of speculators and jobbers, whose ingenuity is exerted in contriving and promoting expedients to obtain public money. The purity of official agents, whether rightfully or wrongfully, is suspected, and the character of the government suffers in the estimation of the people. This is in itself a very great evil.

"The natural mode of relief from this embarrassment is to appropriate the surplus in the treasury to great national objects, for which a clear warrant can be found in the Constitution. Among these I might mention the extinguishment of the public debt, a reasonable increase of the navy, which is at present inadequate to the protection of our vast tonnage afloat, now greater than that of any other nation, as well as to the defence of our extended sea-coast.

"It is beyond all question the true principle that no more revenue ought to be collected from the people than the amount necessary to defray the expenses of a wise, economical, and efficient administration of the government. To reach this point it was necessary to resort to a modification of the tariff, and this has, I trust, been accomplished in such a manner as to do as little injury as may have been practicable to our domestic manufactures, especially those necessary for the defence of the country. Any discrimination against a particular branch, for the purpose of benefiting favored corporations, individuals, or interests, would have been unjust to the rest of the community, and inconsistent with that spirit of fairness and equality which ought to govern in the adjustment of a revenue tariff.

"But the squandering of the public money sinks into comparative insignificance as a temptation to corruption when compared with the squandering of the public lands.

"No nation in the tide of time has ever been blessed with so rich and noble an inheritance as we enjoy in the public lands. In administering this important trust, whilst it may be wise to grant portions of them for the improvement of the remainder, yet we should never forget that it is our cardinal policy to reserve these lands, as much as may be, for actual settlers, and this at moderate prices. We shall thus not only best promote the prosperity of the new States and Territories by furnishing them a hardy and independent race of honest and industrious citizens, but shall secure homes for our children and our children's children, as well as for those exiles from foreign shores who may seek in this country to improve their condition, and to enjoy the blessings of civil and religious liberty. Such emigrants have done much to promote the growth and prosperity of the country. They have proved faithful both in peace and in war. After becoming citizens, they are entitled, under the Constitution and laws, to be placed on a perfect equality with native-born citizens; and in this character they should ever be kindly recognized.

"The federal Constitution is a grant from the States to Congress of certain specific powers; and the question whether this grant should be liberally or strictly construed, has, more or less, divided political parties from the beginning. Without entering into the argument, I desire to state, at the commencement of my administration, that long experience and observation have convinced me that a strict construction of the powers of the government is the only true, as well as the only safe theory of the Constitution. Whenever in our past history doubtful powers have been exercised by Congress, these have never failed to produce injurious and unhappy consequences. Many such instances might be adduced, if this were the proper occasion. Neither is it necessary for the public service to strain the language of the Constitution; because all the great and useful powers required for a successful administration of the government, both in peace and in war, have been granted, either in express terms or by the plainest implication

" Whilst deeply convinced of these truths, I yet consider it clear that, under the war-making power, Congress may appro. priate money towards the construction of a military road, when this is absolutely necessary for the defence of any State or Territory of the Union against foreign invasion.   Under the Constitution, Congress has power " to declare war," " to raise and support armies," " to provide and maintain a navy," and to call forth the militia to "repel invasions."   Thus endowed, in an ample manner, with the war-making power, the corresponding duty is required that " the United States shall protect each of them [the States] against invasion." Now, how is it possible to afford this protection to California and our Pacific possessions, except by means of a military road through the Territories of the United States, over which men and munitions of war may be speedily transported from the Atlantic States to meet and to repel the invader ?   In the event of a war with a naval Power much stronger than our own, we should then have no other available access to the Pacific coast, because such a Power would instantly close the route across the isthmus of Central America.   It is impossible to conceive that, whilst the Constitution has expressly required Congress to defend all the States, it should yet deny to them, by any fair construction, the only possible means by which one of these States can be defended.   Besides, the government, ever since its origin, has been in the constant practice of constructing military roads.   It might also be wise to consider whether the love for the Union which now animates our fellow-citizens on the Pacific coast may not be impaired by our neglect or refusal to provide for them, in their remote and isolated condition, the only means by which the power of the States, on this side of the Rocky Mountains, can reach 'them in sufficient time to 'protect' them 'against invasion.'   I forbear for the present from expressing an opinion as to the wisest and most economical mode in which the government can lend its aid in accomplishing this great and necessary work. I believe that many of the difficulties in the way, which now appear formidable, will, in a great degree, vanish as soon as the nearest and best route shall have been satisfactorily ascertained.

"It may be proper that, on this occasion, I should make some brief remarks in regard to our rights and duties as a member of the great family of nations. In our intercourse with them there are some plain principles, approved by our own experience, from which we should never depart. We ought to cultivate peace, commerce, and friendship with all nations ; and this not merely as the best means of promoting our own material interests, but in a spirit of Christian benevolence towards our fellow-men, wherever their lot may be cast. Our diplomacy should be direct and frank, neither seeking to obtain more nor accepting less than is our due. We ought to cherish a sacred regard for the independence of all nations, and never attempt to interfere in the domestic concerns of any, unless this shall be imperatively required by the great law of self-preservation. To avoid entangling alliances has been a maxim of our policy ever since the days of Washington, and its wisdom no one will attempt to dispute. In short, we ought to do justice, in a kindly spirit, to all nations, and require justice from them in return.

"It is our glory that, whilst other nations have extended their dominions by the sword, we have never acquired any territory except by fair purchase, or, as in the case of Texas, by the voluntary determination of a brave, kindred, and independent people to blend their destinies with our own. Even our acquisitions from Mexico form no exception. Unwilling to take advantage of the fortune of war against a sister Republic, we purchased these possessions, under the treaty of peace, for a sum which was considered at the time a fair equivalent. Our past history forbids that we shall in the future acquire territory, unless this be sanctioned by the laws of justice and honor. Acting on this principle, no nation will have a right to interfere or to complain if, in the progress of events, we shall still further extend our possessions. Hitherto, in all our acquisitions, the people, under the protection of the American flag, have enjoyed civil and religious liberty, as well as equal and just laws, and have been contented, prosperous, and happy. Their trade with the rest of the world has rapidly increased ; and thus every commercial nation has shared largely in their successful progress.

"I shall now proceed to take the oath prescribed by the Constitution, whilst humbly invoking the blessing of Divine Providence on this great people.

"JAMES BUCHANAN.

"WASHINGTON CITY, 4th March, 1857."

After the reading of the Inaugural the venerable Chief Justice Taney administered the oath of office, and the booming of cannon and the cheers of the assembled thousands proclaimed that James Buchanan was President of the United States. The will of the people had been consummated—their sovereignty acknowledged and their decision recognized.

On the sixth Mr. Buchanan sent to the Senate, which had been convened for executive session, the names of those whom he had selected as members of his cabinet. They were duly confirmed, and were as follows : Lewis Cass, of Michigan, Secretary of State ; Howell Cobb, of Georgia, Secretary of the Treasury ; John Buchanan Floyd, of Virginia, Secretary of War ; Jacob Thompson, of Mississippi, Secretary of the Interior ; Isaac Toucey, of Connecticut, Secretary of the Navy ; Aaron Venable Brown, of Tennessee, Postmaster-General ; Jeremiah Sullivan Black of Pennsylvania, Attorney-General. These individuals are nearly all distinguished for eminent services to their country, and enjoy in a remarkable degree the confidence and respect of their fellow-citizens.

GEN. CASS is well known at home and abroad as a statesman of great experience, devoted passionately to the interests of his country, and as perfectly intimate with European politics as with those of the United States. His life is identified with the history of his country for more than half a century, and, though at the advanced age of seventy-five, he has such an astonishing degree of physical and intellectual vigor, that in his arduous duties on "the stump" during the late presidential campaign, he showed a power of endurance of which men half his age might feel justly proud. Mr. Cass is a native of New Hampshire, is of revolutionary lineage, and himself occupied a conspicuous position in the War with Great Britain in 1812. On the field he has distinguished himself for gallantry, and in the civil service has ever shown himself a watchful and jealous guardian of the welfare of his country. He rose to the rank of Brigadier-General in the army, and has occupied subsequently the positions of Governor of Michigan, Secretary of War under Gen. Jackson, Minister to France, and Senator from the State of Michigan, for several terms. There seemed to be no man whom Mr. Buchanan could more appropriately call to the position of Secretary of State, and certainly there was none who would have given so much general satisfaction.

MR. HOWELL COBB, of Georgia, the Secretary of the Treasury, is about forty years of age. He entered Congress in 1842, and rose rapidly as a vigorous debater, an able and expert tactician and parliamentary leader. He was on the floor of the House during some of the most exciting and interesting periods of our history, and in 1850 especially distinguished himself in behalf of what are known as the Compromise Measures of that year. His integrity is proverbial; his personal character spotless, and he must prove an efficient and able support to Mr. Buchanan's administration.

Mr. John B. Floyd, of Virginia, the Secretary of War, has long been known as a prominent politician of his State. He is about fifty years of age, has been Governor of Virginia, but has never before held a national office. He is a man of strong mind, of real ability, and of very decided political opinions. He is an orator of great power and effectiveness, though he has rather shunned than courted a conspicuous position. He brings to the discharge of the duties of his office unsurpassed energy of character and spotless integrity. He cannot fail to exert great influence in the Cabinet.

Mr. Jacob Thompson, of Mississippi, the Secretary of the Interior, has not been in public life since 1850. Previous to that period he had been a member of the House of Representatives during several Congresses, and had distinguished himself as a faithful representative, an eloquent speaker, and a man of more than ordinary practical powers. He is about forty years of age, and is eminently qualified for the peculiar duties of his position.

Mr. Isaac Toucey, of Connecticut, the Secretary of the Navy, has been in political life for a quarter of a century. He was first elected to Congress in 1837, where he distinguished himself as an active and useful member. In 1848, about the close of Mr. Polk's administration, he held the office of Attorney-General, with credit to himself, and with honor to his country. In 1852, he was chosen United States Senator from Connecticut, which office he held up to the time he was invited by Mr. Buchanan to a seat in his Cabinet. During the discussion of the recent political issues, Mr. Toucey has stood forth a bold champion for the right in the face of temporary unpopularity at home. He is about sixty-five years of age, of fine attainments, and of solid, substantial worth.

Mr. Aaron V. Brown, of Tennessee, the Postmaster-General is one of the most marked men in Mr. Buchanan's Cabinet. Few men have impressed their political views more generally upon the people than Mr. Brown. He is about sixty years of age, entered Congress in 1840, where he sat five years, distinguishing himself as one of the most able and indefatigable members. In 1845 he was elected Governor of Tennessee, but since the expiration of the term of that office, he has held no public position. His democracy is of the purest kind, and his ideas have received great currency from the fact that he is the author of the Baltimore platform of principles of 1852, which has become the *magna charta* of the Democratic party. He is an ornament to the Cabinet, and contributes essentially to its strength.

Mr. Jeremiah S. Black, of Pennsylvania, the Attorney-General, is one of the most popular men of his State. He is distinguished for more than ordinary abilities, and is perfectly familiar with the duties appertaining to his office. When called by Mr. Buchanan to his present post, he occupied the position of Justice of the Supreme Court of Pennsylvania, to which office he had been twice elected, the last time running twenty thousand ahead of his ticket. He is known as a democrat of the soundest kind, and as one of the most promising men in the country.

Such is a brief account of the *personnel* of Mr. Buchanan's constitutional advisers. He has instituted his government in the spirit which animated him in accepting the nomination for President, and in accordance with the language in his letter of acceptance, when he pledged himself, should he be elected, to use all the power he constitutionally possessed, "to restore harmony among the States." Ultra the complexion of his

Cabinet is not, yet no one fears that, composed of such men, it will ever barter away substantial rights for mere temporary convenience, or compromise the interests of the country to a time-serving expediency. Of course, it cannot hope to escape the attacks of the active, intelligent, and unrelenting opposition party of the country, but that it will command the respect, confidence, and support of a large majority of his countrymen we cannot doubt. The Democratic party are particularly bound to sustain it, for it evidently owes more to Mr. Buchanan than Mr. Buchanan can possibly owe to that. Under the peculiar circumstances it would have been just about impossible for it to have elected any other man. With the distinct announcement that he will occupy the presidential office but a single term, his enemies cannot reproach him with seeking a re-nomination, and his course can only be influenced by an honest desire to advance the interests of the people, and, as he himself expresses it, "to live in the grateful memory of his countrymen." Thus fairly launched, with the future before it, we take leave of Mr. Buchanan's administration, not doubting that the chapter which shall record its acts, will be an honorable one in the history of our country ; and with the honest conviction that the distinguished man who presides over its destinies, will give renewed evidence of his profound statesmanship, scrupulous integrity, and unsullied patriotism.

THE END.

www.ingramcontent.com/pod-product-compliance
Lightning Source LLC
Chambersburg PA
CBHW031058110726
47900CB00003B/983